A GLORIOUS PASSION

"God help me, Glory, because I can't help myself," Grant groaned as his lips came down to possess hers with all the hunger she had thought only she suffered from.

His kiss left her breathless, and the cold air she dragged into her lungs sent a tingling chill through her that did nothing to quench the fire in her blood. She was dizzy, afraid to pull away from his embrace for fear her knees would give way beneath her. Her hands clutched at his jacket and would not let go.

"Do you know how long I've been wanting to do that?" Grant asked, looking down at her with eyes as bright as black diamonds.

"Since forever," Glory answered, her voice husky with awakening desire. "Just like I've been wanting you to . . ."

LINDA HILTON
SECRET FIRES

ZEBRA BOOKS
KENSINGTON PUBLISHING CORP.

ZEBRA BOOKS

are published by

Kensington Publishing Corp.
475 Park Avenue South
New York, NY 10016

First printing: August, 1991

Printed in the United States of America

Chapter One

Slowly, in groups of two or three, the mourners gathered in the bright sun and brisk wind of early autumn for the burial of Lee Johnson. The preacher from the Community Church, the only one in Greene, Wyoming, stood patiently at the open grave. He held a neat black Bible in one hand and with the other tried to hold his flat-brimmed hat to his head.

Wearing a once elegant black dress, Lee Johnson's widow waited on the wagon seat while the cowboys who had worked for her husband slid the coffin from the back of the wagon. Anna Johnson lifted a black-gloved hand to smooth a loose tendril of brown hair away from her face and blinked away the wind-borne dust that stung her eyes. She glanced at the assembled mourners, most of them total strangers, and felt a grim satisfaction that so many had turned out. Strangers they might be, but at least they had not left her to grieve alone.

"Mrs. Johnson?" The preacher called her name quietly, startling her out of bitter memories. He had moved to stand beside the wagon and stared up at her. "The others are waiting."

"Yes, of course," she whispered. A trace of the Virginia drawl she usually kept so carefully disguised slipped into her voice. "Please, forgive me. I didn't mean . . ."

Her words died unspoken, unnecessary. The pall-bearers had carried the closed pine box to the gaping hole and began to lower it. Anna glanced again at the mourners, not knowing what she looked for, but certain she did not find it. Sympathy? Grief? She saw nothing in the blank faces. The men, the women, even the children seemed so meek, so accepting. The whole scene was like a nightmare, a terrible tableau in which no one did anything, no one cared. Anna wanted to scream at them, to beg them to do something, but she knew it would do no good. Lee was dead, and nothing could bring him back.

Anna offered her hand to the preacher and let him help her down from the wagon seat. When she was standing, he released her, and if she had not quickly gathered the strength to walk after him, she would have been left alone, something she could not bear, not now, not again.

So she followed the minister, whose name she finally remembered was Rupert Clayburn, to the side of the grave. Only four weeks ago, this same young Reverend Clayburn had married Anna Beaumont to Lee Johnson. "'Til death do you part," he had solemnly intoned. Now death had parted them.

"Did you ever think it would be so soon?" Anna asked, forgetting for a moment that Reverend Clayburn could not have heard her thoughts.

"Death comes at its own appointed time, neither too soon nor too late," he replied, his voice as smooth, as emotionless as the faces of the nameless townspeople gathered around the grave.

He left her to take her place beside her stepson Matthew. The tall, gangly fourteen-year-old moved a step or two away from her, but Anna did not let his resentment touch her. He had lost his mother less than two years before, and a month was not time enough to accustom himself to a stepmother. Now his father was gone as well. Matthew was entitled to his grief, his anger, his silence.

The aloneness crept up on Anna again, until she felt

6

she could not have been more isolated if she stood atop one of those distant mountains, covered even now by snow that gleamed white and pure against a cloudless October sky. Why does no one care? she wondered. Why do the women not weep? My husband is dead. He had hopes, plans, dreams that will all go unfulfilled, and none of these people seems to care.

She raised a black-edged handkerchief to her lips, to stifle not a wail of grief but a cry of anger and frustration. Then, as though he too shared the apathy, Rupert Clayburn began the funeral service.

Each time he led the other mourners in a mumbled "amen," Anna whispered into her handkerchief, "Not again." The litany that sustained her through the hours since Lee's body had been brought home, slung over his saddle, held her shattered nerves together. But as the dirt clattered on top of the coffin, Anna struggled to hold on to her determination. Panic made another assault. Her lower lip trembled. Lee was gone, and she was alone.

It was all over so quickly. One by one the ranchers and folks from town hesitantly walked up to the widow and expressed their condolences before they filed off past the church and onto the main thoroughfare of Greene. Anna somehow found the strength to smile the polite, wan smile she knew everyone expected of her. Despite her unwillingness to be alone, she found that she wanted this all to be over so she could escape, back to the ranch that should have been home, and away from the blank, staring faces of people she did not know.

The last to offer her the obligatory sympathy was the man who had stood beside Matthew through the service, a rancher, to judge by his worn, dusty boots, faded shirt, and the weather-stained hat dangling from one hand. He seemed to hesitate, waiting until all the others had gone and only Anna remained by the grave. As she cautiously watched him, wondering why he hesitated to offer the expected platitudes, she realized he wasn't a total stranger.

7

She could not recall his name, but she knew she had seen him before. He was tall, though that meant little. Even Lee, who had been of no more than average height, stood a full head taller than she. Anna tried to remember an occasion when she had met someone considerably taller than Lee, as this man must be. Her overburdened mind struggled but could find nothing in the storehouse of her memories except that vague familiarity.

Experience as well as years in the outdoors had etched those lines around his mouth and the creases at the corners of his eyes, but the strength in those broad shoulders and the pride evident even in his relaxed stance bespoke the vigor of a man in his prime, perhaps thirty-five, no more than forty. And alone among the faces at the funeral, the familiar stranger did not wear that mask of apathy. For a moment Anna stared at him, assessing his strong features, wondering why she had such difficulty remembering him.

His eyes were dark, their color uncertain in the sharp shadows of the noontime sun. The light glinted on undisciplined hair, turning the ends that curled over his ears and the back of his collar a bright gold. The occasion of their meeting must have been very brief, for Anna could not imagine such a man would fail to make a powerful impression. He certainly did now.

When he returned her bold gaze, Anna flushed and lowered her eyes. Yet she did not move. Something inside told her to wait, to let the stranger stare at her as boldly as she had at him. She knew what he saw, but she could not understand what there was about Anna Johnson, twice widowed, that had sparked his curiosity.

Some men had called her striking or even beautiful, but Anna Johnson learned that a woman, especially a widow, should not listen to men's opinions. Her long hair was too ordinary a brown, neither straight nor curly, just stubborn and unruly, like the stranger's but without the sun-bleached highlights. She had been told her eyes held too many secrets in their golden depths, despite her habit

8

of refusing to look shyly away. Her nose, her chin, the way she carried herself despite her unimpressive height, proclaimed too loudly her impatience, her rebelliousness, her defiance. Her father had compared her to a bantam rooster and declared she would have made a fine son, but her mother had prevailed and done her best to turn Anna into a respectable lady. Perhaps she had succeeded.

Then why did the stranger's persistent eyes provoke that always simmering rebellion? And why did she care or even wonder what thoughts lay behind the half smile that softened the lines of his face, yet accused her so knowingly that she felt guilt stain her cheeks? She had no idea what it was he thought she should feel guilty for. Nor, despite combing her recollections about the people she had met since arriving in Wyoming, could she remember who this stranger was.

"You looked like you couldn't quite place me," he said, extending the hand without the hat. His voice was soft, so soft that Anna had to strain even in the quiet of the cemetery to hear him. She detected no mockery, but no sincerity either. The puzzle began to intrigue her. "Grant Brookington, Lee's neighbor to the west at the Diamond B. We met in Conner's Bank a couple of weeks ago."

"Yes, I remember now." She also remembered that Lee had not seemed eager to make the introduction. It had been brief, a mumbled exchange of names before Lee dragged her off. When she questioned him about it, he ignored her. At the time, his silence irked her, but she had no opportunity to pursue the matter and then forgot it, just as she had forgotten Grant Brookington.

She clasped the proffered hand. "I'm sure Lee would appreciate your being here, Mr. Brookington."

He seemed about to say something, then bit the words back. The smile flickered brighter until he extinguished it, but not before Anna recognized that it was a smile without humor.

9

"I wanted to offer my help to Matthew and to yourself."

He released her hand, but it was a long while before her flesh forgot the impression his firm grip had made. She flexed her fingers to dispel a subtle tingling. It did not go away. Neither did Brookington.

He should have. When Anna lifted the square of black-trimmed linen to her eyes, that was the cue for the mourner to make a gesture of sympathy and then depart. It had always worked before. Grant Brookington obviously did not consider himself just another mourner, to be dismissed from the grieving widow's presence with a wave of a lacy handkerchief.

"If you need anything, just send one of the boys over to the Diamond B," he added.

"Thank you, Mr. Brookington. Like everyone else, you've been very kind."

She thought he was going to say something more. That odd smile turned up the corners of his mouth and a twinkle came into the eyes that had studied her a few moments before, eyes she could tell now were a cold, steely grey. The words remained unspoken. Brookington suddenly turned to look behind him, as though waiting for someone. He seemed almost to have forgotten Anna. Only when Matthew approached the grave did Grant Brookington actually step away from Anna.

With mounting curiosity, she watched as the tall rancher reached out his hand to her stepson and then placed his other arm around the boy's shoulders. Neither said a word as they walked toward the wagon together. Grant Brookington did not so much as beg Anna's pardon before he left her, alone except for the two men who leaned impatiently against their shovels in the shade of a leafless cottonwood.

"Of all the nerve!" she muttered before she could stop herself. A flush of embarrassment heated her cheeks as she looked around to see if anyone might have heard her outburst, but the grave diggers were engaged in their own conversation. The only other person in sight was a short rotund man in a brown business suit, walking through the cemetery, careful to avoid crossing a grave.

He, too, looked around, then walked toward Anna, his steps hesitant, timid. He did not look at the hole waiting to be filled.

"Mr. Lytle," Anna greeted him, almost forgetting the obligatory wan smile. "How kind of you to come."

The blue eyes watered behind his spectacles. He dabbed at them with a wrinkled handkerchief every bit as damp as Anna's was dry.

"I heard the terrible news this morning," he rattled nervously. "Please, accept my sympathies and those of my father as well. He's prosecuting that murder trial in Surrey Springs or he'd be here himself, but he wanted me to deliver this to you as soon as possible."

The junior Ambrose Lytle rummaged through several pockets of his rumpled coat to produce a neatly folded piece of paper, which he presented to Anna like a gift.

"In a few days or a week, when you're   when things are settled more, Father will come out to the ranch to go over the details with you," he went on.

Empty-handed, he fumbled for something to do, then finally extended one hand to her. She clasped it, thanked him quietly, and watched as he backed away, eager to escape once his unpleasant business had been accomplished.

Not again, panic whispered in her ear *Not again!* As before, she forced the fear out of her mind and concentrated on getting through each moment one at a time. She stared at the piece of paper young Mr. Lytle had given her. It could only be Lee's will. Though she was cold standing in the October wind, nothing in the world was more important right now than reading that duly witnessed document. It might hold the answers to the unasked questions, the solutions to the unfaced problems. Or it might not. But she had to know.

What's to stop me? she wondered. Already her fingers

were playing with the seal. Lee's dead and almost buried. Terrence isn't here to snatch it out of my hands and tell me he'll handle everything. And Sadie isn't here to beg me to let him. If I don't do it myself, no one else will.

The breeze fluttered the paper and almost tore it from her grasp, and the sunlight reflecting on the white surface forced her to squint. But she had no difficulty reading the senior Mr. Lytle's bold hand. She noted that the document was dated less than three weeks ago, then skimmed the opening statement attesting to Lee's soundness of mind and body. All that mattered were the bequests.

They were few and brief. The entire last will and testament of Lee Cyrus Johnson covered barely half the long sheet of paper. It took only a minute to read.

Though she had been present when Lee ordered the will drawn up, Anna had not known until she read the paper itself that it had been the purpose of Lee's visit to town that rainy afternoon.

He had been in a furious mood. He grumbled the whole time, wishing Anna had been able to ride a horse instead of necessitating the wagon, which made the trip twice as long. And then she had waited, silent and more than a little worried, while Lee argued with the town's only lawyer, Ambrose Lytle, Sr. Lee came out of the office no less angry than when he went in. They drove back to the ranch in gloomy silence.

The next day, Lee Johnson set out on a two-week fall roundup. On the evening after his return from that roundup, the Mexican palomino he took such pride in shied at a jackrabbit, throwing Lee and breaking his neck. His new bride became a widow. It was all very quick, very simple, yet not simple at all.

Lee Johnson had left everything he owned—ranch, house, stock, everything—to his wife of less than one month.

When she reached the signatures at the end of the

document, Anna quietly exclaimed, "Oh, my God," not believing what she had read. She read it again. Her reaction did not change. "Oh, my God," she whispered the second time.

"Mrs. Johnson, are you all right?" He stood silhouetted against the blue sky as Anna looked up, still half blind from squinting against the glare. She had not heard him approach.

"Yes, Mr. Brookington, I'm fine," she answered, though she wasn't sure she meant it. Not when he continued staring at her.

She felt a shiver slide down her spine and she looked away, into the yawning hole with the pine box in the bottom, the lid splattered with clods of symbolic dirt. But she could not escape the mockery in Brookington's eyes, a mockery echoed in his voice. She had caught the sarcasm when he uttered her name.

"I think those men are waiting for you to finish here," he observed with a nod to the grave diggers.

They were probably waiting for her to pay her final respects so they could finish their job and spend their wages at the nearest saloon. Still, she had no right to deny them their reward for the unpleasant work they had yet to do.

"Thank you for reminding me. Tell Matthew I'll be finished in just a minute, if he wants some time alone."

"Matthew's already in the wagon, waiting for you. Unless, of course, you'd rather stay in town?"

"Why would I do that?" she asked, unable to keep a hint of panic from tinging her voice.

She followed his steely gaze to the paper she still clutched in her hand.

At least he wasn't subtle. She did the best she could to smooth the paper, and she folded it to slip into a pocket of her skirt to keep it from being blown away. If that happened, she had no doubt Brookington would retrieve it more quickly than she could, in order to take the

13

opportunity to read the document. Anna decided to deprive him of that pleasure by beating him at his own game.

Before he could reply, she said in a calmer, steadier voice, "Matthew and I will be going home to the LJ, Mr. Brookington. My husband left the ranch to me, so I certainly couldn't think of spending a night away from it."

Something, perhaps a slight narrowing of his eyes or tensing of the muscle in his jaw, told her that he was surprised, though he covered his shock well. She did not cover hers nearly so well when he said, "I'd like to buy the LJ from you. I'll give you a good price, and—"

She interrupted him quickly. "It's not for sale."

Grant suspected she spoke without thinking. She certainly didn't give him a half a second to prepare a reply; more than likely she reacted instinctively and possessively. Though her golden eyes had narrowed with determination, he could detect more fear than caution under the soft drawl.

"Look, Mrs. Johnson, I think once you hear what I have to say, you'll agree with me that—"

"I said, the ranch is not for sale."

He hadn't really expected her to capitulate, but neither had he expected this much resistance. The woman intrigued him. Confused him, threw him a little off balance, but nonetheless she intrigued him. He found that strangely disquieting.

"Everything's for sale, Mrs. Johnson. Eventually, at some price . . ."

"Not the LJ. It's mine. Lee left it to me, and it's not for sale. Not for any price. Good day, Mr. Brookington."

She wasn't angry, or if she was, Grant gave her credit for hiding her temper better than most women of his acquaintance. But she was very, very stubborn.

She was also very attractive. Those dark honey eyes narrowed against the wind but never left him. Her high cheekbones glowed brightly pink in the chill sunshine.

14

She raised a hand to ward off a tendril of loose hair caught in the wind and the action tilted her chin a notch higher. It was a firm little chin, proud and stubborn like the rest of her. And though she had bid him good day, she stood her ground. She wouldn't be easy, but nothing worth having ever was.

Might as well let her know he could be just as stubborn as she.

"Look, Mrs. Johnson, I know this is a bad time." When she opened her mouth to interrupt him again, he raised a gloved hand and to his mild surprise, she held silent. "You got a lot of worries now, and maybe being out here alone you think you have to do it all yourself. Like I said, I'm right down the road at the Diamond B. You need anything, you just holler. And when you decide running a spread like the LJ is more than you can handle, you let me know. I'll take it off your hands."

He wanted to smile but held back any show of the satisfaction he felt while he watched the color rise in her face. She did have a temper, somewhere under that brave front, and she was having a devil of a time hiding it.

Anna took another deep breath and lowered her voice to a husky, furious whisper. The drawl returned, stronger than ever now that she had to expend her concentration to control her anger, but she didn't care.

"No, you look, Mr. Grant Brookington. I know Lee didn't trust you, and suddenly neither do I. I *own* the LJ, lock, stock, and barrel, and I am telling you for the last time, it isn't for sale. And I'd give it away before I'd sell to you anyway."

Without waiting for his reaction, Anna turned and walked toward the wagon.

She knew that if her father had been able to look down from heaven and read her thoughts at that moment, he would have called her mental grin that of the cat that ate the canary. She simply could not help it. Besting the arrogant Grant Brookington alone was cause for the triumphant tilting of her chin, though Anna remembered in time to assume some semblance of decorum.

For a moment, she experienced a pang of guilt. When she searched for the grief she should have felt, there was none. She glanced back over her shoulder toward the grave, ignoring the tall silhouette that still stood beside it.

"I'm sorry, Lee," she whispered more quietly than the wind through the dry grass of the graveyard. "It shouldn't have been like this, but I can't change what's happened."

She turned away again, and the guilt slowly faded. Lee Johnson had been almost as much a stranger to her as the people who had mourned him. She never pretended that she loved him, any more than he had pretended to love her. Their reasons for marrying were probably very different, but neither had questioned the other. Anna knew only that Lee Johnson offered her the freedom that had been taken from her by another man's death too many long years ago.

She had been willing to pay the price for that freedom, the price of being the wife of a man she did not love, did not even know. Now, with Lee's death, she had even more freedom.

She reached the wagon where Matthew waited, his shoulders hunched against the wind that seemed to grow colder with each gust. He glanced at her but made no move to help her up to the uncushioned wooden seat. For a moment she hesitated, unsure of what to do next, what to grab onto to pull herself up.

Gingerly, she lifted her skirt to place a foot on one of the spokes of the wheel. She knew Grant Brookington's steely eyes must be watching her, and she had no wish to fall flat on her face or any other part of her anatomy. She grabbed onto the nearest thing at hand and awkwardly hoisted herself upward. Her landing on the seat was far from graceful, but she had accomplished it without assistance.

Matthew chucked to the horse and the wagon jerked

16

into motion. The wind stung her eyes, and she blamed the tears on that. But she did not wipe them away. She would not acknowledge them in front of Grant Brookington. She knew he had figured out that she wept not for her husand, but for herself, and even then her tears were not of self-pity. They were of fear.

For the first time in her twenty-eight years, Anna Rush Beaumont Johnson was not dependent on anyone else. She owned the LJ Ranch, free and clear. She could do as she damn well pleased.

And it scared her out of her wits.

"So Lee didn't trust me," Grant muttered as he settled his hat on his head and watched the retreating figure. "Well, you can trust me now, Mrs. Anna Johnson, when I tell you that there is one hell of a lot more to owning a ranch than having your name on a piece of paper."

The grave diggers said nothing, just lifted their shovels and walked to the hole. It was hint enough for Grant to leave. As he strode off toward the horse tethered to the graveyard fence, he pulled the hat down further, not only to shade his eyes but to keep it from blowing off. The wind had picked up, colder and sharper, and the clouds on the horizon suggested early snow. He watched the woman and the boy as long as he could see them, down the road and out of town, then onto the narrow track toward their ranch.

"Damn!" he swore, untying the reins. "Damn you to hell, Lee Johnson."

He mounted the black-stockinged bay and turned it toward the same road the wagon had taken. He could, he knew, spur the animal to an easy gallop and overtake the other vehicle in short order. But such a show of bravado was certain to give that silly woman the impression that her triumphant announcement had affected him. It had, much more than she could ever guess, but Grant had no intention of letting her know.

"Damn!" He cursed again, more in frustration than anger. There was no short cut to the Diamond B. The track ran straight across the prairie, passing several nearer homesteads before reaching the LJ and then, eight miles further, the Diamond B. Grant's bay pranced, eager to be off, but he continued to hold it in check.

To judge by the drift of dust behind the wagon, Matthew had urged the nag pulling it to a trot. Grant allowed himself a satisfying chuckle. Maybe a bone-rattling ride back to the LJ would shake some sense into that fool woman's head. Maybe by tomorrow she'd listen to a sensible offer.

The simple logic settled his own anger, and Grant finally touched his heels to the bay's flanks and let the horse bolt to a gallop.

"You cheated me twice, Lee," he muttered as he slowed the bay to a steady canter. He didn't want to come up to the wagon too quickly. "That's twice too often, and I won't let it happen this time. Not again."

Chapter Two

Alone, so cold that her hands ached with the chill, Anna left Matthew to unhitch the horse and stable it for the night, then she returned to the house. It welcomed her with warmth, enveloped her with loneliness. She closed the door behind her and leaned against it with a sigh.

After hanging her black woolen shawl on a peg by the back door, she headed upstairs. She forced herself to concentrate on the list of things to do. If she kept her mind on these tasks, maybe it would loosen its persistent grip on the tall man with the hard eyes. Images of Grant Brookington, his eyes icy, his mouth tight with anger, crowded her mental vision. His words, so bitter, so hurtful, echoed above her footsteps on the uncarpeted stairs. She could not get the man out of her thoughts.

"After I've had some supper, I am going to examine the account books," she told herself aloud while stripping off the black gown. A soft flannel shirt she had borrowed from Lee lay on the bed. She slipped her arms into the sleeves, welcoming the comfort until a wave of guilt and grief washed over her. She did up the buttons determinedly and pushed the other feelings away. She had no time for them.

Talking aloud seemed to help her concentration.

"When I've made some sense out of the accounts and

know how much I can—oh, who in heaven's name is here now?"

The slamming of a heavy door downstairs rattled the panes in the bedroom window and the vibrations seemed to echo ominously in the ensuing silence. Anna grabbed her wool skirt from the bed and stepped quickly into it.

"Who's there?" she called.

"That you, Anna?" a masculine voice asked in reply.

What had been a twinge of fear immediately became a lump of disgust in Anna's empty stomach. There was no mistaking that voice.

"I'll be down in a moment, Lonnie," she answered.

"No hurry. I just came to get a few things."

Subtlety was not one of Lonnie Hewitt's strong suits. His announcement served as warning. Anna raced down the stairs tossing her unbound hair over her shoulder.

She heard the desk drawer slam shut when she was halfway to the parlor. Lonnie, as expected, was leaning with his back to the desk, his hands behind him.

Unshaven, dirty, wearing the same clothes he'd worn on the roundup, Lonnie Hewitt was still the most beautiful man Anna had ever seen. She caught her breath for a whisper of a moment. It took a conscious blink to erase the thoughts before they became desires.

The golden hair needed washing and cutting, but the eyes flashed their bright blue seductively, and his smile beguiled. It was not difficult to imagine him a fairy tale knight like Lancelot or Galahad. A man of such fair features belonged astride a white charger, a Crusader's cross blazoned on his standard. Even now, knowing that Lonnie had probably stolen all the money from the desk drawer again, Anna had some difficulty maintaining her hold on reality.

Her husband's former brother-in-law was indeed handsome, but that didn't keep Anna from loathing him.

"If you're looking for Lee," she began, not knowing whether Lonnie had heard the news.

A drunken smile preceded the expected sarcasm.

"Not here I ain't. In case you hadn't heard, you're a widow, Mrs. Johnson. They buried Lee this afternoon."

She held her head high and refused to turn away from his insinuating stare. "You weren't at the funeral. I didn't know if you had been informed."

He pushed himself away from the desk and staggered a couple of steps, then halted, bracing himself against the back of Lee's wing chair.

"You're drunk," Anna accused.

"Damn right I'm drunk. Been drownin' my sorrow ever since somebody told me about poor Lee." The sarcasm increased, if possible.

"That was two days ago."

"Right. I spent one day mournin' Lee and another mournin' the passing of the LJ Ranch," he sneered, as the sarcasm turned to anger. "This is *my* ranch, always was. My pa built it from nothin' and you got no right to it. Even the name. You think 'LJ' is for Lee Johnson? Hell, no. Pa named it for my mother, Loretta Jeanette, and if Lee hadn't wormed his way into the family by marrying my sister, it'd be mine like it was s'posed to be."

Anna had heard the story before, too many times. She had often wished, in the first days after her marriage to Lee, that he had had the nerve to evict Lonnie, but Lee had guaranteed his first wife's brother a place.

"Then you came along," Lonnie whined.

When he tried to come closer, he discovered his legs weren't completely under his control. He hung onto the chair, leaning forward as though he could stretch far enough to reach her without relinquishing his support.

Anna forced down a mental nausea brought on by the words she knew she had to say. She didn't want to say them, but she had been raised to accept the obligations that came with privilege.

"You are welcome to stay, on the same terms Lee offered. Or we can negotiate, since I admit I'm in a position where I need qualified men to help me."

He spat on the floor.

21

"I don't need to 'negotiate' with you, high and mighty Anna Beaumont from Philly-delphia. I don't need *nothin'* from you that I can't get myself."

"Like the money from the drawer?" she shot back at him, immediately wishing she had kept her mouth shut. Lonnie Hewitt in this state was not a man she wished to anger. In a more conciliatory tone she said, "Go ahead, take it. Regardless what Lee's will said, there will always be a place at the LJ for you, Lonnie."

The nausea became physical as well as mental. Anna could smell the man now; his stink of stale whiskey and old sweat made her stomach lurch.

He waved the tight little roll of greenbacks at her.

"Yeah, I'm takin' the money, but at least I admit it. Not like you, sneakin' into Lee's life and then takin' everything. There's a place for me all right at the LJ. It's the spot you stole from me."

Involuntarily defensive, Anna insisted, "Whatever made Lee write that will, I had nothing to do with it. I didn't even know he had done it until after the funeral."

Lonnie smirked. "I don't believe that any more than I believe Santy Claus is going to slide down that chimney come Christmas. But I ain't gonna stand here and argue. I got more important things to do."

He managed finally to stand without the chair's support. Though still unsteady, he walked slowly across the room toward Anna, almost mesmerizing her with the diabolic gleam in those enchanted blue eyes.

His hand came up to cup her chin. Though Anna turned her head, she could not escape either his hand or the revolting odor that seemed to hang about him like a thick, tangible cloud.

"The LJ is mine, by rights, and I mean to get it," he whispered. His callused fingers tightened on her jaw, turning her to face him. The stench of his breath made her gag. "You might own it now, thanks to your scheming, but it takes more than a piece of paper, no matter how legal it is, to decide who owns a ranch. If I was you, I wouldn't get too comfortable, because when I take this place over, I ain't makin' no 'generous' offers to keep you around."

Lonnie released her abruptly. She waited, eyes closed, expecting a slap, but his footsteps retreated almost immediately, and within a dozen heartbeats of his final remark, Lonnie Hewitt walked out the front door and slammed it behind him.

Anna kept her hand steady long enough to pour thick soup from the pot into Matthew's bowl and then into her own. She had found him in the kitchen when she went to pour herself a cup of hot tea after Lonnie's abrupt appearance and then departure, but both had seemed too embarrassed to bring the matter up.

By then darkness had fallen and Anna found being alone in the house more than she could stand. During the long ride back from the funeral, she had kept silent, uncomfortable with her stepson, but now she knew she would have been more uncomfortable alone. And it was time for supper. She had had nothing to eat all day, and the neighbors had brought more than enough food.

Without a word, Matthew set bowls and spoons on the table, then sat down to spead jam on generous slices of buttered bread while Anna took the soup back to the stove. Unable to bear the taut silence, she set the pot down with a noisy clang. Even that brought no response.

The only way to get answers, she decided, was to ask questions, regardless how unpleasant they might be.

"How much of my conversation with your uncle did you listen in on?" she began as she sat down. She remembered to keep as much accusation out of her voice as possible.

"Most of it," Matthew replied as he selected a slice of bread. "You want to learn to make good soup? Ask Mrs. Oskowitz, the baker's wife."

Anna tasted the rich-looking broth. It was every bit as

delicious as it looked. "Did she make this?"

"Yeah. Good, ain't it?"

"Yes, it is. And please, Matthew, don't say 'ain't.' At least not in the house."

He shrugged and took a ravenous bite from the bread. "You invited me," he reminded her.

"Yes, I did." She set her spoon in the soup but did not lift any to her mouth. "Matthew, we have to talk. I know you don't like me, and I know we'd both like . . . things to have worked out differently, but there's nothing we can do to—"

"I'm glad he didn't stay," the boy interrupted with his mouth full.

"Who? Don't talk with food in your mouth. And don't interrupt."

At that admonition, Matthew looked up from his meal and stared across the table at Anna.

"You sound like Ma," he said quietly. Anna couldn't tell if the statement was an accusation or a compliment. Then, as though shaking off the memory, he added, "I was talking about Uncle Lonnie. I'm glad he left."

"He's an experienced hand and with your father gone, I could have used that experience."

"He ain't—isn't—worth a plug nickel. Grant said the only thing more trouble on the range than Lonnie Hewitt is a stampede. If you really want some help—"

"Wait a minute." Anna rested her forearms along the edge of the table. "Is this Grant Brookington you are referring to?"

He returned to his meal with forced gusto. Anna recalled all too vividly that scene in the cemetery of Brookington with his arm around Matthew's shoulders.

She waited impatiently for an answer to her question. After a moment's silence, the boy spoke again, though he kept his eyes trained on the spoon in his bowl.

"He's a good friend, and he helped us a lot. He taught me a lot of stuff when Pa didn't have time or just plain didn't know. And there ain't nobody here got a bigger or

24

finer spread than the Diamond B. He knows all there is to know about ranchin'. A helluva lot more'n Uncle Lonnie."

Such unabashed loyalty brought a flush to the boy's cheeks, and a note of defensiveness to Anna's reply.

"I don't trust him."

"Does that mean you're gonna tell me I can't see him?"

Anna took a bite of the bread herself and chewed thoughtfully. Matthew said nothing, just waited for her response. At least now he looked at her, though she found his apprehensive stare unsettling. Yet there was honesty and openness in those blue-grey eyes.

"I'm not sure," she answered. "Why? Should I?"

"Pa did."

The boy was almost challenging Anna to make up her mind then and there, but she knew only too well the risks inherent in hasty decisions. She had made enough of them.

"I'll think about it," was the best she could do for now, and that seemed to satisfy him. Matthew returned his attention to his soup and ate noisily for several minutes, as though afraid to continue talking, afraid he'd say something he'd regret. Unsure of herself, Anna likewise remained silent.

She admitted that Matthew had a valid point. Grant Brookington was, in all likelihood, a veritable font of knowledge about the business of running a cattle ranch, and he had generously offered his assistance. That offer came, of course, before he knew that Anna had inherited the LJ. Then all he offered was to buy her out.

Why? she wondered. What made him change his mind, and his mood?

She shook off the mental cobwebs and picked up her spoon. The soup would be cold if she didn't eat quickly.

Matthew had already finished his and got up to refill his bowl. He took his time, stirring the contents of the pot and then ladling steamy broth and vegetables and chunks of meat slowly into the bowl.

"You know," he said, just as slowly, "I think you'd like Grant, once you got to know him."

She shook her head firmly.

"I don't have time for that nonsense, Matthew. Your father left the LJ in my hands, and I've got a lot to learn if I want to hang on to it. And, damn it, I *will* hang on to it."

"I think that's what made Grant so mad. The last thing he expected was for you not to sell it to him." Matthew carefully set the ladle back in the pot and carried the bowl back to the table. "I think you kinda surprised him, too. He was askin' me if you'd had any hysterics, wonderin' what you were gonna do with Pa gone and all. He asked if I needed any help takin' care of you."

"*Men!*" Anna exploded without warning. Matthew froze, a bite of bread halfway to his open mouth. "Every last one of you thinks women are so helpless. Well, you just tell Mr. Grant Brookington the next time you see him that Anna Johnson has, as you put it, a helluva lot more determination than he thinks. He's as bad as Lonnie. And I'll show them both."

The shocked expression on the boy's face registered, and Anna's quickly fired temper just as quickly died. She realized she had risen to her feet like an impassioned orator, and sheepishly she sat down again.

"I got a little carried way," she apologized, but the passion hadn't completely died. "You have to understand, Matthew, how hard it has been for me. Not just since Lee's death, or even since I came to Wyoming."

"I thought you was rich. What's so hard about that?" The bitterness had crept back, but not nearly as deep as before.

Anna shook her head slowly.

"My family did have money, once upon a time, but only because my daddy worked for it. He started with nothing, too, and he raised me like I was his son, to take over his business when I grew up."

26

"How come you didn't?"

"Matthew, you have got to stop interrupting! I didn't because the War came and Daddy lost everything. Every penny. And he was dying. He knew he wouldn't live long enough to build the business back after the War, and he didn't want me to lose it. I was sixteen, not much older than you, when he married me to Phillip Beaumont."

Matthew's eyes widened.

"I didn't know you was married before. Did Pa know?"

"Yes. I told him. When Phillip was killed, I had nothing left, so I had to go live with his brother Terrence in Philadelphia."

She halted, frightened by the emotions her memories had stirred. Anger, frustration, a sense of entrapment, and something even worse. The destruction of her dignity.

"Because I was dependent on Terrence and his family, I didn't dare do anything they didn't approve of."

"Like what?"

Finished with his meal, Matthew leaned his elbows on the table and rested his chin on his hands. His eyes glittered in the lamplight, and Anna suddenly understood that the animosity had melted, at least for now.

"Like work."

"What kind of work?"

"Like cook or clean or laundry or even sewing." What she had found difficult to say before became easy now. Matthew understood, or at least he was willing to listen and try to understand.

"Oh, it was all right to sit in the parlor and monogram Terrence's handkerchiefs, because embroidery was a suitable pastime for a lady of my social standing," Anna explained with no effort to hide her remembered displeasure and disgust. "It didn't make the slightest difference that we were poor as beggars; I could embroider but not mend."

"Sounds like they was pretty stupid folks, to me," the boy observed.

27

"They *were* pretty stupid," Anna corrected, then laughed at the way her correction sounded like an emphatic agreement. Even a little chuckle like that made telling the story somehow easier. "At first I tried to help them. Daddy was a trader in all kinds of merchandise and I learned from him how to strike a bargain, how to tell quality from cheap imitations, how to get the most for my money. Terrence's family didn't believe in that."

"You mean they didn't think you were any good at it?"

"That was part of it, I'm sure. Of course, Terrence's wife Sadie couldn't count her fingers and come up with the same total twice, so maybe they didn't understand that a woman *can* conduct business and make intelligent decisions. Still, I tried to help and they wouldn't listen, so after a while I gave up. For twelve years I watched what they did to themselves, until I thought the frustration would drive me insane."

"Then what happened?"

"I met your father."

Matthew tried but failed to stifle a snicker. "Love at first sight?"

"No, salvation at first sight. Or at least I thought it was."

The memories of more recent hurts, as well as old disappointments and frustrations unhealed by time, finally calmed her. Anna felt drained by her exhibition. After a long moment of quiet, she managed to whisper, "It's late, Matthew." She was suddenly so tired she was afraid if she put her head down on the table the way she longed to do, she'd fall asleep in an instant. "You're welcome to spend the night here, although I'll understand if you'd rather stay in the bunkhouse. And I'd appreciate an hour or two of your time in the morning, if you can spare it. I'd like you to teach me to ride."

"You sure? I mean, yeah, I got time. And I would kinda like to move back in the house. Grant'd say I was 'soft,' but them beds in the bunkhouse is hard, and it's awful cold out there this time o' year."

28

"It isn't any warmer in here. I could see my breath this morning."

He looked at her with his head cocked to one side. The blue-grey eyes blinked.

"Didn't you tell Pa to put the little stove in yet?"

Anna frowned and demanded to know, "What little stove?"

"It's just a little thing. I think Ma made him put it in the cellar in the summer. Said she kept bumpin' into it. 'Course he never got cold, so it was always up to her to tell him when she got chilly at night. He'd check the chimney pipe, and hook everything up so's we didn't freeze at night. It was nice, even though I had to carry the wood all the way up the stairs."

"And where is this wondrous stove supposed to go?"

"On the landing, where the hole for the chimney pipe is in the wall. Lord, you didn't think we slept up there all winter without any heat, did you?"

He laughed out loud, the uninhibited laughter of an innocent child.

There was no sense in her denying her ignorance. He could read her humiliation in her blush and in her silence.

"I guess we'd better get that stove out of the cellar first thing tomorrow morning," Anna suggested when her blush had faded enough to let her speak.

She would pile on the quilts tonight to avoid freezing, and the cold would serve as a reminder of how much she had yet to learn. Holding on to the LJ might not be as easy as she had expected, but Anna refused to give it up without a fight. At least this time she had been given a chance, albeit a slim one. Never again, she had vowed, would she surrender before the battle had even been engaged.

For whatever reason, Lee had put the LJ into her custody. But she realized now that she did not truly own the ranch. Not yet. Ownership was not something that could be written on a piece of paper; it had to be earned.

Chapter Three

Grant stomped the wet snow from his boots before he walked into Conner's Bank, out of the blustery wind at last.

Like most businesses in Greene, the bank was small, but on this Friday morning, the place was busy. Both tellers had long lines strung out from their cages. As much as Grant hated doing business with the bank, he hated waiting in lines even worse.

The only consolation was that old Mr. Conner, founder and president of the bank, allowed his customers as well as his employees sufficient heat in which to transact their business. The snow remaining on Grant's boots quickly melted, and as he took his place in line he removed his gloves. The wait would offer ample opportunity to warm himself after the long ride from the ranch.

"Grant? Is that you?"

He turned toward the slightly husky feminine voice behind him.

"It certainly is," he said with a smile, recognizing the delicate face framed by dark wisps of curls. "Good morning, Nancy. Haven't seen you for a coon's age."

Nancy Reynolds laughed and brushed droplets of cold water from the front of her fur-trimmed cape. She was an attractive woman some few years older than Grant, with

31

dark hair cut unfashionably, but very becomingly, short in curls that betrayed only the first hints of silver.

"You can't blame that on me or Dodd," she scolded. The dimples in her wind-reddened cheeks deepened. "You have a standing invitation any time you're in town. Tonight, maybe? For dinner? You look like you could do with a good meal."

"Sounds mighty good, Nan. I've got a lot of errands to take care of, though, and with the weather as chancy as it is I hate to be away too long."

"Weather's always chancy, and it's been a long time since you and Dodd visited. I thought you might have dropped by the hotel the other day, after Lee Johnson's funeral."

He shifted his weight to his other foot and glanced ahead to see if the line was progressing at all. It wasn't. And the direction of Nancy Reynolds' conversation was making him more than a little uncomfortable. Dodd Reynolds was an old friend whose marriage ten years ago to the town's first schoolteacher hadn't changed the friendship. What changed it, at least for today, were the memories Grant couldn't escape of himself as a defiant young man desperately in need of the advice offered by two older and far more experienced men. They both became his friends, but only Dodd Reynolds remained so. Lee Johnson betrayed that friendship, more than once. And being reminded of it rankled Grant like a raw wound.

As though aware that Grant had made no reply, Nancy Reynolds went on.

"It's hard to think of Lee being gone. And I can't imagine what that poor boy of his is going to do. You've heard, I'm sure, that Lee left the ranch to his new wife. There's been more than a little gossip about that."

"Yes, I heard." He almost told her that that news was one of the reasons for his presence in the bank this morning, but he discovered a sudden and inexplicable reluctance to discuss Anna Johnson. Besides, Nancy

32

prodded him to move up in the line and then she continued talking.

"Lonnie Hewitt claims she chased him off the place with a shotgun even though Lee promised him he could stay."

"When have you been talking to Lonnie Hewitt?" Grant asked, unable to keep his annoyance from adding a tartness to his tone. "And don't believe him. Anna Johnson probably doesn't know a shotgun from a skillet."

"You ought to know me better than that, Grant Brookington. Of course I don't believe Lonnie. Lord, after what he did to Dodd I wouldn't trust that snake any further than I could throw him." She shivered, either from a trickle of melting snow down her back or to settle her obvious dislike of Lonnie Hewitt. "It's about time somebody ran him off, for good. I just don't understand why Lee didn't make some provision for Matthew. After all, the ranch belonged to the boy's grandfather. And you must admit it seems awfully strange that Lee was married to that woman for less than a month and yet he left everything to her."

Looking over the heads of the patrons still waiting ahead of him, Grant wished there were some polite way he could get Nancy off the subject of Lee Johnson. The conversation brought back to Grant that stunning image of Lee's widow proudly declining his offer to buy the ranch. Her defiance, the way she had covered that underlying fear with stubbornness, had shocked the hell out of him.

He told himself he had to get rid of these unfamiliar and very uncomfortable feelings. This time he took the two steps forward without being nudged.

"It happens," Grant said with a shrug. "Lee brought her out here, and I guess he figured he didn't want to leave her without resources. He was getting on in years, you know, and accidents have happened to younger men."

33

A door suddenly slammed on one of the two private offices at the back of the bank, and all eyes turned toward the sound. A ripple of whispered speculation spread through the ranks of those still in line.

"Whoever it is, I hope he doesn't stay in there long," Grant said. "I have some business of my own with the old man."

He was saved from explaining himself by the timely arrival of another woman, who immediately engaged Nancy in excited conversation about someone's new baby. Leaving the women to their gossip, Grant turned to wait, with a little more patience than before. Only one man remained ahead of him. In a few minutes he would have the payroll for the Diamond B in his pocket and begin the wait to talk to Michael Conner.

The silver-haired gentleman behind the massive mahogany desk did not blink an eye when Anna shoved the door closed, but she still could tell her action had surprised him. Her patience, however, had run out. Anna had been pleading her case for almost half an hour. And in that half hour, patience had got her nowhere.

"If you intend to threaten me, young woman," Conner began, but left the sentence hanging as though he had no intention of finishing it.

"No threats, Mr. Conner," Anna said quietly as she returned to the plain wooden chair reserved for clients. Conner's own seat was as massive as the desk, upholstered in black leather, and tilted back to allow the banker comfort as well as the opportunity to display the heavy gold watch chain across the ample expanse of black brocaded waistcoat. "I would prefer some privacy for this conversation."

She hoped he wouldn't ask her why privacy had suddenly become such a concern. Under no circumstances could she tell him that none of the other patrons of his bank bothered her, but when she saw that familiar tall silhouette against the glass front window, she felt invaded. The others were just people, strangers to her as she was to them, and they would take no more notice of her business than she would of theirs. Grant Brookington was another matter entirely.

If her business with Mr. Conner had been proceeding smoothly, even then she might not have jumped up from her chair and shoved the heavy door closed. The frustration was what she did not want Grant to see. Or hear.

"I honestly do not see that there is any point to continuing this conversation," Michael Conner stated as he leaned back in his chair and folded his hands over that ostentatious watch chain. "You are a young, inexperienced woman, and I can see no reason why I should simply turn over—"

Anna leaned forward and grasped the crumpled piece of paper lying on the edge of the polished desktop.

"This is all the reason you need, Mr. Conner," she hissed, afraid she was losing all control of her temper. "My husband's will clearly states that everything he owned is now mine. That includes not only the ranch, the cattle, the horses, the wagon, the house, the furniture, even his clothes, but also whatever sums of money he had deposited in your bank. That money is mine to do with as I see fit, whether you agree with me or not."

She had never intended to make such a speech, but then she had not imagined any need for it. Matthew had told her that morning that he had to go into town for some supplies and she had taken advantage of the opportunity to put her newfound horsemanship into real practice as well as take care of some business of her own. Checking on the ranch's financial situation was one of the first priorities.

When the distinguished and kindly Mr. Conner himself offered his services, she followed him to his office with hopes of having her business taken care of quickly.

35

However, Conner's only service seemed to be the dispensing of advice, advice Anna had no intention of taking.

"I will admit that legally, yes, the ranch and its assets are yours," the banker said, his calm serving as a reminder to Anna of how close she had come to losing her own completely. "However, in your own best interests I must reiterate my suggestion that you sell the property as soon as possible, before it becomes a liability, and return to your family back East."

"How many times do I have to tell you that I don't *want* to go back East?"

Conner's voice and mien took on a more grandfatherly air, as Anna's panic rose, echoed in that murmur of "not again, not again" pulsing through her very blood. She bit the inside of her lip, searching for more patience.

"You are young, Mrs. Johnson, and quite unaware of the risks involved. I am sure that your romantic feelings toward your late husband inspired similarly romantic notions about our way of life in Wyoming."

"Hogwash," Anna interrupted as inelegantly as possible. Somehow, the epithet restored her calm and she was able to continue in a steady, almost unemotional tone. "I am not a silly romantic child, Mr. Conner. My twenty-eighth birthday has come and gone. But age is not just a matter of pages on a calendar, as you and I well know."

So, flattery will still accomplish some things, Anna observed with a sense of satisfaction. Conner unfolded his hands long enough to smooth back the white locks at his temples.

Anna went on with restored confidence. "My father was a businessman, the kind often referred to as 'self-made.' After my mother's death, Daddy treated me like the son who should have inherited his enterprise. There is very little I don't know about running a business. I admit there may be certain details peculiar to ranching that I'll have to learn, but I *can* learn."

"You won't need to go to all that trouble if you sell the ranch," Conner continued to cajole. "Mrs. Johnson, you could make a pretty penny off the sale and return to your family in comfort."

Dealing with this man was no less frustrating than her attempts to reason with her family. Actions, she had painfully learned, spoke far louder than words. But what action could she possibly take with the stubborn, yet powerful old man?

"You haven't listened to a word I've said, have you? I don't want to go back, rich or poor. All I want is to know how much Lee had in your bank so that I can plan my budget accordingly. My family history should have no relevance to this matter." Leaning forward to thump a fist on the unyielding mahogany, she again lost control and begged, "Why, for heaven's sake, won't you cooperate?"

She slumped back, wincing as her shoulder blades came in painful contact with the back of the plain wooden chair. And her fist throbbed, too.

But her tirade had no effect at all. Again Conner assumed that grandfatherly aspect, and Anna thought that if she had chosen to wear a dress, perhaps one of the old black velvet gowns that set off her figure to best advantage, she might have accomplished something. The old man seemed susceptible to feminine wiles, a weakness that had done no more to impress Anna with his business acumen than his present attitude.

But she had worn a pair of Lee's dungarees, and Matthew's outgrown coat, and perhaps Conner thought she was playacting, like a child dressing up in her mother's old clothes.

"Mrs. Johnson, I am only looking out for your best interests," he reiterated with all his detestable calm. "Isn't that what your father would do, if he were here?"

That was the last straw. Snatching the will from the desk once more, Anna got to her feet. She did not need to shake the paper intentionally; anger had her hands

37

quivering. It was only with the utmost effort that she kept from leaping across the desk and strangling that sanctimonious old blowhard. Instead, she strode to the door that she had slammed shut and grasped the knob firmly.

The best thing would be to walk out without another word. But as her hand turned the knob and was pulling the door open, Anna recalled something her father really had said, and it was nothing that Mr. Conner could ever have imagined.

She let the soft Virginia drawl flood back.

"My daddy taught me everything he knew, Mr. Conner. About business and about people. Most important, he taught me dignity and pride. Mama wanted to name me Victoria, after the queen, but Daddy said no. I was a squaller and a fighter, and after three boy babies had died, I lived. So Daddy named me after another queen, one who didn't let anyone or anything stand in her way, certainly not a man." Now was not the time for tears, but they came anyway.

She lifted her chin a fraction higher and tossed back the unruly brown hair. The years seemed to melt away, and instead of Michael Conner's tidy office in Greene, Wyoming, she stood surrounded by the clutter of Andrew Rush's quarters in the heart of Richmond.

Andrew himself, his once handsome features ravaged by grief and loss and disease, sat at the paper-littered desk. His daughter waited in frightened patience. She knew the War that had taken so many of her friends had claimed another victim, but she could not give up hope. Nor would her father allow her to admit defeat, though the low rumble of cannonfire shook the windows in their frames.

Though she saw again the scene in that Richmond warehouse, Anna delivered her exit lines to a very real and present nuisance, silver-haired Michael Conner.

"'Elizabeth' wasn't good enough, my daddy told me; he wanted me to be something special. My name is

38

Glorianna, Mr. Conner, after the queen who earned that title. I intend to live up to it, come hell or high water."

She pulled the door shut with a satisfying though useless bang.

Tears summoned by memories lingered on her lashes, blinding her momentarily. She wiped them away angrily, never slowing her strides. The paper still clutched in one fist blocked her vision for only a second at most, long enough for her not to see the man who had stepped away from the teller's window and then halted when her outburst shattered the quiet of the bank as abruptly as an attempted robbery.

She didn't see him, and if she had, she would not have recognized him, for the sun on the snow outside the plate glass window left even his silhouette blurred against the brilliance. Not until she had run right into Grant Brookington did she realize that her tirade in Conner's office had taken no more time than for a man to wait his turn in line and conduct his business with the teller.

Her furious strides had carried her with such momentum that when she collided with his broad chest, she might just as well have run into a wall. The force of the impact knocked the breath from her for an instant. She would have fallen, too, if Grant's strong hands hadn't caught her, grasping her by the shoulders while she regained her breath and her equilibrium.

It didn't take her long.

"Excuse me," she snapped, sniffing back the last tears as she attempted to retreat a step and walk around the solid barrier that blocked her way. She tried once to look up at him, but that forced her head to an uncomfortable angle that made her slightly dizzy. Besides, she had caught a glimpse of those rugged features set in what looked like a smug smile that would only increase her already substantial embarrassment.

"Are you all right? Is there anything . . . ?"

"I am fine," she insisted. Of all the people to run into, of all the people to bear witness to her failure, her frustration, her tears, why couldn't she have found someone other than Grant Brookington? She struggled to regain her composure and succeeded enough to demand, "You may remove your hands from my shoulders, Mr. Brookington."

He pulled the offending hands back and raised them in a gesture designed to assure innocence. Anna Johnson didn't notice. As soon as she was free of him, she hurried on to the door, her high-heeled shoes announcing each furious step. Finally she was outside, into a bright cold that was all the more bitter for the fire of humiliation raging inside her.

Grant's first reaction was to go after her, to grab her by the arm and demand an explanation right there in the bank, in front of witnesses, if need be. But the shock of seeing her left even that reaction too slow for effectiveness. She escaped before he realized he wanted to know what was going on.

By that time, he also realized it was none of his damned business, which was exactly what she'd probably tell him.

Grant finished tucking the payroll money into his inside pocket and then followed the woman's footsteps out the door. The sun had come out while he waited in line and now blazed in a crystalline sky and reflected off each individual snowflake that whitened the frozen street. When he blinked the glare away, he discovered that Glorianna Johnson was no longer to be seen.

Which, he told himself as he strolled down the sidewalk, was just as well.

But as he meandered through his long list of errands, he found her even more on his mind than before. At the post office, he walked in just as one woman, in conversation with another, exclaimed over a bit of gossip "Glory be!" and instantly Grant recalled that defiant declamation of another woman's name.

Glorianna.

At the barber he submitted to the pleasure of a steaming towel before a shave and haircut. The relaxation brought her image back into his thoughts. Her eyes, like molten gold behind tear-wet lashes, as she looked up at him in shock. Her lips, trembling with barely controlled fury, parted as she gasped for air. And that tangle of impossible hair, like so much fine old brandy spun into silken threads.

Glorianna. Not plain old Anna, a name that could belong to anyone's maiden aunt, but Glorianna. And it fit her, too. Grant wondered with a chuckle how many other men had suffered under the wrath of that glorious temper. At least he knew he wasn't alone. The high and mighty Michael Conner, who had been known to brag that he controlled the purse strings and therefore the lives of damned near everyone in Greene, wasn't immune to the sting of that sharp little tongue.

From the barber's Grant braced himself for the cold outdoors again and crossed the single street to the general store. As he reached to pull the door open, someone inside pushed it conveniently toward him.

"Thanks," said the boy behind a pile of brown paper wrapped packages. Then, seeing who held the door for him, Matthew added, "Oh, hello, Grant."

"Morning, Matthew. Looks like you've been busy."

The boy adjusted the parcels so that they no longer looked like such an unmanageable load.

"You know how it is after a roundup," he said, tucking one rather flat package under his arm. "A few things got lost or broke so I figgered I'd best replace 'em now, before winter sets in good."

Grant nodded his approval and, delaying his own shopping for a while, decided to stroll with the boy. Heaven only knew when he'd get the chance again.

"Are things okay, Matthew?" he asked bluntly. He noticed the boy never missed a step but kept pace with his own long strides. Matthew was growing; pretty soon he'd be as tall as his father. Good God, where had the years

41

gone? "I mean, is there anything you need help with? I didn't expect to see you out so soon, and I thought maybe things were . . ."

They reached the end of the boardwalk, but instead of stepping down to the snowy street, Matthew stopped and faced the older man.

" 'Things' is just fine." The force of the boy's sarcasm set Grant back on his heels. "And just what'd you expect me to do, dress up in black like some widow lady? We got a ranch to run, whether Pa's around or not, and none of the work gets done by folks who sit around and grieve."

He grabbed at a small package that started to slip from his grasp. When Grant moved to help, Matthew's angry glare forced him to retreat. An instant later, the anger melted, and the young shoulders slumped.

"I'm sorry," Matthew mumbled. "Jeez, Grant, I didn't mean to get mad at you. It's just that with *her* not knowin' how to do nothin' and me spendin' half my time doin' things *she* oughta be doin', or teachin' her how, it seems like nothin' at all gets done. Now with the bank givin' her a hard time about Pa's money, well, it's just one more problem when we don't need none."

So that was what had prompted the outburst in the bank. Before he had a chance to think, Grant instinctively offered, "If it's money you need . . ."

Matthew shook his head and began to walk up the street. The snow was melting now, leaving a cold, muddy slush.

"We don't need nothin' right now," the boy asserted. "I showed her where Pa kept the cash so Uncle Lonnie wouldn't get it, and it'll be enough for a while."

"For a while maybe, but it's not even winter yet, son," Grant interjected. "What will you do then?"

"We'll manage. She told me she knows all about runnin' a business and a ranch is just another kind of business." He stopped again, this time halfway across the sloppy street. "Look, Grant, I gotta go."

Matthew didn't have to say that he wasn't sure he

42

wanted to be seen in Grant Brookington's company. Grant understood, and the last thing he wanted was to get the boy in trouble.

"Okay, you go ahead, but you tell her my offer still stands. If the LJ needs my help, you holler. And don't let some foolish notion of pride stand in your way of asking, no matter what your stepmother says. Pride's not worth losing the ranch over."

The boy only nodded. His load of packages kept him from shaking hands, which gave Grant the opportunity to give him a comradely pat on the shoulder, for encouragement as well as to express his faith in the boy's ability.

Watching Matthew walk away, Grant discovered an odd lump in the back of his throat that didn't seem to want to go away. He blamed it on memories of another boy who had been just as fiercely independent.

As Grant headed toward the Cattleman's Club, he separated his past from the present and put the entire situation into what he considered its proper perspective. Matthew Johnson was fourteen years old, not a man yet but no longer a boy, and he had been raised on the ranch, knew damn near everything there was about running it. Though Lee's untimely death may have thrust too much responsibility too suddenly onto Matthew's young shoulders, Grant believed Lee's son could handle it. At least Matthew would know that he had someone to turn to, someone he could trust. Which was more than a seventeen-year-old Grant Brookington had had.

Satisfied with his logic, he hunched his shoulders against a gust of cold wind and slopped his way across the street.

Chapter Four

The Cattleman's was quiet this time of day, the lunch patrons having left but the dinner crowd still to arrive. Grant scraped the mud from his boots before entering, then gratefully doffed the heavy sheepskin jacket and left it in the care of McAndrew. Grant placed two half-dimes in the old man's palm and then walked to his usual table unescorted.

The Cattleman's Club of Greene, Wyoming kept no formal membership rolls. Prices restricted entry to those able to afford twice what the other eateries charged, and failure to abide by the posted rules of behavior—no discharging of firearms, no spitting, no disorderly conduct of any kind—earned a man immediate and usually permanent expulsion.

The decor was the best Greene could offer, which meant polished oak on walls and floor, molded plaster ceiling, gleaming brass lamps, and fine mahogany furniture. It was a good place to do business with a cattle buyer from St. Louis or Chicago, who might appreciate a prime steer but not be willing to ride the ten or twenty or thirty miles to a rancher's home. It was a good place to celebrate the end of a long year riding fences, branding calves, cursing the summer drought and praying for rain to bring the grasses back. And if nothing else, the Cattleman's was a good place just to relax.

Grant settled into the comfort of the secluded booth. He ordered a cold beer, then leaned back against the black leather upholstery and closed his eyes for a moment's rest after the glare and sunshine outdoors. He was just letting the relaxation spread downward from his shoulders when the thunk of a heavy glass mug on the table brought his eyes open.

A slim, dapper man, his dark hair and luxurious moustache liberally touched with silver, leaned on an ivory-headed cane across the table.

"Long time no see," Dodd Reynolds said quietly as he took in the surprise on Grant's face.

Grant smiled at the friendly sarcasm.

"I see your wife's handiwork in this. Join me?"

"Don't mind if I do."

Dodd slid awkwardly onto the opposite bench. The leg shattered so many years ago remained stiff, but Dodd called no attention to it nor did Grant mention it.

"Nan said she saw you in the bank this morning, but she didn't put me up to this. I was on my way to the livery and saw you with young Johnson. How's he doing?"

"About as expected. I don't think it's really sunk in yet."

Dodd signalled a passing waiter with a gesture the man acknowledged as an order for another beer. "Probably not. Especially when it was so sudden. One minute he's got a father, the next minute the guy's dead."

"I didn't mean about Lee. I'm not sure Matthew realizes the ranch isn't his anymore."

A bitterness tightened lines around Dodd's eyes. "Well, it probably should have gone to Lonnie, but I'm glad it didn't."

"Lee had no love for his brother-in-law, either," Grant observed. The waiter returned with Dodd's mug just then. "Here, let me get it. You're no cattleman, so you gotta be my guest."

Dodd started to protest, but Grant had the half dollar out of his pocket and onto the waiter's tray too quickly.

46

"Then let me offer you dinner," the older man suggested. "Nan did say she invited you, so you can't say you weren't warned."

The words declining the invitation were on the tip of Grant's tongue, but he stopped them just in time. Sometimes, he warned himself, the easy way out proves more difficult than the hard way. He knew there'd be no peace if he spent an evening with Dodd and Nancy. The memories would come, the good ones as well as the bad still laced with the same pain.

The easy way to avoid them was to do as he usually did when he stayed in town on a Friday night. After a few beers, he'd order his dinner and eat alone. When he had finished, he'd have McAndrew bring him a fat cigar and a bottle of the smoothest bourbon in the place. By the time the bottle was half empty, Grant would have chosen a girl from the covey who strolled decorously through the club. With the girl in one hand and the bottle in the other, he'd trudge upstairs to the room he always took; and from then until he fell into exhausted sleep, he'd spend every ounce of energy in the pursuit of mindless pleasure.

In the morning the girl would be gone, and he might or might not remember her name. And there would still be so many things that he could not forget.

He spent no more than three or four seconds exploring this avenue, not long enough for Dodd to question the time he spent contemplating a simple invitation to dinner. Yet in those few seconds, Grant recognized that the easy way out left other difficulties to be overcome.

"Sounds like a helluva good idea to me."

"And you'll spend the night." It was a statement, not another invitation. "We can't offer quite all the comforts of the Cattleman's, but—"

"Leave it to a happily married man like you to remind me!" Grant laughed. "I'll survive, I promise."

Grant was about to down the last of his beer when a

47

disturbance at the entrance to the dining room stopped his hand in midair.

"Like hell I will!" a slurred voice snarled. "You'll get the money when I've got the whiskey, the food, and the girl, not before!"

What little conversation had buzzed in the main room a minute ago now ceased. A low, indistinct voice seemed to plead with the intruder, but the conciliatory words went unheeded. Then Lonnie Hewitt swaggered into the room.

"Look, it got paid, didn't it? I don't owe you a red cent, so get outta my way. I'm gonna sit myself down at one of them tables, and you better bring me that whiskey quick."

Grant watched as Lonnie almost stumbled, then collapsed into the booth right behind Dodd.

"Let's go," Dodd whispered. "I don't like—"

"No, wait. He doesn't know you're here."

Grant's initial reaction to Lonnie's arrival had been no different from Dodd's. There was no love lost between them, though Grant, unlike Dodd, could not say that Lonnie had ever caused him any trouble. He simply did not like the headstrong, lazy, and often dishonest Hewitt. And what was it Matthew had said? Something about Lonnie stealing money from the ranch.

"What the hell do you want to stay for?" Dodd asked, his voice still low.

Grant answered in the same hushed tone. "I don't know. Shshsh."

He had told the truth. He didn't know what was making him stay, or why he leaned forward, elbows on the table, his fingers curled lazily around the half-empty mug of beer, to catch any and every word Lonnie Hewitt might utter. The hairs the barber had just cut at the back of his neck prickled.

A waiter brought the whiskey and took the silver dollars Lonnie flipped at him.

"I think I know why Lee left the ranch to his wife,"

Dodd commented. He had lifted the ivory-headed cane to rest it across his thighs, and he never took his hand from it.

"Why? And what's that got to do with Lonnie?"

"Put yourself in Lee's shoes. He's not getting any younger. He's got a boy he can't hardly control, a boy who spends a lot of time with a man Lee would just as soon he didn't."

"Me," Grant confessed. "I couldn't help it. He was Melody's son."

"That's just it. I think Lee was still jealous of you. He took Melody, and after she was gone, he didn't want you to get the LJ. You know as well as I do that Matthew would have turned to you for help if Lee left him the ranch."

"Christ, I already tried to buy it from his stepmother so I could give it to him."

"You did what?"

Grant slumped back. He listened first, to make sure he wasn't missing anything from Lonnie, who was apparently content to toss back one shot of whiskey after another in absolute silence.

"I asked her how much she wanted for it right after the funeral. I figured she'd sell out so she could hightail it back to Philadelphia. But she just flat-assed refused. Said it was hers and it wasn't for sale."

"Do you suppose Lee knew she'd do that?"

"Maybe he did, maybe he didn't. He probably did, and left it to her just to spite me."

Dodd leaned forward and stroked the luxurious moustache thoughtfully. "Or to keep it out of Lonnie's hands. Matthew's only what, fourteen, fifteen years old? Someone would have to be appointed his guardian until he turned twenty-one. Lonnie's his only living blood relative. If Lee named his wife as guardian, don't you think Lonnie would have fought it? And won, on the grounds that he knew better how to protect the boy's interest?"

But Grant had no chance to answer. Again Lonnie interrupted them, this time with a demand for a round of drinks, at his expense.

"It's all right," he chortled. "I got the money for it. Gonna have more, lots more, pretty soon. But I got enough for tonight."

Grant dared to rise from his own seat and watch as Lonnie tried to pour himself another shot of whiskey. Some of the amber fluid sloshed into the glass, but then he lost control and poured more on the table. He set the bottle down angrily.

"My damn glass's broke," he complained, then ordered, "Gimme a new one!" He pounded his fist on the table so violently that the half-full glass toppled, spilling its contents onto his lap.

While the waiter fussed over the mess, Lonnie looked up and around, checking to see who had witnessed the accident and his humiliation. Then he spotted Grant, and a malicious grin spread over his features. Slowly, unsteadily, Lonnie got to his feet.

"Well, now, if it ain't Grant Brookington. I heard you tried to buy the LJ from Lee's wife."

He spat the last words with angry sarcasm.

"I did," Grant admitted quietly. He had dealt with drunks before and knew better than to anger one by ignoring him.

"Didn't work, did it?"

"No."

"You know why? Because the LJ ain't hers to sell."

When Dodd made a move to get up, too, Grant motioned him back. The hatred festering between his friend and Lonnie Hewitt didn't need an outlet now. Not in the club, not in public.

"Isn't it? Then whose is it?"

Lonnie crossed his arms across his chest and belched loudly as he leaned back against the oak divider between his booth and the one where Dodd Reynolds sat.

"It's mine, all mine. Or it will be. Soon's I get my papers filed in court."

He paused, but the pause wasn't long enough for Grant to ask another question. And he had a thousand of them stampeding through his brain. But Lonnie went on, his voice slipping almost to an unintelligible mumble. The eyes, so much like Melody's that Grant couldn't meet them, sagged closed.

"It's like this," Lonnie began, struggling to get his eyes open. "In order to be a widow, a woman's got to be a wife, and so therefore, the Widow Johnson ain't a widow. 'Cause she weren't never Lee's wife. And if she weren't Lee's wife, then she don't own the LJ, 'cause his will said he left it to his wife, and he didn't have one."

Lonnie's head lolled back and he sighed as though drifting into drunken slumber. Then he smiled again, his eyes still closed.

"I shouldn't be telling you this, Brookington. It's my little secret. But I heard she told you off, too. She's a spitfire, she is. But she ain't nobody's wife. Never was. Lee told me just before he went on that roundup."

Good God, what did he say! Grant wanted to scream. He was afraid Lonnie would pass out before he got to the end of his story.

A shudder rippled through Lonnie. He lifted his head and shook it, as though to clear the fuzz from his mind. He even opened his eyes, and finding a fresh bottle and glass on the table, proceeded to pour himself another drink. This time he managed not to spill any, and brought the glass to his lips to throw the liquor back cleanly.

"Damn good whiskey this place serves, you know it?" He looked at Grant and smiled. "I could come to like it here. Good whiskey, fine food, and they say the girls are nice, too. You'd know about that, wouldn't you, Brookington? I'll bet you've had every one of 'em here."

"I've enjoyed the company of some of the ladies, yes."

Lonnie winked slyly and asked in an undertone, "You

51

ever had a virgin? I mean, one you know ain't never done it before?"

Grant's hands clenched into fists, and the rage threatened to explode. He couldn't find an answer, a lie that would keep Lonnie talking, but it didn't matter. Lonnie wasn't listening any more.

"Well, I never did, but I'm gonna. I'm gonna have me my brother-in-law's virgin widow."

He struggled to remain standing, but the whiskey and whatever he drank before he arrived at the Cattleman's had taken effect. Lonnie sank slowly back onto the seat in the booth.

"Sounds kinda silly, don't it?" he mumbled. "But it's true, and I'm gonna prove it. They never slept together, not once. And he told me she never did it with her first husband, neither. Can you imagine that? Married twice, and still a virgin. Beats all, don't it?"

What he said after that drifted into complete incoherence, and a few minutes later Lonnie slumped sideways, his head hitting the padded leather seat with a resounding whack. Grant signalled one of the waiters, but by the time the man arrived, Lonnie was snoring.

"Haul him out of here," Grant ordered, aware for the first time that he had broken into a nervous sweat. Feeling oddly weak, he returned to the alcove where Dodd waited.

"What the hell was that all about?"

"You didn't hear him?" Grant asked.

"Not a word. Oh, I heard him mumbling, but couldn't understand a thing." Dodd tapped on the thick oak panel behind his shoulder. "Not a whole lot gets through these things, and he had his back to me."

Grant sagged onto his own seat and thirstily gulped the remains of his beer. It was warm and flat, but it didn't matter. Nor did it have any effect.

"He was just ranting and raving about the ranch, about how it should have been his and how he's got some scheme to get it away from Glory. You didn't hear him?"

If Dodd had heard nothing, perhaps the secret was safe.

"I told you I didn't. Come on, let's go see what Nan's got cooking. At least her dining room doesn't smell like a rotten skunk's been in it."

The bedsprings creaked as Anna counted the bills again, setting them in neat little stacks beside the coins. She shivered, partly from the cold in the bedroom and partly from the knowledge that her financial resources were considerably shallower than she had hoped.

"How far will ninety-seven dollars and eighty-five cents get us?"

"Not far," Matthew admitted. "But we got another coupla weeks before we need to come up with the next payroll, and we should be able to get that money from Conner. He can't expect the hands to go without pay."

Anna sighed and tried to run her fingers through her tangled hair but failed. As soon as Matthew had departed for his own room, she would have to get out the brush and do her nightly five hundred strokes, which would probably make her head ache worse.

"How are our supplies?"

"Fair, but could be better."

"That's what I was afraid of."

With another sigh, she began gathering up the bills and coins. Matthew yawned loudly.

"Oh, Lord, Matthew, I'm sorry. You've been up since dawn and it must be close to midnight. Go ahead to bed, and we'll worry about this in the morning."

She was relieved he didn't argue with her, as he often did when she gave him orders. He was gone, closing the door behind him, before she had dropped the last of the coins into the little leather pouch.

Matthew could be surly when he wanted to, and stubborn, but as Anna tucked the pouch under her pillow, she murmured a quick prayer of thanks that the

53

boy seemd to be on her side. He could have kept Lee's cache a secret, or taken the money for himself. Instead, he revealed the loose floorboard under the bed as soon as Lonnie had left that horrible afternoon.

She blew out the lamp and removed her heavy robe in the dark, then felt for the edge of the bedspread and deftly turned it back. The sheets were cool, but not uncomfortably cold, and under the weight of blankets and comforters, Anna knew she'd soon be cozy and warm.

And alone.

She rolled onto her side and curled into a tight ball for warmth, and with an effort forced those silly thoughts of loneliness out of her head. They quickly returned.

She blamed them on exhaustion and tossed onto her other side, this time stretching her toes deep into the warmth where the bricks were wrapped in heavy towels. She blamed her confusion on exhaustion, too. Was it thoughts of Grant Brookington that reminded her she had slipped into bed without brushing her hair, or did the thought of her hair bring Grant Brookington to mind?

Never in her life had she been so embarrassed as when she stormed out of the pompous Mr. Conner's office and plowed head first into the man she least wanted to see. Even now, as she pummeled the pillow into shape, she could see the shock in those steel-grey eyes of his. She was certain he couldn't guess why she had practically shouted at him to get his hands off her shoulders, but even that certainty didn't erase the memory of how she had felt his strength and how she had wanted to take advantage of it and let him hold her close while she cried out all her frustration.

The idea was as ridiculous in the dark of her bedroom as it had been in the bank. Grant Brookington had no comfort to offer her, only cash to take away what was rightfully hers. She thought back to the days when she and her father had discussed finances, but she couldn't come up with any acceptable way of finagling the money she needed out of Grant without sacrificing all or part of her precious independence.

A loan would require collateral, and that would give him an interest in the ranch. She didn't want that. Her father had always told her, never take in a partner who doesn't have as much to lose as you do. Grant had nothing to lose by lending her a little money, and everything to gain.

No, she told herself as she flopped onto her back again. Grant Brookington held no answers.

But that didn't get him out of her thoughts, and she could only hope he didn't invade her dreams.

Chapter Five

"Five, ten, fifteen, twenty." Anna counted each bill into the leathery palm, hoping she betrayed none of her anguish. "I'm sorry you feel the way you do, Bob. You'll be missed."

It was not the biggest lie she had ever told, just the bitterest.

"Well, like I said, Miz Johnson, I figger I ought to git out before the money does. I ain't never seen no woman run a ranch and hang on to it, and if I was you, I'd be gittin' out."

There was no malice in the cowboy's pronouncement as he rolled the bills neatly and tucked them into an old tobacco pouch. Without so much as a good-bye, he mounted the buckskin pony and touched his heels to its flanks. It ambled off, toward the road that led to town. Afraid to watch the forlorn little caravan of man and horse, Anna turned her gaze in the other direction.

She immediately regretted it. Like a bronze statue against the autumn sky, Grant Brookington sat on his horse not thirty feet from her.

Oh, God, what can he possibly want now? Anna wondered. She shivered inside the outgrown coat she had borrowed from Matthew.

"Good afternoon, Mr. Brookington," she greeted, walking closer.

57

The horse stretched out his head and snuffled a greeting of his own. Anna captured the steaming velvet nose in her cupped hands, savoring the warmth on her frozen fingers.

"Good afternoon," Grant replied. "Was that Bob Lewis you just paid off?"

Immediately defensive, Anna retorted, "Yes, and I didn't let him go. He asked to leave. Said he didn't cotton to workin' cows for no female."

The man had the temerity to laugh as he swung his leg over the horse's back and dismounted.

"That's Bob, all right." He shook his head, then, when he looked at her again, his expression had changed to one of concern. "Can you get along without him? If you need help—"

"I know, I know, all I need to do is holler. Well, have you heard me holler yet, Mr. Brookington?"

Hands on her hips, she glared at him, challenging him. He halted, the reins loose in his hands. His sheepskin coat molded the broad shoulders and powerful chest Anna had encountered so suddenly last Friday. The memory of that accident in the bank was more of her own embarrassment, but as Anna stared at the man now, in her own stableyard, she could think only of the way her body had collided with his, the unyielding strength she had pushed away, and the cocksure confidence he so easily exhibited when he released her.

"No, Mrs. Johnson, I haven't heard you holler," he conceded.

He flipped the leathers over the horse's head and without an invitation led the beast to the rail fence around the backyard. A gust of wind stirred the fallen oak leaves and swirled a cloud of dust in the yard. The snow of a week ago was gone, replaced by the dry, frozen ground after a hard frost.

"Then I don't need any help."

"Maybe, maybe not. Is Matthew here?"

So that was it. He wanted to see Matthew. Anna didn't

58

like the feeling of disappointment that stabbed at her.

"He's in the bunkhouse, I think," she said.

"Thanks. I need to talk to him as well as to you. How 'bout if I go get him and you put on some coffee in the kitchen?"

Anna saw something in his features that quelled any argument. She had a feeling he brought bad news, and she needed no more of that. Eventually he'd learn that Bob Lewis wasn't the first of her hands to give notice of his intention to seek work elsewhere.

Rats leaving a sinking ship, she had told herself several times in the past three days and again as she opened the gate and walked across the yard to the porch. First Will Parker, then the quiet Mexican known only as Chino had departed, each claiming a week's wages. Yesterday Nate Holt quit, and today Bob Lewis.

Anna pushed it all out of her mind. In the kitchen she pulled off the heavy, ill fitting coat and hung it on its peg by the door, then checked on her stew. This was the first time she'd been able to stand the thought of rabbit stew since the night Lee had been killed, but a steady diet of beef—and her own limited culinary skills—had made her desperate.

She filled the coffee pot and set it on the range, then opened the damper to allow the fire to blaze hotter. The fact that Brookington had had to invite himself rankled, and Anna felt a flush creep up her throat. What had happened to her manners? Her Aunt Phoebe must be turning over in her grave, to think that generations of fine Southern hospitality had come to naught in the person of Anna Rush Beaumont Johnson. As detestable as he might be in other ways, Grant Brookington was still a neighbor who had come to call. The least he deserved was an invitation to warm himself after the long ride.

Coffee was all she could offer him. Even in Philadelphia, poor as they were, the Beaumonts always managed to serve cakes or tarts with the tea offered to visitors. The shelves in Anna's pantry held jars of jam and pickles, peaches and pears and applesauce, all the product of Lee's first wife's labor, but not a single tin of shortbread cookies, not a single slice of cherry pie, not a single strawberry tart.

"Well, what does he expect?" she grumbled aloud as she took three heavy mugs from a shelf and carried them to the table. "I can't learn to run the ranch and learn to cook at the same time. Lord knows there's plenty of beef, so at least we won't starve."

She added coffee to the boiling water and enjoyed the satisfying bitter aroma that filled the kitchen. That simple pleasure faded when the back door burst open to admit Grant and Matthew in animated conversation.

"Hanged 'em both?" Matthew asked, his voice rising with disbelief.

"On the spot. Cinch ring's as good as a running iron, and they each had one." Grant closed the door carefully, shutting out the cold.

It hadn't been easy crossing the yard and climbing the worn steps to the back porch, and he had slipped into the discussion of the summary executions of a couple of cattle rustlers in order to cover his apprehension. Now, standing in the kitchen, he knew he had failed. The smell of coffee, the familiarity of the trestle table, benches, cookstove, even the cast iron pots hung next to the chimney, all combined to send a quiver almost akin to fear through him.

He hadn't set foot in this kitchen in ten or twelve years. Matthew was a toddler that last time, stacking wooden blocks in the middle of the floor while his mother baked bread and apple pies. There had been an ugly confrontation that resulted in the shattering of two hearts, and Grant never returned. The pain should have been gone, faded beyond remembrance, but he felt a sharp twinge nonetheless.

"Coffee's all I've got," the woman said as she poured the dark brew into the three cups on the table. "I'm afraid I don't have much time for baking."

"This is fine. Just something to warm me up. It's getting mighty cold out there."

"Think it'll snow?" Matthew asked.

"Probably. But not much."

How inane. Standing here in this achingly familiar kitchen, surrounded by memories so sweet and yet so bitter, and what did he do but talk about the weather.

He started to pull out the bench to sit at the table, but the woman stopped him.

"Please, let's go into the parlor. It's much more comfortable."

Grant wanted to protest, but he knew he couldn't. What was he supposed to say, excuse me, Mrs. Johnson, but the last time I was in that parlor I made love to your late husband's late wife on a bearskin rug while her son slept in a cradle five feet away from us?

No, that was unthinkable, as were all thoughts of Matthew's mother. Grant forced them from his mind the way he had done countless times before. He picked up his mug, savoring the warmth that oozed into his hands, and followed Lee's widow into her parlor.

The room was poorly lit, but where she sat, on a black wing chair, the weak sunlight came softly through the window like a halo. Not that it made her look much like an angel. Most of her hair was pulled back and tied with what looked like an old ribbon, but long wisps straggled free in languid curls that hung over her shoulders. Only her eyes, wide and cautious, hinted at innocence.

"You said you wanted to talk to me and Matthew," Anna opened. "If it's about buying the ranch, I assure you it still is not for sale."

Grant warned himself to pay attention. He hadn't come all this way just to stare.

He unbuttoned his coat to let in the warmth from the fire and replied to her insistence, "I didn't think it would be. Maybe what I've got to say will change your mind and maybe it won't."

He strolled almost lazily to the fireplace and set the

mug on the mantel. Leaning against the warm stones, he took a few seconds to put his words in order. He warned himself she might not believe him, but he had to tell her.

"I was out riding fences this morning," he began. "Ice storms like the one we had Sunday night can play hell with barbed wire, especially if it's old. Since I had to make the rounds anyway, and since the LJ is a neighbor, regardless who owns it," he said with just a little added emphasis, "I figured I'd check some of yours, too."

She seemed to anticipate the news, but Grant noticed there was no crumbling of her resolve. If anything, she became more stubborn than ever.

"How extensive was the damage?" she asked, pushing one of those tempting strands of hair back over her shoulder. He had a feeling it wouldn't stay there long.

"Considering how bad the storm was, I didn't find too many breaks. What I did find were cuts."

Before the woman could respond, Matthew exclaimed, "Somebody cut our fences? You got any idea who did it? Did we lose any cattle?"

Grant listened to the boy, but his eyes remained on the woman, and she in turn stared at him. He couldn't tell if she accused him of anything other than being the one to bring her more bad news, but there was definitely something in that tawny gaze he couldn't quite fathom.

"From what I can tell," he began, directing his reply squarely at those steady golden eyes, "it happened in the last two nights. There were no tracks, which means the culprits were there either before the storm wiped them out or after the freeze. My guess is the latter, because the cut ends were still clean, with no rust."

"What about the cattle?" she asked, her voice cool and calm, but only through obvious effort.

"None lost. Lee only used that pasture in the spring because of the creek. It's good water for a while, but it dries up by June usually."

"So there was no real damage done."

He shrugged and glanced down at the bare stones of the

hearth. At least the bearskin rug was gone, and the cradle. He wished the memories were as easily disposed of. They crept back, requiring more and more effort to keep them safely buried.

"I can't say, Mrs. Johnson. The fences have to be mended, and that'll take time and men."

"You said the pasture won't be needed until spring. Can the fences wait until them?"

That soft hint of a drawl became more pronounced. Grant had noticed it the other day at the funeral, but it was faint, like certain memories. In the bank, when she yelled at Conner, the accent deepened, as it did now. He suspected she was more worried than she wanted him to know.

"They can wait, yeah, but come spring, the men are going to be busy with other chores. Now's the time to get the fences taken care of, *before* they're needed."

Time she had, men she didn't. Nor did she have the money to buy them. Looking at him, at his relaxed, almost proprietary pose in front of the fire, she knew he understood her predicament as well as she, and probably better.

"I won't pretend with you, Mr. Brookington," she said quietly. "I'm not able right now to spare the men unless absolutely necessary. Where exactly are these fences, and what do I risk if I don't repair them before spring?"

She had already taken the risk of admitting her situation to him, but her father had always told her that success involves risks. Those not willing to take them rarely succeed. And she desperately wanted to succeed at this venture. It was her first, and if she failed, it would very likely be her last. She had little to lose.

Brookington glanced at the boy seated on the sofa.

"Matthew knows the pasture. It's high ground but level, with good grass early in the spring. Lee usually put late-calving cows in there to save having to round them up later. Problem is with the creek. If you don't keep the cattle fenced, they tend to head downstream, where there's a nasty little ravine you can't get them out of. All it takes is a little rain shower and that ravine fills up with water. Two days later, you'll find the dead cows ten miles downstream."

Grant didn't wait for any response. He immediately went on, "There's another risk, Mrs. Johnson. That pasture is at the edge of the LJ. Beyond it is open range. If your cows get out and drop their calves where you can't keep an eye on them, they're fair game for any rancher to brand and claim as his own."

All his earnest warnings had not the slightest effect on her. She replied calmly, "Then it appears to me all I need do is not put the cattle in that pasture."

"A simple solution, if those are the only fences cut. Or if no more get cut in the future."

He waited, letting the suspicion sink in. The thoughts tumbled through her brain exactly as she was sure he wanted them to. The whole thing was far too cleverly planned for her to think otherwise.

"Mr. Brookington, I greatly appreciate your coming to me with this unfortunate information. However, I think it best that in the future you leave the supervision and maintenance of the LJ to me."

"That's all? You aren't going to do anything?"

"What business is it of yours? You did the neighborly thing in letting me know." She got slowly to her feet and took several steps toward the kitchen—and the back door. "Now, if you'll excuse us, Mr. Brookington, Matthew and I have work to do."

He ignored her hint that his welcome had run out. As much as he admired her control, her stubborn pride and determination, he couldn't help but think she was in way, way over her head.

"Damn it, Glory, this isn't something you can ignore. I know what your situation is, I know you can't spare the men. I can. Will you, for God's sake, let me help?"

"No!"

The word exploded from her before she could stop it,

but he had shaken her to her very roots with that one word, the name her father had called her all those years ago. She had almost forgotten it, and the pride Andrew Rush had always put into his voice when he spoke it. Even as a small child, she had wanted nothing more than to be able to live up to that pride and the hopes Andrew had pinned on her.

Now, hearing the name from Grant Brookington's lips, a shiver ran through her, not of fear, but of energy, of reawakening determination deeper and stronger than any she had felt before.

"I don't want or need *your* help." She took a single step toward him, her hands on her hips, and faced him with those wild honey eyes ablaze. "You think you're so clever, Grant Brookington. Now I'm not accusing you of anything, but it seems mighty convenient that you were the one who happened on those cut fences."

"What's so convenient about it? It was damn cold out there at six o'clock in the morning, and I didn't *have* to ride out of my way to check your fences."

"Just like you didn't have to ride all the way over here to tell me about them? Then why did you?"

It finally dawned on him what she was hinting at, and then he exploded.

"My God, you think *I* cut those fences, don't you! Well, let me tell you, lady, if I wanted to sabotage this operation, I'd have been a hell of a lot more subtle about it."

He glanced around the parlor, noting the changes he hadn't seen before. The sofa was threadbare, and the single lamp was a cheap, functional piece with a plain glass chimney. Gone were the elegant crystal lamps and the silver candlesticks Melody Hewitt claimed her grandmother had stolen from an English lord's bedroom. Even the curtains at the window looked shabby, faded and rotted after too many years in the sun.

Grant felt anger well up inside him, not at the woman standing in front of him but at the man who had let a comfortable home disintegrate like his dreams.

"Hell, if I wanted to take this place over, I wouldn't have to do a whole lot. From the looks of things, Lee's run it damn near into the ground since the old man died. But then Lee always was too stubborn to ask for help. Looks like he picked a wife with the same blind pride."

"I'm not blind, Mr. Brookington," she snapped back. "You're blinder than I am if you think I can't see what you're up to. First you cut my fences and do the 'neighborly' thing by telling me about it and offering to help. Next you'll offer to lend me a few of your hands when it comes time to round up my cattle. Then, when you figure you've got me comfortably in your debt, you'll start asking me to pay for all these 'gifts.' And when I can't pay, you'll relieve me of the burden of the LJ, which is what you wanted all along."

"Well, you're at least partly right, you headstrong, independent, ungrateful little—"

"There! You admit it! You're trying to take the ranch away from me."

"I'm doing no such thing! I'm trying to save you a lot of grief. You haven't the faintest idea what you're—"

"Oh, so now I don't know what I'm doing. Did it ever occur to you that just because I'm a woman doesn't mean I haven't any business sense? No, of course not. To you I'm just—"

"Will you shut up a minute?"

Both Grant and Anna looked at the boy who had spoken up and almost in one breath shouted him down.

"Mind your own business," Grant snapped.

"This doesn't concern you, Matthew," Anna added.

"The hell it don't. In case you hadn't noticed, something in the kitchen's burnin', and it smells like rabbit stew."

The stew hadn't burnt at all, though Matthew's warning put an effective end to the argument. When

66

Anna had opened the damper for the coffee, she forgot to close it again, and the stew was boiling merrily, bubbling out of the cauldron to sizzle on the stove.

"It could have been worse," Grant observed, leaning against the door frame as Anna grabbed a towel and slid the damper shut.

"You mean I could have burned the whole house down."

"Well, that, too. Matthew, the woodbox is almost empty. Why don't you go fetch some more." He hoped the nod to the boy would be taken for the signal it was meant to be. He needed a few minutes alone with her.

"I'll have to split some. Might take a while."

"There's enough to last," Anna said. She straightened and moved the kettle to the back of the stove, then wiped the back of her wrist across her forehead. She wasn't going to let Grant Brookington maneuver himself alone with her. Matthew could stay right where he was. "Go ahead and set the table, Matthew. The wood can wait until morning."

"There won't be enough. I'd better go get some more. Grant can set the table."

Before anyone could stop him, Matthew grabbed the old jacket from the peg and was out the door.

Except for the crackle of the fire and the bubbling of the stew, the kitchen fell silent. Too aware that she was alone with the man, Anna looked desperately about her for something to do, something to occupy her so that she didn't have to look at him. His eyes, so hard, so piercingly accusative, sent an unfamiliar shiver of dread through her.

Then, without warning, he said quietly, "I'll get the plates."

"You'd better get three of them. I think Matthew's invited you to dinner."

"I can make an excuse."

She shook her head, loosening more of that wild hair, but she still wouldn't look at him.

67

"No, you might as well stay." Then, when she finally let her eyes meet his, she immediately turned away with a little cry. "Oh, damn, that isn't what I meant to say at all."

In three strides he had reached her, his hands taking gentle hold of her shoulders.

"It's all right," he said with a chuckle. "You don't have to feel obligated."

Sweat trickled down her back, not only from the heat of the stove but the warmth brought on by the pressure of his hands on her shoulders. Did he realize that while they had argued in the parlor, they stood only inches from each other, and that if Matthew hadn't interrupted, she would very likely have pounded her fist in sheer frustration on that broad chest? What was even worse, she didn't want to pound on him; she wanted to lean against him, to have him enfold her in those strong arms and hold her close.

She squirmed out of his grasp and side stepped into the pantry, where it was cooler and darker and she had a moment's privacy to collect her thoughts and settle her nerves.

"Mr. Brookington, please, I would like very much for you to stay to dinner. I have behaved abominably, I know, and if you would rather not stay, I'll understand." She took three plates from the shelf and looked around for a bowl to serve the stew. "I'm not a very good cook, but at least there's plenty of it, and I'd really like the opportunity to make up for the way I behaved."

She emerged from the pantry with the plates and bowl clutched to her chest like a shield.

And all Grant could think was, dear God, Matthew, don't come back now.

If this woman was the innocent Lonnie Hewitt claimed she was, then her husbands had both been fools of one sort or another. How could anyone resist those lips, parted now in apprehension? And that hair, all tumbled around her the color of spilt brandy. What would she look like clothed only in those curls? He wanted to stand perfectly still for a long minute and just study her, to imagine the body revealed as each garment was slowly stripped from her. Then he wanted to touch her, caress her, kiss her until the tawny eyes closed with a sigh of pure desire.

What the hell was the matter with him, letting thoughts like that steal into his mind? It was memories, memories of what he had done with another woman in this house. It wasn't Glory Johnson who made him feel this way. It couldn't be.

"Did you make biscuits?" he asked, surprised at the words as well as the fact that he was still capable of speech. His mouth was dry, his hands sweaty and shaking, but he was under control again.

"No. I don't know how."

She hadn't lowered the shield. The vulnerability was there, behind the pride. And his yearning didn't go away.

"Will you let me show you?"

"If you'll stay."

Chapter Six

It took time to find the ingredients, because the woman simply didn't know where anything was. Grant found himself almost embarrassed for her, though she seemed to take her ignorance in stride.

And what the hell was he doing, he wondered, offering cooking lessons to a tumble-haired widow with a sour temper who couldn't find her way around a kitchen? One minute she was ready to chase him out of her house, the next she was falling all over herself to apologize.

He should get out, while he still could. The only reason he had come was to warn her about the fences, and he had done that. Why, then, couldn't he turn his steps toward the door she had shown him to and leave? Why put himself through this charade of friendliness when it meant nothing?

And then there was the place itself. Being in Melody's kitchen touched painful chords. The years had changed it very little. He found the tin of baking powder in the same place Melody kept it. He didn't know if his hands shook from old anger or remembered passion, but he clutched the can tightly to stop the trembling.

"I can't believe you don't know how to make biscuits," he teased as he carried flour and baking powder to the table. "Don't they have biscuits back in Philadelphia?"

"Yes, they do, and in Richmond, Virginia, too."

71

"Virginia? I thought you were from Philadelphia." So, that explained the drawl. Unconsciously, Grant touched the place on his arm where a Confederate bullet had left a deep and permanent scar.

"I am," she answered easily as she took a mixing bowl and the flour sifter from his hand. If she had been unable to locate the untensils and ingredients, she managed to figure out their functions with little instruction and set to work. "Or at least, most recently I am. My first husband's family moved there after the War."

Grant made an effort to shake off his feelings. He had buried them a long time ago rather than deal with them, and he wasn't about to begin now.

"Matthew told me you'd been married before. You must have been hardly out of the cradle. The war's been over eleven years."

"Twelve," she corrected firmly, then added, "I was sixteen, but not really a child. A lot of us grew up quickly in those years. Phillip, my husband, was killed just a few weeks after we were married."

He took the sifted flour from her and carefully measured two cups into a second bowl. So far, what Lonnie had told him was true. And Grant was beginning to believe the rest of it might be, too.

He wanted to offer some kind of sympathy, but too many memories crowded out the condolences. She wasn't the only one who had lost a loved one to the War, and Grant didn't want to think about his own losses any more than he had to. He returned his attention to the biscuits.

"Next, measure the lard and mix it with the flour before you add the milk. You do that while I check on the stew."

He didn't realize until he walked away from the table how tense he had become. He took a deep breath of the flavorful steam over the kettle as a way of relaxing that tension.

72

"It needs something," he commented after a taste. "Did you put in any basil?"

"No. Should I have?"

"Well, it helps the flavor." He continued stirring the contents lazily. "With rabbit, a little sage wouldn't hurt either. And if you want to keep the carrots and potatoes from going to mush, try not putting them in at the beginning. They don't take as long to cook as the meat."

In truth, she hadn't done too badly, he admitted. And when he turned to see how she was coming with the biscuits, he immediately wished he had given her the compliment first.

Her cheeks were beet red, and for a second or two he thought her lower lip trembled. She kept that little chin up, though, and the only hint of emotion was the slight increase in the tempo of her mixing.

She was indeed a proud little creature. Determined, too, and not afraid of a little work. Well, Grant reminded himself, learning how to make biscuits and stew isn't quite the same as taking on the responsibilities associated with a cattle ranch, but he allowed himself to give her credit for trying.

"Lee never complained," she replied in her own defense.

"Maybe I'm to used to my own cooking. Anyway, I do appreciate the invitation, Mrs. Johnson. A nice hot supper will go a long way to making the eight mile ride home bearable."

She smiled at him, just a little, but when he realized that he was grateful for that smile and her acceptance of his apology Grant also realized he had tensed up again.

Now he wished Matthew would hurry with the damn firewood and put an end to this idiotic nonsense.

The boy did finally show up, just as Grant was opening the oven door so Anna could slide the pan of plump, round biscuits inside.

"It's startin' to snow," Matthew announced. "Not

73

much, but I think I better split some extra wood."

"No!" Grant and Anna cried in a single breath.

The boy dumped an armload of freshly split oak logs into the box beside the stove and shrugged.

"Hey, if you want to freeze tonight, that's your business," he said, "but I ain't about to wake up to a cold house. I'm gonna get the ax now, and—"

"Supper's ready," Anna interrupted.

Grant glanced at her and found the same apprehension in her eyes that he felt in the pit of his stomach. She, too, recognized that tension and wanted it relieved by Matthew's presence.

"Sit down and eat," Grant ordered, "and I'll help you with that firewood after supper."

Again he looked at her, watching for a reaction to his offer, but for a change she said nothing. The rebellion seemed to disappear from her eyes, and Grant suspected she didn't mind his offering to help Matthew. Well, that was good. At least she didn't expect others to suffer for her own stubbornness.

She ordered both of them to sit down while she served, and set a crockery bowl full of steaming stew on the table. Grant gave her an appreciative smile that brought roses into full bloom in her cheeks. She skipped away, disappearing into the pantry again.

"How'd it go the with biscuits?" Matthew asked the instant his stepmother was out of sight.

"They look perfectly edible. And if they're not, you'd better not say anything," Grant whispered back.

The boy grinned and scooped a healthy serving of stew onto his plate.

"I won't say nothin', if you don't!"

Grant raised a hand in a mock threat and smiled back.

Sounds of activity continued to come from the pantry. He had no idea what she was doing in there, but she certainly was making a racket.

He called to her, "Your supper is getting cold."

"I'll be there in a minute. Do you suppose the biscuits are done?"

"Ought to be shortly. You want me to take a look?"

She emerged from the pantry with several small graniteware bowls balanced in her hands.

"No, I can get it. I'm right here."

She set the dishes on the stove and reached to open the oven door. Before Grant could shout a warning, she did what he had been afraid of.

The cast iron seared the unprotected flesh with an audible sizzle, silenced by her cry of pain. Grant's fork clattered to the tabletop as he jumped up, too late.

"God, Glory, are you all right? Here, come over to the table." He put his arms around her and guided her one halting step at a time across the kitchen. "Matthew, go get a pan of cold water. Dip a bucket out of the trough; it's probably the coldest around. *Now.*"

The boy was out the door as fast as his legs could carry him, though the door didn't latch behind him and swung slowly with a gust of bitter, flurry laden wind.

She held her left wrist tightly with her uninjured right hand, her arms and shoulder shivering with the pain. Grant could feel the trembling as she leaned, however reluctantly, against him.

"Get the door," she gasped.

"The hell with the door."

"Get the damn door," she insisted. "I burned my hand, I didn't cut it off."

Her voice was breathless but strong, and she didn't appear in danger of fainting. Grant did not, however, let go of her until he had maneuvered her to the bench on the other side of the table and made sure she was seated. When he did close the door, he looked outside for just a moment to gauge the weather. Snow swirled on a sharp wind, but the flakes were light and small. Matthew was nowhere in sight.

Grant strode back to the table and straddled the bench

where Glory sat, now rocking slowly as the pain deepened. His knee touched hers, but he ignored the contact point rather than draw attention to it by moving.

"Let me see it," he demanded.

Slowly, she extended the hand, her fingers curled almost like claws. The knuckles of her right hand had gone white with their death grip on her other wrist. Grant pried the stiffened fingers open as gently as he could.

The scorched flesh was a yellowish grey slash across the palm and the soft underpart of her fingers and thumb. She flinched from his touch.

"Where the hell is Matthew with that water?" Grant mumbled.

He glanced toward the door but in doing so caught sight of the woman's eyes, filled with an old mixture of pain and something he couldn't quite identify. She stared at him, unashamedly, and he couldn't help staring back.

His grey eyes, once cold and hard as a winter sky, turned to tarnished silver. She could see her reflection in them, so close was his face to hers. She tried to summon up the determination to resist him, but the well was empty, leaving her exposed and vulnerable. When he leaned forward to kiss her, Anna registered no surprise at all.

It was a tentative kiss, nothing like she had expected. His lips were firm but gentle, demanding nothing, taking nothing, only exploring unknown territory. She had no idea what was supposed to happen next, but when the soft pressure on her mouth was suddenly released, her eyes blinked open and she let out a tiny gasp of disappointment.

"What a damn fool thing to do," Grant muttered.

Anna felt the heat rush to her chin and cheeks. And the throbbing in her hand that she had forgotten for those few seconds returned with a vengeance.

"Are you referring to what you just did or to—?"

Matthew's clomping footsteps on the porch silenced her shrewish question. She could not, however, get it out of her mind even after the boy had thrown the door open and kicked it shut again.

"Is it bad?" he asked as he carried the dripping bucket into the kitchen.

"Bad enough," Grant answered.

"I been tellin' you not to grab nothin' on that stove less'n you got a pad," the boy scolded. He set the bucket on the floor at Anna's feet and then dipped a bowl full for her to rest her injured hand in. "Water's a bit dirty, but it's good 'n' cold. I had to break through a skim of ice to get at it."

Grant placed the shallow bowl on the table where Anna could rest her hand in the numbing water and then he returned to his own side of the table, next to Matthew.

"Oh, don't sit down," Anna ordered quickly. "I found some peaches in the pantry when we were looking for the baking powder. They're in those dishes, if I didn't knock them over."

The icy water began to ease some of the fire from her hand, though it did nothing to help that idiotic blush that scorched her cheeks each time Grant Brookington looked at her. What was the matter with her? She had never reacted like this to a man's glance. And certainly not to a glance from a man like Grant Brookington.

She refused to let him get under her skin, even for a minute.

"I think Matthew's mother put these up," Anna explained as Grant brought the three bowls to the table.

He set them down with a nervous little thump, letting go of them as though they burned his hands. Good God, was there no end to the ways this woman could torment him with his memories? He stared at the contents of the blue dishes, remembering how Melody Hewitt had used a much sharper knife to slice his heart as easily as a ripe peach.

The cloud cover was thin, with the brilliance of a full

moon behind it to light the road home. Grant turned up the collar of the sheepskin jacket and hunched his shoulders against the whistling wind, then nudged his heels into the bay's flanks to send the animal loping down the road toward the Diamond B.

What a night! He couldn't remember just how he got through that meal, but somehow he had eaten stew and biscuits and yes, even the peaches. He hoped he hadn't failed to thank Matthew and his stepmother for their hospitality. More than likely he had forgotten, though it probably didn't matter. His chances of being invited back weren't good.

Well, that didn't matter either. What in heaven's name did he want to be invited back for? It sure wasn't for the cooking. Christ, he'd had better food on the trail, cooked over his own fire.

Nor was it the stimulating conversation. He and Matthew had chatted about the rustlers, about the weather, about prospects for the coming year, but the woman had had little to say. She just sat, with her hand in the bowl of cold water, and let the menfolk tidy up the kitchen.

The snow had stopped after depositing just enough of the white stuff to turn the frozen trail to a luminous ribbon in the moonlight. Grant stared ahead, looking for the first faint lights from the Diamond B. The eight miles separating his headquarters from the house at the LJ wasn't a terribly great distance, even in slightly inclement weather, but he had a desperate need to be home, to be away from this place that drove him almost mad with its memories.

He knew now he should never have gone here, no matter what the reason.

"What a damn fool thing to do," he said for the second time that night.

Wrapping a towel soaked in icy water around her hand

78

alleviated the pain, but Anna found that it wasn't only the throbbing caused by the burn that kept her awake long after she had sent a protesting Matthew to his bed.

Grant Brookington and his attempts to take the LJ away from her had not frightened her one half so much as that unexpected and yet unsurprising kiss in the kitchen. It had, for quite some time after the tingling left her lips, left her speechless, almost incapable even of thought. If he and Matthew blamed her silence and her rather blank expression on the pain in her hand, that was all well and good. It simply would not do to have them guess any particle of the truth.

She didn't like the man. He was handsome enough, tall, lean, with rugged features that reminded her of the sculpted crags of the mountains. But Phillip had been handsome, too, and his kisses had not induced mental paralysis. There was no comparing Brookington with Lee Johnson, of course. Not physically at least, but Anna needed no reminding that she had never married Lee for his looks.

Lonnie Hewitt, in fact, offered a better comparison. His nearness, the very thought of his nearness, turned Anna's stomach, yet she knew she had never seen a more beautiful man. So she accepted the fact that Brookington's appearance alone was not enough to stop the beating of her heart.

Yet her heart *had* skipped a beat when his lips touched hers.

"I'm letting silly things affect me more than they should," she scolded herself. "I must be getting old."

The incidents of the past few hours made it quite clear to her that she needed time to think. Everything had happened too quickly, catching her totally unprepared. She had much to learn and hardly knew where to begin.

No, that wasn't quite true, she reminded herself as she checked the fires one last time before settling down on the sofa. She knew exactly where to begin. That was the problem.

With a long sigh of weariness, Anna leaned her head against the sofa back and closed her eyes.

The business with the biscuits was, she realized, far more important than the blushes of humiliation she had suffered. In fact, it was more than an acknowledgement of the enormous task of self-education staring her in the face.

Brookington's instructions had been easy to follow, and Anna was quite certain that she could now produce a satisfactory batch of biscuits by herself any time she wanted to. It was the ease with which he had taught her, not the ease with which she had learned, that puckered a furrow of worry between her brows. Grant Brookington was capable of teaching her an infinite number of skills, especially the particular skills she desperately needed to learn. For crying out loud, he had taken one taste of her stew and told her exactly what was wrong with it!

Culinary expertise was not essential. She wouldn't lose the LJ because her stew tasted bland and her vegetables were mushy. But broken or cut fences were a threat to her survival. Brookington not only discovered the damage, but possessed the experience that had taken him on that early morning inspection tour. Even Matthew, as helpful and knowledgeable as he was, hadn't thought of it.

Neither, Anna acknowledged with a deeper grimace, had her foreman. Or else he just plain didn't care.

"Well, I *do* care!"

That little involuntary cry served as an escape valve, releasing the excess pressure and allowing Anna to regain her calm. And her perspective.

Much as she hated to admit it, she needed help. Grant Brookington had more than once offered his assistance, and she had repeatedly turned him down. No one else had made any similar offers. Looking at the situation realistically, Anna knew that without his help she was virtually certain to lose the ranch and her independence.

With his aid she might still lose it, but at least she had a chance.

The hand began to throb beyond her ability to ignore it. With yet another long sigh, she got to her feet and trudged back into the darkened kitchen, where the bucket sat by the back door.

"It seems so simple," she mumbled while wringing the towel out. "Next time he moseys over, I can just tell him, here's a list of all the things I need to learn to do. Show me how."

If it hadn't been for one small difficulty, Anna might have let it all go at that. But beneath all her worries, all her major and minor problems, lay the worst of her niggling fears.

Grant Brookington wanted the LJ. She had no idea why he wanted it; the reason didn't really matter. This evening, however, he had been only slightly more subtle about revealing that he wanted something besides the ranch.

Anna had not forgotten Grant's quiet exclamation after he drew away from that kiss.

"What a damn fool thing to do," she repeated, wondering again just what he meant.

It occurred to her, while she fished for pieces of ice floating in the bucket, that he might not honor the offer she had turned down so many times. In that case, she'd have cooked her own goose far better than she had the rabbit stew.

Chapter Seven

"You are going to catch your death of cold if you don't wear a coat," Anna scolded, peering under the clothesline strung from one side of the kitchen to the other.

Matthew dumped another armload of wood into the box by the stove and said, "Splittin' wood keeps you plenty warm. And by the way, somebody's comin' up the road."

Straightening from her position hunched over the laundry tub, Anna pressed her wet right hand into the small of her back and groaned. She had been washing dirty clothes since dawn, and with her left hand still too sore from last night's burn to be of much use, the chore had taken twice as long as usual.

"Looks like it might be Uncle Lonnie, but I don't know what he'd be doin' all the way out here. It's probably old man Lytle. You think this is gonna be enough wood for today?"

Anna looked at the nearly full box and at the tub in which the last batch of laundry was waiting to be wrung out and hung up.

"Oh, Lord, I do not need any interruptions now," she sighed. "If the parlor box and the upstairs box are full, yes, that should be plenty."

"Good. Then I'll just split the rest and stack it."

"Can it wait?" Anna asked. "If that is Mr. Lytle, I have

83

a feeling things will go much better if you're here."

"Yeah, sure." He brushed the dirt and wood chips from the sleeves of his flannel shirt and suggested, "You want I should go out and meet him and bring him around the front, so's he don't have to climb through *this?*"

"An excellent idea. Lord, Matthew, I swear I do not know what I'd do without you."

He returned her grin and ducked out of her way before she could reach up to ruffle his already tousled hair.

"Guess you wouldn't have no choice but to ask Grant for help then, would you?"

Anna shrieked her annoyance and threw a wet stocking at the boy, but he had already darted out the door. The stocking landed harmlessly with a plop on the floor.

After retrieving the sock and tossing it back into the tub, Anna removed her apron. Her brown skirt showed traces of dirt where she'd knelt at the laundry tub, and her sleeves, though rolled past her elbows, were wet, but at least the apron had taken most of the soap and splashes. Remembering her manners, Anna checked the coffee pot on the stove. For once it was full.

She walked into the parlor, doing her best to tame her hair. The braid she had labored over this morning was slowly unravelling, with more strands straying over her shoulders than had stayed in the plait. Frustrated, she yanked the piece of ribbon from the end of the braid and ran her fingers through the rest.

"Oh, what does it matter what you look like," she muttered to herself. She brushed the dust from her skirt and glanced around the parlor. "You'd think the lawyer was coming courting or something."

A memory of a young man, nervous in his worn uniform, pushed at her thoughts until Anna shoved it away. She had to keep her wits about her, especially if Ambrose Lytle was anything like Michael Conner.

84

But the man Matthew ushered in the front door bore no resemblance to the autocratic banker.

"Go on out to the barn, boy," Lonnie Hewitt ordered his nephew. "I got business with your stepmama."

Anna halted the sinking of her stomach by lifting her chin a fraction of an inch higher.

"Whatever business you have with me can be discussed in front of Matthew," she asserted. "Do come in, Mr. Hewitt. Would you care for some coffee?"

By then Lonnie had already strolled into the parlor and taken the wing chair. He swung one long leg over the arm.

"Yeah, coffee'd be nice. But the boy goes, less'n you want him to hear about this."

With maddening casualness, Lonnie unbuttoned his jacket and reached into his shirt pocket. The paper was neatly folded, not at all unlike the document young Ambrose Lytle had handed to Anna on the day of Lee's funeral.

She took it gingerly, glancing at Matthew who stood still as a statue just inside the front door. He made no effort to hide his loathing. Anna read quickly, skimming the opening sentences before becoming lost in the welter of convoluted Latin. Her stomach took another sickening drop.

"It's all right, Matthew. You can go ahead and split the rest of the firewood." His scowl made his disapproval clear, but Anna cut off any protest. "I'll let you know when we're finished."

Silence hung in the dim parlor for a moment or two after Matthew slammed the door, but eventually Lonnie seemed satisfied with the privacy and let a confident smile spread across his face.

"How's about that coffee now, *Mrs. Johnson*," he taunted. "Actually, a shot of whiskey would do better after that long ride from town."

"Get it yourself." She struggled to comprehend

unfamiliar terms, but Lonnie would not grant her the time to concentrate.

"Oh, come on, Anna. Where's that Southern hospitality? Wouldn't your mama be all mortified at the way you're treatin' your guest?"

"You're not a guest, Lonnie, so let's not waste any more of my time or yours. What is the meaning of this?"

"Didn't you read it?"

"I read it, and now I'm asking for an explanation." Too many shocks had frozen her where she stood the moment Lonnie had entered the house, but finally Anna found her wits again. She moved to the sofa and sat down, aware that her knees were growing steadily weaker. Oh, God, why did she ever allow Matthew to leave?

"It's only a copy, you know, so tearin' it up won't do you no good, Miss Glorianna Rush. That's right, Anna. You ain't Lee's widow 'cause you wasn't never his wife, and neither was you ever married to that Reb captain, Beauford or whatever his name was."

"Phillip Beaumont. And I most certainly was married to Phillip."

"No you wasn't," Lonnie sneered, "and I can prove it."

He was too confident not to be telling the truth, whatever truth it was. Even another quick perusal of the paper he had given her shed no further light on his madness. Ambrose Lytle's bold script identified only that one Alonso Ward Hewitt was protesting the last will and testament of Lee Cyrus Johnson on the grounds that the woman claiming to be the deceased's widow and heir had never in fact been his legal wife.

"What does Phillip, whether I was his wife or not, have to do with this accusation of yours?"

Lonnie's grin widened, as though she had said something that bolstered his absurd claim.

"You are dumber than I thought, lady," he chuckled. "Which only goes to show how right I am."

Slowly, with all the cocksure conceit he had ever

displayed, Lonnie got to his feet and sauntered toward the sofa. He removed his hat and tossed it beside Anna, then shrugged out of his heavy jacket. It landed with almost proprietorial disdain beside the hat. Though Anna expected Lonnie to join her and his discarded garments, he remained standing, that leering grin more firmly etched onto his features.

"I'm gonna tell you the whole story, Anna, just like I told old man Lytle. And then I'll make a deal with you."

"And if I'm not interested?"

Lonnie shrugged, but the smile never wavered.

"Then you'll lose the ranch. It's real simple."

Anna poured the steaming water into the laundry tub with no heed to the way it splashed on the floor. All she cared about was filling the tub and soaking herself clean. Clean of the grime from working, clean from the filth left by Lonnie Hewitt's presence.

After his departure she went in frantic search for Matthew, only to find the boy had disappeared. He had split no more wood, and none of the cowboys lounging in the bunkhouse had seen him, but his horse was missing from the stable. Not that it mattered, Anna told herself as she trudged freezing back to the house. She could never have brought herself to tell her stepson what had transpired between her and his uncle.

She finished hanging up the laundry, then tried to sort out the disaster that faced her. A desperately needed bath seemed the best inducement of rational thought.

She had had to pump the water herself, though at least Matthew had provided sufficent fuel for the stove. The exertion of forcing the pump handle up and down until the stream of icy water gushed forth provided a temporary outlet for the fury raging through her veins.

Fury and fear. Because, God help her, Lonnie's accusations had not been lies. And as Anna ripped off her clothing and slid into the scalding water of her bath, she

87

knew she had less than twenty-four hours to figure out a way to turn a tragic, honorable truth into a disgraceful, dishonorable deceit.

The answer came to her while she was rinsing the soap from her hair. Hoping there was another, less distasteful solution, she stayed in the bath until the water was chilly and her skin had wrinkled. When she finally got out, covered with goosebumps and her teeth chattering, she had devised no other solution.

After drying and dressing and cleaning up the kitchen, Anna stood in front of the cracked little mirror and drew the brush through her still damp hair. She tried her best to coax the curls into some semblance of order. They refused to obey. She could see how wild her hair looked, and the thought of cutting it became a very strong temptation. She laughed, sharp and bitter in the silence of the bedroom she had never shared with her husband.

Once, when she was twelve and the War had just begun, Anna tried to cut her hair so she could masquerade as a boy and run off to join the army. Aunt Phoebe had caught her in the act.

And what a scolding Phoebe had given! It was the first time, and nearly the last, that Anna heard her aunt use language that she had been taught no "lady" *ever* used.

"Only *harlots* cut their hair," Phoebe cried in her angriest whisper. "Your father, bless his heart, has raised you with some horrible notions, not the least of which is this antisecessionist nonsense, but even he would never countenance his daughter traipsing around like some woman of the streets with her hair all cut off. You, Glorianna, will go to your marriage bed with your hair and your woman's honor intact."

Now, years later, Anna felt her cheeks burn with the heat of a fiery blush, and the threat of tears. Her ears rang with the memories, with the shame Phoebe had made her feel that dreadful afternoon, with the horror she felt now.

"I might as well shave it all off," she muttered angrily to her reflection.

A dull thud from downstairs startled her, but she figured it was only Matthew coming in for dinner. A dinner she hadn't even started to cook. A dinner she would never be able to eat.

When the sounds grew louder, Anna only cursed the boy's temper, knowing it for a reflection of her own.

"Damn it, Matthew, must you make so much noise?" she called.

But the pounding continued, until Anna finally realized they were not produced by an angry teenaged boy looking for something to eat. In her preoccupation with her own problem, she forgot that she had bolted the doors to ensure privacy while she bathed and had never undone them. Matthew, if that was indeed he, couldn't get in.

"I'm coming!" she shouted. "Don't break the door down."

The kitchen was almost dark with the approach of early nightfall. Anna avoided the slippery places where she had sloshed water, but she had to put up her hand to feel for the clothesline still strung across the room. Matthew must finally have heard her, for the fists ceased their relentless entreaty. Ready to chew him out, Anna slid the bolt back and pulled the door open.

"Young man, the next time you—"

Grant Brookington, fist raised to beat on the door again, almost fell into the kitchen.

"Where's Lonnie?" he demanded.

He was furious. His boots pounded on the floor just as his hands had pounded on her door.

"Gone, hours ago. And what business is it of yours?"

Without offering an answer, he pushed past her and strode toward the parlor, expertly ducking the laundry. She followed, every bit as furious, right behind him. He searched the room, even drawing aside the faded curtains to peer out the front window into the twilight.

"I asked you what business is it of yours. If I want to entertain Lonnie Hewitt in my home—"

Grant's short, barked laugh stopped her.

"You weren't 'entertaining' anyone. And as for what business it is of mine, Matthew came and got me. Fortunately, he found me halfway between the LJ and my place, or it would have been another two or three hours before I got here."

Carrying a lamp he had lit in the kitchen, Matthew himself entered the parlor. His cheeks were red, either from the hard ride in cold weather or embarrassment, Anna couldn't tell.

"You had no right," she accused.

"I did *so*," the boy shot right back. "I heard what Lonnie said and I figured you ought to have some help."

Oh, God, Anna groaned inwardly.

"Just how much did you hear?"

"I heard him say that he was gonna take over the LJ if you didn't make a deal with him."

"Did it ever occur to you that maybe I could handle the situation myself? Oh, no, you had to go running for help, for a *man's* help."

"Matthew was scared," Grant explained, some of his anger calmed now that he had assured himself the interloper had indeed departed. But the woman's words were keeping his hackles up. Lord but she was a feisty thing. Independent as hell, or at least she was trying to be. "He said you chased him out, so he came looking for me."

In the lamplight he studied her, searching for any indication that Lonnie had made good on the threat he had bragged about in the Cattleman's the other day. Her hair looked damp, as though she had just washed it, and a lingering scent of soap clung to her. Had she felt so soiled by her forced surrender that she tried to cleanse the stain with a long hot bath?

No, he didn't think so. She seemed too rational to have endured any truly violent attack, but Grant reminded himself that his experience with wronged women was extremely limited. And Glorianna Johnson didn't invite comparison with other women anyway.

"When we got here, all the doors was locked," Matthew added.

"I took a bath. After Lonnie left, I went looking for *you*, but since you had seen fit to take off without telling anyone where you were going, I decided to take advantage of the privacy and had a good long soak."

"Yeah, I seen you used up all the firewood in the kitchen."

"You 'saw,'" she corrected unconsciously. "And the doors 'were' locked."

Locked and bolted with just a single light burning in an upstairs window, Grant wanted to add, but kept his mouth shut. He didn't like the way the sight of that yellow glow had aroused his temper. Horrible images had raced through his mind while he hammered on that locked door. And when she finally answered the summons and he roared into the house, all he could think of was finding Lonnie and strangling him. The images had taken on such reality that he believed them until murder ran hot in his veins.

"As you can both plainly see, I am quite all right," she was telling him, "and Lonnie has indeed gone. I'm sorry you rode all this way for nothing, Mr. Brookington. I would offer you supper but I'm afraid I neglected to fix any."

"I can go out and see what they got in the bunkhouse," Matthew suggested. "I'll bring in some more wood, too."

Before either of them could protest, he had darted out the door.

An uncomfortable silence descended. Anna pushed a hank of tangled hair back over her shoulder and wished she had grabbed a ribbon to tie the whole mess back. But she had no idea Grant Brookington would be the one who

91

tumbled into her kitchen. Now he was here, and she couldn't find the words she desperately needed to say.

Grant let his gaze wander around the room, avoiding looking at her but not wanting to look at anything else. He told himself, as he had on his last visit to this house, that he should not have come. But the boy had begged him, almost in tears, and there was practically nothing Grant wouldn't do for Melody's son.

"This is absurd," Anna observed, startling them both.

"What is?"

"That boy runs out to the woodpile every time you show up, as though he's intentionally leaving us alone together."

So she had noticed it, too. He thought it was only his imagination.

He shoved his hands into his pockets.

"Look, I know it really isn't any of my business, but what the hell was Lonnie doing out here? Matthew said you chased him off last week."

The grey eyes were stern but not angry. He might be worried about his own son, Anna thought, the way he talks about Matthew. And with good reason, considering what Lonnie had threatened. She wouldn't be the only one without a home if he went ahead with his ugly plan.

Grant was also right that it was none of his business, but Anna remembered she had every intention, not fifteen minutes ago, of making it his business. As angry as he made her with his storming into her house like he owned it, she calmed her temper and kept her concentration focused on the incredible scheme she had cooked up while she bathed in the laundry tub.

"I need your help, Mr. Brookington."

The grey eyes narrowed to points of bright steel.

"Was that actually a plea for help from the obstinate Mrs. Johnson?"

"I'm in no mood for sarcasm. Yes, I'm asking for your help."

"How much?"

"How much help?"

"How much money. Lonnie's blackmailing you, isn't he."

"Yes, but not for money." This was becoming much more difficult than she had expected. "Please, Mr. Brookington, this is not a matter I am comfortable discussing, and I would greatly appreciate your refraining from any smart aleck interruptions."

"Anything you say."

He had expected a request for money, and when she gave him that slightly perplexed look, he knew she wasn't lying about Lonnie's demands. If the snake didn't want cash, he wanted something else, and Grant suspected that something else was the woman herself. But why hadn't Lonnie taken the necessary action? Maybe he ought to listen to what she was saying rather than stand here and speculate.

"I may be forgiven the presumption that you find me somewhat attractive," she began, "based on that kiss you gave me when I burned my hand last night."

He almost spoke but remembered he had promised not to interrupt.

"And from the fact that you mentioned having become accustomed to your own cooking and that you failed to mention any wife, I have drawn the conclusion that you are unmarried."

"Are you proposing to me?"

"No!" she cried, her cheeks turning a delicious shade of scarlet. "And you said you wouldn't interrupt."

"Sorry."

Oh, Lord, he had made things ten thousand times worse than they already were. The blush refused to subside, and when Anna tried to speak, she couldn't find the right words. Everything that came to mind sounded so stupid.

"I'm only asking this," she whispered, "because I can think of nothing else to do. Without your help, Lonnie will take the ranch away from me, and possibly—probably—from Matthew as well."

That was an afterthought, but she smiled to herself at the cleverness of it. Brookington had already demonstrated that he cared deeply for the boy, and playing on that feeling wouldn't hurt her own case. Yes, it had caught his attention, she noticed with satisfaction.

"What is it you want me to do?" he asked when the silence stretched out longer and longer. "Kill the lousy little jerk?"

She shook her head, and the brandy-colored tresses shimmered. From where he stood by the fireplace, Grant itched to touch that tousled cascade. His fingers rubbed against each other inside his pocket as he imagined what it would feel like to twist one of those shining curls around his hand.

"He's not worth the risk, although when you've heard my request, you may decide killing him is preferable."

"Quit stalling. What the hell is it you want from me?"

It was now or never. If he left, he took her last and only chance with him.

"Mr. Brookington, I would like you to share my bed. Tonight."

Chapter Eight

"Just like that?"

If she expected him to be surprised or shocked, she was sadly disappointed. He displayed no real reaction at all, either of pleasure or disgust. Well, expecting him to be pleased was rather farfetched, but Anna couldn't help remembering the way he had looked just before he leaned to kiss her.

At least he didn't laugh at her.

"Yes, I suppose 'just like that,'" she replied, trying to ignore the blush that set fire to her cheeks.

"And is there some reason for this, uh, rather unusual request? I'd like to know whether I should be flattered or insulted. I've never stood at stud before."

Grant found he had a very strange reaction to her discomfiture. On the one hand, he enjoyed seeing her less than calmly collected in the face of adversity. Oh, the determination was still there, under that extremely attractive coloration, but at least this time she was struggling. Maybe whatever had driven her to such unorthodox behavior would open her eyes to the seriousness of her entire situation. Maybe, but he had his doubts.

On the other hand, he discovered a very familiar pleasure starting to hum through his veins as he waited for her response. He didn't deny that the thought of

95

having this woman in his bed had crossed his mind on more than one occasion. The first time he'd seen her, when Lee was dragging her alongside him into the bank, there had been an instantaneous attraction. At the time, Grant had put it down to resentment and plain old-fashioned jealousy. But at Lee's funeral, when he couldn't take his eyes off her, he had experienced a spark of desire just looking into her frightened, defiant eyes.

Now, the little vixen was blatantly inviting him to her bed. He could hardly wait to find out why.

"I'm not looking to breed myself, Mr. Brookington," she finally said, "just divest myself on an unwanted honor. And in view of the fact that I turned down Lonnie Hewitt's offer to relieve me of my virginity, I suppose you can be flattered."

The twitching, reluctant smile that seemed to flicker on Grant's lips made her all the more uncomfortable in an already disastrous situation. He mocked her, silently, with just the gleam in those gun-metal eyes.

She didn't wait for him to come up with some stinging sarcasm. It was painfully obvious that he wasn't going to comply. Telling him the whole story might persuade him to accede to her outrageous request, but Anna had her doubts. She also had a very limited amount of time. She would have to do something very quickly, or Lonnie Hewitt would control the LJ by nine o'clock the next morning.

"Mr. Brookington," she began, nervously fingering the top button on her flannel shirt, "I would like to get this over and done with quickly. Lonnie Hewitt has somehow discovered that my marriage to Lee was never . . . consummated and I cannot therefore legally inherit the LJ."

That confirmed his worst fear, and his greatest hope. He had pieced together Matthew's frantic tale with knowledge gleaned from Lonnie's drunken confession, but hearing it from Glory herself was quite another thing.

He swallowed, and licked his own dry lips, and wondered if he was totally insane.

The top button came undone, and then the next. She stilled the trembling of her fingers with an effort. Just a few minutes ago, when this outrageous idea occurred to her, she thought it would be so easy. It was not easy at all, not when Grant Brookington's hard eyes glittered and refused to stop staring at her.

Her fingers reached for the third button. The shirt, one that must have belonged to Lee before his widow appropriated it, gapped enough to reveal the hollow at the base of her throat. She almost seemed to be deliberately separating the halves of the garment to expose as much skin as possible.

When she licked her lower lip and slipped the fourth button from its hole, Grant realized what she was up to.

He took two steps to reach her and grabbed her hands, holding them and the shirt tightly together.

"Stop it, Glory," he growled. "This isn't a game."

She should have gazed at him with grateful, frightened eyes and cheeks flushed with shame. Instead, she slipped her hands free and tugged another button open.

"I know that you are a bachelor of long standing, and I assure you, I am not trying to trap you into marriage." Oh, God, he had called her Glory again, and it sent queer shivers through her like cold fire. She had to keep her thoughts and her words coherent, no matter what kind of insanity assailed her senses. "You need only assist—"

"What's the matter with you?" he interrupted, grasping her hands again. This time his knuckles grazed her skin just below that shadowed hollow where he could see each frantic beat of her pulse. His own seemed hardly more steady. "A decent woman doesn't ask a man to sleep with her, no matter what the reason."

He had a difficult choice in front of him. Let her go, knowing she might continue her attempt at seduction, or continue to imprison her hands in his, which effectively halted her disrobing but also forced him to remain too close to her for clearheaded thought.

And she knew it. He read the glimmer of a triumphant smile on her lips.

He let go her hands as if they were hot as the cookstove.

She unbuttoned another button.

He took one step backward and halted, mesmerized by the sight of a plain linen camisole trimmed with a single ruffle of black lace.

"I've spent twelve years living the life of a 'virtuous' widow," she told him. Something was growing inside her, something over which she was afraid she had little control. Another force urged her onward, one that, instead of fighting her determination to seduce this man, actually encouraged her.

She finished with the buttons and then tugged the shirttails free of her skirt. "I was poor, humiliated, bored, and altogether disgusted by that life. Lee Johnson gave me the opportunity to escape, and I am not going to let it slip through my fingers for the sake of a virtue that has done me little good in the twenty-eight years I've maintained it."

"Good God, woman, you're serious, aren't you?"

His voice was lower, rougher, almost hoarse.

She lowered her own voice to just barely above a whisper.

"I most certainly am."

She slipped one arm free of the sleeve, then the other. The shirt fell softly to the floor. Her heart was pounding, and she hadn't felt so terrified since the night the hands brought Lee into the kitchen, his neck broken. But what she had started could not be stopped.

She fumbled with the buttoms on her skirt because she didn't dare take her eyes from him, and she couldn't see the damn fastenings.

"And don't try to tell me you don't find me attractive, Mr. Brookington. I may be innocent, but I am not ignorant. I did not ask for that kiss last night; you gave it freely, and I don't think you regretted it."

She was crazy, and he must be even crazier because he wasn't doing a thing to stop her.

The plain brown skirt slithered over her hips to land soundlessly at her feet.

"Did you think about that kiss while you rode home last night, Mr. Brookington?" she asked as she stepped over the skirt. He was no more than two feet away from her now, almost close enough to touch. She was surprised to find that she wanted to touch him, to know him. It was a strange wanting, completely outside the rational need for independence that had forced her to these extreme measures.

Worse yet, reminding him of that kiss also reminded her of it. "I thought about it. In fact, I lay awake for hours, wondering why you had done it."

"You mean you've been planning this since last night?"

All that hair tumbled around her shoulders was enough to drive a man wild, but when the shoulders were bare except for the narrow straps of her camisole, the wildness raged beyond control. Grant licked his lips and swallowed a choking lump.

"Oh, no, I didn't plan it at all." Was that a lie? Didn't she feel that she had been thinking about him, imagining what it would like to be with him, forever? She had to shake off these musings, concentrate on her objective. "You still haven't answered my question. Did you think about that kiss?"

He couldn't tell her the truth, that he'd thought of little else last night, this morning, and most of the day as well. Such information would only add fuel to an already raging fire.

But neither could he deny it. And her reminder brought the memory of that particularly pleasurable moment of madness almost to the present. That same tempting mouth was just inches away, moistened by the

99

tip of her tongue so that her lips glistened in the dim afternoon light. Her nostrils flared with each breath, and her eyes had gone as dark as molasses. If he didn't escape now, he'd be entrapped forever.

"This is crazy. Tell me what the hell is going on with Lonnie and we'll try to work it out. But you've got to stop this, Glory, you've got to."

He watched as the first of her petticoats traced the same path as her skirt.

"That's the second time this afternoon you've called me that, Mr. Brookington. Why?"

She set her right foot on one of the andirons and leaned down to unlace her shoe. All that magnificent hair tumbled over her head, baring her back above the black ruffle. Grant groaned.

"I should never have had supper with Dodd," he muttered, finally tearing his eyes away and looking at the ceiling. "I should have stayed at the Cattleman's, spent the night with Angela, and then this wouldn't be happening."

"I believe your mind is wandering, Mr. Brookington. This is the second time I've had to repeat a question. Why do you keep calling me 'Glory'?"

Surprised and puzzled, he looked at her again only to find that she had pulled her remaining petticoat up to her knee and was in the process of rolling down a plain black stocking. Inch by silken inch, she bared her calf, then her ankle, and finally a small, narrow foot and five slender toes.

"I don't know why," he stammered, unable to concoct a lie. "In the bank last week, when you gave old man Conner hell, you stormed out of there bragging about being named Glorianna after some damn queen, and I guess I just thought Glory fit you better than Anna, like somebody's old maid aunt."

"So, you don't deny that you find me attractive."

She was working on the second shoe.

100

"No, I don't. But I find a lot of women attractive without taking all of them to bed with me."

"You take Angela to bed. You said so yourself."

She hadn't looked up yet, having encountered a knot in the lace of the second shoe, but Grant didn't consider that fortunate. The sleek lines of her back, the taut muscles that bunched and flexed under skin like ivory satin with her every move, teased him, reminded him that she was capable of her own kind of strength.

But without the hypnotic depth of her golden eyes drowning him, he regained a little of his composure.

"Angela's a whore. You're not. And for Christ's sake, you could get pregnant. Then what?"

The knot came free. She took her time, however, untying the lace. She had not, she realized with a start, considered the possibility of conceiving a child.

"I'd claim the child was Lee's, of course," she stated quickly.

"But I'd know it was mine. What if I wanted it?"

She removed the shoe and then the stocking, as slowly and captivatingly as before. Her answer didn't come until she had straightened and tossed her hair out of her face.

"Then I suppose you'd have to marry me, tomorrow or the day after, and I'm sure neither of us want that. I assure you, however, that I do not expect to conceive a child so easily. I am, after all, twenty-eight years old, well past the prime of my youth."

"My mother was thirty-two when I was born."

She didn't like arguing with him. His confidence unnerved her, because it was so natural, so much a part of him, where she had to struggle for hers. And then she couldn't count on it.

"Well, my mother was twenty, and I was her fourth and last child. But don't change the subject." He very nearly had, which would have defeated her purpose. Having a baby was less of a worry to her than losing the

101

ranch. "Surely you must be awfully warm in that heavy coat."

When she came up to him and reached for the buttons on his coat, he discovered he had backed all the way to the stones of the fireplace. There was no escape, short of pushing her away from him, and that would mean putting his hands on the uncovered skin of her shoulders. Looking at her, smelling the fresh, soapy scent of her, was trying enough; touching her would drive him completely over the edge.

His next mistake was to look down to capture her hands again, except that instead of her hands, his eyes found a more delectable sight, the valley between her breasts, just barely visible where her camisole fell away as she brought her arms together.

He groaned, part in a kind of pain and part in surrender. His mouth came down on hers while he was still struggling to get his arms free from the coat.

This was no tentative kiss like what he had given her while she quivered with the pain of a burned hand. Now he explored, slipping his tongue past lips parted in surprise. And it was then, when she realized that she had welcomed his kiss, that Glory knew she had lost control of the situation. Now Grant Brookington was in charge, and he would not readily relinquish his position.

There was possession in the way he inexorably pulled her body against his, the way his tongue teased against hers and wouldn't let her escape. For a fleeting instant, Glory wondered if he would turn her trick to his complete advantage, destroying her independence before she had even won it. Was there something she had overlooked, some strange legal technicality that Grant Brookington, so knowledgeable about so many other things, would use to force her into the same pathetic compliance Terrence Beaumont had?

In that split second of panic, she found a morsel of logic. No man whose heart beat as wildly as Grant's did against hers, no man whose mouth demanded such complete surrender, no man whose hands trembled when they touched a woman's shoulders could possibly be in control. And it didn't matter, because neither was she.

Her stifled bit of giddy laughter became a soft, drawn out sigh as he released her.

She tasted like tea and sugar, all sweet and warm and melting in his mouth. He wrapped one arm around her, holding her to him while he shook the coat off his other arm. Her eyes were closed, the lashes thick against her cheekbones. Still parted, her lips glistened, tempting him to kiss their swollen fullness again. He resisted.

He slid long, strong fingers into the thick hair at the back of her head and grasped a handful of the tangled tresses, forcing her head back. The molten honey eyes flashed open.

They were filled with panic.

She had cornered him like a hunted animal until his instincts took over and he fought back the only way he knew how. But instead of defeating her, he became more trapped in her seductive web. Even now, when the fear turned her passion-glazed eyes glittery with tears, he had no control over the hand that slipped down her back to her waist and pulled her sharply to him. He would not let her pretend ignorance of what her teasing performance had done to him. She had pushed him this far; now he'd show her what happened when he pushed back.

What happened was that a pair of slender arms wound themselves around his middle and tightened the embrace.

"I won't let you go," she told him. The soft drawl crept back, adding to the seductive whisper that was all she could manage. Yet underneath it all lay that same determination, and that same bewildering need that she could neither ignore nor resist. "I know what I'm doing, Mr. Brookington, and I mean to see it through."

She pressed herself more tightly to him. There was no

103

denying the hard ridge of arousal under the buttons of his trousers. Her hips moved ever so slightly to the left, forcing a short, sharp gasp from him.

"You've got to stop this, Glory," he begged. "For God's sake, Matthew might come waltzing in here at any minute and how would you feel if he found his stepmother sprawled on the floor?"

"Are you just now thinking of that possibility?"

She smiled and grasped the heavy wool flannel of his shirttail to pull it out of his pants. All fear was gone, all hesitation. That nameless, unknown *hunger* alone remained, driving her inexorably forward.

"Matthew won't come back until one or the other of us goes after him," she explained. "He's playing matchmaker, has been since the first time you showed up here after the funeral. Now, we both know he's going to be disappointed in that, so don't you think we owe it to him to keep his rapscallion uncle from taking away his home?" She had the shirttail free enough to slide her hands underneath. She encountered skin, smooth and slick with the fine perspiration of passion. "And if you're really afraid of being 'disturbed,' we can always go upstairs to the bedroom and lock the door."

It didn't make the least difference to her if he took her here on the rough stone hearth or on the sofa or carried her dramatically up the stairs to fling her on the bed and ravish her in comfort. In fact, she preferred one of the former locations, because the stairs were too narrow for such theatrics and the time spent climbing them might give him the opportunity to cool his ardor and change his mind.

Already she felt him beginning to marshal his scattered forces.

She licked her lips and murmured, "I know there's no love involved, but would it be so bad, making love with me this once?"

"No, oh God, no, Glory, it wouldn't be bad at all. It's just that . . ."

Searching for one last reason that might change her course, Grant realized the alternative was worse. What if she went after someone else, one of the cowboys who worked her cattle? Lonnie's threat had sent her into the arms of a man she disliked as much as she disliked Grant Brookington. His refusal might make her desperate enough to explore even more dangerous options.

And he couldn't deny the desperation such possibilities aroused in him. He wanted her, in his arms, in his bed, taking his flesh into hers and feeding his frenzy with her own. He would be her first, and for a while at least he would be the only man to possess her. The idea that someday in the future there might be another man in her life crossed his mind. As he disentangled himself from her desperate embrace and led the way to the stairs, he did not think about any future beyond this night. Tonight she would be his and his alone.

The stairway was narrow, but not too narrow to negotiate with a slender woman in his arms. Scooping her up so the froth of her hair tumbled over his arm and shoulder, he carried her up to the landing and through the open door to the bedroom. She said nothing, not a word of protest, no exclamation of excitement. The gleam in her eyes brightened, though, and Grant felt a shudder of anticipation shiver through her.

The room was bright and warm, and a hairbrush lay on the bed beside a length of blue ribbon. Grant set Glory on her feet beside the bed, then watched as she picked up the brush and ribbon and put them on the dressing table. Her nonchalance surprised him, until he saw how her fingers trembled. Nervously, she smoothed the ribbon for a moment before turning to face the man she had set out so competently, and so successfully, to seduce.

"Having second thoughts?" he teased.

If she was, she chased them away with a shake of her head.

She ignored his question and offered, "Shall I help you with your boots?"

"No. Like you, I am quite capable of removing my own clothes."

The sarcasm reminded her that her power over this man could easily be wrested from her. Anger was every bit as powerful a drive as sex, and physically Grant Brookington remained much stronger than she. So she bit back a retort of her own and leaned against the dressing table to watch him.

She did not waste any effort trying to deny his good looks. Not when he seemed to take special delight in displaying his charms to her as tantalizingly as she had done to him.

Methodically, with no sign of special emotional involvement, he sat on the bed to pull off his boots and socks. He might just was well have been getting ready to go to bed alone; he didn't look at her and he gave every indication of a man who was totally unaware of a woman's presence. He set the two boots side by side just under the edge of the bed before stuffing the socks inside them.

But he was aware of her, acutely. When he stood and stretched with a lazy yawn, he made sure she noticed the unmistakable swelling below his belt.

"Do hurry," she urged. Her tongue made an unconscious swipe across her lips.

"Are you that eager?"

It was cruel of him to tease her, but she had it coming.

"I want it over and done with, Mr. Brookington. The sooner the better." That little pink tongue flicked out again, evidence that part of what she said was a lie, whether she knew it herself or not.

He laughed, low and softly, as he unbuttoned the shirt.

"No, you got that all wrong, Glory. The longer the better. I mean, why waste it? Why rush through it when you can make the pleasure last and last?"

"I'm not interested in pleasure." Then why is my heart pounding? Why can't I seem to breathe enough air

106

into my lungs? Why do I miss the touch of his hands on my skin? "This is strictly business."

He flung the discarded shirt in the general direction of the foot of the bed, where one trailing sleeve snagged on the footrail. The shirt hung like a banner of ownership.

"Look at me, Glory," he commanded in a husky whisper. "You wouldn't let me turn away from you."

She watched because she could not help herself. She knew now why he felt like a brick wall when she crashed into him at the bank that morning. His chest was broad and muscled as befit a man who had worked hard all his life. Under the shadow of dark hair, the skin was deep gold, bringing to Glory's mind the image of him in the summer sun, bare-chested as he swung an ax to split wood for the cookstove or tossed a saddle on the back of a horse.

There was a deep scar on one arm, another, less obvious, on his belly. Yet they were not disfiguring, but rather evidence that he had been hurt and survived. Glory thought of the other scars, the kind that could disfigure the heart, the soul, the mind, and wondered if she would ever regard hers with as little concern as Grant paid the marks on his body.

Then he held out his left hand, beckoning her to join him. Trancelike, she obeyed.

The balance of power had shifted. Now Grant was in control, clearheaded, confident, his right hand steady as he unbuckled his belt and unbuttoned his trousers.

"You started it," he told her with just a lascivious nod of his head to indicate the blatant physical evidence of his arousal. "And you'll finish it, but on my terms."

He didn't wait for any sign of agreement from her. She put up no resistance when he took hold of the black-ruffled camisole and began to pull it up over her head. He let her tug her arms free before the camisole was off, leaving her effectively blindfolded and defenseless, a state he had to take advantage of.

"Hmm, nice breasts."

She yanked the undergarment off and glared at him. "I beg your pardon!"

Buck naked, so thoroughly aroused he was almost afraid he'd humiliate himself, he couldn't help but laugh out loud at her outrage. Good Lord, she even had her fists on her hips.

But they were awfully nice breasts. Round and full with tight little nipples that would feel all crinkly against his tongue.

"I said, we're on my terms now. I'll do what you want, Glory. I'll stand in for the husband who couldn't do what he should have and make a woman of you so you can keep the damn ranch, but by God, I'll get some pleasure from it. Now, take off that petticoat and whatever the hell you've got under it. I won't make love to a woman wearing clothes."

Her face felt as scorched as her hand. The blush refused to fade, too, because she knew her anger was causing her to take deep and rapid breaths that only drew more attention to the portion—or portions—of her body that prompted the man's humiliating remarks. Well, it didn't matter. In fact, she reasoned as she jerked the drawstring on her petticoat to free the knot, his unforgivable conduct served to dispel those threats of romance that had whispered in her mind's ear while he carried her up the stairs.

She stepped out of her underdrawers and kicked them out of her way.

"I'm ready," she announced.

"No, not yet I don't think. You gotta relax. Come on, lie down on the bed and I'll help you relax."

He turned down the spread and blankets and sheet, but she ignored the invitation and walked around the bed to climb in on the other side.

"No, my dear, no covers. I want to see you, all of you, while I touch you and taste you, and everything else I'm going to do to you."

The pink started at her throat and rose to her cheeks

108

and then to the roots of her tousled hair, before it spread lower, flushing those proud breasts and turning the peaks even darker. Grant lay down beside her, his head resting on his left arm, and tentatively touched the tempting nipple nearest him.

"Relax," he crooned when she shivered. "I'm not going to hurt you."

"I'm a virgin, Mr. Brookington," she reminded him, trying to keep her gaze fastened on the ceiling when what she really wanted to do was stare at him, gaze into his eyes and find something wonderful and welcoming. She knew it wouldn't be there, though, and she didn't like the ache that knowledge brought. "Of course it's going to hurt. I'm quite prepared for it, however." Better to stick to reality, however unpleasant, than try to make silly dreams come true, even for a brief moment.

"I said I'm not going to hurt you, and I mean it. Does it hurt you when I touch you like this?"

He ran the tips of his fingers over the topaz jewel crowning her breast.

Her answer was breathless.

"No, it doesn't hurt, but I do wish you wouldn't."

"Why?"

He reached across her still tense body to caress the other gem no jeweler could have set more perfectly. She shivered again and arched her back just slightly, as though fighting against the instinct that sought the pleasure he offered.

"Now I'm the one repeating questions. Why don't you want me to do this?" He ventured to wrap his hand around the fullness. Then he squeezed very gently and brought his mouth down on the peak. It was every bit as crinkly against his tongue as he had thought it would be. "Doesn't it make you feel good?"

"Yes," she gasped "No, not good. Just all strange and warm and like I was melting inside." The edges between dreams and reality were no longer clear and sharp. They, too, were melting.

"That's exactly the way you should feel. Because you *are* melting inside." He slid his hand down her stomach, past the soft curling hair between her legs to the warmth she tried to hide from him. "Inside here."

At his nudge, she relaxed her thigh muscles just enough for him to push her legs apart. The sigh of useless protest which escaped her soon turned into a moan of burgeoning ecstasy. He was touching her, then sliding his finger into the place where she felt that liquefying glow.

"It's good, isn't it?"

His voice seemed a million miles away, or perhaps so close that it came from inside her.

"Yes, it's good. Ah, Grant, please. Please."

There was something out there, in the velvet darkness that engulfed her, a brilliance she felt but couldn't see. Blindly, guided only by the instinct this man's intimate touch aroused, she reached for that brilliance.

She tugged at his arm, trying to pull his body atop hers, but he was too strong for her.

"No, Glory, not yet. I said I didn't want to hurt you."

She struggled against the tide of sensation to hold on to her sanity.

"But I need you," she begged, each word a separate gasp. She pushed against his hand, increasing the pressure of his probing fingers. "You said you would. Make me a woman."

"I will, I will. Oh, God, Glory I will."

And then the darkness shattered, and she cried out at the brilliance that overwhelmed her. It was like lightning and thunder when a storm breaks the sullen heat of a summer night, frightening and soothing at the same time. It crashed all around her, blinded her, deafened her, terrified her. And it was the most wonderful terror she had ever known.

While the thunder still echoed in her blood and the lightning still shimmered along her nerves, she felt the weight beside her shift. It was his knee that nudged her this time, spreading her legs further apart to accommodate his body between them.

"Now, Glory, when you're all warm and wet with your own pleasure, now I'll take mine and make you what you want to be."

He found and entered her and even pushed past the fragile barrier of her virginity so easily that she hardly noticed the pain. Not that it mattered. Through the fading luminescence of fulfilled passion, Glory knew the goal was at last achieved.

She blamed gratitude and relief for the way her arms wrapped around him, but the rest of her body responded in other ways that she did not understand and could not control. She opened herself to the hard, swollen length of him with a wonderous welcome.

"Ah, God, you're good, Glory," he sighed with a randy smile and a gentle thrust that drove him deeper into the sweetness he hadn't known he could crave so desperately.

"I know," she sighed right back.

He kissed her smiling, beguiling mouth once, brief and hard.

"But only for me, Glory, only for me."

He moved faster, plunged deeper. He was her whole world now, the pleasure he had given her, the pleasure he was taking from her.

She was lost, and she knew it, and she didn't care. Tears trickled from the corners of her eyes, tears of joy, tears of regret, tears of a thousand confused emotions that ravaged her heart and soul while Grant Brookington ravaged her body. And yet there was no pain, neither the brief, sharp pain that she had expected nor the deeper, twisting agony that she sensed lurking in wait. There was only the pleasure, the sweet, rippling pleasure of being a woman, the fiery ecstasy only a man could give. She would hold it to her as long as she could.

"Oh, damn, Glory, I wanted it to last," he whispered against her cheek, his breath a series of gasps, "but it's so good, oh sweet Christ, Glory, it's so damn good."

Chapter Nine

A light tapping wakened Glory from a sound sleep. She blinked, momentarily disoriented, then answered, "Yes, who is it?"

"Just me," Matthew called. "I got breakfast almost done."

The room wasn't dark; she estimated the time to be near seven o'clock, more than an hour after she was accustomed to rising. She threw off the blankets and let the chill on her naked flesh chase the last grogginess—and the remnants of last night's ecstasy.

She steadfastly refused to think about what she had done except as a business deal successfully concluded. Whatever feelings she had felt were nothing more than relief. They *couldn't* be anything else. She wouldn't let them.

She found the clothes she had shed the evening before draped neatly over the end of the bed. The very neatness brought a silly smile. Grant had been so solicitous last night, when he left her drowsy and half asleep. It was he who had brought her clothes from the parlor, and he who had gone out to the bunkhouse to bring Matthew back to the house.

And it was Grant who explained everything to the boy, or at least as much as Glory allowed him to explain. She had listened to fragments of their conversation that

113

drifted up from the kitchen, but she couldn't quite remember if she stayed awake long enough to hear Grant's horse ride away or if she had just dreamed it.

The important thing, however, was that she had secured the LJ. Seducing Grant Brookington had been a long shot, yet she had done it. She could keep her appointment with Lonnie and the lawyer with no fear. The fact that the accomplishment of her mission was not at all unpleasant was a fortunate bonus, but since there was no need for it to happen again, Glory intended to dismiss it completely.

Dressed in a pair of Lee's dungarees and the shirt Grant had tried unsuccessfully to keep on her, she skipped down the stairs and into the kitchen. The scents of hot coffee and bacon and eggs assailed her and aroused an appetite that had gone without supper.

"You feelin' better?" Matthew asked as he brought a steaming mug of coffee to the table. "Grant said you was feelin' kinda sick last night. Headache or somethin'."

So that was the lie he had told the boy.

"I was worried about Lonnie, I guess. All I needed was a good night's sleep. And a good breakfast. Goodness, Matthew, where did you learn to fix all this?"

He shrugged and slid two eggs onto her plate.

"After Ma died, there wasn't nobody else. Sorry. *Anybody* else. You even got Grant tellin' me how to talk now."

Half an hour later, fortified with the best breakfast she'd had since leaving Philadelphia, Glory buttoned up her hand-me-down coat and tugged on her oversized gloves. She had barely enough time to ride to town to keep her appointment.

Matthew argued that she shouldn't go alone, but she insisted. She saddled the mare herself and mounted without any assistance, then set off toward Greene.

The weather had relented, with a magnificent clear sky, brilliant sunshine, and just enough breeze to whisk away the dust the mare's hooves raised. The mountains

114

were snowier now than they had been the day of Lee's funeral. Someday, Glory promised herself as she dug her heels into the mare's flanks, I'm going to ride into those mountains myself, just to see what they're like. Perhaps Grant could show her the way.

His constant presence in her thoughts irritated her. She resolved again to keep her mind on her own business, which did not include Grant Brookington.

The ride left her refreshed and cleansed, as though the crisp air had rinsed away the cobwebs of worry. When she dismounted and tied the horse to the rail in front of the bank, Glory knew she was smiling. Her victory last night had restored her confidence, to say nothing of strengthing her determination.

The bank was less crowded than the last time she had been there. Good heavens, even the bank lobby reminded her of him! Scowling, she strode across the almost deserted space to the room at the back where Ambrose Lytle waited.

The lawyer rose at her entrance and extended a hand across the desk.

"Mrs. Johnson, good morning. I'm afraid Mr. Hewitt hasn't arrived yet."

"I have time," she replied. "I can wait."

"Fine. And may I introduce Dr. Poole?"

She turned to face the other gentleman seated at the far end of Lytle's desk, which was only a little less impressive than Michael Conner's.

Poole was in his mid to late fifties, spare of frame and hair, with lines that might have come from laughter or worry crinkled around bright blue eyes. He got to his feet slowly.

"Mrs. Johnson, how do you do? Forgive me, but the cold weather has left a few joints rather stiff."

Lytle coughed and took a cigar from the carved walnut humidor at his left elbow.

"I do not know how much you know about why Mr. Hewitt requested this appointment," he said to Glory as he struck a match and touched it to the end of the cigar. "Oh, do you mind if I smoke?"

She shook her head.

"I know exactly why I'm here, Mr. Lytle. And I know why the doctor is here."

Lytle had the decency to look away from her. It didn't matter. She would submit to the most humiliating examination so long as it proved she had indeed been with a man, any man. Lonnie's claim rested on her virginity, and she had given that to Grant Brookington.

The lawyer puffed on his cigar and the doctor dozed off, snoring quietly. The clock ticked off the seconds, then the minutes, and still they waited for Lonnie. He had told her yesterday to be at the lawyer's office at nine o'clock, and it was now almost half past.

"Mr. Lytle, how long do you suppose I ought to wait?" she asked at length. Unlike the lawyer, her nerves were calm. He tapped the ashes from the cigar and coughed again.

"I can't see any reason to keep you any longer, Mrs. Johnson. As you know, the protest he filed clearly states that you were to be here at nine o'clock this morning, and you were."

"Then if you don't mind, Mr. Lytle, I should like to get on with it. I have other business to attend to this morning."

Lytle looked at Poole, and the doctor shrugged.

"Here, or at my office?" Poole asked.

It took fifteen minutes at the most, fifteen of the worst minutes of Glory's life, but then it was over. While she pulled her clothes back on, the doctor wrote his deposition. He explained it to her, but she hardly heard beyond his acknowledgement of the ruptured hymen. He informed her, with a censuring frown, that there was evidence of sexual activity too recent to have been with her late husband, but he wouldn't put that in the report.

It wasn't germane to the legal matters presented.

She didn't care what he thought of her conduct. No one now could ever prove that she hadn't been Lee's legal wife, and nothing else mattered.

And Lonnie never showed up. Glory wondered, after she had left the bank and was heading for the general store, if somehow he had found out about Grant. Had the sniveling worm hidden himself somewhere to watch all the hours Grant had stayed?

Oh, what did it matter! He'd have to find some other means of stealing the ranch, and she was certain she'd be able to defeat him again, no matter what he did.

The general store smelled delicious, almost as delicious as the kitchen when Matthew cooked breakfast. Leather and dry goods, pickles and cheeses. Tobacco and cinnamon, salt beef and apples. Glory breathed deeply as she stood just inside the door.

How good it felt, to be surrounded by all these things for sale, things she could buy and put to use on her ranch. She wandered, in a pleasant sort of daze, amongst all the haphazard displays.

There were garden tools, hoes and rakes and shovels, and she wondered if she ought to buy them for the garden she would plant come spring. From all the fruits and vegetables put up in the pantry, she knew that Lee's first wife must have had a garden somewhere. Surely there must be tools, in the barn perhaps. But she gazed wistfully at the shiny new tools, wishing for everything to be new now that the LJ was hers.

She fingered a massive leather horse collar, a slender spiderweb spun from one side to the other. She lifted the cover on the pickle barrel and drank in the pungent garlic smell. She hefted a hammer, surprised at how the weight gave her a feeling of power and authority.

"Can I help you, ma'am?"

The shopkeeper's voice startled her and she almost dropped the hammer.

He looked at her in her borrowed clothes and sniffed.

117

"The dress goods are over here, if that's what you're looking for."

"Not at all. I need some pants, some shirts, a pair of boots, gloves, a coat, if you don't mind."

Obviously, he did mind, but he showed her where the dungarees were stacked in neat cubicles, arranged by sizes. He looked at her with a withering stare when she demanded to try a pair on, but he held aside the shabby curtain that screened off a closet, and there she pulled off the old pants and tried on the new.

They were stiff and scraped her legs, but she loved the newness, the crispness. And she remembered what Matthew had said about the fabric shrinking. So she noted the measurements of the pair that fit, and when she walked back into the store, gathered four pairs of the next size and carried them to the counter.

Beside the dungarees, she piled shirts, three of smooth chambray to be worn next to her skin to protect against chafing and three of heavier wool flannel. Then there were socks and gloves, and finally the boots.

But no coat. The shopkeeper didn't have one in her size, and the ones he did have were of inferior construction. Glory smiled smugly when she examined the garments and discovered that they had been put together so cheaply. The skills her father had taught her all those long years ago had not been forgotten.

She munched on a juicy pickle while the shopkeeper added the various prices. He tore off a piece of brown wrapping paper and wet his pencil with his tongue as he scribbled. She caught his first two errors, one in his favor and one in hers, but then decided to ignore his miscalculations in favor of devouring the pickle.

"That comes to fifty-five dollars and twenty-seven cents," he announced. "Including the pickle."

"Just put it on the account for the LJ Ranch," she told him, wiping her fingers on the seat of her pants. "I'm the new owner."

"Lee Johnson's widow?" he asked, without surprise.

"Well, I'm very sorry, Mrs. Johnson, but your husband never was all that good about paying his bill, and frankly, I don't feel I can entrust a sum this large to a woman running the ranch."

She hadn't expected this. Everything had been going so well, from her seduction last night to proving it this morning. Now this merchant who couldn't even add up his sales correctly was telling her he didn't think she could pay him!

No temper tantrums, she warned herself. Just get the job done.

"I shall return, sir," she said quietly. "You may wrap the parcels for me while I fetch the *cash* to pay for them."

The bank was even more deserted than when she had left it earlier. One of the tellers leaned back on his stool reading a newspaper. The other was cleaning his fingernails with a pocketknife.

"I wish to withdraw one hundred dollars from the account of the LJ Ranch," she instructed the second teller when he had closed the knife and put it away.

"I'll need to get approval," he stammered.

"Then get it."

She didn't wait at the window but followed the man as he walked from behind his cage toward the office of the president. While the teller conferred with his employer, Glory strode into the next office, where Ambrose Lytle was putting on his coat preparatory to leaving for lunch.

"Mrs. Johnson. What can I do for you?"

She gestured in the direction of Conner's office and said, "You can tell *that man* that Lee had over a thousand dollars deposited in this bank, and I want one hundred of those dollars to meet my living expenses."

But before Lytle could walk to the adjacent office and present her demands, Conner himself had come out with the clerk.

He smoothed the silver hair with a plump, spotted hand.

"There seems to be some misunderstanding, Mrs.

119

Johnson," the banker apologized. "You may have the funds at any time you need them. There's no reason to—"

"Thank you," she interrupted, surprised at his abrupt change of attitude, but without the time to contemplate it. "I'll take it *now*."

When she returned to the store, her purchases sat on the counter exactly as she had left them, unwrapped. She looked around for the storekeeper and found him assisting another customer, a woman in a fur-trimmed cape who was buying lamp oil, wicks, and a chimney to replace the one she said her husband had broken. She laughed as she detailed the accident, and Glory couldn't help but envy the woman her delightful relationship with a husband whose clumsiness didn't detract from her love for him.

She stood aside as the woman came to the counter to pay for her purchases.

"Excuse me, aren't you Glory Johnson? I'm Nancy Reynolds. My husband Dodd and I run the Greenbriar Hotel."

"How do you do, Mrs. Reynolds," Glory stammered.

"Oh, heavens, I'm sorry. I must have surprised you, since you don't know me from Adam. Dodd and Grant Brookington are old friends and Grant was telling us all about you the other night."

"He was?" Damn the man! She couldn't even shop without being reminded of him.

"Incessantly. I know you must be busy, but could you find time for a cup of tea or coffee? I'd like to get acquainted with the woman who has managed to get Grant Brookington talking about something other than steers."

It was all too sudden, and this Reynolds woman seemed to know too much, where Glory knew far too little. Besides, how could she sit down to tea, wearing old pants and a shirt with holes at the elbows, with a woman as fashionable and elegant as Nancy Reynolds? Not and talk about Grant Brookington, who despite all her efforts, had been in her thoughts all day.

Glory called on the habits ingrained by a stubborn Aunt Phoebe. "Perhaps some other time, Mrs. Reynolds. I really am pressed today."

Nancy smiled as though she understood.

"Next time you're in town. Tell Matthew I'll give you the recipe for my brownies, and he'll be sure you have time for a visit."

The sunshine faded beneath a murky cloud cover by the time Glory was halfway back to the ranch. The weather matched her mood. She scolded herself, often and loudly, about the silliness of her feelings, but nothing erased the sense of inadequacy that Nancy Reynolds had given her.

The mare's ears turned backwards when Glory spoke, then pricked forward again at the sound of distant thunder.

"I know, she was just being friendly, and I can't blame her for that."

The horse tossed her head.

"I just felt so, well, so dowdy. I mean, there she was, not a hair out of place, not a smudge or spot on her skirt, and me in the menfolk's cast-offs. And I suppose you're thinking I ought to get used to it. After all, it was my idea to hang onto the ranch, and that means giving up fancy clothes and riding into town in a carriage. I can't have my cake and eat it, too.

"Hell, I can't even bake a cake!"

The temperature dropped as the clouds swirled and thickened. A brisk wind replaced the breeze, gusting now and then. Glory could just make out the trees and buildings at the LJ when she felt the first hard drop of rain.

By the time she had the mare unsaddled and rubbed dry and filled the manger with a generous scoop of grain, the rain had turned to a slushy sleet. Glory tucked her parcels under her coat and dashed across the muddy, slippery stableyard.

There was no light burning in the kitchen, a sign that Matthew was out. Glory opened the door and stepped into the darkness. It was cold darkness. And a bitter, smoky one.

She dropped her parcels to the table and groped for the matchbox on the wall. She had been expecting a warm kitchen and her disappointed body shivered. The first match snapped in two, and she swore angrily.

The second sizzled and settled to a steady flame. She lit the lamp and turned the wick up and coughed at the acrid smell that filled the room.

It was the smell of burnt meat. She knew instantly what had caused it.

"Oh, *damn!*" she cried.

She set the lamp down just carefully enough to keep from breaking it, then ran to the cold stove. On top of it sat the kettle, every bit as cold, and coated on the inside by a vile-looking, bitter-smelling black concretion that was to have been supper.

She drew back her foot to kick the impassive hunk of cast iron that had conspired against her again, but caught herself in time. "No, I won't give you the satisfaction," she told the stove.

There was nothing for it but to start from scratch and light another fire. Her stomach growled, reminding her she had had no lunch and would have to wait longer still for supper. They were frustrations, inconveniences, nothing more. She had handled worse problems.

But the half frozen rain that had pelted her when she ran from the barn to the house was seeping through her clothes now, chilling her to the bone and adding to her frustration. When she looked into the woodbox and saw only chips and slivers, the frustration finally became too much.

Self-pity overwhelmed her. She had done and endured

more than was fair, only to meet with yet another defeat. Too cold and exhausted to fight anymore, she gave in to tears.

The sleet was well on its way to becoming snow when Grant and Matthew dashed up the stairs to the shelter of the back porch. They brushed the icy pellets from their coats and shook the worst of the wet from their hats before Matthew reached for the doorknob.

"I am frozen clear through," Grant complained. "I shouldn't have let you talk me into fixing that last gate."

"Yeah, but it got you an invitation to supper, didn't it?" the boy teased back.

Grant snarled and followed Matthew into the kitchen.

They reached Glory, who was sprawled at the table, at the same time, but Grant was the first to speak.

"Glory?" he whispered to the blanket-shrouded form. "She okay?"

"I don't know," he answered, puzzled at the way she seemed to have fallen asleep so soundly in a room that was as icy as the barn. Then he saw the bottle lying on the floor under the table.

"She's drunk," he said, as though he couldn't believe it himself.

Matthew picked up the bottle and looked at the spill on the floor.

"She can't be too drunk. That was Pa's bottle, and it didn't have but an inch or two in the bottom."

Grant glanced around the kitchen as though looking for an explanation. Slowly, he began to piece all the little details together. The encrusted pot on the cold stove, the empty woodbox, the wet kindling heaped in the stove, and the remains of a dozen matches all told the story.

Glory raised her head and tried to open her eyes. They seemd stuck together. When she finally did get the lids up, the light hurt so bad she had to squint just to see. And still nothing came into focus.

123

"Is that you, Matthew?" she asked, her voice loud in the silent kitchen.

"Yes, ma'am. Me'n Grant been out fixing some of those fences."

"I thought you were going to fill the woodbox this morning," she accused. "I came home and the fire was out and I couldn't even light another because the woodbox was empty."

"Well, I was going to, but then Grant came by and he—"

"I don't give a damn about Grant. Besides, don't you spend most of the time while he's here splitting wood? That's where you always run off to, like you think I don't know what you're doing. Well, it isn't going to work. I don't need him anymore. What I need now is some firewood."

The pain Grant felt at her abrupt disregard surprised him, but he put it down to ordinary male pride. Besides, she was drunk. Though he had heard the saying about there being truth in wine, he had heard more than enough lies come from bottles.

She sat up straight. The blanket started to slip off her shoulders, but when she reached for it she encountered something warmer than expected. She looked down, fighting to clear her vision, and managed to distinguish a large hand. The hand slowly lifted the quilt back onto her shoulders and tenderly tucked it around her.

She looked up. She didn't need to focus to recognize the steel grey eyes that met hers.

"Oh, it's you. Again." She almost felt as if he had been with her all day.

"Yes, it's me, again." He pulled the bench a little further out from the table and straddled it, just as he had the night she burned her hand. "What the hell happened?"

He took one of her hands in his, trying to transfer some warmth to her. Her lips were almost blue, and her teeth

124

were starting to chatter. And she had the nerve to tell him she didn't need him anymore.

"I forgot to close the damper on the stove this morning when I left, so the stow burned down to nothing and the fire went out."

"It's a wonder the whole place didn't burn down."

"I don't need that, not from you," she snapped.

"That's right, you don't need me at all anymore, do you?"

She couldn't be too drunk. That remark brought a fierce blush to her cheeks. It served her right, too.

Ignoring his barb, she continued, "I was going to light the fire again but there was no wood and no kindling. So I went outside . . ."

"Without a coat."

"Well, it was already wet clear through."

"But your shirt wasn't, until you went out without a coat."

"Yes," she shot right back at him, "I went out without a coat. Are you going to scold me and send me to bed without any supper?"

He almost reminded her that he had put her to bed last night without supper and she hadn't complained at all. In her present frame of mind, however, there was no telling how she'd react to being reminded of last night. And Grant wasn't sure he wanted to think about it any more than necessary.

"All right, so you went outside. Then what happened?"

She sniffed and looked around, then reached for the bottle he had set at the end of the table.

"Oh, damn," she moaned. "I spilled it, didn't I. Well, anyway, I found some kindling but it wouldn't burn and by then I was too damn cold. So I got the blanket from the bed and went looking for Lee's whiskey. Terrence always said there was nothing like a stiff shot of whiskey when things were going bad, and I suppose he ought to know since things so often went bad for him."

A sharp crackling sound and the smell of burning wood reached through the fog of whiskey and cold. She sniffed and brought her numb fists to her eyes to rub them and make them focus.

Matthew was on his knees in front of the stove, blowing gently on a pile of flaming sticks and shavings. Beside him on the floor was a stack of clean, dry wood.

"Where'd you get that?" she demanded to know.

The boy looked over his shoulder at her, then glanced to Grant with a question in his eyes. The man just shrugged.

"It was in the parlor," Matthew answered rather sheepishly.

"In the parlor?"

He nodded.

"The parlor box was clear full."

"You mean, I went out in that horrible weather, burnt my fingers on a hundred matches, and damn near froze to death when there was a box full of nice dry kindling in the next room?"

"You sure did."

The shocked expression on her face warned Grant to expect tears and self-recriminations, but she said nothing. She slumped. A forlorn tremor went through her. Hesitantly, Grant put one arm around her shoulders and pulled her closer to him.

She didn't fight him at all. As much as her earlier words had hurt him, he discovered that her display of weakness, her surrender to despair, touched him more deeply. He liked her better when she snapped like flames on dry wood.

"It's all right," he soothed. "Everybody has days now and then when nothing seems to go right. Tomorrow you'll look back on it and laugh."

"No, I'll just make more mistakes, make a bigger fool of myself. I just can't do anything right."

This had to be the whiskey talking, not the proud, defiant Glory who stood up to everyone and everything.

126

"Did you have any lunch today?" Grant asked.

"No. That woman in the store invited me, but I told her I didn't have time."

"What woman?"

With no lunch and no supper, he wasn't surprised the shot or two of whiskey had hit her so hard.

"Some friend of yours. She was going to give me a recipe."

Everything seemed so absurd. The warmth of his embrace penetrated the quilt, easing the cold and making Glory drowsier. Involuntarily, she snuggled closer to him and let her eyes fall closed.

"Must have been Nancy," he said. "If it was the recipe for her brownies, take it. That's one of the best kept secrets in the county."

"Oh, Grant, I feel terrible."

"Sick? Like you're going to throw up?"

"No, just terrible. Stupid. Incompetent."

"Don't be silly. Look at all the things you've learned. I saw how you took care of the horse tonight. Rubbed her down and fed her and gave her water before you came in the house. Two weeks ago you didn't know a bit from a bellyband."

"But I still can't cook, and I ruined the kettle to boot. And then to sit here, crying about not having any wood when there was a whole box—I just can't do anything right."

"If you're looking for pity from me, lady, you're not going to get it."

His harshness startled her. She looked up, most of the alcohol-induced haze dissipated now, and he met her gaze with hard, cold eyes.

"For a woman who says she doesn't need any help, you are doing one hell of a lot of whining," he told her. There was no pity, not even gentleness, in his voice. "Matthew's got the fire going in here and he's working on the fireplace in the parlor, so let's you and me rustle up something to eat."

127

"There isn't anything. I put the last of the beef in the stew that burned up."

"Then we'll fry some potatoes, heat some beans and bacon, bake a pan of biscuits."

There he was again, offering help she had no choice but to take. How cleverly, how subtly he forced her words back down her throat.

She refused to let him have the last word.

"See," she whined, wishing she hadn't. "I can't even come up with an alternative to stew. Just name one thing I *can* do right, Mr. Grant Brookington."

She disentangled herself from the quilt and his embrace and staggered to her feet. The floor seemed a little uneven, but the feeling of light-headedness passed quickly, as though the effect were more from rising too quickly than from a few swallows of whiskey.

Standing over him, though not by much, she looked bedraggled and miserable and bewitchingly desirable. Oh, she needed him, all right; she was just too stubborn to admit it. A man had no choice when confronted by such a contrary female but to show her the error of her ways.

"Well, you're not the greatest cook west of the Mississippi, that's true," he replied slowly. "And I have a feeling you still hold onto the saddle horn every time Lucy jumps to a canter."

She blushed, affirming each of his statements.

He stood, still straddling the bench, and tossed the quilt to the floor.

"But I swear, Glory, there is no woman on this earth who makes finer, sweeter love than you do."

She turned a deeper, more delectable shade of red just before she burst into tears and ran for the stairs. Grant was still shaking his head when he heard the bedroom door slam shut.

Chapter Ten

The hangover wasn't enough to slow Glory down. Under the headache burned the fires of humiliation, stoked by the memory of a man's soft, seductive laughter and his praise for a skill no one had needed to teach her. Like a locomotive under a full head of steam, she charged through the morning, grabbed a hasty lunch, and attacked the afternoon.

When night fell, she collapsed into bed exhausted. Matthew had helped her with supper, teaching her how to fry a slice of beefsteak, boil and mash potatoes, and make gravy, so she went to bed with a full stomach, for the first time in several days. Neither exhaustion nor a full belly kept her from lying awake for hours.

During the day, she contrived to stay busy enough to forget last night and the words she had hurled at Grant Brookington. But at night, when her muscles quivered as they tried to relax, her spite returned to haunt her.

"I don't need him anymore," echoed over and over in her mind. Was it the whiskey that prompted her reckless declaration of independence? Had the liquor peeled away the layers of doubt to let her proclaim once and for all that she would never be forced to rely on someone else again? Was she trying to convince him—or herself?

She pulled the quilt up to her chin and tucked her shoulder into the pillow. For an instant, she thought she detected just a whiff of a lingering masculine scent, but when she tried to recapture it, there was nothing but ordinary pillow. And why not? Grant hadn't slept there.

Angry, and frustrated because she was tired and yet couldn't go to sleep, Glory pounded the pillow, then reached for the other. She dropped it on top of her own, to cover up any hint of a reminder of Grant Brookington's presence in her bed.

Ah, but this pillow was the one he had used, and now the scent was stronger, unmistakable. She couldn't define it, just knew it was there. Finally, aware that she had wrapped her arms around the pillow and hugged it to her, she drifted into sleep.

The next day, two more of her hands left. Without a word, Matthew joined the remaining crew for chores, and when a blizzard blew in that night, Glory, too, pitched in. She shoveled grain into wagons to be taken to the corrals holding the market steers. She carried wood to the house and bunkhouse, kept the fires burning, cooked for herself and Matthew as well as the men. She fed the chickens and the three ferocious hogs, tried to milk the cow, and tended the horses until she couldn't pitch another forkful of hay down from the loft.

There seemed to be no end to the work. In the evenings, she pored over the slapdash records Lee had kept. Trying to sift the truth from his frequent errors often brought tears. More than once she slammed the ledger book shut and lay her head on her arms to fall asleep still weeping.

It took her every moment of three weeks to put the books in order, to assemble an accurate inventory of supplies and livestock, and to calculate what kind of profit to expect when she sold the cattle. On the evening before she was to accompany the herd to Greene, she closed the heavy book with a sigh of relief and satisfaction instead of a cry of despair.

"I do believe we have made it, Matthew," she announced.

"Made what?"

"Enough money to see us through the next year. Now that Mr. Conner has relented about the bank account, I won't have to keep so much cash around the house."

Matthew, lounging on the sofa, yawned. Glory noted that the boy looked older, too old for his fourteen years. Not once had he complained, though she knew he must have been thinking about the assistance they could have had from Grant Brookington.

"What difference does it make if it's in the bank or the house?" he asked.

"Lonnie can't get it if it's in the bank."

By her estimates, based on Lee's erratic bookkeeping, Lonnie Hewitt had skimmed nearly all the surplus from the ranch's operation since Melody Johnson's death. Matthew's mother must have had some control over her brother, because the depredations on the cash hadn't started until she was gone.

"Well, I don't guess we got much worry about Lonnie," Matthew observed. "He ain't been around here for what, three weeks? Either he found some other tree to pick, or he's starved to death by now."

Glory didn't share Matthew's confidence. The sense that Lonnie was lurking, waiting to strike, had never left her for a single moment. The memory of her degradation, of the physician's moral scorn, and of Lonnie's failure to appear had all left an indelible mark.

Still, Glory couldn't suppress a cautious optimism.

"By this time tomorrow, we will have those steers driven into Greene, sold, loaded onto a railcar bound for who knows where, and a tidy sum to put in Mr. Conner's bank. There might even be enough left for a celebration dinner. Where's the best restaurant in Greene, Wyoming?"

The boy sat up, enthusiasm replacing the day's-end lethargy.

131

"I s'pose the Cattleman's, but I ain't sure they let ladies in. Well, that is, ladies like you."

Glory arched an eyebrow.

"And just what kind of 'lady' am I?"

Matthew's face flushed watermelon pink.

"Oh, Lord, I didn't mean it that way. See, they got ladies in the Cattleman's that, well, the kind of ladies men like to visit once in a while."

"Prostitutes," Glory said to get the boy out of an obviously uncomfortable situation. "I am quite aware of their existence and their purpose. In that case, what's the next best restaurant in Greene?"

He almost looked disappointed, as though he expected her to defy convention again by marching into the sacrosanct Cattleman's and demanding service.

"Grant took me to the Greenbriar once, and it sure was good."

The name rang a familiar bell in Glory's mind, but she had to think for a minute before she remembered Nancy Reynolds, Grant's friend, was the owner of the hotel. Well, Grant hadn't been around the LJ for three weeks, so there was no reason to deny herself the pleasure of a night on the town.

"The Greenbriar it is. As soon as we get those cattle sold, you and I, Matthew Johnson, will go out for dinner. Why, I may even wear a dress!"

Glory checked the fire in the upstairs stove before she closed the door to her bedroom. The wind was howling around the house again, and the murky sky hinted at snow. Though the steers had to be driven only a few miles to the freightyard in Greene, those miles could be miserable if the weather was bad.

It seemed there was always another obstacle, another difficulty to be overcome. On the eve of victory, Glory worried about the last obstacles. On paper, everything looked good, but she knew there was still no guarantee.

She almost wished she hadn't proposed a celebration until after the cattle were sold. Overconfidence had skunked more than one business deal.

She tossed and turned, unable to sleep. If there had been any lingering reminder of Grant on the pillow, she had long since caressed it away, yet she hugged the feather-filled substitute to her and tried not to think about him. It had been three long weeks since she had last seen him. Three long weeks since she had told him she didn't need him. Three weeks since she had realized how much she did need him.

She dreamt of mountains and snow and screaming winds, of cattle that bawled and called her name. She dreamt of incessant thunder that rattled the windows and shook the house to its foundations. And all the while the cattle cried out, "Glory! Glory! Glory!" until she pressed her hands to her ears and begged them to stop.

But they didn't, and slowly she realized that part of the dream was real. Only it was Matthew who kept calling her name, and the thunder was his relentless pounding on her locked bedroom door.

She was up before she could even answer him.

"My God, Matthew, is the house on fire?"

"Worse, I think. Somethin' stampeded the steers."

She pulled her nightgown over her head, then grabbed the pants she had tossed at the foot of the bed.

"What happened?" she asked as she shoved her arms into shirtsleeves and fumbled blindly with buttons.

"Dunno," Weed Usher, her foreman, answered from the other side of the door. "Woke up to, uh, heed a call o' nature and I heared a funny kind o' noise. At first I thought it was a gunshot, only muffled. I listened for it again, and that's when I heard the steers. Even on snow, there ain't nothin' else sounds like panicky cows."

Dressed, Glory opened the door and stepped into the hallway. She didn't waste time asking why there had been no one guarding the steers. With every hand needed to drive them to town, she had taken the risk of letting all the men get a good night's sleep. Weed had warned her, but now he said nothing. There was no time for recriminations, only for work.

The weather granted them a small respite. Though the wind hardly lessened, the cloud cover thinned enough to let an iridescent moonglow illuminate the whitened countryside. Stepping down from the back porch, Glory could see three horses saddled and waiting, with one of the cowboys mounted on a fourth nearby.

"The rest of the boys are already out, Weed," he told the foreman. "I hate to say it, but it looks like somebody did this deliberate. Spooked 'em and then scattered 'em."

And scattered them good. By the time the sun came up, blood red behind the thinning clouds, Glory began to assess the damage. Her optimism of the night before faded as the day grew brighter.

She endured the cold silently, riding to follow Weed's or Matthew's instructions. She learned more in those two days than she could have been taught in a month, but the lesson was painful.

The cold was not the worst. This was November, the very beginning of winter. Had it been February, she doubted she could have survived the bitterness. Yet her legs and face still went numb, and her fingers lost the ability to clench and unclench around the reins, so that she just held the leathers for hours at a time, never letting go.

She couldn't decide if the sun was friend or foe. For a few hours during the middle of the day, it lent warmth enough to thaw the worst of the frozen body parts. At lunch, Matthew insisted she head back for the chuck wagon or at least a hastily kindled campfire for hot coffee. By then she could bend her fingers enough to hold the tin cup and sip the scalding bitterness to warm the inside of her. Then, like the men, she stubbornly got back in the saddle and chased the steers that were her only hope of survival.

But the same sun that shed welcome warmth also cast a blinding glare on the pristine snow. Cheek muscles screamed with the ache of squinting, and at night Glory felt the tenderness of sunburn from the reflected brilliance. She lay in bed and cursed the sun, hoping it would not rise again.

Despite her curses, and prayers, the sun came up the next day, and the next. Two days after the stampede, Glory and Weed and Matthew counted the animals packed into the corrals that had been repaired enough to be usable.

"We lost fifty-two head," Weed announced grimly. "Plus three more dead."

The loss was staggering. It meant nearly all the profit Glory had counted on. Still, she calculated they would suffer no huge deficit. If nothing else, they'd all dine grandly on prime beef instead of the tough carcasses of culls. She'd be no better off than when she started, but neither would she be any worse.

"We'll take them into town first thing tomorrow," she told Weed and the boy as they mounted for the quarter-mile ride back to the house. The sun was going down already; it would be nearly dark before she was home. "We'll post a guard tonight. I'm taking no more chances."

Matthew offered to take the first watch, but Glory refused. He had done enough already and, like herself, was virtually asleep in the saddle. But he did not give up easily.

"It's only for a coupla hours," he insisted as they trudged up to the house. There were no lights burning, no drift of smoke from the chimneys. "And I wouldn't be alone. I got my rifle, too."

"No. You're too young to be sitting out there waiting to shoot someone."

"Ah, c'mon, you don't really think he'll come back, do you?"

"'He?'" Glory echoed, opening the door to the cold, empty kitchen. "I suppose you've been speculating as to the identity of the person who ran off my cattle?"

"Weed and Bob think it was Uncle Lonnie."

The thought had crossed her mind too, more than once during the cold, miserable hours she had sat on that horse.

"Maybe it was, but how would he know we didn't have a guard that night?" She unbuttoned the heavy coat and tossed it toward the table. It fell to the floor, where she let it lie. "You start a fire in the parlor; I'll do the stove."

Matthew did as he was told but he did not, however, leave off his argument.

"Well, I still think it was Lonnie. He'd be just mean enough to do something like this."

"Mean enough, maybe, but what purpose did it serve? No, Matthew, if Lonnie was behind this, he'd have done something more destructive, more permanent. Like stealing the whole herd, not just driving off a few head that will probably come wandering back or turn up at the spring roundup."

"Who else has any reason to stampede the herd the night before we were gonna sell 'em?"

She had no answer, at least none she was willing to give. Even later, after they had eaten a quickly thrown together supper, Glory resisted the thoughts that tried to sneak into her mind. But when she had sent Matthew to bed and was alone again, she couldn't help the unpleasant answer from making a concerted attack.

Grant Brookington had more than one reason to stampede her cattle.

A hot bath, a few hours' sleep, and a hearty breakfast worked a minor miracle, and the sight of her steers stretched out in a solemn line headed for Greene and the railyard raised Glory's spirits even more. She had wanted to ride at their head, proudly bringing them suc cessfully to market, but neither she nor her horse was up to it and she elected to bring up the rear in relative comfort.

They arrived just before noon, when the yard was its busiest. Weed, who had gone ahead to locate the buyer with whom Lee had contracted last year, was already waiting.

"His name's Walt Hackett, and he'll be here soon's he's done with the beeves from the Witch's Hat."

Glory nodded. Steve Peake's ranch lay south and a little east of the LJ, bordering the Diamond B as well.

"I told him he was gonna have to deal with you, so he ain't gettin' any surprises."

"Thank you." She tried to breathe a sigh of relief at having got this far, but the exhilaration was too much. Her heart was pounding; her cold hands sweated inside the gloves, making the blisters sting. "And, Weed, thank you for everything else. If we come out of this okay, I'll make it up to you and the others."

He said nothing, just turned his horse away to help the rest of the hands finish corralling the steers.

She didn't have to wait long for Walt Hackett, nor did she need anyone to identify him. Something suggested he was only comfortable around beef when it was on a plate in front of him.

"Mrs. Johnson?" he asked. He was a short, plump man, closer to fifty than forty, with a neat beard and bushy sidewhiskers. He wore a black derby hat that left his ears exposed to the cold, and they were as red as his cheeks and bulbous nose.

She extended her hand and noticed with satisfaction that her grip was considerably firmer than his. Perhaps he had shaken too many hands already in Greene.

"Mr. Hackett. I'm sorry we didn't make our appointment the other day. A bit of trouble the night of the storm."

He nodded, as though he understood, perhaps too much.

"My condolences on the loss of your husband. Mr. Usher, your foreman, explained everything to me."

While he talked, Hackett walked around the corrals, first just looking and then taking a small notebook from inside his coat to scribble in. He had to hold the pen inside his glove to keep the ink from freezing, but that didn't stop him from writing several pages of notes.

"The contract, of course, was for fifteen hundred head from the LJ Ranch," he explained. "Have you brought fifteen hundred?"

"Almost. Fourteen hundred seventy two, to be exact."

Would Hackett void the contract because she hadn't delivered the full quantity? If he did, what on God's green earth would she do with the steers then?

But she couldn't think like that.

"And they're prime, Mr. Hackett. They've been on hay and grain the past month."

"Except for the past two nights."

"Well, yes," she stammered. "But what difference can two days make to an animal that's been well fed for a month or more?"

He turned to look at her, staring down a nose that gave him little if any dignity.

"Mrs. Johnson, I applaud your courage in bringing these cattle here to fulfill your late husband's contract, but obviously you know very little about the business. Two days and nights in this kind of weather can do enormous damage to an animal."

"Such as?" She wouldn't let Hackett know the extent of her ignorance, but she was damned if she'd be as ignorant next year.

"A steer expends an enormous amount of energy, which lowers its weight. Also, some of these animals appear to be injured."

138

She couldn't deny either statement, but before she began defending her steers, she wanted to know exactly what Hackett's stand was.

"What does this mean in terms of the contract my husband signed with your company?" she asked. She managed to sidle around Hackett so that he had to face her, or turn around and go back the way he had come.

He sniffled and tucked his notebook away again. Glory would have given almost anything to have seen what he had written.

"The contract was only for the delivery of the steers, you understand."

"I understand."

"And you were two percent short of the quota."

"No, Mr. Hackett, I made ninety-eight per cent of the quota."

"Same thing, isn't it?"

"Not at all."

He gave her an odd look, as though to say, well, she's only a silly female, and who can begin to understand the way they think?

"What I want to know, Mr. Hackett, is how much you're going to pay me for the steers."

Out came the notebook again, and the pen.

"I have been prepared to pay thirty dollars a head," he said slowly, still scribbling. "Deducting for the shortfall on the contracted quantity, weight loss due to inadequate feeding, and projected losses due to injuries, I can give you twenty-two dollars each for these steers."

"But that's twenty-five percent!"

The cattle buyer smiled indulgently and chuckled.

"No, Mrs. Johnson, it's just under ten percent. Here, let me show you."

Glory had no idea what kind of mathematical chicanery Hackett was going to try on her, but she did not have the time for it. She grabbed the piece of paper he tore from his notebook and wadded it angrily into a little ball.

"If you had offered me a reasonable price, I'd have taken it." She kept her voice low, despite an urge to scream at the top of her lungs. "But not this robbery. Not without evidence."

"Evidence? I don't know what you mean, Mrs. Johnson. And I assure you, I meant no dishonesty."

"I'm sure you didn't, Mr. Hackett. At least none that you thought I'd ever catch."

The rest of his face turned as red as his nose and ears.

"Now, what I suggest is that we take a few of my steers over to the feed store, where I know they've got a nice big scale, and we'll weigh them."

"Weigh them? Whatever for? I don't buy beef by the pound, Mrs. Johnson."

"No? Then why were you ready to deduct from the price for the weight loss? As I was saying, I suggest we find out the average weight of five of my steers and compare it, to, say, five from the Witch's Hat that are being loaded on the railroad cars right now. Mr. Peake received full price for his steers, didn't he?"

It was an outrageous scheme, almost as outrageous as seducing Grant Brookington, but Glory ruefully reflected that that scheme had worked out quite successfully. Why shouldn't this one?

Chapter Eleven

Over the first three weeks in November, Grant found a dozen reasons to pay another visit to the LJ, but he talked himself out of the long, cold ride every time. Sometimes it wasn't easy. By the middle of the month, after several snow storms, he started to worry about the LJ cattle. He had never given them a second thought when Lee was alive, but now that Matthew and Glory were depending on those steers, he worried. And he didn't dare do a thing about it.

So he rode his own fences, fed his own steers, sat up nights and played poker with his own men. He didn't even leave the ranch for a visit to town, because he knew the road would take him past the LJ, where he might by chance encounter Matthew or Glory.

And he was damned if he'd give her the satisfaction.

He had let her make a fool of him, let her use him and then cast him off like a worn-out boot. It would never make any difference to her that he had left the comfort of her bed to hunt down Lonnie Hewitt and make a few threats of his own. He had wanted to share with her the triumph he had felt when Lonnie's sneer became a disbelieving frown. She, however, wasn't likely to want to share; she wanted everything for herself.

He had hoped his announcement that she'd have no more trouble about Lee's bank account would delight

141

her, but he discovered too late that his effort had been another mistake, one that at least he didn't compound by bragging about it to her. It had taken just a hint to old man Conner that there was a lot of Diamond B money on deposit that could be very easily withdrawn and taken somewhere else unless Lee Johnson's widow was treated with a little more respect.

Unfortunately, Glory didn't care if a job got done; she wanted to do it herself. She'd rather be a martyr than allow anyone to help her. And there was nothing he could do about that.

He wished he could.

Just like he wished he could get her out of his mind.

And finding thirty head of market steers with the LJ brand on them on the Diamond B range was not the way to get Glory off his mind.

Nor did he have any choice but to deliver them to her.

They made a thoroughly incongruous parade: Glory, Matthew, Walt Hackett, Steve Peake, and ten grumbling steers. As they passed down the main street from the rail yard at one end of town to the feed store at the other, they drew everyone's attention. Customers from the stores came out to the boardwalk to see what was going on. A man with a half-lathered face and a barber with a razor in his hand gaped from an open door. Even silver-haired Michael Conner left his opulent office to stare through the bank's plate glass window.

Much of the crowd followed them, excited by the prospect of something new and different, of a tale to tell on the cold winter nights that were just around the corner. Glory didn't care who watched or how many, so long as she had witnesses.

By the time they reached the feed store, gamblers were taking bets.

Like Peake's, her steers were in good condition. Lee, and his father-in-law before him, had imported Eastern bulls to improve the meat-producing capability of the longhorn cows driven along the treacherous trail from Texas a decade ago. Fully half the herd now were shorthorn crosses, including four of the five that bawled and bellowed in the street in front of the feed store.

Steve Peake accepted the congratulations of the crowd after his five steers were weighed. His reputation as one of the better cattlemen in Wyoming had not gone unnoticed when Glory selected him as the standard against which she would be measured. She wanted no excuses.

Then one by one her five steers were loaded into the leather sling and hoisted off their feet just enough to tip the scale.

Landon Smith, who owned the store and demanded a dollar apiece for weighing the animals, announced each weight in a mock solemn tone. When the fifth and final LJ steer had been set back on its hooves, he announced the winner.

Glory listened, though she already knew the results. Somehow, it wouldn't be true until Smith proclaimed it.

"Average weight for Mr. Peake's Witch's Hat steers is fourteen hundred forty-three pounds. For Mrs. Johnson's LJ steers, the average is fifteen hundred and twelve pounds."

Matthew, Weed, and the LJ cowboys exploded, with whoops, hollers, and a few gunshots that nearly stampeded the ten steers. Glory felt an urge to do likewise, but she left the celebrating to the others while she graciously accepted Walt Hackett's ungracious apology and his cash.

"All right, Mrs. Johnson, that's thirty dollars a head for fourteen hundred seventy-two steers."

His pen scraped slowly on the paper. She watched him, even as she mentally multiplied and compared the figures to her earlier estimates. Halfway through her own calculations, a familiar voice behind her interrupted.

143

"Better make that fifteen hundred and three steers, Walt."

She couldn't help herself. His name and an unexplained joy burst from her in one breath.

"Grant!"

Glory spun around and came face to face with a velvet nose that knocked her hat off her head.

"No, ma'am, I'm Grant. The horse's name is Rusty."

He was laughing at her, teasing her, making fun of her in front of men whose respect she had just won, and she didn't care. Even embarrassment at the hands of the man she had tried for three weeks to forget failed to wipe the smile from her face. And it was a smile she could not let him see.

She turned away to retrieve the hat, careful not to bend over and provide him another target for amusement. She reminded herself to be careful about everything she did, everything she said. That involuntary delight she had experienced could not be allowed to continue. There was no room in her life for it.

"I found some LJ steers wandering on my range," he explained as he dismounted, "so I brought them in for you. I figured you'd do the same for me."

The smile that had lit up her whole face and warmed his own heart was gone. At first he thought she had hidden her joy to avoid embarrassment in front of the others. Then he realized she was just back to business, as usual.

"And at thirty dollars a head, that comes to an nice even forty-five thousand and ninety dollars."

The cattle buyer was still scribbling with a reluctant pen.

"Er, yes, that's correct, Mr. Brookington." Hackett looked up at the tall rancher and asked, "How would Mrs. Johnson like the transfer of funds accomplished?"

Grant shrugged.

"How should I know? Ask Mrs. Johnson. It's her money."

144

If he had caught her off guard, she didn't show it. But neither did she give Hackett a chance to turn his attention elsewhere.

"Your credit has cleared the bank by now, hasn't it, Mr. Hackett?" Glory asked, all supreme confidence and control. "A draft on your account will be fine. We'll just walk over to the bank and finish this up."

Without waiting for Hackett, she turned quickly and headed in the direction of the bank, leaving Weed and the other hands to herd the ten confused, bawling steers back to the depot. Grant watched her go, a bit peeved that she hadn't bothered to thank him for finding her strays and bringing them to town or given him the chance to invite her to lunch. However, the sight of her trim little bottom, encased in dungaree pants that fit like a passionate man's caress, drove almost all the anger from him.

It also made him even more determined not to let her get the best of him again.

There were bills of sale to sign, and the draft to deposit, and then Hackett surprised Glory by producing a contract for the following year. She signed, after getting the buyer to take two thousand head.

She followed Hackett out of the bank, then stood on the sidewalk to watch him hustle down the snowy street. Never in her life had she felt so proud of her own accomplishments.

She did not have time to savor her triumph. She had a long list of supplies to buy before she could meet Matthew for dinner. The boy had his own errands to run, he claimed, though Glory suspected he intended to spend most of the day in the company of Grant Brookington.

Dark had fallen by the time she finished, and there were three other wagons waiting to be loaded ahead of hers at the feed store. That meant at least a two-hour wait.

"Might as well spend the night at the hotel," Matthew

145

suggested. He sat on a wooden crate and scratched in the dirt at his feet with a stick. "Grant said there's a big party goin' on tonight."

"I don't have time for parties," Glory protested. She had no intention of playing along with Matthew's matchmaking by attending a party with Grant Brookington.

Matthew shrugged and gestured to the waiting wagon. "Suit yourself, but it don't make no sense to ride all the way home tonight and have to come right back in the morning."

"Weed or Charley or one of the others can bring it."

"Nope," Matthew said with a stubborn shake of his head. "Ernie 'n' Old Ken already went back, you gave Young Ken a couple days off to go to Surrey Springs courtin', Spruce is stayin' in town to have that bum tooth pulled, Weed'll be too hung over to drive, and you swore last week you'd never let Charley handle the wagon again as long as you lived."

The boy's serious expression was all innocence, but Glory knew the kind of scheming that went on behind the guileless eyes. Matthew was determined to keep her in town. He probably had an answer for every objection she could raise.

Reluctantly, she told him to go ahead and take two rooms at the hotel. Confirming all her suspicions, he gave her an I-told-you-so grin and ran down the street.

The day had been long and exhausting, and she looked forward to a hot bath, a supper someone else had cooked for her, and a few extra hours of sleep. Even if they had been able to get the wagon loaded, she doubted she and Matthew would have had the energy left to drive all the way home. It was just as well Matthew had insisted, she admitted to herself after she gave final instructions to the men at the feed store and headed for the hotel.

Grant saw her before she saw him. He had been watching for her ever since Matthew trotted up and informed the rancher of his success in persuading his stepmother to spend the night in town.

"I still think you shoulda told her," the boy argued for the tenth time. "She's gonna be madder'n hell when she finds out."

"Maybe she won't find out. And maybe I will tell her, when the time's right. At least it kept Lonnie from getting the ranch. Now look, son, you go in and get those rooms. I want to talk to her alone for a minute, all right?"

Matthew grumblingly agreed, but as he walked away, he warned Grant one more time.

"Lyin' ain't the way to make her like you any better."

Having Matthew touch so precisely on the heart of the matter made Grant even more conscious of what he had done. Glory would indeed be furious if she discovered the truth. As he watched her cross the street toward him, he decided there would never be a better time for telling her than tonight, when she was in such a cat-with-the-cream good mood. Maybe, just maybe, she wouldn't get too upset.

She marched up the steps from the street, her hat tilted back to let the setting November sun brighten her cheeks and sparkle in her eyes. And all about her, that profusion of wild, unruly hair.

He wanted her. Not just sexually, though that particular desire was probably the most obvious, to him if not to anyone else. There was also an unquenchable urge to take care of her, to keep her from making needless mistakes and taking ridiculous chances. He blamed Lee for leaving her alone and vulnerable, but the worst of Grant's frustration came from knowing that no matter how much he wanted to take over the responsibilities left by Lee's death, he couldn't do a thing unless Glory gave him the right to. Lee had left her the means to assert the very independence that Grant feared would be her ruin. And he couldn't seem to make her understand that.

She walked up to him with an innocent half-smile on her lips, obviously proud of her day's work. Didn't she have any idea of the feelings the sight of her aroused in

147

him? No, she couldn't, or if she did, she casually disregarded them. He didn't even suggest they go somewhere less conspicuous, less public. Grant waited only until Matthew was inside the hotel and out of hearing, and then he let loose.

"What the *hell* were you doing?" he demanded. "Do you have any idea what risks you were taking trying to round up those steers yourself? My God, you could have been killed!"

A cowboy on his way into the hotel gave them a curious look, but Grant hardly noticed and never paused in his tirade.

"I told you if there was any trouble, you should send for me. Why didn't you?"

Though she knew she had no reason to argue with him, and certainly no need to justify her actions to him of all people, she calmly insisted, "There wasn't any trouble we couldn't handle ourselves. Besides, you have no right to tell me when and to whom to turn for help. The LJ is mine."

"Not without a little help from me, it isn't."

She glared furiously at him, her hands on her hips, but she kept her voice level.

"Fifteen minutes in my bed doesn't give you any authority over me, Grant Brookington."

He grabbed her arm, his grip a vise she couldn't slip out of.

"Watch your mouth, Mrs. Johnson," he growled. "You may have no concern for your reputation in this town, but damn it, I do. And before you go spouting off in front of every citizen of Greene, think about Matthew for a minute, instead of just yourself."

He took small satisfaction from her silence. At least it proved she had some sense of decency. Her refusal to give in, however, made him realize she was right. He didn't have any authority over her, and as far as she was concerned, she'd probably rather be trampled in a stampede than give up her independence.

A woman like that almost dared a man to make life easy for her, just so she could laugh in his face and tell him she didn't need him.

"You could at least have thanked me for bringing your steers in," he said suddenly.

"I could thank you to leave my work to me and my men," she shot right back. "And in case you hadn't noticed, we're attracting the kind of attention that is bound to ruin my reputation, which you are so concerned about. Would you mind letting go of my arm?"

Instead of releasing her, he shoved open the wide door to the lobby of the Greenbriar Hotel. When he tried to propel her inside, she planted her feet as stubbornly as a mule and refused to take another step.

If she had felt awkward over her appearance that day in the general store when Nancy Reynolds introduced herself, Glory felt worse today. And she knew she looked worse, too. Grant's sheepskin jacket was no less worn than hers, and his denim pants were considerably more worn, yet his appearance did not seem the least incongruous; hers was an insult.

"I'd just as soon not," she said, her voice down to a whisper.

Grant stared at her in the fading light. What happened to all her spirit, her fiery pride, her uptilted chin and tossed back shoulders? Where was all that temper she had been so ready to unleash just a minute ago? Why did she slowly remove her hat and shake her hair, not back over her shoulders but forward, as though to hide behind the cascading tangles?

"What's wrong with the Greenbriar? The food's the best in town, and you must be hungry. I know you didn't have any lunch."

"I look like hell," she confessed angrily. "And I smell of horses and steers. They'll probably kick me out for offending the other guests."

He should have gloated over her embarrassment, but

149

he couldn't. Not when most of it was his own fault.

"Nobody'll mind. Besides, I didn't think you were the kind who cared about appearances. I thought you were a rancher, like me." He cursed his own temper, his own pride for having tried to drag her in here. He was as guilty as she for thinking only of himself.

Before Grant could find a way to apologize, Steve Peake, whom Glory had expected to be bitter over her victory, strode up and interrupted the conversation with a congratulatory and not very gentle slap on her shoulders.

"You should have seen her, Grant," the older rancher said with honest admiration. "It was like she brought those steers in and just *dared* Hackett not to pay her full price."

"I did nothing of the sort!"

Peake laughed good-naturedly.

"Naw, I guess you didn't, but jeez, I'm sure glad I got my money from old Walt before you showed me up. How much you wanna bet next year he starts paying by the pound?"

"Then you better make sure your steers are nice and fat," Glory warned.

"I intend to, ma'am, believe me," Peake responded just as solemnly. Then returning to a lighter tone, he said, "You know, this sort of thing calls for a celebration. It isn't every day a man gets beat at his own game by a very lovely lady."

Glory blushed at the unexpected compliment, but Grant thought he detected a hint of panic under her reddened cheeks. He decided to offer a little assistance.

"Keep it up, Steve, and you're likely to get beat by another lovely lady. Patsy's Irish temper isn't very forgiving when it comes to her husband squiring other women around town."

Glory barely stifled a loud sigh of relief. She cast Grant a look that made up for her earlier lack of gratitude.

"I didn't mean it *that* way," Peake hastened to explain.

150

"In fact, I was going to invite you both to join Patsy and me for dinner. Be a good chance for Mrs. Johnson to meet folks, too. Sam and Daisy Wood'll be here, and Mike Parrish with his new bride."

As he had before, Grant left the decision up to her.

"If you're inviting, consider me invited," he said to Peake. "How about it, Mrs. Johnson?"

He felt no guilt putting her on the spot like that. He seemed in fact to enjoy throwing her a new challenge.

"I do appreciate the invitation, Mr. Peake," she said quietly. "I'm afraid I'll have to decline, however. Matthew and I have supplies to take back to the LJ, and we need to get started first thing in the morning."

Grant shook his head and used a sly smile to let her know her excuse wouldn't suffice, but it was Steve Peake who urged her to ignore her responsibilities for one night.

"I know it might not look right, you coming to a party so soon after you lost your husband," he said. "But out here folks don't expect a woman to mourn her man too long. And besides, you owe it to yourself to have a good time now that the cattle are sold. Especially after the way you whipped old Walt."

Unless she admitted that her only reason for resisting the invitation was Grant and the conflicting emotions he was stirring in her, she didn't stand a chance against Steve Peake's persuasive smile.

"All right, Mr. Peake, I accept. But I have to finish my shopping and, uh, clean up first."

"Just like a woman after all!" Peake laughed. "I'll save you two a place," he said and, without any other leave-taking, walked into the hotel.

Grant tried to hide a grin of enormous satisfaction. Not only had Steve Peake happened along at a most opportune time, saving Grant from making a complete fool of himself all over again, but the man Glory had beaten had managed to talk her into joining him for dinner, with Grant included in the invitation.

151

"It won't be so bad," he assured her, lowering his voice to a soft whisper to match the gentle caress of his finger against her cheek as he pushed one of those wild strands of hair back from her face. He couldn't seem to keep his hands away from her. If he didn't get her into the hotel or out of his presence, he'd just have to kiss her here in front of God and everyone. "Look, Matthew just went in to get a couple of rooms, so why don't I order you a nice hot bath while you finish your shopping?"

I can't resist him, she realized with a flash of panic. I'm going to do exactly what he wants me to do because he's made *me* want to do it, too.

His touch left her cheek warm, then cold when he drew his hand away. She felt hypnotized by his gaze and his smile. When he began to walk away from her and said, "I'll meet you in the lobby in an hour," Glory found her feet wanting to follow him, as though some part of her couldn't bear to be parted from him.

Cold common sense returned as she walked back down the sidewalk. She shook her head and laughed, at herself. If there hadn't been other people around her, she probably would have scolded herself out loud for falling so easily into the trap Grant Brookington had laid.

There were compensations, however. An invitation to dinner was just the excuse she needed to buy something for herself, something she didn't really need but wanted just the same: a new dress. She hadn't had one since Phillip died, when everything she owned had been dyed black.

She forced herself to remember that she was a widow again and propriety, even by Wyoming standards, did not permit her to indulge in something extravagant. But she wasn't going to dinner with Grant Brookington unless she had a dress.

Disappointment awaited her at Foley's Fashion Emporium, the only purveyor of ladies' apparel in Greene. According to the hand-lettered sign in the window, the store closed at six o'clock. After struggling with the locked door and peering into the darkened shop through already frosty glass, Glory took Lee's watch from her pocket and snapped it open. There was just enough light from the saloon next door for her to see that the store had closed half an hour ago.

"Damn!" she swore.

"Is that any way for a lady to talk?" Grant asked, walking up behind her.

She had heard his footsteps, though she hadn't known it was he until he spoke.

"When she's as mad as I am, it most certainly is. I spent all day on ranch business, and then when I finally get a little time for myself, the shop is closed."

"Foley's? What do you want in there? They only sell dresses."

He took a chance teasing her, especially when she was already angry. It was too dark to see her clearly, but he suspected the instant of silence after his taunting remark spoke of a blush on her cheeks.

"I did not want to embarrass your friends by appearing at dinner in dirty dungarees and one of Lee's old shirts," she replied. "I thought a dress would be more appropriate, and I had the extra funds—thanks to your assistance this afternoon—to purchase something suitable."

She was flustered; he listened to the drawl deepen with every word she spoke. He rested his forearms on her shoulders in a casual embrace and chuckled.

"Well, wouldn't that have been a sight for sore eyes. Glory Johnson in a dress. Can it be there's a little bit of feminine vanity under that cowboy hat?"

He must have touched a nerve with that barb, because she didn't have a rejoinder. Rather than give her time to think of one, he gambled again.

"Come on, let's go down to Abel's," he suggested, reaching out his hand to her. "You can buy a new pair of

153

dungarees, a shirt with pearl buttons, and a fancy belt all studded with silver conchos."

Heads turned as Grant and Glory strolled through the dining room to Steve Peake's table, but Grant doubted she noticed the attention. He, however, had seen the appreciative smiles. It wasn't often a man got the pleasure of watching a pair of shapely legs in pants, and Glory's were certainly shapely. And the masculine tailoring of the crisp white linen shirt emphasized rather than minimized her femininity. Grant couldn't hide a secret smile of his own. After all, he enjoyed her company; the others could only stare.

The restaurant was crowded and noisy, with a three-piece "orchestra" providing dance music. Steve and Patsy and their other guests apparently were on the dance floor, because the table was empty. Glory released a little sigh of relief.

Grant held her chair, then sat down beside her. For a moment neither of them said a word, until, in a single breath filled with apprehension and expectation, they spoke together.

"Look, I'm sorry."

The whole room seemed to have gone silent, then the tension collapsed in two quiet chuckles.

"I started it," Glory said, shaking her head in self-mockery. "I do owe you an apology, and a great deal of thanks. Those thirty head meant a lot."

To say nothing of those fifteen minutes in my bed, she wanted to add, but wisely held the words back. She wished she could stop thinking about that night. Being with Grant seemed to keep the memory in the front of her mind.

"Like I said, you'd have done the same for me, wouldn't you?" he teased.

"Yes, I suppose so."

154

"And I had no right to talk to you the way I did. I'll accept your apology if you'll accept mine."

He reached his hand across to her and she had no choice but to accept it. She knew she'd feel that same tingling that even his most casual touch caused. She shook his hand briefly, then quickly tucked hers back onto her lap.

The music ended to polite applause, and a few moments later, Steve Peake ushered his wife and guests back to the table. At first Glory felt the same humiliation that had assailed her when she entered the dining room, but Patsy Peake's friendliness put her immediately at ease. The vivacious redhead never said a word about Glory's stiff new denim pants or the shirt whose pearl buttons seemed to draw too much attention.

All Patsy did care about, it seemed, was getting every detail of the incident with the cattle buyer. The tale of Glory's victory over the unscrupulous Mr. Hackett had spread quickly, with appropriate exaggerations, and Patsy was only the first of several people to offer congratulations.

One stern-visaged matron who came up to the table shortly after dinner had been served did not even introduce herself.

"It's about time a woman stood up to a man," she expounded. "I outlived four husbands, but not one of 'em gave me credit for having a lick of brains."

And with that she clapped Glory soundly on the back and then marched off.

"Margaret 'Don't call me Maggie' Hancock," Patsy explained, "with husband number five-to-be in tow."

The man tagging along behind the redoubtable Mrs. Hancock was half her size, a mouse to her moose, and Glory couldn't stifle a giggle.

"Too much champagne?" Grant asked.

"No," Glory answered. "I've barely had any. I am *not* going to let you get me drunk, Grant Brookington.

155

You've already talked me into too many things that I didn't want to do."

He winked at her and murmured, "And haven't you been guilty of doing the same to me in the past?"

She giggled again and immediately wondered if perhaps she was just slightly tipsy.

Steve Peake's extravagant purchase of the enormous bottle as a salute to Glory's outsmarting the cattle buyer obligated her to have at least one glass. She avoided any more of the bubbly wine through the late dinner, but afterwards, Steve proposed another toast, and Glory allowed Grant to fill the glass again.

He lifted the magnum bottle and poured just enough for the toast.

Glory was relaxed, the first time he had seen her that way since he left her lying asleep and satiated in her bed three weeks ago. She laughed, and the sound was the sweetest music to his ears. The soft Virginia drawl crept into her voice as she relinquished some of her control.

Grant wanted to ask her to dance, but didn't dare. Once he had her in his arms he'd never be able to let her go. Steve did ask her, when Patsy protested that her feet couldn't stand another. Glory accepted, but only after a quick glance at Grant. Was she asking his permission? Or was she hoping he'd ask her himself? He just nodded and smiled. There was envy, but not jealousy, in the way Grant's steely stare followed his friend and the woman in the tight dungarees to the dance floor. Glory never noticed.

But when Peake brought her back to the table, she did notice. The look in Grant's eyes as they greeted her return was one of open, undisguised hunger. Glory recognized it because it was nothing more than a reflection of her own desire.

She wanted to blame her suddenly rapid pulse on the champagne, her dizziness on exhaustion and a whirlwind waltz, but the lie remained a lie. Grant Brookington made her heart pound, turned her knees to jelly, sent chills down her spine and fire into her vines. It didn't matter that she didn't want to respond like this to him; she had no control over her reaction at all.

She could not spend another minute in Grant's company without risking more than she could afford to lose.

Please, God, get me out of here, she prayed.

But it was Grant, not God, who came to her rescue.

"Are you all right?" he asked as he got to his feet. "You look like you could use some fresh air."

She could hardly speak.

"I'm afraid I'm not accustomed to champagne," she whispered.

Almost before she knew what was happening, Grant had made excuses for their early departure and was escorting her through the crowd. In the nearly deserted lobby he helped her into her jacket and then ushered her out into the crackling cold night.

She had taken no more than three steps away from the door when his arms went around her and enfolded her in a desperate embrace.

"God help me, Glory, because I can't help myself," he groaned as his lips came down to possess hers with all the hunger she had thought only she suffered from.

Chapter Twelve

His kiss left her breathless, and the cold air she dragged into her lungs sent a tingling chill through her that did nothing to quench the fire in her blood. She was dizzy, afraid to pull away from his embrace for fear her knees would give way beneath her. Her hands clutched at his jacket and would not let go.

"Do you know how long I've been wanting to do that?" Grant asked, looking down at her with eyes as bright as black diamonds.

"Since forever," Glory answered, her voice husky with awakening desire. "Just like I've been wanting you to."

Someone came out of the Greenbriar just then, reminding Grant that a public thoroughfare was no place to begin making love.

"We've got to get out of here," he said.

She curled closer to him, resting her cheek against his shoulder. "I have a room at the hotel," she whispered.

He loosened her hold on him and held her at arm's length.

"You're not drunk, are you?" A sober Glory Johnson would never have capitulated so easily. Grant didn't think she had that much champagne, but as tired as she was, it probably hadn't taken very much.

She shook her head.

"Sober. Cold sober." She reached up and placed her finger against his lips. "No, let's not talk about it. I don't understand it any more than you do, and I'm not going to try."

Despite the frosty air, he was sweating. He didn't know which he wanted to do more, lock her in her room and run as fast and as far from her as possible, or lock himself in her room and make love to her until the sun came up.

Then she fastened her hands behind his head to pull him down for another, even hungrier kiss. The decision was made for him.

"There's an outside stairway," he murmured against her mouth, nibbling at her lips between each word. "Have you got the key to your room or do you need to get it at the desk?"

"I've got it. Oh, Grant, this is so crazy! Why can't we stop it?"

"I don't know. I wish to Christ I did."

The room was dark, except for a circle of yellow spilled just inside the open door from a lamp in the corridor. Grant located the bed, then shut the door.

"Grant?"

"Yes?"

She was a voice, disembodied in the darkness. He held his breath, praying she wouldn't ask him now to leave. He wasn't sure he had the power to.

Then she was a warmth, reaching for him, pressing herself against him until he returned her embrace with the same passion.

"I couldn't see you," she whispered. "I was afraid you had gone."

"No, love, I couldn't leave you. Not now."

He would have added "Not ever" to that vow, but he could not form words when his lips and tongue and teeth were concerned only with kissing her.

They pulled off articles of clothing, their own and each other's, with no heed to where the garments fell. The only sounds were of buttons clattering on the floor as

160

shirts dropped to the bare wood, and of gasping breaths as two mouths struggled to stay joined.

Then, finally, frantically, there was nothing between them.

Blind, Glory let her sense of touch imprint on her fever-heightened imagination every detail she could not see. Trembling in passionate exploration, her fingers grazed his face. She traced the wings of his brows, stroked the hard line of his jaw, caressed the hollow in his temples where his own pulse raced.

She reached behind his head to hold him inescapable and pressed her body the length of his. His hands slid down her back from her shoulders to her waist and then lower, to cup her buttocks and pull her more tightly to the throbbing core of his desire.

There was no denying this kind of hunger. Glory felt her feet leave the floor as Grant lifted her. Instinctively, she wrapped her legs around him, opening her warmth to him greedily at the same time she cried out at the force of his entry.

She tried to think, to make some sense out of the sensations that had overcome her in so few minutes, but her mind could not hold a coherent thought. She knew only that she did not want to stop the sweet, deep pleasure he was giving her.

He took a step backward and found the bed. Without breaking the wanton bond that made their two bodies one, he sank down and back until he lay on the quilted spread with Glory astride him.

It was insane, it was beautiful, it was ferocious, it was delicious, but it couldn't last; their need was too great. Glory ground her hips against his and drove him into the depths of her soul. A few frenzied thrusts brought him to a hasty climax just a heartbeat before Glory gasped at the explosion within her own body.

She collapsed atop him, her breathing ragged, her heart thudding in her chest. Gradually she became aware that though the room was cold, their bodies were slick with sweat. They had not even bothered to open the bed; there were no blankets to pull up for warmth. Only where her tangled hair covered her shoulders and where Grant's hands rested still possessively on her bottom was she warm. She shivered and tried to burrow closer.

He stroked her back, feeling gooseflesh.

"If you'll get off me, I'll find the blankets," he whispered. "Or light a fire. Unless you'd rather freeze to death."

"I think I've already died," she sighed, but managed to ease herself away from him though her arms quivered weakly. An involuntary little wail escaped her when she broke the union of their bodies.

The cold set her teeth to chattering now that she had completely lost Grant's warmth. She wrestled with the quilt and blankets and sheets and finally slid under the covers up to her chin. The sheets, however, were little warmer than the room. Glory reached out for Grant. She encountered only an additional expanse of chilly linen. Before she could call his name, a brilliant flash of light startled her.

He had struck a match and was touching it to the wick of a lamp on the table beside the bed.

"I want to see what I'm doing," he said. "Keep the bed warm; I won't be long."

He gave her a lazy grin that spoke of pleasures yet to be enjoyed. A shiver rippled down her spine, but she hadn't the strength to turn away from him, much less to get out of the bed and leave him, the way her better judgment urged.

The glow of incandescent passion was fading, dimmed by the bright light of reality. Common sense told her she had committed an unforgivable folly. What had happened three weeks ago was excused by the exigencies of survival, but what had happened here tonight had no excuse, no rationale. As her pulse returned to something approaching normal, Glory sensed that persistent, sustaining rhythm. *Never again*, it whispered.

162

Never before had she had a choice. Always the dependence had been forced on her, because she had had no resources with which to fight free. She felt anger rising within her, anger directed at herself because she couldn't seem to pay any attention to her own better judgment when it screamed at her to put as much distance as possible between herself and this man who posed the greatest threat to her independence.

But how could she pay attention to better judgment when Grant paraded naked about the little room?

The muscles of his back, chest and arms glided smoothly under skin still tanned from the summer sun. Though his legs and buttocks were paler, Glory detected a lingering hint of gold on his flesh. The thought of him swimming naked in a mountain stream and then lying in the summer sun to dry brought a flush to her own skin. She blinked, but her eyes came open almost instantly, and she could not turn away, not even from the blatant sexuality his very casualness exuded.

He seemed no more aware of his nudity than of the cold that raised gooseflesh on his arms and turned his nipples to tiny pebbles of bronze against the gold of his chest. Yet when he glanced over his shoulder toward the bed and caught her staring at him, she knew his exhibition was completely deliberate.

He closed the fire door on the stove and stood up to face her.

"No, Glory, don't turn away," he begged. "I want you to look at me, so you'll know exactly who's making love to you this time."

In the sharp lamplight he might have been a gilded statue, all smooth skin and hard muscle. Even the hair on his chest, which she knew was darker than the rumpled curls on his head, seemed touched with gold.

"I don't know what you mean," she whispered. "Grant, you know you're the only one who ever . . ."

"Ever what?" he demanded, though he kept his voice as soft and low as hers. While she scrambled for any

163

answer but the one he would insist upon, he took the few steps to the bed and slid lazily under the covers beside her.

"You think I'm the only man who's ever made love to you, but you're wrong, Glory."

Her eyes widened and he had to kiss her to keep her from crying out a desperate denial.

His mouth moved skillfully on hers, possessing without demanding. For a second or two she fought him, determined that he should not accuse her wrongly, but at the first teasing flick of his tongue across her lips, she surrendered all over again. When he drew away, she moaned at the loss and opened eyes she could not remember closing.

Propping himself up on one elbow, he began again, "That night three weeks ago, that wasn't making love. It was a cold, calculated seduction, and I admit I was a most willing and even cooperative victim." He traced the outline of her still parted lips with the tip of his little finger. Her tongue slipped out to moisten her lips and it was all he could do not to kiss her again. "A few minutes ago something hot and wild and wonderful happened, but that wasn't making love, either."

Grant slid his arm under her and pulled her closer under the warmth of the blankets, so that he lay on his back while Glory curled against him with her head on his shoulder. She rested one arm on his chest, feeling the rhythm of his heart under her hand.

Then she felt a warmth over her own heart and realized it was Grant's hand on her breast. His palm gently rubbed her nipple, sending a spray of sensation through her nerve endings.

"But now, Glory, I *am* going to make love to you," he whispered.

He was lost, and he knew it. Her eyes, golden in the lamplight, had trapped him as surely as a fly in molten honey. No rope could have bound him more tightly than the strands of mahogany silk spread in lustrous tangles on his shoulder. He twisted his fingers in them and pulled her mouth to his with a groan of reluctant surrender.

She arched toward him as his lips left hers and trailed down her chin and throat to her breast. He took the proud peak into his mouth, circling it with just the tip of his tongue. She shivered.

"Are you cold?" he asked, though he made no move to pull up the blankets he had pushed down to expose her breasts.

"Yes, and no." Where his tongue had moistened her skin she felt a chill; where his hand caressed her flesh she felt only warmth.

She expected a repeat of the fiery passion that had so suddenly and completely consumed her. In the haze of repleteness following that blaze, she believed she could fend off his next assault. But his caresses were gentle, soothing, relaxing. Whatever resistance she might have mounted was battered down by the relentless tenderness of his attack.

She did not recognize its power to arouse until it was far too late. She had sworn she would not, no matter how much she wanted to, give in to him again, but she surrendered before the battle began.

"Don't fight it," Grant urged, murmuring the words against her throat as she threw her head back with a cry of agonized desire. "Just let it be, let it grow."

He stroked the silken flesh of her inner thigh until she sought the pressure of his hand elsewhere. He complied with her unspoken wishes and let his fingers find the warm spring from which her desire flowed.

It wasn't supposed to happen this way. After three weeks of unexplained desire, Grant had excused it all as the result of unfinished business. Taking her to bed again would, he believed, cure him of this insanity. Instead, now that he had tasted of her passion again, he wanted her more than ever.

Why did she have to be so willing? Despite her attempts to resist him, he knew she wanted every caress,

165

every kiss he gave her. And that undeniable response that came from so deep within her left him unable to ignore his own. Perhaps there was a part of her, that fiercely independent part that exasperated him at the same time it made him admire her guts and stubbornness, that would have prevailed against him, but he wouldn't—couldn't—give it a chance.

Then she touched him as he was touching her. Her cool, innocent hand surrounded his hardness to draw a cry from him that she muffled by lacing the fingers of her other hand into his hair and cupping the back of his head to pull his mouth down to hers.

Body, mind, and soul, she lived only for the moment, for the explosive brilliance that Grant Brookington generated in her. Her body cried out for him. Her breasts ached for the swirling delight of his tongue on her nipples. She craved the sweet capitulation that only he could command. Even as he moved to cover her body with his, she tugged frantically on the hard, satiny shaft in her hand to bring him closer and could not release him until she had guided him to the threshold.

"Take me now, Grant," she pleaded, raising her hips in an effort to capture him.

Tousled hair hung over his forehead, shadowing but not hiding the glitter in his steely eyes. A rapt smile curved his mouth. With deliberate slowness he slid into the eager warmth of her.

"I take no more than I give, Glory."

And what he took was time, to draw out the pleasure. At first she found it unbearable, to be teased and brought only by infinitesimal steps closer to the satisfaction she craved, the satisfaction only he could give her. Then, as he spoke softly to her, telling her of the delights he wanted to share with her, she settled into the slow rhythm of deepest passion.

It wasn't like before. This time she could feel so much more, not only of the body that joined to hers, but of the other sensations that could not be tasted or touched. The

166

security of his arms along her sides. The affection of a whispered kiss on her cheek. The flutter of a blush when he murmured a shocking intimacy into her ear while he drove himself inexorably deeper into her soul. The shiver of anticipation when he brought the rapture closer.

And when at last she shuddered in the throes of that sweetest of ecstasies, she could not remember any existence of which he was not a part.

They had lain in replete silence for several minutes. Now that the intoxication was wearing off, Glory could turn her thoughts in other directions.

"You weren't worried about getting me with child this time," she remarked as Grant's hand wandered to the hollow between her ribs and then to her belly.

She couldn't see the way his lips curved into a satisfied smile.

"Oh, I thought about it," he replied. "I thought maybe it wouldn't be such a bad idea."

"You thought *what?*"

Glory scrambled away from him, tangling herself in sheets as she tried to escape his mesmerizing touch. She sat up and for a stunned moment did not even realize that in doing so she had bared herself to his hungry gaze again. And the cold air, after she had grown comfortably warm under the blankets, immediately crinkled her nipples.

He chuckled and tried to kiss her hip, which was the closest portion of her anatomy to his mouth. When she drew away and would have bent her leg in belated modesty, he scowled up at her.

"You aren't pregnant, are you?" he asked as he eased her down beside him again and pulled the covers up over her.

"And if I were, what difference would it make? I'm quite capable of raising a child by myself."

It was extremely disconcerting to try to hold such a conversation with a man whose fingers were stroking her

167

thigh while his lips nibbled at her shoulder.

"And run the ranch, too? Don't you think you might just need a little help?"

"No," she insisted firmly, and rolled over, an unsubtle hint that she would like to get some sleep. "I don't need anyone. Besides, there's no child so it doesn't matter."

Apparently Grant didn't take her hint. He, too, rolled onto his side, but instead of turning his back to her, he wrapped his arms around her and slowly eased her against him.

"Maybe the first time it didn't work, but what about tonight? What about the next time?"

"There won't be a next time."

A ripple of fear went through her even as she spoke. There was no denying the evidence of Grant's seemingly unquenchable desire. Nor could she seem to control the surge of anticipation that brought fresh heat to her loins when he reached around her to fill his hand with the fullness of her breast.

He buried his face against the back of her neck, letting the wild strands of her hair tickle his nose and tease his eyelids closed.

"There'll be a next time, Glory. You know it and I know it. One of these days you're going to admit how much you need me, even if it takes a baby in your belly to prove it." He lowered his hand to her stomach and exerted just enough pressure to force her more firmly against him. "Maybe he's there already, and if he is, you need to get your sleep. Good night, Glory. Sweet dreams."

It was a long time before she did sleep. She blamed part of her insomnia on the strangeness of having someone else in her bed after all those years of sleeping alone, but there was much more to it than that. Grant's words had taken root and, like some persistent weed, would not be dislodged. She admitted that she hadn't given much thought to the possibility of conceiving a child, but now, he had made her think of it.

Eventually, exhaustion and a deep satiety combined to bring on drowsiness. A yawn and a stretch were followed by a relaxed burrowing into the mattress and pillow. Somehow, on the edges of sleep, it didn't seem so strange that she was naked, that there was an equally naked man beside her, and that her hand had reached down to cover his where it rested firmly on her belly.

Glory rose at the first light of dawn. She expected Grant to be long gone, but he slept soundly beside her, never moving even when she struggled to extricate herself from the sheets that were tangled about their legs. The fire had died hours ago, and Glory let the cold floor on her bare feet wake her and steel her to her decision.

If last night's lovemaking produced a child, she would not let it change her life the way Grant wanted it to. She certainly would not need to marry him. If she could run the ranch, then she was perfectly capable of raising a child. After all, hadn't she spent enough time with Sadie's children in Philadelphia?

In that respect she was probably more prepared for motherhood than most women. She held no illusions about cooing bundles of joy; babies could be, and frequently were, demanding nuisances. They expected to be fed whenever they were hungry, without the slightest regard to anyone else's wishes. Extra care had to be taken to keep them from spoiling one's clothes with the products of their bodily functions. They could ruin one night's sleep after another and then snore contentedly through the entire day with a perfectly clear conscience.

Yet despite all their bad qualities, they could easily insinuate themselves into everyone's heart with a single smile.

And they could just as easily break those hearts by falling victim to some dread disease, some childhood accident. Glory paused while stepping into her trousers and wiped away mental tears. The anguish of loss when Sadie's firstborn had succumbed to whooping cough remained even though the little girl was nine years in her grave.

Was it the memory that stung her eyes and tightened the back of her throat? Or did she unconsciously touch her hand to her belly and send up a wordless prayer to keep any child growing there safe?

She shook off all such thoughts and concentrated on getting her clothes on. As soon as she was dressed, she cautiously opened the door and slipped as silently as possible into the hall. Downstairs, she found Matthew waiting for her in the dining room.

Grant waited until the sound of her footsteps faded down the uncarpeted stairs before he flung the blankets back and let the cold air set his teeth to chattering. It should have chased the blatant arousal that had driven him almost insane while he listened to Glory pulling on her clothes, but nothing so paltry as a cold hotel room could cool this insatiable wanting.

Though he had a persistent suspicion that Nancy Reynolds would be delighted to discover Grant Brookington had spent the night with someone other than a prostitute whose name he would probably never remember, Grant decided discretion was more important. He gathered his own clothing and thrust weary arms and legs into the garments as quickly as he could. And when he was done, he made a careful survey of the room to be certain he left no evidence of his presence behind.

He almost didn't see the faded cotton shirt in the dim light. It lay on the floor halfway under the bed. Grant picked it up, knowing it wasn't his own. It was too big to have been Matthew's, and too well-worn to be a recent purchase.

His curse was a bare whisper, but nonetheless violent. "Damn you, Lee Johnson!"

The shirt tore easily in his angry hands. He ripped it again, ignoring the buttons that scattered on the floor, the scraps of fabric that settled on the bed.

"It wasn't enough you stole Melody. It wasn't enough I had to see her boy every day and hate him because he was yours and not mine. It wasn't enough you brought your new wife to town and practically dared me to lust after her the way I did after Melody."

He flung the tattered remnants of the shirt to the floor and kicked at them in a vain attempt to expel the frustration.

"You had to go one step further and make her utterly dependent on me just long enough to make her completely independent. Just long enough to make me want her more than I've ever wanted anything."

The sound of a door opening and then closing somewhere down the hall interrupted his diatribe long enough for him to get control of his temper. But when Grant looked down at the torn pieces of Lee's shirt, he could not force himself to gather them up.

"I'm damned if I do and damned if I don't," he muttered.

Chapter Thirteen

The Greenbriar's dining room was busy, as cattle buyers and ranchers began their day's business over fresh eggs and ham and golden flapjacks. Glory scowled as she mumbled her order to the harried waitress.

Matthew's plate was already empty, except for a puddle of maple syrup and a bit of gristle from a thick slice of ham. Having missed supper, he must have been ravenous.

"I'm sorry about last night," he apologized while Glory sipped scalding coffee. "I only meant to lie down for a few minutes. I didn't think I'd fall asleep that easy."

"You were dead tired," she excused him. "You've been working harder than anyone these past few weeks."

"Yeah, but you didn't have nobody to eat dinner with. I didn't mean to leave you all alone with a bunch o' folks you didn't know."

Unable to meet the boy's eyes, Glory looked in vain for the waitress, but it was too soon for the order to have been filled.

"It was all right. Grant invited me to join him and some of his friends."

Matthew seemed to sigh with relief then, as though he'd been afraid she would blame him for her having to dine with Brookington.

"Since I'm done here, why don't I go down to the

173

livery and get the wagon?" the boy suggested. "We can head on home as soon as you're done eatin'. Less'n you got other things to do."

"No, that sounds like a good idea. Thank you, Matthew."

His presence had made her nervous, as if his quiet blue-grey eyes were looking for signs that would tell him she had spent the night with a man she professed to hate. She knew that sexual satisfaction itself left no outward evidence, save perhaps a blush that she couldn't seem to control, but there were other signs an observer might find unmistakable.

Had her voice hesitated when she spoke Grant's name, or had she called it out? Did she sit too straight on her chair, proclaiming her brazen actions, or did she slump with shame? Was her hair, never very tidy under the best of circumstances, the wild banner of a wanton, or was Glory's fruitless attempt to confine the curls in a shapeless knot an obvious effort to conceal what could not be concealed?

Her breakfast arrived, hot and inviting, but she picked at the food without interest. Only when she saw Nancy Reynolds strolling through the dining room did Glory make an attempt to eat, using the action to screen her flaming cheeks from Nancy's scrutiny. If anyone would know that Glory Johnson had not slept alone last night, it would be the hotel keeper's wife.

And when Nancy became engaged in what appeared to be a lengthy conversation, Glory seized the opportunity to escape. She paid her bill quickly, then slipped out the door to wait on the boardwalk for Matthew.

Matthew had charge of the wagon and the supplies it carried while Glory rode Lucy. The wind had stayed steady, blowing spits of intermittent snow directly into their faces. The horses bent their heads to it, and both Glory and Matthew hunched their shoulders down into

174

their coats. Conversation was impossible; they rode home in silence.

By the time they reached the LJ, Glory's toes were numb and her face felt frozen. But she helped her stepson with the animals, releasing them from harness and saddle, drawing fresh water, pitching sweet-smelling hay down from the loft. The labor warmed her enough that she did not feel quite as disappointed as she would have had she entered the frigid kitchen immediately after dismounting.

Though it was well into the afternoon before Glory had the stoves fired and the house warming, she did not allow herself to rest.

She worked until she could no longer see, until her legs screamed for her to sit down, until her back shrieked for her to rest. Newly washed clothes dripped a weary monotone onto a floor that would need scrubbing the next day; the pantry shelves looked less bare now that the supplies had been put away.

She had sent Matthew to bed hours before, over a string of half-hearted protests. After bringing what seemed like half a forest of firewood into the house, Matthew had helped Glory fix a hasty supper of beans and fried sausage. Then he had pumped every bucket and kettle full of water to heat for his own bath, and just before accepting that luxury, he had filled them all again so there'd be plenty of hot water for the laundry. As soon as he had finished his bath, Glory had taken advantage of his drowsiness to hustle him upstairs. She promised to follow him soon, but instead she plunged back into work.

Only when her vision blurred and her legs refused to hold her up anymore did she give in to exhaustion. Collapsing on the sofa, she used the weakness of her legs as an excuse not to climb the stairs to her bedroom, but as she drifted into the welcome arms of sleep she knew the real reason for not seeking her bed was the loneliness that waited for her in it.

The following day, she maintained the same routine.

175

From sunup, when she stretched the stiffness from her neck and shoulders, to long after the early sunset, Glory lost herself in work. At supper, Matthew asked her if something was wrong, but she shook her head and insisted that she was simply doing what had to be done.

And there was much to be done.

Glory had thought her success dealing with the cattle buyer would have instilled the men with more confidence in her ability to hold the ranch together, but instead it cost her another worker. Dan Brower, who had stayed at the ranch that morning they took the steers to town, heard the story from Weed and the others when they returned. Dan had packed his things and left that same afternoon.

Glory refused to think about it. The rest of the men seemed loyal, if not friendly, and on occasion one or two seemed almost willing to help when she asked for assistance. She dared to hope the worst was over.

It wasn't.

With no legitimate excuses to offer Matthew, Glory had returned to sleeping in her bedroom, though she waited until she was on the verge of collapse every night before she could bring herself to slide between the sheets. Even then, her last thoughts before falling asleep seemed always to be of Grant, no matter how hard she tried to concentrate on something else. There had been no word from him, not even a visit when he rode, as he had to have, past the LJ on his way to the Diamond B.

The night the first storm hit, the howling winds kept Glory awake long after she should have fallen into oblivion. During the day, she had watched the clouds building, obliterating the distant mountains, and she had taken Matthew's predictions of heavy snow seriously. The winds began shortly after a dreary sundown, though the snow held off until later. But when it came, it left no doubt that this was no light flurry.

Glory wakened to a world she could never have imagined.

"Oh, this ain't nothin'," Matthew told her as he

176

gobbled hot oatmeal. "Sorry. This isn't anything. It gets worse in January and February."

She stood at the kitchen window, her back to the room and the boy. Beyond the glass panes there was nothing but white. The air, the sky, the ground had disappeared behind this all-enveloping shroud. The wind still whistled, blowing snow through cracks around the window until Matthew showed Glory how to use a knife blade to stuff rags into the cracks. Yet even that could not keep out the bitter cold.

"How will you get to the barn? Or the bunkhouse?" she asked, not turning from the blankness beyond the window.

"I won't. That's why I loaded up the porch with wood. Until this blows over, we're goin' nowhere."

The wind finally died down that evening, and the snow stopped soon after. By the time Glory trudged to her bedroom, the moon had come out, an eerie specter behind the tattered clouds.

She blamed the isolation for the thoughts that kept her awake. Memories of stories of families found frozen to death under monstrous blizzards came back to haunt her. She dreamt of being discovered, an icy corpse in her cold bed, and of steel grey eyes laughing at her as strong fingers swept the snow from her frozen face. When she forced herself awake, she knew she had reached out for the someone who had once slept beside her, the someone who had mocked her in her dream.

She admitted to fear, and even asked Matthew if there wasn't something they ought to do to avoid disaster should another blizzard strike.

"Do we have enough firewood?" she asked two or three mornings later. The porch had been swept clean and there was now a narrow path from the house to the barn and bunkhouse.

"Between what we got in the house and what's on the porch, we can last two weeks easy, and I don't recall ever bein' snowed in that long."

Glory was kneading dough for bread, enjoying the

177

resilient texture in her hands and the warm yeasty smell. Over the past few weeks, she had become reasonably proficient at least at this skill, and no longer worried each day if what came from the oven would be edible.

"What about supplies? Food, for instance. Oil for the lamps."

Matthew shrugged.

"I don't know about that. Depends on what's in the pantry and so on. There's plenty of beef, and it'll stay frozen. Same with the pork. And 'course we got the chickens, if you ever feel like cookin' one."

Glory shuddered. Cooking chicken meant killing one, and she had not yet been able to bring herself to do that chore. So the chickens still clucked around her when she went out to feed them or gather the few eggs they produced this time of the year, but they did not provide any dinner meat.

"I suppose I ought to take inventory of what we have," she sighed. "Maybe you could help me with that after I put the bread in to bake. Then we'll have to see about getting into town."

They made out the list—it was longer than she had expected—but her journey into Greene was delayed by yet another storm.

This one blew up almost without warning. At noon the sky was a brilliant blue, the sun blinding on the snow; by two o'clock the first flakes had started to fall from a leaden sky. When the clouds cleared shortly after dawn the next day, another seven inches of snow lay on the ground.

Two days passed, and by then Glory knew a trip into town was imperative.

"I've got to go," she insisted as she sat on the bench by the kitchen table and tugged on her boots. "We're almost out of flour, and I used the last of the coffee this morning. There's enough salt to last to the end of the week, maybe. But I discovered last night that we need lampwick."

178

"We got plenty of candles. Look, you can't just go riding into town by yourself."

She stood and pulled down the sleeves of her wool flannel shirt. "There aren't more than a dozen matches in that box. Neither of us knows how to make soap, and there's barely a sliver left, enough for one of us to take a bath."

She was right, and he knew it, but she could tell he wasn't giving in without a fight.

"All right, look. We can't afford for me to go with you until the chores are done. I'll go help with the cattle and then I'll go with you. Okay?"

Now it was his turn to have presented undeniable facts. The LJ was dangerously short of help and if both Glory and Matthew got stranded in Greene by another storm, there simply would not be enough men left to handle even the most essential chores.

"We'll have to hurry," she said, thinking out loud. "We can't leave here any later than noon, or we'll be riding back in the dark."

"Full moon tonight. On this snow, it'll be like daylight."

"Fine. But you'd better be here by noon anyway."

She had no doubt that Matthew was back at the house long before noon, but by then Glory was riding down the main street of Greene, on her way to the general store.

No amount of effort could wipe the grin from her face. She had, without anyone's help at all, saddled Lucy, and ridden all the way into town. And when she encountered Nancy Reynolds in the store, Glory discovered her pride did not diminish.

"It's only ten or twelve miles," she explained as she hefted a sack of flour to the counter.

"Still, I'm not sure I'd be brave enough to try it alone," Nancy commented.

Glory shrugged. She might not be as elegant as Nancy

179

Reynolds in her fur-trimmed cape, but neither was she afraid to do what had to be done. The LJ was a responsibility she had taken on willingly, risks and all. Having succeeded at one accomplishment, Glory felt confident enough to shrug off some of the risks.

"I knew I could stay in town if the weather looked threatening. A storm usually takes a couple of hours to build, and that's enough time to ride home. It's still clear, so I should have no trouble."

"Well, I'm glad you did venture in. I didn't get a chance to talk with you when you stayed with us a few weeks ago."

There was a serious undertone to Nancy's voice that sent a warning shiver through Glory. She strolled away from the counter and headed for the bins of coffee beans, but the storekeeper's voice called her back.

"Oh, Mrs. Johnson, are you sure this twenty-five pound sack will be enough flour? I've got plenty of fifties, and I can have one of my boys take 'em out to your pack horse."

She had barely turned around by the time the man finished his statement. Without a doubt, Nancy Reynolds saw the furious flood of red that swept up Glory's throat to flame in her cheeks. Every ounce of that hard-earned pride seemed to melt, like the snow that had turned to sloppy puddles around her feet.

"The twenty-five will be plenty," she stammered. "I didn't bring a packhorse."

Matthew would have thought of it, had she waited for him. She knew there was no longer any road for the wagon, but the idea of bringing another horse had never occurred to her.

The storekeeper shook his head. Glory saw the disapproval stamped on his face. She refused to let him think her incompetent, even though she had to admit she was, at least in certain areas.

"I wasn't planning to come in for supplies," she explained, squaring her shoulders and lifting her chin. "I

180

just thought I'd pick up a few things in case this weather got worse again. A little insurance, if you will."

The man looked at her, as though he didn't quite believe her. To emphasize her point, she strolled around the store and selected a few items of a decidedly nonemergency nature.

"I noticed this little copper tea kettle the last time I was in your store, Mr. Abel," she said as she lifted the pot down from a shelf. "I get so tired of coffee all the time. But what I really need is another heavy woolen shirt."

She set the copper kettle on the counter in front of the storekeeper and met his scowl squarely, daring him to question her ability to take care of herself. She would rather he think her frivolous for making an expedition in such chancy weather than that she didn't know what she was doing.

If Nancy Reynolds had any further comments, she kept them to herself, but Glory remained acutely aware of the older woman's puzzled contemplation. She did her best to ignore it, adding a red plaid shirt to her purchases. She remembered everything she needed without resorting to the hastily scribbled list that lay in a crumpled wad in her pocket. She didn't dare bring it out; it was evidence that she had lied about her purpose in coming to town.

"I hope you got enough cash for this, Mrs. Johnson," the storekeeper mumbled as he slowly totalled up the amount of her bill.

"I'm sure I do. If not, I can get more from the bank. At least Mr. Conner isn't giving me any trouble about my finances, unlike some of the businessmen in this town," she added accusingly.

"I hate to say it, Mrs. Johnson, but the bank's closed."

A hint of panic flared in the back of her mind, a panic Glory was certain became instantly visible in her eyes. She knew it wasn't Sunday, because there were no signs of activity around the church. Had the bank failed, like so many had in recent years? But the town seemed too calm to be in the grip of financial disaster, so Glory dismissed that fear. Something else had forced Michael Conner to close the bank's doors on an ordinary business day. Whatever it was, it could bode no good for a woman struggling to make her way in a world dominated by men like Jethro Abel, whose jowly face seemed to light with a malicious smile.

He grinned at her, and looked down at the pile of items she had purchased.

"You got everything you need, Mrs. Johnson? Didn't forget nothing?"

In addition to the flour and lampwick, the matches and coffee and salt and other necessities, Glory had treated herself to more than a few luxuries. Beside the shirt and socks she had folded a bright plaid scarf to wrap around her neck against the December wind. The copper kettle required a pound of exotic tea in a tin painted with indecipherable Chinese writing and a lovely scene of an arched bridge over a placid stream. Matthew could make do with ordinary soap, two bars of which sat wrapped in plain brown paper beside the tin of tea, but Glory couldn't resist the rose-scented decadence of a cake imported from France.

What was there about such items that would cause a wicked sneer to twist the shopkeeper's face?

"No, I've forgotten nothing," she said. "If you'll let me know the total, I'll pay you and be on my way back to the ranch."

"Total comes to twenty-seven dollars and fifteen cents."

As she pulled the coins from her pocket and spread them on the counter—a total of thirty dollars in gold— the hairs on the back of her neck seemed to stand on end. Something was wrong, very wrong.

"There," she said, hiding a quaver in her voice. "That should be enough."

Abel scooped the money into his hand and headed for the till.

"More'n enough," he said with strange relish, "but it

don't leave much for Christmas presents. And like I said, the bank's closed. Conner always lets his people go home early on Christmas Eve."

In her haste to escape the store and Jethro Abel's laughter, Glory twice dropped the copper kettle with a resounding clatter that echoed in her already ringing ears. How could she have been so stupid?

It was bad enough that she hadn't known to bring a pack animal. Then she had to compound her ignorance by wasting money on luxuries for herself, on the day of all days when she should have been buying gifts for others. Stupid and selfish, that's what Abel must think of her, and Nancy Reynolds, too.

Glory stuffed the new shirt into one saddle bag, along with the coffee and salt. The other items, except for the flour, she crammed angrily into the leather pouch on the other side of the saddle before balancing the flour sack across the pommel. The kettle she hung on the horn, having no other place to put it. The canister of tea fit nicely, but noisily, inside.

Through the glass window of the store, Glory saw Nancy Reynolds engaged in what looked like an argument with Jethro Abel, the elegant woman's fist raised to point an accusing finger at the storekeeper. But it didn't matter. Whatever they argued about had nothing to do with the widow Johnson and the utter fool she had made of herself—again.

Yet as she untied Lucy's reins from the rail in front of the store, Glory cast a single glance back to that window, just in time to see Nancy Reynolds wave frantically to her.

"No," Glory mouthed sternly, letting no sound come from her lips. She felt tears prick the back of her eyelids, and she would not give in to tears. They would only be another reason for Jethro Abel—and Nancy Reynolds—to laugh at her.

But Nancy wasn't laughing. As Glory swung the leathers over the horse's head, the other woman dashed out the door and called to her.

"Wait! Please, I need to talk to you!" Nancy cried.

"I haven't time, Mrs. Reynolds. Good day to you, and Merry Christmas."

Because of the precarious position of the floursack, Glory couldn't kick Lucy to a wild gallop and speed away from the site of her most recent humiliation. That gave Nancy Reynolds the opportunity to plead with her for another few seconds.

"Abel owes you an apology, and he'll give it, if you'll only come back," she begged, half running along the boardwalk to keep up with Glory. "And I must talk to you."

Later, Glory would blame her hesitation on the weakness of feminine curiosity. But when she tugged gently and brought Lucy to a patient halt, she told herself she was only being polite and avoiding a scene in the street on Christmas Eve.

"Mrs. Reynolds, I don't think I have to explain to you how important it is that I return at once to the LJ. And I have no wish to face Mr. Abel at this moment, apology or not."

"Abel is neither here nor there, Mrs. Johnson. It's Grant Brookington I need to talk to you about."

"I have nothing to say to you or anyone else about Mr. Brookington."

Risking the loss of the desperately needed flour, Glory dug her heels into Lucy's flanks and the mare jumped to a startled canter.

Glory heard Nancy call her name again, but she did not turn or even slow Lucy's pace until she was well outside town, beyond the church and the graveyard.

The lingering heat of embarrassment kept her from feeling the cold for a while, but Glory quickly realized that the road home was into the wind that had been at her back earlier. She pulled off her gloves and dug the soft woolen scarf from the saddlebag. With it wrapped around her neck and tucked into the front of her coat, she kept the wind off her throat. She was also able to pull the scarf up over her mouth and nose to warm the air she breathed.

"It'd probably be better if I froze to death out here," she muttered, reaching into her pocket for the gloves again. In only a few minutes, her fingers were getting numb and stiff.

And one of the gloves was gone.

"Oh, damn it!" she screamed. "Damn it, damn it, *damn it!*"

The wind tore her words away.

She turned Lucy back in the direction of Greene. Surely the glove had fallen from her pocket while she was fishing for the scarf. It couldn't be far behind.

But she couldn't find it. Even on the bare white track, where a lone glove should have been perfectly visible, she could see nothing.

"The wind probably picked it up and covered it with loose snow," she grumbled, shoving the bare hand into the pocket. "Well, it's a fitting penance for my extravagance."

The cold and her inability to stop blushing, even out here in the middle of nowhere where no one could see her, should have been enough to keep her mind off Nancy Reynolds' parting words. But even the depths of humiliation offered no escape from the feelings stirred by just the mention of that man's name.

"I am twenty-eight years old," she declared to the stark landscape around her. "I have entered into two marriages that have ended disastrously for all concerned. I spent twelve years of my life in a virtual mausoleum erected to the memory of a man I barely knew."

Poor Phillip. It was hard now even to remember what he looked like. She wondered when she had so completely forgotten him.

"I will not let any man, for any reason, take charge of my life. And that is exactly what Grant Brookington wants to do. Which is why I *refuse* to fall in love with him."

She shouted her declaration to the silent snow and sky, to the sharp line of mountains in the distance. Not even an echo returned to her. It was as though the vast emptiness had absorbed her words and would not give them back.

"I made a mistake today," she admitted. "In fact, I made several mistakes. But I learned from them. If I turned everything over to Grant Brookington and let him handle my problems for me, I'd be no better than Sadie."

She had pitied her brother-in-law's wife for a while, until she realized Sadie enjoyed being helpless. Worse was the respect such helplessness brought Sadie from the rest of the family. In that entire pathetic congregation of parasites, Sadie was the worst, and they had loved her the most.

"And they hated me," Glory mumbled, feeling again the loneliness, the disparaging glances, the whispered apologies. "Oh, God, what if everyone here hates me, too? What if I fail, and there's no one left to turn to?"

It wasn't a thought she could face just now. Not when she was cold and embarrassed and very close to that soul-destroying self-pity that had once driven her to drink. At least she'd never make that mistake again. Nor, she promised herself with a setting of her shoulders, was she going to fail.

The land between Greene and the LJ appeared flat, but the soft undulations were deceptive. The town nestled in a shallow valley that was virtually out of sight less than a mile down the road. Glory had left the metropolis far behind when she came to the first fork in the packed snow. Around her was nothing but snow and sky, with the mountains in the hazy afternoon distance.

The parting of the road was a familiar gauge, marking the halfway point between Greene and the LJ ranchstead.

Relieved that she now had no farther to go than she had already ridden, Glory glanced to the west and the line of snow covered peaks that serrated the horizon.

She saw no clouds, but the lazy angle of the sun surprised her.

"Better speed it up, Lucy," she told the mare as she tapped her heels against the animal's ribs. "We might have a full moon tonight, but I don't feel like riding in the dark. And it's going to be dark sooner than we think."

The mare responded by jolting to a trot and then an easy, loping canter that would have brought them home in no time, had they been out feeding the cattle or checking the fences. But Glory knew that the mare couldn't keep up this pace all the miles ahead, and it would be dangerous if she worked herself into a sweat. So after an easy jaunt that brought them perhaps half a mile closer to home, Glory pulled on the reins and slowed the mare once again to a steady but frustratingly slow walk.

And the sun continued to slide closer to the mountain peaks.

"We'll walk to that stand of cottonwoods," Glory told the mare. It helped to talk, just as it helped to set a goal after which she would make her next decision. "Then we'll try another gallop. Not too much. Matthew would skin me alive if anything happened to you."

The furry ears wiggled back, and Glory patted the mare's neck. Before she could get her bare hand back in her pocket, a hawk circling in search of prey let out a screech that startled her. Her involuntary jerk on the reins, coupled with a tightening of her knees around Lucy's middle, brought the mare to an abrupt halt. Glory held her seat with little trouble, but she couldn't get enough of a grip on the sack of flour. With a dull thwack it fell to the ground.

One seam split open, not completely but at least three or four pounds of flour now lay in a powdery puddle on the packed snow. By the time Glory found a piece of string to tie the corner of the sack shut and hefted it back

187

onto the front of the saddle, her fingers were completely numb, and even her face seemed to have lost its sense of feeling.

She struggled to mount, but as though the horse sensed her frustration and worry, Lucy skittered nervously until Glory felt hot tears trickling down her frozen cheeks.

"I've got five more miles, damn you, and I am not going to walk them," she swore as she pulled the scarf up over her nose again.

But the sun rode still lower in the sky, and Glory realized it was better to walk than to stand and fight with a stubborn horse. She squared her shoulders and headed for the LJ.

Chapter Fourteen

The sun disappeared behind the sharp teeth of the mountains just as Glory began the climb up the last slow rise to the house. The wind that had stung her eyes and chapped her cheeks died with the last light, but as darkness fell, so did the temperature. She tried to walk faster, to generate body heat from the exertion, but her feet refused.

"Damn you, horse, will you hold still?" Glory begged for the hundredth time. Once more she tried to mount the normally placid mare, but once more Lucy skittered away.

After three and a half miles, more or less, what was another mile?

Yet with every step of that last mile, Glory cursed out loud. She brought down a thousand damnations not only on the uncooperative horse but on her own stupidity, the weather, Lee (for getting himself killed), Matthew (for not coming to look for her), and most of all Grant (just for existing and insinuating himself constantly into her thoughts). She found reasons to consign to perdition Jethro Abel, Michael Conner, Lonnie Hewitt, and even such innocents as Weed Usher, Steven Peake, and Nancy Reynolds.

She went so far as to mutter a mild blasphemy against the God who had allowed her to make so many mistakes and end up in such a terrible situation on Christmas Eve, for crying out loud.

Anger worked, and she kept putting one foot in front of the other until at last she topped the rise. In the distance, just barely a quarter mile away, lights gleamed gold in the silver moonlight.

Leaving Lucy tied to the backyard fence, Glory stumbled through the gate and up the porch stairs. She fully expected to find Matthew sipping a cup of hot coffee after a nice hot supper. The stove would be hot, too. The mere expectation of warmth after so many hours in the cold was the only thing that gave her the strength to open the door and step into the kitchen.

"Where the hell have you been?"

It was a greeting she would have expected from Grant, not Matthew. Too weary to take another step, she sagged against the door frame and blinked in the bright light.

"I went to town," she explained. The scarf still covered her mouth, but she hadn't the strength to pull it down, much less unwind it from her neck and take it off. "For supplies."

Just being indoors was enough to start Glory's frozen extremities to thawing. As the pain began to replace the numbness, she eyed the bench at the table and tried to walk to it. She took one staggering step.

Matthew caught her before she fell, and he dragged her to the table. She noticed that there was no supper ready and waiting for her, not even a cup of coffee.

She didn't protest when he untied the scarf and pulled off the remaining glove.

"I just got back half an hour ago," he told her. "I figured you'd be here, waitin' supper and madder'n hell 'cause you couldn't get to town. Instead, you're gone, and nobody knows where. I was worried sick."

He took off her hat and then began unbuttoning the coat. She tried to help, but her fingers simply wouldn't cooperate.

"There's a sack of flour, some coffee and a few other

190

things," she whispered. A new numbness came to replace that which was slowly fading as she grew warm. No one had worried about her for a long time, not since her father died. That Matthew had been concerned enough to swear at her gave Glory an odd feeling.

"But what took you so long? Somethin' happen to Lucy?"

"No, except she wouldn't let me get back on."

"Why not? And what were you doin'—"

The kitchen door burst open, and Weed poked his head inside.

"Hey, Matt, Lucy's tied out back and—oh, she's home."

Glory couldn't tell if there was relief or disgust in her foreman's announcement.

"She just got here," Matthew added. "Said she's got some supplies out there. You wanta bring 'em in? Then you and the boys can go ahead."

"Yeah, sure. You goin' to the party? I mean, now she's home safe, don't seem no reason to miss it."

The boy shrugged. "I don't know. Oh, and could you take care of Lucy, too?"

Weed nodded.

"Sure. Glad to see you're okay, Miz Johnson. Saves me 'n the boy riding out after you. 'Specially on Christmas Eve."

He touched his hat and was gone again.

An uneasy silence settled over the kitchen.

It did not last long.

Matthew waited until he was sure Weed wouldn't hear, and then he exploded.

"What in tarnation possessed you to go riding into town alone? Hell, you didn't even tell nobody where you was goin'!"

Being chewed out by Grant would have been one thing, but to have a fourteen year old boy give her a dressing down made Glory even more humiliated. And more angry.

191

"I didn't tell *anybody*," she corrected him automatically, then corrected herself just as quickly. "No, I did tell someone. I told Ken, when I saddled Lucy, I was going to town."

"Old Ken ain't in the message-bringin' business. Besides, it's Christmas Eve and he's half drunk already."

"I'm sorry. And I didn't know it was Christmas Eve."

"Didn't know?"

The boy got to his feet and threw his hands in the air.

"What kind of idiot have I got for a stepmother?" he shouted. "She don't even know what day it is! She heads off by herself, don't take no packhorse to bring home any decent amount of supplies, loses her damn glove, and Lord only knows what other stupid thing she done. And she can't even get back on a horse by herself!"

Flustered, unable to understand Matthew's fury, Glory tried to explain, without falling back on lame excuses.

"I was foolish, I admit that, but I had no choice. We *needed* those supplies. And it's just as well I did go, because you said yourself you just got back, which means I'd have been waiting here all day for you, and tomorrow, being Christmas, we couldn't have got anything. The shops will be closed."

Feeling was coming back into her fingers and toes. She lifted one foot to begin pulling off the worn, wet boot.

There was an awkward knock on the door, and when Matthew opened it, Weed stepped in, his arms laden with an assortment of packages.

"Ain't much left of the flour," he observed. "Coffee spilled, too, but most of it's still inside the shirt. Might taste a bit woolly, but I guess that's better'n no coffee a-tall."

"Thanks, Weed," Glory sighed. "Go on and enjoy your party."

"Yes, ma'am. And you have a good time, too. Tom said they got two of the biggest turkeys he ever seen cookin' over at the Diamond B."

Glory turned to look at Matthew, who shrugged again, and when she turned back to hurl an accusing question at Weed, she caught only the closing door

She pulled off the other boot.

"I am not going anywhere. All I want to do is get into some warm clothes, eat something even if it's just bacon and eggs, and go to bed."

She was sitting, and Matthew was standing, which gave him the illusion of authority. He used it to full advantage.

"We ran into Tom Cashion while we were fixing some fences, and he told us Grant was having a big do at his place."

"No. I'm not going."

"Everybody'll be there," Matthew pleaded. "It's not that late, not really. I can have a couple of horses saddled in less time 'n it takes you to wash up and put on somethin' fancy, and we can make it over to the Diamond B in less time 'n that."

"No. It wouldn't look right for me to be attending a party so soon after your father's death."

Her conscience tweaked her for falling back on propriety she had never believed in before.

Knowing he had the upper hand now, Matthew argued, "Nobody pays no attention to that sort of thing out here. I oughta know. Ma wasn't gone two weeks and folks were pushin' Pa to get married again."

She had to remain firm. "It's different for a woman. And anyway, I'm not in the mood."

She got to her feet and walked to the stove, where a blazing fire was beginning to radiate its heat into the rest of the kitchen. Three large kettles sat on top, filled with water that was already lukewarm. Still, it would be a long while before that water was warm enough for bathing, and by then it would be much too late to set out for the Diamond B.

But when Glory turned around and opened her mouth to point that out to the boy, the heartbroken disappointment so evident on his face defeated her every protest.

"How can you not be in the mood?" he asked quietly. "It's Christmas Eve."

Matthew had taken on so many responsibilities over the past few weeks that Glory sometimes forgot he was still just a boy. Oh, he thought he was all grown-up all right, even grown-up enough to chew his stepmother out, but something about the Christmas season stirred the excitement, the wonder, the innocence of the child in him.

"I think I can find a pair of Ma's mittens," he said, as though he knew he had her on the defensive. "And I think I can talk Weed into lettin' you ride Granite. He ain't as slow as Lucy, so we could get there quicker. And really, it's only a little past five now. We might miss dinner, but Grant'll save some. Even leftovers'd be better'n what we got here."

They both looked at the sack of flour Weed had deposited on the table. Of the original twenty-five pounds, not more than ten remained, discounting the portion that had gotten wet from melting snow.

"I won't tell nobody about what happened today," Matthew promised.

"You won't tell *anybody*," Glory corrected again with a sigh of abject resignation.

His eyes widened, and a smile hesitated on his lips.

"Does that mean we're going?"

She took a deep breath and unfastened the last buttons on her coat.

"Yes, Matthew, we're going."

Weed used the excuse that being in charge of the LJ in Glory's absence, he couldn't very well relinquish the best cow horse on the ranch, so instead of Granite, Glory rode Old Ken's crossbred Morgan mare, April. After the long walk with the obstinate Lucy, Glory found riding considerably more comfortable, especially when Matthew tucked a heavy fur robe over her lap.

194

"Buffalo hide," he explained as he mounted. "Ain't nothin' warmer."

"Ain't nothin' smellier, either," she commented.

"Quit yer complainin'!" he laughed. "You wanna freeze?"

Though cold and dark, the ride to the Diamond B was shorter than Glory expected. April had a smooth, ground-eating canter that seemed to skim her across the snowy trail as if she were flying. There was no time for conversation, hardly even time to look around at the frozen, moonlit countryside.

And when they arrived at the Diamond B, Glory still didn't have time to look around. One of Grant's hands was waiting to take care of the horses the instant Matthew and his stepmother dismounted. He whispered something to Matthew, who chuckled but said nothing. The boy did, however, glance in Glory's direction, and that brought an answering grin from the other cowboy.

"What was that all about?" Glory asked as they walked together across the yard to the two-story stone and log building that was the main ranch house at the Diamond B.

"I didn't say a word about this afternoon," came Matthew's defensive answer. "Norm was just asking me if you had any trouble with April."

Glory didn't believe him, but she couldn't argue because they had reached the house and Matthew was opening the door.

Beyond the dim, lantern-lit vestibule, which was a good-sized room in itself, the enormous living room was crowded with people and light and music. Glory hung back, reluctant to enter that ocean of warmth and good feeling. Her own mood, a complex of exhaustion and lingering embarrassment and a sudden shyness, didn't seem to fit in with the atmosphere that would envelope her the moment she stepped into that room.

She knew she could not hide here in the foyer forever. Already Matthew had taken her coat and added it to the pile that all but buried a handsome pine deacon's bench. Any second now he would come back and nudge her in the direction of the party.

But he didn't. For a long moment, Glory just waited and stared, taking in the sight of so many people, so much light, so much warmth.

The living room was huge, three or four times the size of the parlor at the LJ, and the ceiling rose two full stories above the floor. Around three sides of the enormous room ran a second-floor balcony, the railings festooned with pine boughs and sprigs of wild holly. Their spicy aroma mingled with the scent of wood smoke and food.

Glory's stomach growled. She turned to look for Matthew, but the boy had disappeared.

Instead, Grant Brookington stood a few feet away, leaning against the wall by the deacon's bench.

"Merry Christmas," he greeted with a lazy smile. "You're just in time for dinner."

He was glad he had seen Matthew first and had time to meet Glory before she walked into the living room. He needed those couple of extra minutes to compose himself. He couldn't have done it in a room full of people.

The last time he had seen her in female attire was the evening she had slowly stripped out of skirt and shirt and everything else. Tonight she was far more prim, in a black skirt that had probably seen better days and a shirtwaist of a color Grant could only describe as dark lavender, trimmed with ivory lace. Mourning colors, though he doubted she wore them for Lee.

Her hair was wildly dishevelled from the ride, and her cheeks glowed with the cold. He couldn't stop looking at her.

"Merry Christmas," she murmured back. The way he stared at her was doing strange things to her insides. Remembering that night at the Greenbriar, Glory took a step toward the crowded room. If she stayed too long in Grant's company, the same thing would happen again.

196

She could feel the fiery mood building already.

"I'm sorry we were so late. I rode into town this afternoon and it took me longer than I expected to get back."

Grant walked closer. The whiteness of his dress shirt contrasted to his weathered complexion, making him seem civilized and barbaric all at once. "You rode into town? But Tom said he had run into Matthew and Weed. Who went—?"

"I went by myself," she answered quickly. "And Matthew has already scolded me enough, so you don't need to."

"I wouldn't think of it."

But he would think of a thousand other things he'd like to do to her. She read the essence of those thoughts in his eyes. Someone else might think that glitter was merely the reflection of lantern light, but Glory had seen the spark of easily aroused passion before in those steely depths and she recognized it now.

Or did she? When she realized Grant had taken one of her still cold hands and linked it through his bent arm, she also realized her eyes were closed and her lips were parted, expecting his kiss. The music that had filled the house was only an echo now, drowned out by laughter and applause. Glory turned her gaze in the direction of the crowded dance floor only to see that the dancers stood still.

And everyone was looking in her direction.

Steve Peake, his arm draped around his wife's shoulders as though the last dance had exhausted him, was the first to speak.

"Well, Grant, the Johnsons are here now, so can we eat? I'm starved."

Glory's blush deepened from scarlet to crimson. As though Grant suspected her uppermost desire was to find the nearest hole and climb into it, he clasped his other hand over hers and held her more tightly. Then he escorted her down two stone steps into the living room.

197

"You had us all worried," he told her in a voice meant to reach the farthest corner of the crowded room.

"Worried and hungry," someone called out, drawing general laughter.

"Next time I'll leave word with someone more reliable than Old Ken," Glory assured everyone. That brought another chuckle, and a measure of relaxation.

It even made Grant relax his grip on her hand, though she had no illusions about his willingness to let her go completely.

He led her to the opposite side of the room, where an immense stone fireplace dominated the wall. And on two long trestle tables in front of the blazing fire was spread out the most wondrous feast Glory had beheld in years.

"Oh, Lordy," she breathed, with every soft murmur of forgotten Virginia back in her voice. "I have not seen a Christmas like this since before the War. Those are indeed the biggest turkeys I have ever seen."

She had been cold and hungry too long, and she didn't care if she made a complete pig of herself. Grant handed her a plate and then proceeded to ask her if she wanted some turkey, and she said yes. Then there was a ham, glazed with honey and brown sugar, and she wanted some of that, too. And mashed potatoes and sweet potatoes and creamed corn and cornbread and gingerbread and baked apples and peach cobbler and on and on until the plate was overflowing.

"You can come back for more if this isn't enough," Grant whispered, but not very quietly.

He steered her back into the living room and then toward the staircase that led to the balcony, where tables and chairs had been arranged overlooking the dance floor, so that the guests might dine without the risk of a boisterous reveler upsetting the plates or, more important, the beer and other potables. Grant chose a place nearest the chimney of that great fireplace.

"The warmest spot in the house," he said, setting down her plate and then holding the chair for her. "Now,

I order you to eat and get warm, and not worry about a thing. It's Christmas Eve, and worrying isn't allowed anymore."

They ate, not in silence because no one else would let them, but they did not talk of worries. Yet the worry was there, the fear that refused to go away. Glory would chat with someone who stopped by their table for a moment or two and when she looked back, Grant would be staring at her, and she could almost feel his eyes caressing her, making sure she was all right. He had been worried, no matter what else he might say.

Again, she felt a strange tingle spread through her at the thought that someone cared. Even if that someone was Grant Brookington.

After dinner, while the adults relaxed and let their meal settle comfortably, Grant called out all the children. He led them in games, from toddlers to teens, and when the little ones cried, he bounced them until they laughed. One plump little girl in a faded pink dress just couldn't keep her blue eyes open any longer, not even when Grant tried to bribe her with a stick of peppermint candy. So he lifted her in confident arms and carried her to her waiting mama.

The older children, like Matthew and a few even younger, begged to be allowed to stay with the grown-ups as dancing resumed, and few parents protested. The musicians, who turned out to be neighbors like everyone else, picked up their instruments once again.

Glory lost all track of time. She danced with everyone, except Grant. He just waited for her, offering her a drink of untainted punch after a particularly energetic polka that wily old Clint Bascomb claimed her for, or helping her to her chair when it was obvious that Silas Sellers had done her blistered feet no good. When the next man, young or old, shyly approached the little table by the chimney and asked if Miz Johnson would care to dance, Grant merely smiled and graciously shared her. Glory did not ask why. She was afraid of the answer.

199

She didn't like the idea of Grant laying claim to her, and yet she had done nothing all evening but bolster that impression. It was as though her mind said one thing, but another part of her steadfastly contradicted that assertion.

As children dropped off to sleep and parents began to consider heading for their own distant homes, there were farewells to be said, and a final gathering in front of the dying fire in the living room.

The candles that decorated the buffet tables had burned low, and some of the lamps had gone out, dropping the room into gentle shadows. Herman Schultz was packing his fiddle into its worn case while his wife tried to gather their six children, including the little blonde in the pink dress. The eldest daughter resisted her mother's calling and dawdled in the farthest corner with, to Glory's mild surprise, Matthew Johnson. Other guests were bundling into coats and hats and gloves, while Tom Cashion and the cowboy named Norm brought word of each horse or wagon or sleigh that had been readied for departure.

"We should sing a song, you know," Trudy Schultz suggested, tucking her child's blonde curls into a heavy knitted cap. "A Christmas song, all of us."

And so they gathered around the fireplace, where Grant had placed another log on the embers, to raise untrained voices in a single hymn of a baby laid in a manger. When it was over, someone gently intoned a blessing on all who would be travelling home that night. And then, amid wishes for a merry Christmas and hopes for a prosperous new year, the guests departed.

Glory stood in the empty vestibule for some moments before she remembered she, too, was a guest. The feeling Grant instilled in her earlier had taken firm hold, and she knew she had acted the hostess without thinking.

She was still struggling to escape the role when Tom Cashion ducked back into the house and brushed flakes of new-fallen snow from his shoulders.

"Everybody get off all right?" Grant asked his foreman.

"Had a bit of a fight with Stu Hancock. Insisted he's a better driver drunk than his wife is sober."

Glory bit back an argument. She couldn't even remember which of the two dozen men was the conceited Mr. Hancock, but she was certain Grant's response to Tom's information would echo the usual male opinion.

"You get him to give the reins to Becky, or did you have to knock him out again?"

"No, she got 'em, all right. I think she'd have hit him over the head before we had a chance. After last year, she wasn't taking any chances." He waited a moment, as though not sure what he was supposed to say next. "Well, I guess I might as well hit the hay myself. Cows don't know it's Christmas tomorrow, so I gotta get up and feed 'em just like any other day. G'night, and merry Christmas, Mrs. Johnson."

"Merry Christmas to you, Tom."

She stood still, knowing Grant had put his arm around her, and waited until Tom had closed the door and the foreman's footsteps faded away.

"Are you tired?" Grant whispered, his lips against her hair.

"Yes, but there's a lot of work to be done."

"You're not going back to the LJ tonight."

"Oh, I know that," she acceded. "But look at all these dishes. And there is popcorn all over the floor and . . ."

"And I have people who get paid to take care of things like that."

Surprised, Glory twisted out of what was becoming a more and more intimate embrace.

"You do? You have servants, out here?"

He laughed, softly, and drew her close again, this time with both arms around her waist.

"Not exactly what you're used to, but I do have a cook, a stubborn little Frenchman who refuses to allow anyone else in his kitchen except for his wife, a Shoshone woman

201

twice his size who works as my housekeeper. And they will be highly insulted if you try to do any of the work yourself."

She was not unaware of the way Grant was guiding her toward the stairs again. She had been tired even before she came to his house, and now, after a sumptuous meal and hours of dancing, she could almost have fallen asleep on her feet. Though something in the farthest corner of her brain continued to warn her against the surrender she had already made, she was only able to register mild curiosity when Grant strolled past the stairs and headed for a door leading off the living room.

He didn't need to tell her this was his study, the place where he carried on the heart of his life, his business. Her father had been the same way: his office was his kingdom.

The fireplace was smaller, but made of the same rough stone as its larger companion in the living room. To one side of the warm hearth stood a massive walnut desk, the papers neatly stacked and held in place with a chunk of shiny quartz. Drawn in front of the steady blaze was a sturdy leather sofa, the kind a man would retire to after attending to the business of his ranch. There was a needlepoint-covered stool for his feet; and a heavy afghan, crocheted in bold-colored squares, lay in a neatly folded pile at one end of the sofa in case the fire failed to disperse all the chill.

Wearily Glory sank down onto the sofa. When Grant sat beside her and pulled her down so that her head lay on his lap, she did not struggle. Her eyes drifted closed.

"Don't go to sleep yet," he begged.

"I'm not sure I can help it. I'm not used to walking five miles in freezing cold weather and then dancing half the night away."

He stroked her hair, spreading the shining strands out across the leather beside him.

"What were you doing walking? I thought you rode into town."

"I did. Only Lucy—"

"She didn't throw you, did she? Lucy's never done anything like that before, but—"

"No, she didn't throw me. She just wouldn't let me back on."

Though she was growing sleepier and sleepier by the moment, Glory gave in to Grant's demand that she tell him the whole story. By now it was no longer even embarrassing, just an annoyance that she had had to endure.

The embarrassment returned when Grant began to chuckle.

"If Lonnie Hewitt hadn't already skedaddled, I'd run him out of town all over again."

"What's Lonnie got to do with my not being able to get back on my horse?"

"Well, it's all Lonnie's fault. You said you put the tea inside the kettle, didn't you?"

"Yes, but what has *that* got to do with it? Oh, Grant, make it quick, because I just can't stay awake another minute."

"All right, all right. Must have been ten years ago, when Lucy was just barely saddle broke. Lonnie got drunk one night and tied a couple cow bells to her bridle before he rode her into town. I don't know what the hell he was thinking about, doing a dumb thing like that, but the poor beast never forgot. Not too long after that, Melody tried to put sleighbells on her saddle, and Lucy wouldn't let her on, either."

"But I had no trouble mounting in town. It was only after . . ." She yawned and then answered her own question. "After the tin and the kettle had been clanging for four or five miles."

"Hey, you couldn't have known. I don't think Matthew even knew about it."

It was such an easy, companionable conversation, and yet when it faded and they both lapsed into silence, the comfortable feeling remained. Grant reached for the afghan and spread it over the woman lying beside him,

203

half expecting her to protest. But she didn't. She just snuggled into a more comfortable position and sighed.

Sleep was just around the corner. Yet it hesitated, and she remained awake, aware of so many things that she would have ignored had she been able to succumb.

Maybe it was just that she had been so cold for so long that Glory relished the tingle of the fire on her face, the scratchy pleasure of wool against her cheek. She felt safe and secure in the presence of a man she had once considered her mortal enemy.

Oh, Lord, it would be so easy, she admitted silently. He could do it all, and I'd have no more worries. He'd take care of me, right down to having someone to wash the dishes for me. It would be so damn easy.

But nothing came with a guarantee. She had married Lee Johnson expecting that same kind of security, and it had been destroyed in the blink of an eye. As painful as the lessons she had to learn might be, she'd learn them and stand on her own two feet.

"Glory?"

His whisper slowly penetrated her thoughts.

"Yes?"

"I thought you had fallen asleep."

"No, I was just thinking."

"About what?"

She almost said "About us," but caught the words just in time.

"About the ranch."

"You don't have to, you know."

She was so relaxed she didn't react immediately, but something in the back of her mind alerted her to the danger.

"Oh, Grant, please, not now," she begged drowsily. "It's not for sale, and I'm too tired to argue with you."

He continued stroking her hair, brushing the edges of his fingers against her temple, and his words seemed to follow the same soothing, seductive rhythm.

"Then marry me, Glory, and—"

In such a rush that she nearly tripped on the afghan and fell over the footstool, Glory was on her feet and backing away from the sofa where Grant just stared at her. His eyes, his mouth, even the way his hands were poised from his last caress, bespoke infinite patience.

It was as though he had read her thoughts, and nothing could have frightened her more.

"No," she gasped, as much in denial of his proposal as in disbelief.

Chapter Fifteen

"You don't have to answer so quickly. Think about it, at least until tomorrow."

Glory tried to untangle herself from the afghan but stumbled again, and Grant was there to catch her. The instant his arms went around her and drew her tightly against him, she knew she was lost

He could have kissed her, but he didn't. He just held her, one hand cradling her head against his shoulder.

"Don't do this to me, Grant," she pleaded. "You don't know what it's like, being afraid and alone and not knowing if you're going to get home safe or die out there. I was so scared, and I knew it was my own fault, but that didn't make me any less scared, and now you've made me scared all over again."

"You don't have to be afraid of me," he crooned. "And yes, I do too know what it's like to be scared." And alone.

He had been wrong to ask her, at a time when she was at her most vulnerable. He had done it without thinking, as though driven by some unknown need.

"It's easier for you. You didn't have it all thrust upon you with no warning, no preparation." She wiped at her eyes and sniffed back unwanted tears. "You knew all along what you had to do. I'm lost, with no one to turn to."

"You've got me."

She detected the note of bitterness that had crept into his voice and stiffened in his arms. Grant allowed her to escape the confines of his embrace.

"I should go home," she murmured.

"No, it's late and it's been snowing for a while already. Besides, I sent Matthew to bed."

There was no argument she could make, but when she refused to give in completely, Grant reached deep into the pain he had buried and brought out the wounds he never thought he'd have to show anyone.

"Sit down," he ordered. "And stop feeling so damned sorry for yourself all the time."

Gently grasping her upper arm, he turned her toward the sofa and she sat, gracelessly. The exhaustion that had left her momentarily defenseless had departed. She was awake, but without energy, without strength, filled only with an apprehensive numbness.

Grant began slowly, the words not coming as easily as he had thought they would. But he kept his eyes trained on her, holding her as firmly as if he had not taken his hands from her.

"I homesteaded the Diamond B when I was seventeen years old. My mother managed to squirrel away a thousand dollars before my pa could drink it up, and she left it to me when she died."

There, now it was getting easier. He ran his fingers through her tousled hair and turned away from the woman on the sofa as the memories flowed back. He could face them or her, but not both at the same time.

"I bought a few head of cattle, built myself a cabin, and called myself a rancher. Now, I'm not telling you this so you'll feel sorry for me, being a kid on his own. But I didn't come from a family with any ranching experience. My mother was a schoolteacher from Ohio. Pa ran a dry goods store, so he didn't hardly know one end of a horse from another, let alone cattle."

He heard the intake of her breath as she prepared to argue with him, but he was in no mood to listen to her.

This was his turn to indulge in self-pity; she had had her share and more.

"Don't get that look in your eyes wondering what brought them out to Wyoming, because I don't know myself," he said, his eyes meeting hers once more.

"And this isn't about them anyway. I was stubborn, just like you. I could have gone to work for somebody, but I wanted my own place. It damn near killed me, too, until I had the sense enough to ask for a little help. Matt Hewitt ran the next place over, the LJ he called it after his wife, and he took a little pity on me. He was a big Texan, been raised with cattle, and I just seemed to soak up everything he told me."

Glory wished she could turn away from Grant's steady stare. She knew what he was thinking. If he had been able to swallow his pride and accept help, she ought to be able to, too.

"I took a chance. I trusted Matt Hewitt, even though he might be a conniving thief who'd steal every penny I had. He showed me how to judge cattle, how to buy just the best cows and breed them to the right bulls. He could have been lying and laughing behind my back, but I didn't have any choice."

Just like me, she knew he expected her to say, but the words wouldn't come.

"And don't talk to me about scared, lady."

His voice had changed again, dropping to a whispered, remembered terror. A log popped in the fire and he flinched, as though the years had somehow slipped away.

He slipped out of the dark blue coat he had worn all evening and unbuttoned the cuff of his left shirtsleeve. While he rolled the sleeve up, he continued to talk, still in that strange, haunted tone.

"When you've spent a cold, rainy night behind enemy lines, with a Confederate bullet turning what blood you've got left to poison while you hide under a pile of the bodies of your best friends, then you can tell me about being alone. And when the doctors tell you that the only hope for saving your life is to cut off your arm, then you can tell me about being scared. And when some drunken surgeon, who's so tired of hearing young men scream when their bodies are mutilated and their lives destroyed, comes up to you and offers you a chance at saving yourself if you'll let him run a red-hot poker into your flesh, then tell me about not having any choices."

She had seen the scar before, but against the mature musculature of his arm and the rest of his body, it had seemed so insignificant. And there were other scars, though none nearly so twisted and puckered as the five-inch long strip of untanned skin that marked his left arm just below the shoulder. He pulled the fabric of his sleeve higher, exposing the whole length of the disfigured flesh.

Grant waited, barely breathing, and Glory wondered if he would speak again. He seemed lost in thought, trapped in memories too painful to be shared. She reached out, her fingers barely able to touch the hand that hung, almost lifeless, at his side.

Then suddenly he was on his knees before her, not in supplication but to drag her to the floor with him. Kneeling, their thighs touching, he circled her horrified face with trembling hands and kissed her softly, yet possessively.

Against her lips he whispered, "I've known fear you can never know, and God grant you never do. All I want is to protect you, to keep you safe. Never, ever to hurt you."

There was no fur rug on the hearth, only a coarse crocheted blanket between their bodies and the unforgiving slabs of slate.

It was like a dream, a fascinating yet terrifying nightmare that Glory could not escape, for she wasn't sure she wanted to. She felt everything, from the scorching firelight on her naked breasts to the chill of the stone beneath her back, through a haze of unreality. Was she making love to Grant, driving away his own demons resurrected from the grave of a frightened and forgotten

210

youth, or was he wrapping her in a cocoon, sheltering her from the horrors of a future she could not begin to envision?

When it was over, when they lay still tangled in each other's arms and legs and the fire gleamed on the slick perspiration of sexual fulfillment, they needed no words. To name the justification would have been to give it validity, and neither Grant nor Glory, at that moment, had the strength to face it.

Grant made no effort to persuade Matthew and Glory to stay longer then breakfast on Christmas morning. The light snowfall overnight had left another inch or two on top of what had already fallen, but the leaden sky promised more. As she let Grant tuck the buffalo robe more tightly around her legs, Glory bit back a cry and put a holiday smile on her face.

"Merry Christmas," she wished him. "And thank you, for everything."

"Think nothing of it." He shrugged in the cold and shoved his bare hands into the pockets of his pants. "Just get home safe before this storm hits."

Then he slapped the mare's rump before Glory could say anything else.

She didn't look back. Leaving him had been almost impossible as it was.

And yet there had been no other choice open to her.

They had made love again in front of the fire, never saying a word, just devouring each other in a thousand tiny morsels. Kisses, touches, the look in fire-gleamed eyes, the catch of passion-shortened breath: those alone sufficed. And when, exhausted in body and soul, Glory had fallen asleep, Grant carried her to one of the guest rooms on the second floor.

She wakened there, alone, with but one thought on her mind. That single notion left her preoccupied through breakfast, during which she was introduced to Maxim,

211

the very businesslike Frenchman who had charge of Grant's kitchen. She remembered wishing Maxim a *joyeux Noel*; the meal and the hour she spent in Grant's company were a blur.

Then, riding against the wind that was growing colder and colder by the minute, she still could not get that nagging litany out of her head. The big mare's hoofbeats, muffled on the snow, drummed it into a persistent cadence so that when at last the familiar buildings of the LJ came into view, Glory wondered how she had kept from screaming the two horrible phrases aloud just to stop their echoing in her mind.

He asked me to marry him, she had silently repeated to herself a thousand times since last night, *but he never said he loves me.*

If she thought she would rid herself of the warning by burying herself in work, she was sadly mistaken. And she came to realize, within a few minutes of arriving back in her own familiar kitchen, that Grant Brookington had no intention of her forgetting anything.

Matthew shook the snow from his shoulders before removing his jacket and hanging it on its peg by the door.

"Looks like *somebody* snuck a Christmas present in your saddlebag." The boy grinned as he held out the brown paper package. "Go on, open it. I'm dyin' to see what it is."

Glory was not so eager. It was bad enough Grant had got her something when, though he didn't know it, she had completely forgotten Christmas and had bought no gifts at all. And he knew her so well he had had to resort to making Matthew the bearer of the gift, just to ensure she wouldn't refuse it.

That did not mean she had to open it right away. She set it on the kitchen table and proceeded methodically to check the fire in the stove. Meanwhile, Matthew waited, standing at the end of the table as though guarding the precious package.

"You gonna open it?" he queried when Glory passed right by the table again.

"When I'm good and ready."

"Hell, that might be next Fourth of July! Come on, open it while it's still Christmas."

Slowly, deliberately, Glory untied the string and folded back the paper. Inside was a thick book, bound in red with gold stamped on the spine and cover.

"Oh, Lord," Glory breathed, not trusting herself to say any more.

The book was *Miss Clark's Everyday Cookbook and Housekeeping Guide.*

The storm predicted for Christmas Day did not materialize. After a few brief flurries, the clouds cleared and by nightfall the stars glittered against a velvet sky. The break in the weather allowed Matthew to take two packhorses into town the next day and come back with sufficient supplies to get through the worst of winter. Neither he nor Mr. Abel said a word about some of the items on the list Glory had sent with him.

Her first attempt at an apple pie was less than a total success, but Matthew took a second slice without being asked. He was a growing boy, and a hard working one, too, so that even at her worst, her cooking had rarely put him off his food. But with Miss Clark's assistance, Glory found Matthew's enthusiasm grew when mealtimes approached.

On New Year's Eve, she spent the entire day planning and preparing what she fully hoped would be a masterpiece. Just as she was ladling creamy smooth potato soup into bowls for herself and Matthew, heavy footsteps pounded up the back steps.

Without being asked to enter, Weed Usher opened the door and poked his head in to announce, "We got a fire, Miz Johnson."

She set the ladle back into the kettle deliberately,

without panic, and walked to retrieve her coat. Matthew was already on his feet, headed in the same direction.

She smelled the smoke even before she reached the porch, and there was an eerie orange glow silhouetting the barn. Her heart stopped, and just as Grant had fallen into the nightmare of remembered horror, so Glory felt the past creeping up to enfold her. She ran across the yard, not waiting for Weed or Matthew, and felt none of the cold wind that whistled around the barn and cut through to her bones.

Though she could see that the flames were licking hungrily only at a small shed, in her mind's eye the image of Richmond engulfed in the fires of hell was much clearer. Terrified sobs surged up, and she struggled against an overpowering urge to run, to flee mindlessly without direction, so long as she left the horror all behind her.

She was shaking, and though she stood well away from the rapidly consumed little wooden structure, she felt every degree of the heat. It seemed to radiate from some volcanic core within her, threatening to spew destruction over all it touched.

"Looks like it's under control," Matthew commented.

Had he said anything else? How long had she stood here, watching the hands fling buckets of water against the wall of the barn to keep it from catching when they knew the shed was a quick and total loss? Glory had no idea. She was trembling with fear and with cold, but she could not guess at how much time had passed.

Weed turned his backside to the fire for warmth. In the eerie light Glory saw that his clothes were wet and his face was streaked with soot.

"It'll take a while to die down yet, but I don't think the barn's gonna catch."

"Any idea what happened?" the boy asked. He, too, bore smudges on his cheeks and forehead, and Glory noticed he had a white rag of some kind tied around his hand.

The foreman shrugged.

"Old Ken come back from checkin' the young cattle and said he smelt smoke. It was damn near dark then, and hell, we got a dozen fires goin' here in the middle o' winter. An' you know how Old Ken is. Always worryin' about somethin'."

Glory heard them, but she said nothing. It must have taken them half an hour or more to protect the barn while the shed continued to burn; now it was only a glittering shell, the hand-hewn timbers crumbling in upon themselves and the miscellany stored within. And all that time Glory had stood, transfixed, silent, mesmerized by fear.

"Ain't no great loss," Weed said.

"Coulda been, if the barn'd caught."

Still staring at the flames, Glory became aware that someone else had walked up beside her.

Without looking, she knew it was Grant. Instinct guided her to him and the arm he extended to wrap around her shoulders. Yet even as she accepted the warmth and comfort, another part of her stiffened in defiance and suspicion. Silently, with frequent glances over her shoulder to watch the last flames, she let Grant lead her away.

"I was on my way home with Tom when I saw the fire," he explained after giving Matthew the care of his horse and heading toward the house. The orange glow had died now, leaving the yard in ghostly shades of snowy grey and midnight blue. "Does anyone have any idea how it started?"

Glory shook her head and opened the back door. She had heard his question and understood it, but her mind was wrestling with other thoughts. She had no answer for him.

"Do you think someone set it deliberately?"

She walked automatically to the table, where the

215

supper she had prepared had turned cold and inedible in the dishes. Matthew would be hungry when he came in after seeing to Grant's horse, but fortunately there was plenty still warm on the stove. The meal wasn't a total loss.

Why am I worrying about a pot of potato soup, she asked herself, when I should be worrying about who burned down one of my buildings?

But that question, which she had asked herself long before Grant raised the possibility, meant that she would have to face the truth: That someone was threatening her.

Grant didn't move from his position by the door. He knew she had heard his question, and he wasn't going to make the answering any more difficult by repeating it. So he just watched her, his eyes studying every movement as she took the dirty dishes off the table, went to the pantry to fetch clean ones, and set three places.

She still hadn't responded when Matthew pushed the door open. The boy said nothing, though he gave Grant a questioning look that received only a shrug in reply. Then he tiptoed to the bench at the table to remove his boots before the sooty snow melted and made a mess. His big toe poked through a hole in one sock, and the other was on the verge of springing a leak. He carried the boots to an old rug set by the back door and dropped them with a thunk.

"Is the fire out?" Glory asked suddenly, as though once the silence had been broken, there was no sense trying to put it back together.

Matthew answered while taking his customary seat at the table again. "Just about. Good thing it wasn't windy, though, or the barn would've gone for sure."

A shiver ran down Glory's back. She set a fresh bowl of hot soup in front of her stepson and then glanced at Grant with an unspoken invitation. For a moment she thought he was going to excuse himself and leave, but he unbuttoned the heavy jacket and hung it on a peg, then bent down to remove his own dirty boots.

The ham was so done it fell in tender chunks from the bone when Glory tried to slice it, and the glaze on the sweet potatoes had turned to a sugary crust, but it looked as though nothing was ruined. Glory set the various dishes on the table and then took her own place, across the table from Grant and Matthew.

She helped herself to rather skimpy portions of food, and even then just toyed with it. Once in a while she'd glance up at either Matthew or Grant.

They did not exclude her from their conversation, but she did not join it, either. She listened, and tried to keep a tight rein on an imagination that was rapidly running away with her.

"Oh, yeah, it was set, no doubt about it," Matthew said, his mouth full of ham. "Weed said it musta started inside the shed, and there weren't nothin' in there— oops, sorry. There wasn't anything in there but old tools and some broken wagon wheels and a couple beat-up old saddles Pa never got fixed. Nothing that'd catch fire by itself."

"He's sure it started inside the building?"

"That's what he said. By the time he got there, it was kind of exploding, or falling in on itself 'cause there wasn't anything to hold it up anymore."

She noted the ease, the naturalness that existed between the man and the boy and wondered—for the briefest of moments—what it would be like to sit this way every evening, the three of them almost like a family.

It was tempting, almost too tempting. Glory shoved a large bite of ham into her mouth and chewed angrily. Thoughts like that could drive her to make disastrous mistakes.

"I don't know how he could've," Matthew said. He reached for the sweet potatoes. "The door wasn't locked, so anybody could've got in, but somebody would've seen him for sure."

"Seen whom?" Glory asked, forcing herself to pay

217

attention to the conversation and not let her mind wander.

Blue eyes and grey ones turned at once to her.

"Where you been all night?" Grant teased. "We were speculating on the possibility that Lonnie set the fire."

She shook her head in firm denial.

"I'd have seen him. I spent all day right here in the kitchen. And why set fire to a dilapidated shack with nothing in it?"

"Several reasons. Main one would be to scare you, give you some idea of what he's capable of, but at the same time not destroy anything of value. Torching the barn would have defeated his own purpose: Why burn down the very thing he wants?"

"That still doesn't explain how he did it with no one seeing him."

She was struggling against the reality, against having to acknowledge that she was frightened. But the fear was there, in her eyes, and it twisted a knot in Grant's belly.

Didn't she have any idea what it did to him to worry about her day and night? He wanted to scream at her, take her by the shoulders and shake some sense into her.

But he couldn't make a scene in front of Matthew. It didn't matter that the boy probably knew every detail of their crazy relationship. Matthew was still Melody's son, a reminder of another relationship that hadn't turned out the way it was supposed to.

Yet when Matthew yawned and Glory sent him to bed, Grant felt no better. The tension now was ten times worse without someone standing between them.

He helped her with the dishes and tried to keep up a stream of conversation to cover his nervousness. He had no illusions that she was any more relaxed than he; they seemed to reflect and magnify each other's feelings.

The last plate had been returned to the pantry. Grant hung the damp dishtowel on a cupboard doorknob. Glory slumped at the table, her apron wadded in front of her.

"Helluva lousy New Year's Eve, ain't it."

218

She looked up. There were shadows of sleep deep in her golden eyes. If he hadn't spoken, she might easily have nodded off.

"And I brought a bottle of champagne just to celebrate," he added.

"So this wasn't a chance visit?"

He had the grace to grin and blush. Glory noticed that he was freshly shaven and no longer had sun-bleached hair curling over his collar. A haircut, a barbershop shave, and a bottle of champagne: Good God, he was courting her! He had proposed, she had withheld her decision, so now he was turning on the charm to pressure her.

"No, this wasn't a chance visit," he admitted, walking toward her. "Though I never really said it was."

She didn't like having to look up at him like this. But she hadn't the energy to get up.

Until he took gentle hold of her elbow and raised her to her feet.

"The champagne ought to be good and cold now," he whispered as he guided her to the parlor.

Not a lamp had been lit, and the fireplace provided only a sullen glow from the embers on the grate. The room was still warm, though, and the dark was almost welcome.

"You've been sleeping down here?" Grant asked with a nod to the quilt folded over the back of the sofa.

"Sometimes." Please, she begged silently, don't ask why.

He didn't. Maybe he had already guessed, maybe he didn't care. He just took the quilt and, when Glory sank down onto the sofa, he draped the comforter over her lap.

"Don't move," he ordered. "I'll be right back."

She heard the kitchen door open, then close, and surmised the bottle had been chilling just outside on the porch. Grant brought it into the parlor and set it gently on the table beside Lee's wingback chair.

"Glasses in the dining room?" he asked.

219

Drowsy with warmth, Glory only nodded. She wasn't about to tell him she had lived in this house over three months but had never set foot in the dining room. Obviously he knew more about the house and its contents than she.

Strange, she thought. Lee never mentioned the dining room, nor did Matthew. Only when Glory had asked Lee what was on the other side of the closed door that led from the parlor had he told her it was the dining room, along with the comment, "We don't use it." And that was all. End of discussion.

In those few turbulent weeks of their marriage, she had wondered about the closed room, but since Lee's death, too many other things had claimed her attention. Someday, she promised herself, she'd explore the dining room, and the attic, and the rooms behind the locked doors on the second floor. For now, however, it was infinitely easier just to relax, to drift, to dream.

"Happy New Year."

The bubbles from the glass he held under her nose tickled, rousing her from delightful grogginess.

"Hold these while I add some wood to that fire. And then make some room for me under that quilt."

A queer feeling came over her as she took the glasses from his hands, her fingers barely brushing against his in an easy, familiar way. It was like that moment earlier, while they ate dinner, when she had involuntarily mused on the possibility of having Grant at her kitchen table every evening. Only now the feeling was much more intense.

It was a feeling that Grant Brookington belonged here, in her parlor. The realization startled her, and her immediate reaction was to tilt the glass to her lips and drink, as if the tart tingle could drive such seductive thoughts out of her head.

It didn't. She watched him, so calm, so confident as he lifted another log into place, poked at the embers to stir little tongues of flame from them, and then rocked back

220

on his heels to wait and be sure the fire had taken hold. He did look right, placing his broad hands on his knees to stand and set the poker back in its rack. He looked even more right turning and walking back to the sofa, where she waited.

Glory swallowed another sip of the champagne before she handed Grant his glass and pulled back the quilt so he could take his place next to her. Already the flames were licking at the fresh logs, and the heat radiated sharply, making the quilt almost unnecessary. Glory was about to say something when she noticed that Grant had unbuttoned his cuffs and rolled the shirtsleeves up, exposing the telltale red wool of his underwear.

She couldn't control a little giggle.

"What's that all about?"

"Nothing."

"Don't lie, Glory. You've been quiet and glum all evening, and now all of a sudden you're getting silly." He checked the level of wine in her glass. "And even you couldn't possibly be drunk on three or four sips of champagne."

But she was tired. Too tired to fight anything.

"I'm trying to imagine you in that union suit."

"What's so funny about that? Hell, lady, it gets cold out there, riding damn near twenty miles to town and back. A man's gotta do something to keep from freezing to death."

For a moment, she was able to resume a serious tone and keep her face from splitting into a grin.

"I understand completely. And I certainly wouldn't want anything to happen to you."

It was a slip, brought on by exhaustion and worry and something else that Glory wasn't ready to identify. Grant knew that, but he wasn't ready to face the implications either.

He placed his left arm around her shoulders and drew her closer to him. There was nothing seductive in the move, at least not seductive in the way Glory expected.

221

Yet that very unexpectedness caught her off her guard.

"Would you like to see me in my union suit?" he asked in a teasing whisper.

"No!"

He sipped his own champagne nonchalantly.

"Why ever not? Of course, I suppose after seeing me in considerably less, my underwear wouldn't be nearly as . . . exciting."

She squirmed against him, not trying to escape, but more in an effort to get comfortable.

Then she whispered, "Grant, I, um, I can't, not tonight."

She didn't breathe, waiting for the embarrassment to fade. And in that momentary silence, she heard Grant catch his breath, too, and then let it out in a long slow sigh of disappointment.

He hadn't known how strong his hope was until that moment. He had let the possibility lie safely buried for the past week but had given it little conscious thought until tonight. Then, while he rode hell-bent for election toward the orange glow he knew to be a fire, he couldn't help but think of the incalculable loss if anything happened to her. He had even caught himself praying, for the first time in a decade or more, wanting her only to be safe, whether she became his or not, whether there was a child or not.

He shook his head at his own vanity.

"I didn't come here for that," he told her honestly. "I came to celebrate the new year." He kissed the top of her head and gave her shoulders a gentle squeeze.

Glory lifted her glass, half empty now, and waited for Grant to touch it with his. "So here's to the new year 1878. And you don't even have to worry about a baby; there isn't any."

He was still wondering why she sounded so disappointed when he took the empty glass from her limp hand and set it beside his on the floor. A few seconds later, he too fell asleep.

Chapter Sixteen

In Richmond, the first day of a new year had been a day of celebration, of parties and ringing bells, of visits paid and guests received. On the LJ, it was just another day of work.

The fire had burned itself out, leaving a dirty pile of ash and cinders and twisted metal. Wrapped against a biting wind, Glory stomped her feet to keep them from freezing while she surveyed the wreckage in weak sunlight.

"I think you're right, Matthew," she agreed. "It was set, and it was carefully planned."

"Had to be. And who else would do it that way but Uncle Lonnie?"

But Glory wasn't so sure she wanted to agree with him on that point.

Matthew was insistent. As he walked alongside her to the house, he repeated everything he had told her earlier, whether she wanted to hear it again or not.

"It was set deliberately, right? Just wasn't any way for it to start by itself. So the question is, who done it?"

"Who *did* it, Matthew."

"Yeah, right." At least he had got the "any way" right. "Had to be somebody who knew nobody used that shed, so he could get in there and set everything up without worryin' about somebody breakin' in on him. It'd also

223

have to be somebody who knew just what was in that shed, 'cause he'd have to work at night."

"You didn't mention that before."

"What, that he'd have to work at night?" The boy shrugged and unlatched the gate to the yard. "I just figured you figured that out already. Hell, anybody who saw Lonnie comin' outta that shed'd have to get suspicious. So he'd have to work at night, when he could come and go without bein' seen."

"Unless it was someone whose presence wouldn't arouse any suspicion."

Matthew paused with his hand on the back door knob. His brows knit together in a half-angry frown.

"I hope you aren't accusin' any of the LJ hands," he warned.

"No, I wasn't."

"That's good, 'cause I know none of them did it."

The kitchen was a jungle of laundry again, making the trip to the parlor a wet, cold obstacle course. As Glory ducked her way through the maze, Matthew continued his speech.

"Nobody with any sense would burn down the ranch where he works; that'd be plumb stupid," he insisted. "And none of the guys here wants to work for Lonnie, you can bet your last nickel on that."

Even Matthew didn't feel like reiterating the fact that if anything happened to Glory, Lonnie Hewitt would end up in charge of the ranch. Matthew was too young to run it, even though he'd be legal owner by inheritance. And Lonnie, as the boy's nearest relative, would have no difficulty gaining control.

She took off the cumbersome jacket and hung it over the back of Lee's chair, to warm by the fire. Then she sank wearily onto the chair itself to sort out her thoughts. Matthew dropped onto the sofa, in just the spot Grant had dozed last night.

He leaned forward, elbows on his knees.

"You were sayin' before that it didn't make sense for Lonnie to do it. But it does, really."

224

Glory shook her head.

"Not to me it doesn't. If he wanted to scare me off, burning down an old shed isn't likely to succeed. He knows I'd never sell to him, so scaring me isn't going to get him anywhere. And another thing: he doesn't have the money to buy it."

"You got a point there."

"One more fact is that Lonnie hasn't been seen anywhere around these parts for over a month. Last week at Grant's I heard Mr. Peake say that Lonnie had been hanging around the Witch's Hat, looking for work after your father died, and they'd all been glad when he disappeared."

Matthew leaned back, stretching his arms along the back of the sofa. One arm rested on the folded quilt, and Glory felt a second of panic, wondering if the boy could smell the lingering scent of Grant's sheer masculinity on the cover. No, that's crazy, she told herself. It's just an old blanket, for crying out loud.

But she worried about it long enough that she missed Matthew's next argument.

"Hell, there's one not more'n five miles from here, closer even than the Diamond B. It's not much, and I sure wouldn't want to stay there in the winter with only a little cookstove to heat the place, but if you're real desperate, I guess you'll take anything."

"What are you talking about?"

"You gotta learn to pay attention," he scolded. "You sick or something?"

"I'm not sick. I was just thinking. Now, what were you talking about?"

"I said that if Lonnie was stayin' in town, everybody'd know about it, so he'd have to be holed up someplace else. Only place close, and out of the way so nobody'd notice him, would be a line shack. There's one about five miles from here, in one of the summer pastures alongside the Witch's Hat."

And Lonnie was known to have spent some time relatively recently at the neighboring ranch.

"But I don't guess he's gonna strike again for a while at least, so we can breathe easy. I'm gonna go help with the cattle, and then if there's anything you need me to do around the house, I'll be back at lunchtime. That all right with you?"

She had drifted off again, her mind unable to concentrate on anything but the possibilities of who had threatened her last night.

"That would be fine, Matthew," she said. But she never heard him leave the house. In just a second or two, she was right back with her murky speculations.

She couldn't argue with most of Matthew's logic. Whoever had set the fire had indeed known exactly what to do and where and when. The best determination she or the boy or any of the hands could come up with was that someone had kindled a small, quickly burning fire in a pile of combustible material shortly after dark had fallen. That allowed for the detection of the fire and prevention of its spread to the far more valuable structure next to it.

Lonnie had motive enough, Glory didn't deny that. But so did someone else, someone who had the temperament, the patience, the sheer intelligence to concoct a subtle scheme of this nature.

She didn't want to believe Grant was capable of such a thing, but there was a part of her that felt relieved, too. When Grant was around her, she lost all track of reality, of her dream. He made her almost want to be dependent again, to be free of worries and risks, of cares and responsibilities.

Yesterday, when she had wakened to learn that her fears of conceiving a child were groundless, she had experienced that same confusion of emotions. How was it possible, she wondered, to feel relief at the same time as disappointment?

The same was true now. The pain of believing Grant guilty of cutting her fences, of driving off her cattle, of setting fire to her building was slightly mitigated by the notion that she couldn't possibly have tender feelings toward such a man. Anger and hatred would soon, she believed, change her shameful desires as well.

It still hurt. As she got to her feet, she sighed with regret and determination. Part of her had truly longed to make Grant Brookington a permanent part of her life. Part of her had truly wanted his baby to be growing in her womb. Both of those wishes, seen now in the bright, harsh light of day, were the worst possible threats to her hard-won independence. She forced herself to ignore her emotions and concentrate on more important, more practical matters.

She checked the laundry in the kitchen, found the dungarees still damp but the shirts dry enough to begin ironing. She added wood to the stove to keep the kitchen warm, and then set her mind to another task, one she decided would turn her attention to thoughts far removed from Grant Brookington and his unconscionable betrayal.

The door to the dining room wasn't locked, but the mechanism of the latch had seen little use, save Grant's opening of it last night. Glory struggled to turn it, cursing Lee all the while, until finally it gave. The hinges, too, resisted, but a sharp push with her shoulder sent the door swinging into the cold, dim room.

She looked around until she spotted a lamp on the sideboard across the room. Striding toward it, she took in the details of the long, narrow room that ran the depth of the house at this end.

A single window, tall and narrow, faced south, but sun-rotted velvet draperies blocked what little winter light would have come in. Braving a chance encounter with a spider, Glory tried to pull the tattered fabric aside. The whole mass disintegrated, collapsing with an eruption of dust while she held a torn fragment in her hand.

She coughed and sneezed, but noted no spiders, though webs festooned the now bare window. And outside, like another web, the leafless branches of a cherry tree swayed in the winter wind.

At least now she could see something. It was just as well, too, because a closer inspection of the lamp on the sideboard revealed that its bowl was empty of oil, and its wick had burned down to a stub. She'd have to get another.

But for the moment, the light from the window was enough. It allowed her to see the large painting hung on the wall above the sideboard, its gilt frame draped with cobwebs like everything else in the room.

Half expecting a wedding feast to be laid on the long table like in Mr. Dickens' *Great Expectations*, she turned cautiously. But there was no moldering multitiered cake, no dust-encrusted china and silver and crystal waiting for revelers who never came. There was only an oak table, attractive in its simplicity. The top was scarred here and there beneath the layer of dust, and its slightly imperfect lines suggested that it had been made by an amateur, a grandfather perhaps, to be given as a gift.

The matching chairs, ten of them, were tucked neatly around the perimeter. Glory ran her hand along the top rail of one, feeling the invisible imperfections the hands that had fashioned it left in the wood. Someone had labored long and patiently over these pieces. Why had they been shut away?

She moved slowly across the bare wooden floor, around the table to the china cabinet against the other wall. The beveled glass in the doors was all spotted with fly specks and grimy with dust. She had to open one door to peer inside.

Though the doors had been closed for untold years, the dust had crept in anyway. There were two neat circles where two wine glasses had rested all that time, the glasses that Glory had surreptitiously washed this morning and hidden behind jars of pickles in the pantry. Even in the dark last night, Grant had known exactly where to find them.

If he knew where to find two wine glasses in a room that had been shut up for years, certainly he would know which buildings were in constant use and which were virtually never entered. He'd know the habits and quirks of everyone on the ranch. He'd know—too much.

Glory's shiver had little to do with the cold. She looked about and spotted the small fireplace, its hearth swept clean after the last fire. Now there was only dust, and webs. And questions.

She left the dining room and closed the door carefully behind her. Tomorrow, or the next day, she intended to give the room a thorough cleaning. It might take the rest of the week to wash all those dishes, to dust and wax the enormous table and the intricate carvings on the chairs, to clean the windows. Glory didn't care. She looked forward to the labor.

In the kitchen, she took the dry laundry down from the lines and set the sadirons on the stove to heat. There was another basket of laundry to be hung up, too. The work seemed never ending. Once upon a time, a little girl in Richmond, Virginia had had an army of servants to do these things for her. Glory pinned one of Matthew's shirts to the rope strung from one end of the kitchen to the other and wondered whatever had happened to that little girl.

She also wondered what had happened to this house she lived in now, and what connection it had to Grant Brookington.

The snow that had started while Glory explored the dining room continued to fall through the afternoon. Matthew carried armload after armload of split firewood to the porch after filling all the woodboxes to overflowing. Even then he wondered aloud if it would be enough. Glory, finishing the last of the ironing, assured him it was, unless he intended to fill the pantry with firewood as well.

He didn't laugh.

By darkfall, the wind had picked up, until it was howling around the house like a wild demon. Despite a roaring blaze in the parlor fireplace, the room remained cold. After supper Glory went looking for a copy of Mr. Dickens' *Great Expectations* that she thought she recalled seeing on the little bookshelf by the desk, and when she found it she curled up on the sofa and wrapped the quilt around her to read for a while before facing the bitter cold upstairs.

She hadn't gotten very far when Matthew, standing by the window, muttered something about Grant.

"What was that?"

"I said, I hope Grant got back from that line shack before this storm hit."

"Why would he be going up there?"

"Well, when I mentioned the possibility of Lonnie hiding out up there, he said he thought maybe he'd go check it out. It's outta his way, so I was hopin' he got there early and headed home before the storm hit. A man'd have a hard time surviving being caught in this one."

Glory slept very little that night, and when she slept, dreams wakened her instantly. She blamed the visions on the fact that her bed was cold, even with an extra pair of heavy comforters. But she did not dream of being cold herself; her nightmares were of a man being trapped in a snowbound cabin, with grimy windows covered with dust and cobwebs. There were no curtains on the windows, just tattered remnants of red woolen underwear. And Glory no longer laughed at the thought of Grant's red underwear.

In the morning she wakened, still exhausted, to a world of silence. The snow still fell, though the wind had died. Nothing moved beyond the windows, and everything was the same color: white.

Grant left the tiny cabin exactly as he had found it: cold, dirty, and reeking of the whiskey that had spilled from the bottle on the floor by the bed. He had no doubt the place had been inhabited last night, and possibly for two or three days beforehand. The remains of several meals lay scattered about the crude table, with a skillet of scorched beans left on the cold cookstove.

After taking one last look around the place, Grant pulled the door shut and latched it securely. Then he tugged his hat down firmly on his head against the snow that was just beginning to drift from an ominous sky.

As he brushed the first flakes of snow from his saddle and then mounted the patient bay gelding, he swore at himself.

"Damn good way to get caught in a blizzard," he muttered. "And no damn good reason for it, either."

Someone had indeed been staying at the line shack, but the spilled whiskey and slovenly habits did not unquestionably identify the someone as Lonnie Hewitt. And even if Lonnie had left his name scrawled in the dust on the table, that wouldn't prove that he had ridden to the LJ last night and set a fire in an old outbuilding.

"You're not thinking straight any more, Brookington. You spend one lousy night with the woman and you can't get her out of your head. Matthew tells you she suspects Lonnie's been hiding out at the line shack, so what do you do? You take it upon yourself to risk life and limb to check out her harebrained theory."

He kicked Rusty to an easy lope, which the horse had no trouble maintaining despite the snow. The trail from the main road to the cabin had been trampled enough over the past few days to make it reasonably easy to travel. That trail was another reason to suspect Lonnie: between the line shack and the headquarters of Peake's was nothing but an untouched expanse of virgin snow.

The problem with Glory's harebrained theory was that it hadn't been harebrained at all. In fact, Grant had come up with the same idea, but had said nothing to her for fear of frightening her. Yet it wasn't until Matthew brought the subject up that Grant thought about checking it out.

"She used me," he told the horse. "And I'll end up freezing my damn butt off just to put her mind at rest."

The snow grew heavier as the sky darkened. There was no wind, which, though it might have made the weather more dangerous, would at least have given a hint of direction. Grant worried that the blizzard might become so thick he couldn't see landmarks through it, and Rusty, much as he could usually be depended on to find his way home, would more than likely just put his head down and ride out the storm, which Grant knew he himself wasn't capable of.

He grew more bitter with each easy, rocking stride the horse took.

He had been used, and not just once. One time, he could forgive her, maybe even twice. But feisty, stubborn, independent little Glory Johnson had used him too often to count.

It wouldn't have mattered, he argued silently, if he hadn't let himself fall for her. And fall hard.

"Hell, I even asked her to marry me!" he shouted. "Oh, I'll bet she loved that one. Probably laughed 'til she cried."

That helped. Anger eased some of the disgust he felt. The trick would be to stay angry long enough to erase the other feelings.

He had risen shortly after dawn, must have been around six-thirty or seven. Glory was still asleep, so he had helped her into a more comfortable sprawl on the sofa and tucked the quilt around her before he tiptoed out the back door. He was just saddling Rusty when Matthew appeared and told him of Glory's suspicions concerning Lonnie.

That held up his departure, until maybe eight at the very latest. Another three hours to get to the cabin. But how long had he been riding since leaving there? He had no idea. And the sky was getting darker all the time. The ride back to the Diamond B was long, and if he didn't reach home by dark, he'd be a goner for sure.

"It's just a storm," he reassured himself as well as the horse. "We've been through lots of 'em, haven't we, old boy? And look, there's the sign for the Fortescue place up ahead."

He felt better knowing for sure where he was, but the

fact that he still had a good long ten miles to go was far from reassuring. Especially with the damn snow getting thicker and thicker. Snowflakes were sticking to his eyelashes, and the gelding's chin whiskers were coated with ice.

"And I'll bet you that damn woman is curled up cozy as a mouse in front of a big fire, with a cup of tea at her elbow. Probably lookin' through that cookbook I bought her to figure out what she's gonna fix for herself and Matthew for supper."

He gave up. He couldn't concentrate on guiding the horse, so he let Rusty pick his own way through the blur of snow. All that filled Grant's thoughts now was the rage and bitterness, the hurt and the loneliness, the memories and the pain.

"Oh, damn you, Melody, why didn't you wait?" His mind was still coherent enough that he recognized the signs of danger. His mouth was growing stiff with the cold that he barely felt. The words came only with effort, but he could no longer keep them inside. "And damn you, too, Glory, for being so damn much like her."

Grant was numb by the time Rusty came to an exhausted halt by the stable door. The horse's thick winter coat had insulated him well, leaving a solid layer of snow on his head, shoulders, and rump. He shook it all off as soon as his rider had dismounted, and then Grant had someone else to swear at.

Tom Cashion opened the door and stepped back as his boss led the tired horse into the relative warmth of the stable.

"Where you been? I expected you back last night."

"I got delayed," was Grant's terse answer. He had taken Rusty into his stall and was struggling with stiff, unfeeling fingers to remove the saddle.

"Was it much of a fire?"

The foreman, half a head shorter than the man he worked for, leaned his forearms on the top of the stall door.

"An old shed. It was damn near out when I got there."

233

"Then how come you stayed?"

The cinch strap was half wet and harder than hell to undo. But it gave Grant a good excuse for not turning to face Tom Cashion, who was a good friend as well as a good foreman.

Tom's worst vice, and maybe his only one, was that he was too good a friend. He knew too much about Grant Brookington. He had silenced the rumors that hummed all over the ranch after Christmas, but only because Grant ordered them silenced.

There hadn't been a woman in Grant's life for a long, long time. Of all the hands who had been with Grant, Tom knew the most about the reason why. Therefore, it was Tom who found the possibility of Grant teaming up with Lee Johnson's widow to be sweetly satisfying.

"Matthew needed some help cleaning things up afterward. And he wanted me to check it all out this morning, make sure there wasn't any danger of the barn catching."

"I see." Tom paused, as though he had caught the note of warning in Grant's voice. The subject was not to be pursued. "You look froze half to death. Go on up to the house and I'll take care of Rusty."

Grant didn't wait for the offer to be withdrawn. Without even thanking Tom, he left the big gelding and strode out of the stable and toward the house.

He had but one thought on his mind now: to get warm, and then get as drunk as possible as quickly as possible. He had done the same thing when he had come home from the war, the wounded hero, only to find that rumors of his death had preceded him, and the woman he loved was married to his best friend. He had thought he could never feel so hurt, so betrayed, again.

He had been wrong.

Chapter Seventeen

The dining room took three weeks to clean, but before the end of January, Glory had the room restored to its former splendor.

And splendid it was indeed. The old table was solid oak, turned a soft golden color over the years. Under the grime, she found that the ten chairs had needlepointed seats, each in a different pattern. When asked, Matthew informed her that his grandmother had made them long before he was born.

He was less forthcoming when prodded with other questions.

"Pa just didn't use it, after Ma died," he mumbled one bright sunny afternoon while he watched Glory return the crystal goblets and tumblers and snifters to the cabinet. "He said it was too much bother, there bein' just him and me."

The explanation made sense, but Glory suspected there was more to the story.

"We don't have to eat in here every night, but once in a while, it wouldn't hurt. Maybe on Sundays?"

The boy didn't reply to that suggestion. Perhaps it was the enforced idleness brought on by winter's isolation that had Matthew reverting to the surliness with which he had greeted her arrival several months ago.

At first she hadn't noticed it, but after the three-day

235

blizzard was over, she found that Matthew left the house as early as possible and started taking some of his meals in the bunkhouse with the hands. When he did come home, he spoke little and went to bed as quickly as practical.

Today, while helping her with the crystal, he had been a little more open, but she had no difficulty detecting an undertone of the old hostility.

"You'll still have to keep the door closed," he warned, "unless you want to keep a fire goin' in here, too. The fire in the parlor can't heat both rooms."

That was another aspect Glory hadn't considered. She wondered when she would ever learn to take everything into account the way Matthew seemed to do automatically. It seemed not a single day went by that he didn't catch her up on some display of simple ignorance that left her with tingling red cheeks.

But she had learned much and gradually gained a sense of emerging competence. She set the last wine glass in its place and closed the cabinet doors with a satisfied click.

"Thank you for your help, Matthew. If you have other chores, go ahead and tend to them. I can finish up here."

He didn't hesitate to escape.

The dining room was bright, with brilliant sunshine reflected off the deep snow outside. Glory had removed what few shreds of draperies remained, leaving the window uncovered until she could find replacements. In the light she could see the details of the oil painting that hung, freshly cleaned, over the sideboard. It was an English landscape, with a thatch-roofed cottage by a stream, puffy clouds in an azure sky, soft and golden and tranquil.

All very unlike the life that Glory led.

Still, she could count the dining room's transformation a triumph. There had been far too little of those lately.

She closed the door behind her, its hinges now smoothly oiled, and confronted a disaster in the parlor.

"It's called mending," Matthew told her while he

deposited an armload of clothing on the sofa. "I ain't got a sock without holes, and all my shirts is missing at least one button. I got two pairs of pants with rips, and my long johns need patchin'."

He stood, in his own red wool union suit, with one knee poking through a hole. When Glory turned away, embarrassed, Matthew fired another shot.

"It don't bother you none to see Grant in his underwear, or less, if I figure things right."

She whirled back to face him, her cheeks burning with as much humiliation as anger. "That's enough, young man!"

"No, it ain't enough!" he shouted right back. He grabbed a pair of dungarees from the pile on the sofa and jammed first one leg and then the other into them. "There's work to do around here, lady, lots of it. And it's things that *need* doin', not just fancyin' up a dining room we don't never use."

He buttoned up his pants, then took hold of a flannel sleeve sticking out from the bottom of the heap of mending. When he pulled the shirt free, half the rest of the clothes tumbled to the floor. Matthew made no move to pick them up.

"Just 'cause it's winter don't mean we ain't got work to do outside, neither," he continued, thrusting his arm into a sleeve with such force that Glory heard the worn fabric give way. The tear didn't stop Matthew. "Ain't no time in the summer to do all the fixin' that needs done, so it all gets piled up for now, when we got the time."

He bent to finish buttoning the shirt, only to discover that in his anger he had buttoned it crookedly. While he unbuttoned it and started over, Glory's own temper came to a boil.

She took several strides toward the boy and, when he looked up, cracked him soundly across the face with the flat of her hand.

"Don't you *ever* talk to me like that again."

Matthew glared down at her now with his blue-grey

237

eyes wide with shock. The mark of her hand stood out on his cheek; he raised his own hand to the stinging and rubbed it in surprise more than pain.

"I came here with no idea what was expected of me." The quiver in her voice had spread to her whole body now. "Until someone tells me, I will continue to be ignorant. Not once in the past five or six months have you brought me a single piece of mending. Not once in the past three weeks, while I have scrubbed and waxed and scraped and scoured, have you mentioned other chores that needed attention."

She waited for him to reply. By the look in his eyes, he had lost none of his own anger. If anything, he had become more furious. The wide eyes narrowed and his mouth tightened, as though he were holding back a torrent of abuse.

"I don't know what's gotten into you, Matthew Johnson, but this kind of behavior is unexcusable. You can march yourself right up to your room and stay there until I'm good and ready to tolerate your presence."

He laughed at her.

"That's just what I mean," he spat. "You ain't got enough hands to work this place as it is, and then you go and send me to my room, like you was back in Philadelphia where nobody had no more work to do than flickin' the ashes off a fat cee-gar. Well, I ain't goin' to my room. I got work to do. And you better be glad I'm doin' it, too, 'cause you sure as hell couldn't."

He grabbed two socks, both with holes in the toes or heels, and stomped out of the parlor and into the kitchen, where his boots and jacket waited. Stunned, Glory remained where she was, surrounded by the boy's clothes.

She had read all of Miss Clark's book, and though it contained many helpful hints, some of which she had put to use cleaning the dining room, there were no instructions on how to mend a worn-out stocking.

Nor were there any instructions on how to deal with a

fourteen-year-old boy whose attitude could change as dramatically as Matthew's had.

Glory heard the kitchen door slam shut and Matthew's feet pound down the porch stairs. He was right, she admitted as she sank slowly onto the sofa and picked up a sock with both the toe and heel worn to spiderweblike frailty. The LJ was short of manpower, and she needed every bit of Matthew's help she could get. She was surprised he hadn't reminded her of all the offers Grant had made, offers that would have made everyone's work considerably easier.

Was that the reason for the boy's growing sulkiness? The more she thought about it, the more she believed his change in attitude had begun right after the first of the year, and the last time Grant had paid them a visit.

"You can't expect a man to ride twelve miles in a blizzard just to see how things are going," she scolded herself. She picked a shirt up off the floor and examined it, finding two buttons missing and the elbow of one sleeve torn. "He has his own ranch to run."

Though she hated to, she had to admit that over the past few weeks she had caught herself frequently going to that dining room window and staring out over the snow-covered landscape in the hope of seeing a big bay horse loping down the road toward the LJ. She used every ounce of cold, pure logic to lay the blame for the fire and the other "accidents" at Grant's feet, but logic didn't change the way she served dinner to herself and Matthew and wished there were a third place set at the table.

Nor did logic explain the sleeplessness that assailed her unless she clasped that other pillow close to her. The nights were cold, no matter how many quilts and blankets she piled on her bed, until she brought up the quilt that had lain on the back of the parlor sofa, the one she and Grant had slept beneath. It made no sense at all, not logically.

Matthew's behavior made no sense at all, either. Perhaps it was just "cabin fever." Everyone got a little

239

fed up and cranky as the winter wore on. Maybe Matthew had developed a friendship with that little girl Glory had seen him with at Grant's and now was antsy about seeing her again.

That, however, did not excuse his behavior. He had accused her of ignoring the necessary mending while she entertained herself cleaning the dining room. Yet he had helped her with that cleaning, and not once during all that time had he said a single word about missing buttons or threadbare stockings.

It was almost, Glory thought suspiciously, as if he had waited until she experienced a moment of triumph to shoot her down.

He was at least right about one thing: He hadn't a single garment that didn't need some kind of repair.

She carefully sorted and folded the clothing he had deposited on the sofa, then when everything was back in order, she got up and headed for the stairs.

A week ago, while looking for rags, she had made a cursory investigation of the two closed rooms on the second floor. Like the dining room, they had been declared "off-limits" when Glory first inquired after their contents. But now Lee wasn't around to tell her, "Nothing there you need to bother with." Curiosity was a strong motive, but a need to see if there was anything of use or value provided a more logical one.

The door to the first room opened with little effort. Lifting her lamp high, Glory discovered the room contained old furniture. Only a large, comfortable looking rocking chair with a tattered cushion looked serviceable. The assorted odd chairs and small tables all needed repair, and Glory did not possess the required skills. Otherwise that room was almost empty.

In contrast, the second room was a veritable jungle. Chests and crates and baskets were crammed into every available space. On top of one chest Glory had found a pile of rags, just exactly what she needed for polishing

240

the old oak table and chairs in the dining room, and she had left the room quickly.

But she had not forgotten it, or the treasure trove it might contain. As she opened the door again, she felt the cold of long neglect.

Matthew's mother had undoubtedly taken care of her family's clothing, so her sewing utensils had to be somewhere in the house. Glory already knew the contents of the other rooms; that left only this jumble as the repository for Melody Hewitt Johnson's possessions.

Glory set the lamp on the chest where she had found the rags and turned the wick up just a little. The light spread into the far corners, though that wasn't really very far. The room wasn't large, perhaps the same size as Matthew's bedroom. But it seemed larger because of all the stuff stored in it.

An eerie shape hidden behind an upright steamer trunk confirmed Glory's suspicions. She worked her way toward it, climbing over other crates and boxes to reach the dusty silhouette of a dressmaker's mannequin.

She had a queer feeling when she touched the padded cloth shoulder.

"You were taller than I," she said quietly, knowing that this was all that was left in this house of the physical form of her predecessor.

A strange urge suddenly swelled within her, a desire to meet Melody Hewitt Johnson face to face and ask her, no, demand of her the answers to all the questions. The curiosity had been there, probably from the very instant Glory entered the house where Melody had been born and raised, married and gave birth and finally died. It was as though over the years the house had absorbed Melody's essence, inescapable, inextinguishable.

The sensation grew stronger, and Glory snatched her hand away from the headless, limbless dummy. She wanted no ghost to help her search for practical items such as needles and thread and shears.

241

She found a thousand other things first.

One trunk yielded children's clothing, everything from an infant's christening gown dripping with hand-made lace to several pairs of woolen knickers that must have fit Matthew at the age of nine or ten. They looked hardly worn, and Glory could imagine the boy protesting the dandified clothes his mother insisted on. There was even a little hat.

Glory carefully repacked everything and shut the trunk, moving on to the next crate.

Her heart caught in her throat as soon as she lifted the lid. The clothes here had not been so tenderly folded and laid inside. The blouses were wrinkled, as though someone had washed but never pressed them. Glory took just one out, holding it up long enough to know with absolute certainty that the garment had belonged to Matthew's mother.

She thought of her own shabby wardrobe, sup-plemented now by flannel shirts and dungarees, and a momentary wish entered her mind. Melody had been taller, and perhaps a little broader through the shoulders than she, but Glory could easily have worn the blouse, and the others that filled the crate. But she knew she'd never do it. Certainly not in front of Matthew.

She opened several more boxes and found them all filled with discarded clothing. There were men's suits and shirts that had belonged to a man much taller and heavier than Lee, and Glory surmised these had come from Melody's father, Matt Hewitt. He was the man, she recalled, who had taught the young Grant Brookington everything he knew.

Fascinated, Glory went from one box to the next, opening each and going through its contents. Even after she had located Melody's sewing box, with spools of various colored threads, an assortment of needles, and dozens of spare buttons, she kept searching out of sheer curiosity. She knew she should stop, that the mountain of mending in the parlor wasn't shrinking by itself, but

242

she could not resist the desire to know more about this house, and about the woman who had lived in it.

But the next thing she found revealed no secrets. She lifted the lid on a box of lead soldiers, many of them missing limbs or even heads. They looked too old to have been Matthew's; she guessed Lonnie must have played with them when he was a boy growing up in this house. She put them away quickly.

There was another wooden crate filled with uncut fabric, from fine white linen meant for a man's dress shirts to heavy woolens and bright gingham cottons. Glory found several pieces suitable for skirts and dresses, but she had no patterns and wasn't even sure she felt capable of tackling such an undertaking.

She located the patterns in the very next box. But while she sat on the floor and sorted through the yellowed envelopes containing the fragile pieces of tissue paper, she grew aware of the growing chill in this room. Her enthusiasm had kept her warm, but now the cold came in again.

She looked up at the window and discovered that the sky had grown dark. The entire afternoon had passed while she did nothing more constructive than snoop through a room of family memorabilia, a family that wasn't hers.

After brushing the dust from her skirt, she tucked the box of patterns under one arm and picked up the wicker sewing box to take to her own room. Then, when she came back for the lamp, she took one last look at the closed trunk on which it had sat all afternoon.

"It's late," she reminded herself. "There's no supper on the stove and Matthew will expect a meal."

But curiosity about that trunk was too strong to ignore.

"Five minutes, that's all it'll take to open it up and look through it. Probably more clothes, anyway, nothing much."

Something, perhaps her conscience or the sense of

responsibility that Matthew's accusations had reawakened, sent her down the stairs first. She added wood to all the fires, placed several potatoes in the oven to bake, set a skillet on the stove to heat for the strips of beefsteak she intended to fry. Only then did she dash back to the storeroom where that last trunk lay waiting, taunting.

She moved the lamp to the top of a crate she had already explored, and then lifted the lid of the heavy, brass-bound trunk.

On top were several plain nightgowns of warm, serviceable flannel. The others Glory had seen were pretty things, trimmed with ribbons and lace, not like these. Yet they were undoubtedly Melody's. No sense of age clung to them, and they had not taken on that yellowing that the years gave to garments no matter how carefully stored.

Glory knew that Melody had died after a long illness some two years before Lee's trip to Philadelphia. Lee had, in fact, made that trip to settle certain affairs concerning property Melody had inherited from her mother. Coming out of the First Mercantile Bank of Philadelphia, Lee had literally bumped into Anna Beaumont. Two nights later, after an uncomfortable dinner at Terrence Beaumont's house, Lee had proposed.

She folded the nightgown preparatory to replacing it in the trunk. The reason for her curiosity was suddenly very clear.

"All I wanted was to belong here, Lee," she said to the haunting silence. "I wanted to be a part of your life, not just an ornament, not just a reminder of the past. I wanted to live."

When she saw the corner of the small, inlaid wooden box, she should have ignored it. Her curiosity seemed sated, and she did have work to do, work that needed doing. But it was the last unexplored corner of the room. Better to get it all over and done with, and then she could get on with the rest of her life. Whatever Lee's intentions toward her might have been, his death had forced her to take charge of her life in exactly the way she had wanted to. Willingly or not, she was indeed learning how to live.

The box was larger and heavier than she had at first thought. Seven or eight inches high, it was at least two feet wide and approximately eighteen inches deep. Made of a dark material, walnut or old cherry she supposed, it was decorated with inlays of flowers in lighter woods like maple and oak and ash. The hinges were so heavily tarnished that they could only be of silver.

Glory settled herself on the floor, her back leaning comfortably against the trunk, and lifted the lid of the beautiful little chest.

She let out a little laugh at the sight of a delicate carnelian cameo surrounded by gold filigree. It was the only piece of jewelry, reminding Glory that in the back of her mind had been the wish to find a chest full of diamonds and rubies and pearls.

There was a small Bible bound in cracked white leather, with a length of faded and frayed red ribbon marking a passage. Beneath the Bible lay an embroidery sampler only half finished, still in its frame, the needle with a strand of apple green floss rusted permanently into a corner of the fabric.

Two oval frames held photographs, the first of an elderly man who could only be Matthew Hewitt. Even posed for the portrait, he had seemed incapable of holding still, as though he had too many things to do. For a moment Glory studied the small picture, trying to find some trace of Matt that had been passed on to his grandson. The stubborn jaw, perhaps, or the wide-set eyes. The boy must have taken after his mother, because he certainly looked nothing like Lee, and there was only the faintest resemblance to his grandfather.

The second portrait drew a gasp of satisfaction from Glory.

Here was Melody Hewitt Johnson, holding on her lap a child of five or six years in a prim little sailor suit. It was Matthew, all right, but Glory paid little attention to the child. She was mesmerized by the woman whose place she had taken in this house.

Melody was beautiful, with a cloud of pale hair around a serene face that could have been a Madonna's. There was a faraway look in her eyes, probably a trick to help her hold still for the photographer, but it gave her an ethereal, almost angelic aura.

Glory felt a sharp pain in her chest. She knew now why Lee had treated her the way he had. Lee wanted Glory to replace that delicate goddess, to decorate his home as Melody had. The revelation unsettled her.

She set the portrait aside and continued rummaging through the contents of the box. What remained, however, was disappointing, though it gave her a clue as to the background of the collection.

There were a small needlework scissors, a sheaf of stationery, a handkerchief with the letter M clumsily monogrammed in one corner, and an empty bottle that had probably contained laudanum drops. Glory could easily picture all these things, including the Bible and the photographs, occupying the table beside Melody's bed. Perhaps she even kept them in the box, so that when she was gone, someone—Lee, Matthew, a well-meaning friend—just closed the lid and packed everything away.

It gave Glory an odd feeling, wondering if that had in fact happened. She took more care, tucking the photographs gently between layers of an unfinished sampler. Then, though she knew she ought to be downstairs preparing supper, she set the heavy box beside her on the floor and opened the Bible to the place Melody had marked.

The page was stained, as though pain-weary fingers had traced the lines over and over.

"'The Lord is my shepherd; I shall not want.'" Glory whispered the familiar words that had given her comfort too, in days almost forgotten. She ran her finger over the page just as Melody must have.

And she felt something behind the page, something

246

that drew her curiosity without thinking.

She recognized the stationery as a sheet from the bundle in the inlaid box. It had been folded once, to fit snugly behind the marked page.

The letter was dated August 9, 1874. Glory shivered and folded it once more, to give herself a moment for composure. She knew from the marker on Melody's grave beside Lee's that she had died on the tenth day of August, 1874.

After taking several deep breaths, Glory unfolded the sheet again and began to read. She did not breathe again until she had finished.

"I am so afraid," the unsteady hand had written. "I know that I do not have much longer, and as many times as I read the words of comfort on this page, I am still frightened. There are so many things I should have done differently. Now it is too late. My life has been a lie, and I am certain I will know the torments of Hell. So it is not for your sake that I make this confession, but because I do not want to go to Hell.

"When I am gone, I will give Matthew into your keeping. He is yours, and he is the one good thing I have done with my life. You, too, have done well with him, better by far than the man he calls his father.

"I love you, as I always have, even though I know it is not enough."

There was no signature, only a scrawl where she must have dropped the pen.

Glory closed the letter and with numb fingers replaced it in its hiding place. She knew as surely as she knew anything else that Melody Johnson had intended to finish the letter and give it to the man who had fathered her son. Death had prevented her, and she had taken her secret to her grave.

Glory put the Bible back in the box and closed the lid. Then she picked up the lamp and carried it back to the bedroom she had taken it from. She remembered nothing else until Matthew burst in the back door just as she was turning over a slab of beefsteak in the skillet.

"Sorry I'm late," he mumbled. "The bull got out."

She couldn't help it. Her eyes seemed glued to his face, even when he turned around to hang his coat on its peg.

"It's all right. I was busy and didn't get supper started until late."

"You're just now cooking it? What the hell you been doing all day? It's damn near eight o'clock."

He poured himself a cup of coffee from the pot on the stove, so that he was standing right next to her. Still unable to look away from him, Glory dropped the meat back into the skillet.

"I said I was busy. I had to find the sewing things, and it took a long time."

Matthew carried his cup to the table and sat down, sipping morosely at the black liquid that had to be stronger than lye soap after sitting on the stove since morning.

"You coulda asked me. I knew where Pa put all Ma's stuff."

"Well, you coulda asked me to do some mending, instead of dumping it all on me at once."

She didn't even know where that spark of temper came from. Consciously, she had only one thought, only one burning, blazing realization.

And she wondered how she had failed to see it before.

Matthew looked so much like his father that it brought a painful lump to her throat and the beginnings of tears to her eyes.

Chapter Eighteen

Matthew's open animosity turned to brooding silence, so that he seldom spoke at all, even when another blizzard kept them housebound for four days in February. And Glory, afraid of giving away her secret, was just as taciturn.

The bull was dutifully returned two weeks later, none the worse for his adventure. Grant had found the confused, belligerent beast wandering on the Diamond B side of a snow-downed fence. Glory watched from the kitchen window while he delivered the animal into Matthew's keeping, but she did not venture out to talk with him.

She seethed. What a fool they had taken her for! What a fool she had been.

Any idiot could have seen through the closeness between Matthew and Grant. The rest of the pieces fit together so neatly, too, that Glory wondered how, in the name of heaven, she could have been so blind.

Lee must have known, too. That explained his obvious hatred for his neighbor, as well as the way Lee treated Matthew. Changing his will to give the ranch to his new wife was just another way of spiting the boy.

Glory turned angrily from the window, and put a plate in its place on a pantry shelf. But as she took another plate from the dishpan, her feet wandered to the window once again.

Oh, yes, Melody's letter explained so many things. It explained why Grant was so eager to buy the ranch before Lee's grave had even been filled. It explained all the strange accidents that had occurred since Glory had taken possession of the ranch. The cut fences, the stampeded cattle, even the burning of the shed: they'd all been carefully orchestrated by Grant Brookington to get Glory out of the way so he could buy the place for Matthew, the son he couldn't acknowledge.

It didn't explain, however, the reason for the lump in her throat as she stood, wiping a damp dishtowel idly over a dry plate, and watched the man and boy together. She couldn't hear what they were saying, and though she knew she ought to go outside and thank Grant in person for bringing the errant bull back where he belonged, she hung back.

Grant hadn't come alone. The shorthorn bull was a hulking thing, a good breeder but mean and strong. It had taken Grant, Tom Cashion, and Lyle Nutter to keep the bull under control on the long trek back to the LJ. Once there, however, Grant relinquished his job to one of the LJ hands so he could have a few words with Matthew. Glory, Grant noticed, was nowhere around. He should have been grateful, but he wasn't. Still, he could delay his return to the Diamond B for a while and chat with Matthew.

"You're going to have to tell her the truth." Grant draped his arm around Matthew's shoulders. The boy was growing like a weed, he realized. Together they watched Young Ken help the other two hands cajole the bull into a corral specially cleared of snow. "You saw the tracks: someone cut the fence and led the bull out of here."

"Wouldn't do no good. She don't believe nothin' I tell her anymore."

"Wouldn't do *any* good."

The boy wriggled out from under the comforting arm and turned like a mountain lion at bay, spitting and hissing.

"First Ma, then her, and now you! It don't matter none how I talk! I ain't gonna be nothin' but what I am now, and anyway, it ain't none o' your business, I'm obliged to you for bringin' the bull back, *her* bull, that is, so now you can just leave."

Grant raised his hands as though to take hold of the boy's shoulders again and maybe try to shake a little sense into him, but he never touched him. Instinct told him that wasn't the right tactic.

Glory had seen the action, though she had no idea what had prompted Matthew's outburst. Nor did she have any idea why she felt this aching in the pit of her stomach. Was it because now she had seen them together, father and son, for the first time since learning Melody's secret? Was it because her own loss of family made her more sensitive to the emptiness Grant could fill in Matthew's life?

She stepped away from the window, afraid to watch more. Her hands were shaking, and her knees felt strange, rubbery, like the night they brought Lee home and told her he was dead.

As the truth slowly dawned on her, she stumbled to the bench and sat down heavily.

Her grief was different this time, but she recognized it all the same. Poor Lee. She had taken advantage of him with no thought to what he wanted from her. And she had ignored the old proverb: Beware of wanting something too much, for you might just get it. She had wanted freedom, and Lee's death had given it to her in spades. The shock she had experienced that night came from her involuntary recognition of that sad truth.

Now she recognized another, even sadder.

She wanted Grant Brookington. Not just because he could help her with the ranch, although that was part of it. He represented both her chance at freedom and her greatest risk of losing it, but still she wanted him. Nor was her desire the same raw, devouring sexuality that had driven her that night at the hotel. Oh, that feeling of heat

251

was there, in the pit of her stomach, but it was different now, subdued, controlled, and growing stronger all the time.

Underneath it all, underneath the fear and the wanting, the anger and the desire, was that seductive whisper. Not again, it warned her. Never again.

The warning came too late. Glory realized she had already fallen in love with Grant Brookington.

Slowly, gaining back her equilibrium and forcing her hands to steady themselves, she rose and returned to her post by the window.

They were embroiled in a heated argument, their breaths forming clouds of steam in the clear, cold air. Both seemed to be shouting at the same time. Then Grant threw up his hands and turned his back on the boy. Matthew took another step toward him, and said something else.

"You wanna tell her? Then you go right ahead, but I ain't sayin' a word! Let her figure it out for herself. She ain't stupid, like Ma was."

The words stung. Grant froze, as though someone had just poured a bucket of icy water over him.

"Don't say things like that. Your mother was never stupid, Matthew." There was ice in his voice, too, and he felt a coldness seeping inside him.

He had left the bay gelding tied to the backyard fence, and he walked toward the patient animal, intent only on escape.

Blocking out the sound of Matthew's voice, he untied the reins and tossed them over the horse's head, but when he grasped the saddlehorn and put his foot in the stirrup to mount, a queer feeling came over him, as though someone stood just behind him and stared. It sent a chill down his back, and he glanced over his shoulder, but there was no one there.

Even after he had swung up onto the gelding, the sensation of eyes boring like a slowly twisted brace and bit into the sensitive spot between his shoulder blades persisted.

252

Matthew approached Grant and stood, feet planted slightly apart, hands on his hips, blocking the path.

Keeping his voice low, the boy asked, "If Ma wasn't stupid, then how come she married Lee Johnson? Weren't for his money, 'cause he didn't have a pot to piss in. Weren't for his looks, neither."

"You weren't there, Matthew. You don't know." Then he choked on the next sentence and, rather than have the boy see and hear the torment he had caused, Grant dug his heels into the bay's flanks and bolted out of the stableyard.

"What was that all about?" Glory asked Matthew when he stormed into the kitchen half a minute later.

"Ask *him*," came the sullen reply.

Muttering something that sounded like either "stupid" or "stubborn," the boy tromped through the house to the stairs and then pounded up to his room.

He didn't speak to her for a week. Not a single word. At breakfast he ate what she put in front of him, then immediately went out to attack his chores. Often Glory didn't see him again until supper time. After one or two futile attempts at conversation, she gave up. Her questions received only grunts or shakes of his head for answers, never a coherent word.

"I'll lose my mind," she told herself aloud one afternoon as she settled on the sofa with the dwindling pile of mending. "One day, after months with no one to talk to, I will become suddenly insane. Matthew will come in and find, not supper on the table, but his stepmother, sitting in mindless silence in her parlor, with a darning egg and a holey stocking in her hand."

She looked down at the objects and swallowed the threat of tears.

It wasn't the mending she hated. It was the fact that the work, once she had mastered it, required no thought, leaving her mind free to wander. Even the frequent pricks to her finger didn't help her concentration. What

253

bothered her more than anything and often made her set the work aside long before she had done her daily quota was the feeling that came over her every time she set Melody's sewing basket beside her on the sofa.

What really had happened? She picked up a thimble and wondered about the woman who had worn it. Grant had told Glory about being in the War: had he gone off, leaving Matthew's mother pregnant and with no other way out of her predicament but to marry the first man who came along?

She had no idea, and no one to ask. The loneliness, the frustration, the sheer curiosity and the tedium of day after silent day ate away at her sanity. February gave way to March, with longer days and shorter nights, snowstorms and days warm enough for the sun to melt the snow, and yet there was no change in Glory's routine.

And yet there eventually came a day when the routine itself ran out. The mending was done; the laundry caught up. Bread was baking in the oven along with a cake. The house was clean, from the bedrooms upstairs to the dining room downstairs. And Glory found herself standing, rather forlorn, in the parlor with nothing to do.

It was six months to the day since she had arrived in Wyoming and wed Lee Johnson.

In all that time, she had not once written to her family in Philadelphia. Too many things had happened, and too quickly, but she resolved to remedy the situation at once.

The letter rambled, for she spent the entire afternoon on it, detailing to Terrence and Sadie, to Terrence's parents—who had been her own mother- and father-in-law for a very brief time—the strange course her life had taken since she had left them. She would enclose a bank draft by way of repayment for all they had done for her over the years. It was the least she could do, and she sincerely hoped they would not refuse her generosity.

Lord knew they could use the money. Lord knew, too, that she had taken enough from them, though she would gladly have done so much for them over those same many years.

Over dinner that night, which she served in the dining room rather than the kitchen, she outlined her plans to Matthew. It had been a month now since Grant's last visit, a month since Matthew had done more than grunt at her.

"It's a hundred dollars, and I know that's a great deal of money, but I feel I owe them that much."

The boy just shrugged.

"If you think it's too much, if you think we can't afford it, I'd be willing to listen," she prompted, afraid she was going to cry and plead with him to speak to her before she lost her mind completely.

"'S your money," he muttered, never looking up.

"Yes, but I feel your opinion is valuable, Matthew, or I wouldn't have asked for it."

"Don't make no never mind to me." Then he belched rudely, pushed his chair back, and left the room.

Glory lay awake for hours, angry and hurt and ashamed. She had done something, though she had no idea what, and he wasn't forgiving her for it.

By the next morning, she felt no better, but at least her day had some purpose. The weather was clear, though cold, and promised to remain fine for several days, more than long enough for the first trip into town since January. Supplies were running low, as expected for this time of year, and Glory was eager to escape the ranch and its denizens for a day.

"Where you think you're goin'?" Matthew asked as she rode out of the barn an hour after breakfast, packhorse in tow.

"Town. We need supplies, and I have that letter to mail. There's leftover meat and potatoes you can heat up for supper, or eat with the boys in the bunkhouse. I may not be home until morning."

In fact, as she left the boy standing, mouth open, in the yard, Glory decided that she definitely would not be home until morning. She was tired of cooking for herself, of washing her own dishes, of turning down and making her own bed. She owed herself a night of relaxation, a night at the Greenbriar.

Besides, Nancy Reynolds had repeatedly invited her, and Nancy Reynolds just might have some answers to some very puzzling questions.

At the bank she purchased the draft made to the order of Terrence Beaumont, and then strolled across the street to the post office. Whether Terrence or his stiff-necked parents accepted her payment was now their business: she had at least gone this far to erase the debt.

She felt a new spirit of freedom as she walked from one errand to the next. From the post office she went to Abel's General Store and ordered a long list of essentials to be packaged and ready for her in the morning. Jethro's pinch-mouthed wife was keeping the store, which relieved Glory of having to face the man who had caused her such humiliation on Christmas Eve, but Mrs. Abel's suspicious stare over her pince-nez spectacles was hardly less discomfiting.

On the way to the Greenbriar at the opposite end of town, Glory couldn't avoid stopping at Foley's Fashion Emporium. Well, she could have, but it would have meant crossing the street for no reason. She might have done that to avoid Grant Brookington, but not the dress shop.

She stood just inside the door and took in the sights, the smells, even the subtle sound of the shop. There was a lingering echo from the tinkling of the bell over the door, and the floor squeaked and groaned at the slightest shift of Glory's weight. Like every other business in Greene, Foley's sported a cast-iron stove that lent a quiet crackle to the background as well as the scent of smoke and hot metal.

And the clothes! By the standards of the Richmond she

256

had grown up in, Glory found Foley's Emporium shabby and pathetic. Nothing within the small space remotely resembled the bright satins and silks, the rich velvets and elegant laces of that long gone place and time. The dresses were simple and functional, of practical fabrics suited to the world of Greene, Wyoming Territory. Bombazine, gabardine, serge, and flannel. Dark blue, dark green, brown, and black. So sad, so drab, and even so, Glory felt at once enormously out of place.

She was even more drab, more sad, in her dungarees and boots and misshapen hat.

"May I help you?"

Startled, Glory turned around. A tall spare woman whose iron-grey hair was pulled back in a sleek chignon stood in front of a swaying black curtain that concealed a back room. Her navy serge skirt showed not a single crease, nor did the sleeves of her crisp white linen waist.

She walked, or glided, toward her customer with a look of pure disdain on her sharp features. The brown eyes gave the younger woman a thorough inspection, and gave Glory a chance to notice that Mrs. Foley squinted. Vanity, no doubt, kept her from resorting to spectacles like Mrs. Abel.

"I'm looking for a dress. Something simple, suitable for a widow but not too, ah, too morbid."

Mrs. Foley's brows arched in surprise.

"You must be Mrs. Johnson," she said, with the same disapproval in her voice that had been in her look.

"I am. And I am also very busy, with little time to waste. Can you help me or not?"

The older woman sniffed and seemed on the verge of dismissing her customer, but Glory was the only person in the shop at the moment, and, she suspected, perhaps the only one in all day. And if Mrs. Foley knew who she was based on gossip, then she also knew that Lee Johnson's widow had the hard cash to pay for her purchases.

An hour later, Glory departed the dress shop. Though

she carried no packages under her arm, she wore a satisfied smile on her face. The alterations necessary would be finished before the store closed at six, and instead of dungarees and a man's shirt, Mrs. Glorianna Johnson would be able to sit down to dinner in a brand new green gabardine dress, with a lace collar and lace cuffs and carved pearl buttons all the way down the front.

Until then, however, she had plenty of time to kill. Lunch ought to be the first item on her agenda, since her stomach was already growling annoyingly. Besides the Greenbriar, Glory had noticed two other eateries that a woman might enter unescorted, but she decided on the hotel dining room nonetheless. For one thing, she planned to retire to her room for a leisurely bath—which she would not have to draw for herself nor drain afterwards—and for another, she intended to speak to Nancy Reynolds. And where else would the hotelkeeper's wife be at lunchtime than, presumably, in the hotel dining room?

When Glory arrived, however, the room was virtually empty save for two elderly women who toyed with dishes of soup and slurped innumerable cups of tea. Still, they stole frequent glances to the woman in pants, making her stammer when the waitress came to take her order. She felt their censoring eyes throughout the meal and thus lost most of her enjoyment of the luxury. Instead of savoring the food, she gulped it, eager only to finish and leave the place to the old women and their tea.

After stopping at the desk to order her bath—which would not come with an audience—Glory proceeded up to her room. It was not the same she had taken the night she had sold the cattle, thank God, or she would never have been able to enter it. Instead, she had a pleasant sunny room in the front of the hotel, overlooking the main street. She was standing at the window, watching the traffic below from a new and somewhat fascinating perspective, when someone knocked on the door.

Supposing it was only the bearer of her bath, she called, "Come in. The door's unlocked."

She did not turn when the door opened, until a quiet feminine cough alerted her.

Nancy Reynolds greeted, "Good afternoon, Mrs. Johnson May I join you for a few minutes? I brought some coffee, unless you'd prefer tea."

Without waiting for an answer, the older woman proceeded to the table by the window and set down the tray. Over the quiet sounds of pouring coffee, she continued to talk.

"Are you in town on business this afternoon? I was hoping we'd have some time to talk, since it seems you've always been in a hurry the few times we've met."

There was something that kept Nancy Reynolds' voice from being totally welcoming. Glory wondered, even while phrasing her reply, if that animosity had always been present or if it was something new.

"Now that there's been a break in the weather, I came to stock up on some things. It's been quite a while since we've been able to get into town, and we were running low."

Nancy rested her elbows on the edge of the table and leaned forward just a bit. "I was worried about you. Is everything going all right for you and Matthew?"

Glory's head snapped up from her concentrated stirring of her coffee.

She had expected Nancy to ask about Grant, not Matthew. She reminded herself to be doubly cautious in her reply.

"As well as I can expect," she answered, but she knew her tone was too hesitant to convince her hostess. "Why do you ask?"

"Lee had a lot of trouble with the boy the past couple of years, since his mother died."

Glory suddenly wasn't sure if she was the cat or the mouse in this tense little game. For each tidbit Nancy Reynolds offered, she seemed to exact a price of additional information.

But Nancy hadn't exactly asked a question, and rather than volunteer an answer, Glory remained silent.

Her hunch paid off.

"They were never very close, for a father and an only son. Of course, Lee was a bachelor a good many years more than most men before they become fathers. And Melody Johnson kept a tight rein on her boy, so when Lee pulled him out of school and put him to work full-time on the ranch, Matthew had a lot of adjusting to do. I'm not sure he ever really accomplished it."

"I wondered why he wasn't in school. He's a bright boy, but I wasn't sure there even was a school here in Greene."

"Not a high school, but he could board in Cheyenne and go to school there."

It was indeed a game, one in which the rules were vague to begin with and changed constantly. Was Nancy seeking information about Glory's financial situation? Or something else? Cautious, Glory pondered half a dozen possible replies. Her delay cost her dearly, for it gave her opponent the opportunity to change the rules again.

Nancy set her spoon down beside her coffee and, just as Glory had an answer formulated to her last question, Nancy asked, "Have you seen Grant lately?"

Glory lost all ability to think.

"N-no, I haven't. Not for several weeks. Is something wrong?"

She knew immediately that she had given away far more than she should have, but she couldn't call the words back. And the anxiety in her tone of voice revealed even more than her words. Now the roles in the game were clearly defined. Glory was on the defensive, without even a hole in the wainscoting to escape through.

"We're all opportunists, Mrs. Johnson," Nancy said quietly but with a fierceness that left no doubt about her intention. "I came to Wyoming because teachers were in short supply and I needed a job. So I don't hold it against you that you married Lee for reasons other than love. Few women can afford that luxury."

"You did."

Glory felt a glow of satisfaction at the surprise on Nancy's face.

"I did, and I count my blessings every night. But I earned the right, and I paid for the privilege."

Now it was Nancy's turn to have said too much, and Glory took swift advantage.

"You were in love with Grant, weren't you," she stated. "And he wouldn't have you?"

"Quite the opposite. He would have married me, but he'd never love me the way I wanted to be loved. Someone else had got to him first. I knew I'd always come in second best."

"Melody Johnson."

Nancy nodded, and suddenly all the fight was out of her. Her eyes seemed to swell with unshed tears, and a soft pleading came into her voice.

"Melody used him, and his love, until he didn't have anything left. She played him against Lee so that she always got her way. When her father was still alive, she used all three of them, and then threw Matthew into the fight, too. It damn near killed Grant."

Glory began to understand. And she wished again that Grant were here, or at least accessible, because the need to talk to him, to pour out the burgeoning feelings within her, was becoming overwhelming.

Nancy rose and stood looking down at her guest. Steadiness returned to her voice.

"I'm sorry, Mrs. Johnson, to have taken so much of your time. I had no right to presume upon you like this. But having done so, I cannot leave without a final request."

Her lower lip trembled, and Glory knew then that the love Nancy Reynolds had once borne for Grant Brookington had not died.

"Don't use him. Don't hurt him. Or I swear to God, Glorianna Johnson, I will kill you myself."

Glory would have left the hotel and headed immediately home after that devastating interview, but the supplies wouldn't be taken to the livery and loaded on the packhorse until morning. There was no reason to skip the luxuries of a hot bath, dinner served in her room, and the new dress which was delivered precisely at six o'clock.

But she found no pleasure in any of her luxuries.

She could not even sleep. After blowing out the lamp, she slipped between crisp clean sheets and then lay awake, eyes staring at the ceiling for hours.

Finally, unable to stand the restless tossing and turning another minute, she got out of bed and padded across the bare floor to stand by the window.

It was past midnight, but a full moon illuminated the empty street below. All the shop windows were dark, and the only sign of life in Greene at that hour was the drifting of woodsmoke from the chimneys of the houses on the side streets behind the stores. Even the two horses tethered in front of the saloon across from the Greenbriar seemed lifeless, frozen statues in a painted landscape.

Then movement caught Glory's attention. From the far end of town, almost out of her line of vision, another horse trotted in the moonlight. Instinctive hope flared in Glory's breast, but in an instant she knew it wasn't Grant on the faithful Rusty. The moonlight shimmered on the pale splotches of the painted horse's coat and sparkled on the silver conchos of the cowboy's hat.

She watched, too horrified to back away from the window, as Lonnie Hewitt dismounted and tied the familiar pinto beside the other two horses in front of the saloon.

Chapter Nineteen

The ride back to the LJ in the cold of predawn was nearly as difficult as the afternoon of Christmas Eve. Glory pushed Lucy and the packhorse every inch of the way, with constant glances behind her to see if the painted horse followed. So intent was she on escaping any pursuer that she did not notice the red gelding in the stableyard.

Grant, however, must have been warned of her arrival, because he was standing on the porch when she crossed from the barn to the gate.

"Something's wrong," she said, pausing at the bottom of the porch steps. "I can see it on your face."

He managed a slight smile at her astute perception.

"There's been an accident, but this time you can't blame me."

"Oh, God, what is it now?"

She raced up the steps and pushed past him into the house.

Nothing had changed from when she left yesterday. The kettle still sat on the stove; the woodbox was half full. Abruptly, she turned when Grant at last followed her inside and closed the door behind him.

"Matthew?" she asked in a terrified whisper.

Grant nodded, and an almost overwhelming urge to take her in his arms and comfort her rushed through him.

"It's nothing serious. He and Old Ken were repairing a wheel on the chuck wagon and something slipped. Matthew's got a badly sprained wrist is all. He's upstairs resting, if you want to go see him."

She was torn, wanting to check on the boy and yet held as if by some eerie magnet to remain in Grant's presence.

"What—what are you doing here?" she finally managed to ask after a long silence. "Were you just riding by, or did someone come get you?"

"Neither. Or both."

Oh, Christ, he was blushing. And stammering like an eight-year-old caught with his hands in the cookie jar. Why did just the sight of her do that to him? All he could think of was her. Her face, all flushed with exertion and the chill of a March afternoon. Her hair, tousled and blown by the wind so that it hung in wild wisps all around her. Her hands, one splayed on her hip, the other clenched into a fist at her side.

He could have stood there and studied every detail of her. It seemed impossible that he hadn't seen her for over a month; it felt like years, or like only seconds.

"I was here when it happened," he finally said, remembering that she had asked him a question. "I came to find out what your plans were for the roundup."

Matthew had suffered an injury, and Glory knew her first duty was to see him, to make sure he was taken care of. But her feet wouldn't move, and neither would her eyes. They drank in the sight of Grant Brookington, standing a few feet away, hat in hand. He was talking, no doubt about something important, and she heard nothing above the frantic pounding of her heart.

"Is Matthew all right? Should he have a doctor? Is there anything I can do?"

The words tumbled from her. Someone else moved her lips and drew sounds from her throat; the real Glory existed only to be aware of the man who had walked back into her kitchen and into her life.

"He's fine. I wrapped the wrist and gave him a couple shots of whiskey before I put him to bed."

Consciousness, or something resembling it, slowly returned. Glory tested her muscles and found that they still functioned. She was able to remove her coat and hang it up, then turned to the stove where fresh coffee sent up a welcoming ribbon of steam.

"Then it probably would be best if I let him rest for a while," she said while steadying her hands to lift the coffee pot preparatory to offering some to Grant. "I haven't exactly been one of his favorite people lately anyway."

She hadn't meant to say that, and she noticed the quizzical look on Grant's face right away.

"No, he'll think I don't care if I don't check in on him," she mumbled as she set the coffee pot back down. "Please, help yourself, and I'll be back in just a minute."

She took the stairs two at a time. At the top, she paused, her hand on the railing, and tossed her hair out of her eyes. With a long deep breath to calm herself, she strode to the open door and stopped just inside Matthew's room.

The boy lay flat on his back; his right arm, swathed in neatly wrapped strips of a torn bedsheet, rested on top of the quilt. Though his eyes were closed, there was a certain tenseness about his features that suggested a couple shots of whiskey had not been enough to put him to sleep.

She whispered, just in case he had dropped off. "Matthew?"

He opened his eyes slowly.

"You get everything in town all right?" If the liquor had slurred his words, it had also taken away some of his bitterness.

"I got everything. Don't you worry about that, just rest and get that wrist well."

The boy yawned, and mumbled something that sounded like, "You gotta let Grant help you now," but his voice faded so at the end that Glory wasn't really sure what he had said. He let out a long sigh and drifted at once into deep, sound sleep.

Pain and exhaustion shadowed his eyes. Glory wondered how long he had been pushing himself beyond his limits, and if that were not the root cause of the accident. Feeling a tug of guilt deep inside, she backed out of the room and tiptoed to the stairs.

"He's worn out," Glory said as she sat down at the table with Grant and a cup of coffee. "I let him do too much."

"No more than you did yourself." Grant waited for the thought to sink in, and then he said, "Will you accept some help? In a few weeks, you've got to be ready for the spring roundup. You're already short several hands, and with Matthew out of commission, you're going to need help. There's just no way Weed and Ken and the others can do it all."

He was right, and she knew it. The voice that had cried out within her at the welcome sight of that big bay horse and had urged her to fling herself into those strong welcoming arms flatly refused to be silenced.

But another voice, older, wiser, and persistent if not loud, continued to whisper in her mind's ear.

"I can send a couple of my men to help fill in until Matthew's wrist is healed," Grant suggested. "You can even pay them, if it'd make you feel better. It might be easier, though, if I just stayed and helped out for a while."

He had given her an escape clause. But it was Glory who came up with the face-saving justification for a choice her heart insisted upon.

"Oh, God, Grant, there's so much to do around here. If I waited for you to ride back to the Diamond B and send a couple of hands over, we'd be another day behind." She smiled and stretched her hand across the table. "I'll pay you twenty bucks a month and board."

"You just hired yourself a hand, Miz Johnson."

Grant allowed her no excuses, not even apologies. He

pushed her relentlessly, from the instant they entered the barn where Weed and Young Ken were sorting the bags and bundles of supplies they'd taken from the packhorse.

"Hell, Glory, this place is a mess!" he exploded, storming into the dim, rich-smelling building. "When was the last time you cleaned it out? You can't leave horses standing in old manure for months at a time."

He found a shovel leaning against a stall gate and damn near threw it at her.

"Start down there, with the cow. Get everything out, down to bare dirt. Then put down a good foot of fresh straw. It's a wonder you didn't get some disease drinkin' milk from a cow wallowin' in shit like a damn hog."

She bit her lip, first in shame and then in anger. What right had he to come into *her* barn and tell her what to do? She had a deep urge to fling the shovel back at him, especially when he had walked ahead of her and presented such an inviting target.

But he was right, and she herself had given him the right to tell her so.

So while Grant continued to yell and curse and grumble, Glory opened the stall door and led the placid milk cow into the corridor and tied her to a post. The animal never made a sound or sign of protest, didn't even blink to acknowledge the stream of invectives Grant Brookington was loosing into the air. She just waited until the woman had tied her tether to the post and then the cow lifted her tail and deposited a fresh pile of manure at Glory's feet.

Grant saw the gesture and almost lost control. It would have been so easy to laugh and slip an arm around those dejected shoulders before he sent her back to the warmth and comfort of the house. But he had sworn too often to himself on too many sleepless nights that he'd never give her the chance to take advantage of him that way.

He'd play the game, but by his own rules. And if she won, he'd consider himself the real victor.

267

He found a broken-handled wheelbarrow at the other end of the barn and pushed it towards her.

"When you get this full, take it out and dump it in the garden. And don't just pile it up in one spot. Try to spread it around a little. I'll see if I can find something to fix the handle, but in the meantime you'll have to make do with it like this."

He dropped the wooden contraption to its legs with a clunk and turned his back to her without waiting for a reply.

Tears stung Glory's eyes, not only from the ammonia-laden manure she shovelled into the wheelbarrow.

Grant should have been ecstatic at her capitulation. This brutal animosity was the last thing she had expected. But with each shoveful of rank, rotten straw she pitched into the barrow, she reminded herself that she had no one to blame but Glorianna Johnson.

Reminded or not, she still felt the pain of each scathing attack he made on her incompetence. He seemed to be searching for any and every excuse to mock her, humiliate her, scold her, make her look ten thousands kinds of fool.

"Aw, jeez, Glory, will you look at this? When's the last time you had these horses shod?" His voice was muffled by distance and the walls of the various stalls in the barn, but he made sure she heard and understood every word. "Cripes, woman, did you think one pair of shoes was supposed to last forever, just 'cause they're iron?"

Her face burned; her ears felt as if they'd melt right off the sides of her head.

"It's a wonder you didn't lose everything you had loaded on this packsaddle. Half the leathers are split beyond repair. Somebody should've cleaned and oiled 'em good and they wouldn't have got ruined. The boys down at the livery must've had a helluva time making it all secure. Either that, or you were just plain damned lucky."

She heard him slap an animal's rump and move the

beast out of his way and thought she detected a lot more compassion in the way he addressed the horse than in the way he reviled her.

She stabbed the shovel into the floor and got a jolt when it hit hard-packed earth instead of moist straw. A single tear dripped out of her eye and slithered down her nose.

"I'm doing the best I can," she muttered under her breath. She wouldn't argue with him, and risk losing his desperately needed help. Nor would she deny that much of—no, *all* of what he said was true. "I'm ignorant, all right? Is that what you wanted to hear? I told you from the beginning I didn't know anything about this business, but I can learn. Look at what I've learned already. Don't I get any credit for that?"

Apparently she didn't, because Grant found one thing after another to bemoan as he made his inspection of the barn.

"Who the hell left a lantern sitting on top of a wall? Never, ever put a lantern where it can fall and start a fire, especially in a barn. Course, with all this wet straw, there probably isn't much danger of fire. Nothin' this wet would burn."

Glory wanted to explain that she had put the lantern there several days ago, empty and in need of a new wick. She knew, however, that no explanation would placate Grant's temper. It seemed to feed on each fault, each error.

She reverted to mumbling to herself more and more, just to cover up the sound of his voice.

"Damn you, Grant Brookington. You don't have to rub it in quite so hard."

She threw another shovelful into the wheelbarrow and eyed the contents. If she filled it to the rim, she'd probably not have the strength to push that heavy a load outside to the garden, wherever that was.

Testing the uneven handles, she discovered she could manage without too much difficulty, but she didn't dare

269

add any more. Better to leave it half full and make more trips than risk not being able to control it and having to clean up the same pile of manure again.

She leaned the shovel against the wall, carefully out of her way, and pushed the barrow out into the barn. There was, she recalled, a patch of plowed earth just east of the house that might well have been used as a garden plot. It was as good a spot as any, she guessed, to spread this smelly mess.

She got as far as the barnyard before Grant stopped her.

"And what were you planning to use to spread that?" he drawled. "Or were you planning just to dump it in a pile?"

She dropped the wheelbarrow and whirled to face him, fed up to her eyeballs with his arrogant attitude.

"Maybe I was *planning* to spread it around with my bare hands. What difference does it make to you? It's *my* ranch, *my* garden, and *my* manure!"

The silence lasted two seconds, maybe three. Steel grey eyes hardened, golden ones blazed. Then, when Grant was certain the red in her cheeks came from the realization of exactly what she had said, he let the long-withheld laughter explode. Still holding the shovel handle, he doubled over in hysteria.

Glory froze.

"Oh, God," she groaned. It was bad enough to have him yelling and swearing at her, but nothing hurt more than his laughter.

"What's goin' on out here?" Charley, poking his head out of the bunkhouse door, looked from Grant to Glory and back again.

Neither of them had an answer, not even when Weed and Old Ken pushed Charley aside and wandered out to watch for themselves.

"Oh, God," Glory whispered again. She had to escape. She'd make a dignified exit if nothing else. She turned

270

her back on the men, all of them, and grasped the handles of the wheelbarrow.

If the ground hadn't been half-thawed, her plan might have worked. But the legs, under the weight of the manure, had sunk into the mud deeper than Glory expected, thus lowering the handles. That should have been to her advantage, giving her more leverage. Except she had forgotten one salient point.

She set her back to the task and lifted with every ounce of effort she could summon, Grant's laughter still ringing in her ears. But the barrow didn't budge. There was just a resounding crack as the other handle broke.

Grant dropped the shovel and ran, hoping that she'd maintain some kind of precarious balance long enough for him to reach her before she landed in the mud herself. He almost made it.

He caught her just under her upraised arms, but by then she had gone too far backwards. Her momentum took them both, hard, all the way to the ground.

Matthew, drawn from his nap by the noise, stood groggily on the porch.

"I hope you brought clean pants," he called to Grant, who was rubbing his forehead where Glory had accidentally swatted him with the short length of broken handle. "She don't do laundry but once a week on Monday, and today's only Wednesday!"

It had been a long, hard day. There wasn't time for a relaxing soak in a deep tub of hot water; there wasn't anyone to heat the water anyway. Matthew helped put something together for supper, but both Grant and Glory insisted he get back in bed as soon as he had eaten some bread and a slice of pan-fried beefsteak.

That left only Grant and Glory to clean up the kitchen after they'd done their best to clean up themselves.

He *had* brought extra pants, in the hope that she'd

271

finally accept his offer, so at least he didn't have to parade around her house with a sheet or a blanket wrapped around his middle. Now, lying in the dark in the parlor, where he'd made a temporary bed on the sofa, he wished he didn't feel so all-fired pleased with himself.

He had, he reasoned, no reason to be pleased. Nothing, absolutely nothing, had gone as planned.

He had humiliated her, shown her just how ignorant and incompetent she was, and let her make a complete fool of herself in front of the few hired hands she had left. That much had followed his carefully constructed strategy. But instead of collapsing on his mercy, the stubborn little witch just got more stubborn. She had actually sat there, in the mud, comfortably ensconced in the V of his widespread legs, and dared to demand that he help her to her feet!

So why, in heaven's name, did he have this grin plastered all over his face? He hadn't beaten her, he had no reason whatsoever to feel so damned victorious. If anything, she had beaten him, and royally.

And that, certainly, was no reason to feel the way he did.

She had gone upstairs while he was still plumping a musty-smelling pillow, and he listened to her now as she moved around in her room. He could imagine her skinning off her dungarees and slipping off the flannel shirt, but he wondered, with the expected and uncomfortable results, what she wore underneath her masculine garb.

He heard the squeak of a drawer opened and closed. Was she taking out a nightgown and then wriggling it over her head? He squirmed, but couldn't find a more comfortable position in his makeshift bed. The next sound to reach him was the creak and groan of bedsprings, but not in the bedroom where Glory slept. Confirming his assumption that Matthew was restless, Grant heard the soft patter of bare feet cross from one room to the other.

"Are you all right, Matthew?" she whispered, not sure he was still awake.

"Yeah, I'm okay. Just not used to havin' to sleep on my back is all."

"The wrist doesn't hurt too bad?"

"Naw." The only light came from across the hall, but it was enough for Glory to see the truth behind his lie. "Well, it's kinda sore. Grant said it'd be worst tonight. He told me to drink some more of that whiskey. Said it'd help me sleep, but I ain't too sleepy right now."

She needed no other proof of the effect the liquor had had on him. The fact that he was speaking to her, rambling even, was obvious evidence that something had destroyed his carefully constructed wall of silence.

"It really was an accident," he went on. "I know you think I done it on purpose—"

"'Did' it," she corrected automatically, though she doubted he heard or cared.

"—to get Grant over here, but honest, I didn't. I might've, if I'd thought of it. You shouldn't be so mean to him, you know? He's my best friend, best in the whole world. And you know why?"

The words were slurred, as much by sleep as the couple of shots of rotgut Grant had forced on the boy to get him some badly needed rest. Fuzzy or not, each syllable rang clear in Glory's ears.

"Hush," she urged gently but firmly. "You need to sleep, Matthew. We can talk more in the morning."

"Pa was mean to him, too. Wouldn't let him come over here, wouldn't let him take me fishin' up in the mountains like he used to. Remember that big trout I caught that one time? Just about pulled me in the stream. And it was a good thing he was big, too, 'cause we didn't catch nothin' else that whole day."

He was drunk, as only a fourteen-year-old on his first drunk could be.

"Come on, Matthew, roll over on your other side, so you don't hurt your arm, and go to sleep."

273

She tried to nudge him, and when that failed, she slid her hands under him to try to force him into a position more conducive to sleep. That, however, failed as well. And Matthew seemed to have only begun.

Time and reality lost all meaning for him. He slipped into the past as easily as he slipped back into the present, and sometimes he mixed them together. Though he never raised his voice above a whisper, Glory was certain even that quiet sound carried too easily in the night silence of the house.

"I used to think you were just like Ma, wantin' somebody to take care of her all the time. Always had to have everything just her way. And when things went wrong, you always had somebody else to blame, didn't you? Uncle Lonnie or Grandpa or Pa or Grant. Nothin' was ever your own fault, was it?"

"Oh, Matthew, you don't know what you're talking about. Please, just go to sleep."

She had been helpless before, sitting in the mud with half a dozen cowboys fit to bust a gut laughing at her, but listening to Matthew's rantings filled her with helplessness and panic. She dreaded what she might hear, dreaded worse what Grant might hear.

"I tried to tell Grant you wasn't like that. Why don't you like him? You were gonna let Uncle Lonnie stay around here, and he's worthless as pig snot, but you don't want Grant to help. I don't get it. You never used to mind him comin' around."

Glory shivered. The boy was confusing her with his mother, and she sensed there were forbidden words about to be spoken, words she had no way to stop.

"But it'll be different now, I promise. He's here, and I mean to see that he stays, no matter what you say. And, Ma, you'd be proud of me. I didn't tell nobody he's my pa. Not a soul. It's still just our secret."

274

Chapter Twenty

In less than thirty seconds, Matthew was snoring, soundly and blessedly asleep. Stunned and suddenly aware of how exhausted she was, Glory tiptoed to her bedroom. Despite the emotions rampaging through her, she too was asleep almost before her head hit the pillow.

In the morning Grant wakened her with the delicious aromas of frying bacon and fresh coffee from the kitchen. He allowed her ten whole minutes of lying comfortable in her bed, savoring the prospect of breakfast already on the table. Then, with no respect for her privacy or propriety, he climbed the stairs and stood in her doorway to bang a spatula on the edge of a tin mixing bowl and announce it was time to get up. He didn't leave until she had left the bed.

· He drove her relentlessly, from before sunup until after dark, every day. Just when she thought she was getting accustomed to the rigorous routine, when she thought she had mastered a particular skill, he would spring something new on her.

"We gotta get those horses shod today," he told her over breakfast. The kitchen window was still pitch black, and they ate by the light of a single lamp on the table, just as they had done every morning and every evening for the past week.

Glory almost jumped at the chance to escape what had

275

become, to her, worse than slave labor. "I can take them into town as soon as it's light. Do you think the smith can have them done in one day?"

She didn't like the way the lantern light illuminated Grant's grin over his coffee cup.

"Don't have time to take 'em into town. The LJ's got a forge, and there ought to be enough blanks to shoe nine horses and a couple mules."

He waited, cup still poised an inch or so from his mouth, for her reaction. It wasn't long in coming.

She shook her head, slowly at first and then more firmly.

"No. I will not, I cannot become a blacksmith. I have cleaned the barn, and I have repaired harness. I have hammered and sawn and scraped and dug and hauled and loaded and unloaded, but there is no way on God's green earth you are going to get me into a smithy."

She stared across the table at him, her determination rising the more his steely eyes glittered with glee. All this past week she had sensed him laughing at her, waiting for her to realize that this was one hilarious joke, of which she had been the butt. Well, he had gone as far as he was going to go.

"I'll assign one of the men to do it," she announced imperiously. "There's no law that says I have to do everything myself."

Grant set his mug down and scraped the last of his scrambled eggs onto his fork. Eating that last mouthful gave him a cover for the very satisfied smirk that was beyond his power to control. He had pushed her almost to his own limits, but the scheme had worked. He had finally broken her.

"Fine," he said, wiping his mouth on a napkin. "I'll take my week's pay and head back to the Diamond B then, Mrs. Johnson. The agreement was that you'd do it my way, no arguing."

He saw panic flash through those golden eyes, but not a sign of the defeat he expected.

When she did begin her argument, her voice was quiet and soft and hesitant.

"You don't understand, Grant. It isn't that I don't . . ."

He could have interrupted her when she let the sentence hang unfinished, but he waited, patiently, for her to have her say. He already had his reply well rehearsed.

She didn't pick up her thread of thought for a while; it was as though she had to tie some loose ends together first. She took another sip of her coffee then set the cup down and ran her fingers through the tangles of her hair. It was a ritual Grant swore he'd never get used to. Each morning she had come down to the kitchen like that, dressed but with her hair uncombed, tousled just as it was from sleep. And each morning it had driven him crazy.

She had no way of knowing how many times he regretted his decision. It was just as well she thought him a veritable slave driver for the way he pushed and provoked her hour after hour. The rational part of him insisted he was doing it for her own good. Eventually she'd realize just what an enormous responsibility she had taken on and she'd quit. For her sake as well as his own, it was better that she realize she could not possibly run the LJ successfully. The harder Grant drove her, the sooner she'd accept the truth and relinquish her foolish dream.

That, after all, was exactly what he wanted. He'd give her a fair price for the ranch and send her back to Philadelphia in comfort.

Or at least, that was what the rational part of him thought.

The other part of him thought no such thing.

The other part of him wanted her to stay. And he couldn't think of a single rational reason why.

"If it is so important that we get the horses shod, wouldn't it be better if I simply took them to town and

277

had the job done there?" she asked, startling him from his confused thought.

"I don't see why, when you've got everything right here to do it."

He didn't like that slow, methodical way she spoke. It emphasized her drawl a little more than usual, and it made him wonder just what scheme was brewing in that sharp little brain of hers.

"If you take the time to teach me, it would tie up your time as well as mine, and there'd be the chance that I'd do something wrong that would cost us dearly during the roundup, correct?"

He wanted to deny her logic but couldn't.

"If, however, I take the horses to a qualified blacksmith, I'd be out of your way so you could do other things that need doing around here, and we'd have the job done just as quickly and certainly much better."

She leaned foward with her elbows on the table and her chin propped in her palms, a perfect picture of wide-eyed innocence waiting for an answer.

Grant didn't have one.

And Glory knew it. She could have clapped her hands for joy. She had beaten him, even if it did mean a long, lonely ride to town with a string of horses behind her. It was worth the long ride just to be out of Grant Brookington's company for a day. Though she didn't really look forward to a dull day in Greene, it was better than . . .

The memory of her last trip to town came rushing back.

What if Lonnie was waiting there for her?

She shook her head, chasing the thought away. If Lonnie wanted to harass her or threaten her, he had had a whole week in which to make his move. Poor Lonnie. As much as Glory disliked him, she had to feel a little sorry for him. She had blamed him for so many things, and suspected him of so many more, when there wasn't the slightest bit of proof.

And when Grant Brookington was every bit as suspicious.

She blinked, letting him know she was still waiting for his reply to her suggestion. He finally came up with one.

"Nope, I don't think it's a good idea. You don't know horses well enough yet, and if something spooked the whole string and they bolted, you'd be in trouble."

She might be hurt, and being hurt as well as alone was not a pleasant prospect. It irritated Grant that the silly woman never worried about herself but left it always to him to watch out for her safety. Worse still was the possibility that the horses might simply head immediately for home, and then Glory would have to return, shame-faced, to retrieve them. Grant tried to rationalize his objection on the grounds of not wanting the time to be lost, but he knew that he was really trying to spare her additional humiliation.

"I'll help," she agreed reluctantly, "but don't expect me to do very much. I'm—I'm not very good around fire."

Puzzled, Grant cast his mind back to the night the shed burned and the way she had stood stiff and terrified in his arms.

"Better get used to it," he forced himself to say gruffly. "C'mon, let's get started."

They spent most of the morning hunting for the tools Grant needed, hammers and tongs and other odd-shaped implements, as well as the preformed horseshoes that would be shaped to the specific needs of each horse. Then and only then did Grant enter the open-sided shed that had once served as the LJ's forge.

There were twelve horses and four mules to be shod, and when Grant looked at how sadly the animals had been ignored, he shook his head and turned back to the bellows.

"Maybe I shoulda let you take 'em into town. We'll be at this all day and most of tomorrow, too," he grumbled.

"Matthew never said a word," was Glory's excuse as

she led Lucy to Grant and held the mare while he lifted a hoof and rested it on his knee to remove the old shoe.

"The boy's overworked. And his father wasn't the best teacher in the world either."

Glory patted the mare's neck and breathed a sigh of relief that she didn't have to face Grant while he said those words. He had his back to her, while he trimmed and filed the mare's hoof with the confident skill of an expert.

"It's my fault. He begged me time and again to accept the help you offered, but I was too stubborn, and too ignorant. I didn't realize how much I didn't know."

Admitting her ignorance was easier when Grant wasn't looking, but she didn't go any further.

He moved to another hoof and went slowly through the details of how to remove the old shoe and trim the hoof so that the new one would fit properly. With the horse's halter tied securely to one of the poles holding up the forge's roof, Grant told Glory to try the next hoof herself.

She was slow and awkward and clumsy, but Grant showed only patience. He corrected her mistakes, helped her until she had everything right.

When they had finished, he set Lucy's hoof down and strode to the pile of shimmering hot coals. A few strokes of the bellows brought the flames to life, revealing the iron shoe already red-hot in their embrace. He grabbed the tongs and lifted the shoe from the coals with a shower of sparks.

Glory jumped back as a crackling ember popped in the air just in front of her face. Grant tried to ignore the fear in her eyes as he took the shoe to the anvil and reached for the hammer.

He pounded on the red-hot iron, sending more sparks flying. Lucy shifted her weight from one back leg to another and dozed peacefully, but Glory felt her own pulse beginning to race through her veins. The fury in

280

Grant's motions, the anger in each thwang of metal on metal, sent a warning through her. She sensed that this was his way of working out a problem, and she dared not add to it.

In silence he worked, except for occasional instructions. When he was finished with Lucy, it was nearly noon, and the day had grown pleasantly warm. But in the forge the fire and the exertion had brought a sheen of sweat to his brow, and his shirt was damp with it. While Glory was gone to bring the next horse, he untied the leather apron and lifted it off to remove the flannel shirt. He'd be more vulnerable to the little burns from the sparks, but he needed the freedom to move, and the respite from the heat.

He seemed tireless. Silently, steadily, he drew one iron shoe out of the fire after another, hammered them to the precise shape for each neatly trimmed hoof, and then plunged them into the quenching trough before nailing each in place. His chest and arms, shoulders and back glistened with sweat that ran in charcoal rivulets through the smoke and coal dust that had settled on his exposed skin. Even his face was black, and there were places where stray sparks had burned his hair.

Through it all, he said nothing. Even the instructions faded away, as Glory knew instinctively what to do next. She learned when the fire needed replenishing, when the water had grown too hot, even when to bring Grant a cool drink for himself. He took the tall glass from her hand and drank it down in what seemed a single gulp, then wiped the back of his hand across his mouth, smearing the grime until he looked like some demon straight from hell.

The work he did, however, was her salvation.

On the other hand, watching him was becoming more of a temptation than she could stand.

He winced as a spark lit on his shoulder, and Glory instinctively wanted to take a cold wet rag and ease the momentary pain. She held back, not daring to interrupt him. When the day grew longer and longer, and still there was work to be done, he flexed the arm with its ghastly scar, and she knew it ached. Again, she did not give in to the urge to beg him to stop, to rest, to leave the final labors until the next day. He would only take it as a sign of her own weakness.

She could not let him even suspect that her weakness was of a different kind.

It took a day of watching him sweat and strain and curse uncooperative animals and swear at her when she didn't understand his orders, for Glory to admit finally and without reservation that she had fallen in love with Grant Brookington.

"What are you doing just standing there and staring at me for?" he snapped. "I'm done with this mule; where's the next one?"

She blinked, brought rudely out of thoughts she wished she hadn't thought.

"I'm sorry," she stammered. "I wasn't staring. I'll get the other mule." She began to lead the shod animal back to the barn and realized that night had fallen completely. The yard was lit only by the moonlight. And the air had grown cold.

Footsteps hurried up behind her.

"No, let it go," Grant said as he placed a hand on her shoulder. "The fire's burning down and I think I've done more than I should have for one day. We can finish in the morning." Taking the mule's lead rope from her hand he added, "I'll put Brownie away, you go on back to the house and see if Matthew has anything ready for us to eat."

She could see only the whites of his eyes in his dirty, smudged face until he managed a weary, half-hearted grin that gave her a glimpse of his teeth. She reached up to swipe a finger teasingly down his nose.

That half an instant of contact sent a searing river of liquid fire all through him, hotter than the coals in the

282

forge by several thousand degrees. It was enough to make him wish he had just sent her back to the house alone, so he could finish the shoeing of the last few animals by himself.

Sitting across the dinner table from her one more night was certain to drive him stark raving mad. This past week he had been able to control his feelings with logic. Tonight, however, logic was no match for the desire flaring in him.

He watched her as she walked away from him, headed for the kitchen. For the first time since leaving the forge, he felt the chill in the air on his naked skin. A shiver rippled through him; he tugged on the mule's lead and practically dragged the animal into the barn. Yet despite the cold that raised gooseflesh, Grant took his time putting the mule in its stall.

By the time he did reach the kitchen, his teeth were chattering and his lips had turned purple.

"What were you doing out there, trying to freeze to death?" Glory scolded. Without giving him a chance to answer, she told him, "I figured you'd want to clean up first, so your bath's all ready. There's a nice warm towel by the stove, and I got clean clothes from your saddlebag. Don't worry about making a mess; we can eat in the dining room and take care of all this later."

The next thing he knew, he was standing there, in the middle of the kitchen beside a tub full of steaming water, alone.

He bathed and he dressed in clean clothes and he walked into the dining room without being aware of anything. He ate a meal that consisted of he knew not what dishes. Matthew might have cooked old boots and clods of dirt for all Grant tasted.

He wanted her. It didn't matter that she had used him just exactly the way Melody had. It didn't matter that she would go on using him until she didn't need him anymore.

It didn't matter that everything between him and the woman across the table from him was based on greed and some misplaced desire for revenge.

He wanted her, and he intended to have her, on any terms he could manage.

Glory bathed quickly, knowing Grant was just on the other side of the door in the parlor. She had tried during dinner to bring up the subject of moving him into the upstairs bedroom, but he and Matthew had talked almost incessantly about plans for the roundup. So she excused herself while they were still eating and prepared her own bath.

She was drying her hair with a towel when she heard Matthew call a tired good night to her before he trudged up the stairs. Despite his still aching wrist, the boy had done his own chores as well as the ones she had neglected while helping Grant. There had to be a way to relieve Matthew of all this responsibility. She hoped she could learn enough in the next week or so to take the burden from the boy herself. If she could get through the roundup and the summer, she'd have a full year of experience, enough perhaps to give Matthew the freedom to go back to school.

She had been daydreaming when she should have been combing the tangles out of her hair.

But she had left her brush upstairs. She preferred to sit in front of the parlor fire and slowly loosen the knots and snarls, but even if she had remembered the brush, she certainly couldn't indulge in that kind of vanity while Grant Brookington lounged on the sofa. Teasing him with a finger down his soot-smudged nose was one thing, but even she wasn't cruel enough to taunt him further.

She cinched the belt on her bathrobe tighter and slowly eased the door to the parlor open.

With his head resting on one arm of the sofa, his

284

stockinged feet still hung over the other arm. There was no way he could be comfortable in a position like that. His left hand rested on the floor beside him, but even while Glory stood staring in amazement, he moved the other arm in an effort to find a place for it between his body and the back of the sofa.

She strode to him and shook him firmly by the shoulders. At least he hadn't undressed yet.

"Grant, wake up," she ordered. "You can't sleep like this."

He grunted and snorted and tried to roll over onto his side away from the nuisance that invaded his slumber. Unfortunately, the nuisance persisted.

He opened his eyes and scowled.

"What do you want now?" he demanded. "I have enough trouble sleeping on this thing without you waking me up in the middle of the night."

"It's not the middle of the night. You've barely fallen asleep, Grant." She took hold of his hand and tried to pull him to his feet. "Why didn't you tell me the sofa was too short for you? Come on upstairs and you can have my bed."

In a blink of an eye, everything changed. He was sitting up now, but she still held his hand between both of hers. When she realized that he was fully awake, she tried to let go. She couldn't.

"If I go upstairs, you're coming with me," he said quietly. "If you're not prepared to do that, then I suggest you hightail it out of this room right now. I want you, damn it, Glory. I can't be around you all day and then have you come up to me at night—"

The hell with trying to reason with her. What he felt went beyond reason anyway.

He stood and took her face gently in his hands, then brought his mouth down on hers in a kiss so soft, so possessive, that it took any and all protest from her. His tongue probed against her lips until she welcomed his

285

seeking, his tasting of her. He threaded his fingers into the cool wet mass of her hair and cupped the back of her head to hold her to him, inescapable.

A single kiss was enough to leave him breathless, his blood racing through his veins to fill every portion of him with desire. Yet holding her against him, he held back the furious onslaught of arousal that would rush him beyond the boundaries of his control.

"We need to talk, Grant," she whispered against his chest. He could feel the movement of her lips through the fabric of his shirt like a series of delicate kisses. The idea of just talking to her was slipping farther and farther from his mind "We're tired now, both of us, and not thinking straight."

"Hell, woman, I never can think straight when I'm around you."

Only when she lifted her head away from his muscular chest did she realize she had twined her arms around his waist. From shoulder to ankle their bodies were molded together as instinct had drawn them.

The lamplight from the kitchen cast oblique shadows, turned eyes to silver fire and golden flame. Wet tendrils of hair framed her questioning face, with a teasing curl plastered to her cheek. He leaned forward to kiss the twisted strand of hair, then ran the tip of his tongue along its curve.

"I can't think at all half the time," he groaned. "I set out to do one thing, and as soon as I lay eyes on you, I know I'm gonna do something entirely different, something I don't even want to do, something I know I shouldn't."

"You don't want to be here?"

She bumped his nose with her cheekbone.

"No, damn it, I don't." With his thumb he traced the line of her jaw, then stroked the edge of her lower lip, trembling now as she waited for him to continue. "You can't imagine how many times I've wished I never laid eyes on you, that Lee hadn't died and left you with all

286

this, that you'd at least have sold the place and gone back East. My life was a lot easier before you entered it."

"But I didn't," she protested. "You entered mine. You came up to me that day, you offered to buy me out and—"

He hugged her to him before she got the wrong idea.

"Glory, I wanted you from the first instant. Not that afternoon when we buried Lee. You probably don't remember that other time, in the bank. You were all wet just like you are now, your hair stringy and wiggly under that bedraggled old bonnet."

She remembered, and her silence told him she did.

"All I could think was damn it all, he took Melody away from me and now he had you. Hell, I didn't know your name or anything else, but just because you were his, I wanted you."

He felt her stiffen, angered and hurt by his confession, but he tightened his arms around her and would not let her leave.

"When I offered to buy you out, it was because I was still jealous of poor dead Lee."

"How sad," Glory whispered. "He was so jealous of you."

She looked up, and her eyes met his. Her own longing was mirrored there, but in the dark depths she found uncertainty and caution, just as she knew he would see in hers. Yes, they needed to talk, but not now, not when their minds were clouded with this crazy desire they could not deny.

"Go on to bed, Glory," Grant ordered. He eased her away from him reluctantly but kept his hands clasped around the upper part of her arms. "I'll finish shoeing the horses in the morning, and then maybe Matthew and Ken can help with the chuck wagon. If all goes well, we should get done early enough that you and I can sit down and talk this all out, the way we should have done a week ago, or maybe six months ago."

Glory reached up to touch his cheek, her fingers

trembling and tentative as she whispered, "Yes, we need to talk. But right now, you need sleep, and you won't get it here on this sofa. I've slept here before and I can do it again, so you just march yourself up there and—"

"No, not without you," he reiterated. "I won't leave you down here alone."

Puzzled, she took half a step away from him. The edge of her bare foot came in contact with something very cold and hard. She looked down and saw the dull gleam of metal and realized the gun lay within the reach of Grant's hand while he had lain sleeping.

"I think we'd better talk now."

Grant took a deep breath and spent half a second debating with himself whether to tell her the truth or not.

"Lonnie's back in town, swearing he'll take the LJ away from you one way or the other."

The old doubts came rushing back to her. Was Lonnie the enemy, or was Grant just using him as a decoy? She shook her head and tried to turn away, but Grant held her fast.

"Damn it, woman, when are you going to get it through that thick, beautiful head of yours? Lonnie, or one of his goons, would just as soon kill you as look at you. He will not stop at anything, not even murder, to get this ranch."

She wasn't accepting it, though she had stopped struggling to get free of him. Grant lifted his face to the dark ceiling and sighed again, lowering the volume of his voice.

"I don't know what I can do or say to convince you. You remember your theory that Lonnie was hanging around this winter, somewhere close where he had easy access to the LJ, so he could set that fire? Well, you were right. Smart, but stubborn, that's what you are."

"What theory? What are you talking about?"

"Matthew told me. I checked it out the next day and damn near froze my butt in that storm. That line shack of Steve Peake's was his hideout, and if there wasn't any

288

direct evidence that Lonnie had set the fire, there sure wasn't any other good reason for him to be holed up in a place like that in the middle of winter."

The middle of winter never sent a shiver down Glory's back like the one she experienced now. The cold reached right through her, clutching at her belly and her heart.

"I don't know what Matthew told you," she whispered, "and I don't know anything about Lonnie and a line shack either."

Now it was Grant's turn to be puzzled. Finally, he released her arms and gathered her once more against him.

"Oh, God," he prayed, "I don't know what to do with you, but I can't do anything without you either. I know you're just as scared, just as confused as I am, and there isn't a damn thing we can do about it."

For a long moment, silence descended upon them, wrapping itself around them just as their arms twined around each other, holding bodies close. The creature in his embrace smelled of soap and fresh water and that unmistakable fragrance of woman, of desire, of hunger. He buried his face in the tangled damp hair and drank in the scent, then let his breath out softly, caressing her ear with the words he whispered.

"I can't argue with you anymore. We'll go to bed, and in the morning we'll talk. And what happens in between, we won't fight it."

She got the lamp from the kitchen while he checked the locks on the doors once again, then she led the way up the stairs to the darkened room. Across the hall, Grant pulled the door to Matthew's room closed after a quick look to make sure the boy was asleep. When he walked back to the other room, where she waited, he paused in the doorway.

She had untied the belt to her robe. The garment hung open, revealing the white of a plain flannel nightgown. In one hand she held her brush and raised it to pull it through the tangled hair.

289

"No," he managed to whisper. "Leave it like that."

He crossed the floor to stand in front of her and take the brush from her. Her hands dropped limply to her sides. She made no attempt to stop him when he slid the robe off her shoulders and let it fall down her arms to pool at her feet.

"It hasn't been easy for me either," Glory told him. She felt his hands at her throat, searching for the little buttons that fastened her nightgown. Her eyes never left his, bright in the darkness now. "Oh, Grant, what if it isn't the ranch that I want, just you? Sometimes that's how I feel."

They made love with all the tenderness required of something so fragile and delicate. There were no cries of passion, no frantic demands for fulfillment. But afterward, when they drifted off to sleep in a cocoon of satiety and exhaustion, neither could forget that on the floor, within easy reach of Grant's hand, lay the cold, deadly steel of a loaded gun.

Chapter Twenty-One

Grant pulled the cinch strap tight around Rusty's belly with a grunt of satisfaction. The past weeks had been hectic, and at times he had come very close to panic, and even closer to giving it up entirely, but somehow, with Glory's help, the LJ crew was ready for the spring roundup.

The air was fresh and clean after a thunderstorm during the night. Now morning was only moments away. The sky to the east glowed bright gold where the sun would soon explode upon the world.

There had been no more sign of Lonnie. Still, the last thing Grant checked before mounting the bay was the gun at his hip. He had worn one ever since he could remember, so that it seemed as much a part of his clothing as his hat and boots, the faded bandana around his throat, or the gloves that protected his hands. But today he was more aware of the firearm than ever.

He hoped he'd never have to use it.

"You ready?" he asked Glory who for once looked down at him.

"Whenever you are," she answered with a grin. The wild hair was pulled back and tied with a length of leather thong, but stray strands floated on the morning breeze to flutter around her face. Her hat shaded her eyes, but nothing could hide the golden warmth of them, a warmth

Grant remembered from firelit nights and stormy afternoons and the soft twilight just before dawning.

He smiled at the memories and swung into the saddle. With a nudge of his heels, he turned the gelding toward the open range. Memories would have to hold him for the next two or three weeks.

Glory breathed deeply of the crisp, clean air and kicked her mount, a buckskin mare named Cleo, to a trot to catch up with Grant. Despite the long hard day's ride ahead, she felt free, unfettered, and she reveled in it. She had earned it.

"Assuming nothing's happened to the chuckwagon, we should arrive at camp late this afternoon and have a hot meal waiting for us," Grant said when, after the first exuberant burst of speed, he slowed Rusty to a walk and let Glory catch her own breath. "The real work will start early tomorrow, after everyone's had a good night's sleep."

They had dropped behind the others, who found the open country an invitation to races and other impromptu competitions. The yells and whoops, the startled whinnies of horses urged to greater speed, faded into the distance as the cowboys from the LJ and the Diamond B galloped over the next rise, toward the mountains and the open range that spread out at their feet.

An hour's easy ride took them beyond territory Glory could call familiar, and she began to take in the sights and sounds and smells of the open range. Here there were no roads, not even a narrow beaten path across the grassland. Above, the sky was clear, with only a few high streamers of clouds, leaving the sun to make sharp shadows as the day brightened. The horses picked their way surely across open meadows, up and down low hills, over icy swollen streams.

"It smells so good," Glory exclaimed as she knelt to refresh herself from one of those rushing torrents. "I never knew water could smell so fresh and clean. It always just smelled like—like water."

"You owe your very existence to that water, coming from the snow up there." Grant pointed toward the mountains, still grey in the morning haze. Though the horses had brought them many miles westward, the peaks seemed no closer. "See how the banks are bare on either side of the creek? That's how high it can rise when there's a flood."

"Does that happen often?"

He shrugged.

"Often enough. It takes a combination of heavy winter snow, a quick melt, and some rain to boot. This year spring's been slow and steady, so we shouldn't have a big rush of melting, but a cloudburst can still swell these little creeks to deadly rivers. I've seen it happen."

He pushed Rusty to a comfortable lope, and Glory had to dig her heels into Cleo to get the mare to chase after him.

She no longer clung to the saddle horn when her horse broke to a run; she leaned into the speed and became part of it. The wind pulled at her clothing, at her hair, stung her eyes until tears of exhilaration slipped out the corners, and she loved it.

Freedom sang in her blood to the throbbing rhythm of her pulse. The past three weeks were all but forgotten; she had survived the frustration, the drudgery, the constant bickering with Grant and sometimes with Matthew, and now she raced with that wild wind across the prairie. Never in her most fantastic dreams had she ever envisioned this kind of intense joy.

Crouching over Cleo's neck until the mare's mane blended with the wind-whipped strands of her own hair, Glory urged the horse to even greater speed. And when, alerted by the pounding of hooves on the thick turf, Grant reined in Rusty, Glory let out a shriek of uncontrolled ecstasy.

She swept past him. At first, he thought the mare had taken the bit in her teeth, but before he could spur his own horse after her, he saw Glory crack the end of the

293

reins on Cleo's shoulder. She and the long-legged buckskin were having the time of their lives.

Grant caught up to them as they approached a grove of cottonwoods clustered at the bend of a wider stream. Cleo resisted Glory's control and tossed her head, but she settled down to a tight trot and finally a lazy walk as she followed her flaring nostrils to the refreshment of water.

The rasping cry of a hawk broke the late morning stillness. Satisfied that she had her horse in hand, Glory threw her head back and squinted to find the bird high in the endless blue. Then she looked around and discovered a whole new world.

"Where are we?" she whispered.

"About twelve, fifteen miles northwest of the LJ. And a couple miles off course for camp."

He shaded his eyes and glanced overhead, then looked down to check the length of his shadow.

"It's damn near noon. I'd suggest we stop and have a picnic under those trees, then hightail it back to where we're supposed to be. Everybody else is way ahead of us by now."

Ahead, behind, it didn't matter. She could see no one in any direction. Only grass and sky and the mountains that kept one from touching the other.

Wonder tinged her voice as she asked, "Why does it look so different here? The mountains are the same, and there are stretches on the road into town where you can't see a building, but it isn't the same."

"Maybe it's just knowing that when you get to the end of the road, there'll be a town. Out here, there isn't even a road."

Glory leaned over to look at the ground beneath Cleo's hooves. There was grass, thick and green and not even bruised by the passage of other horses ahead of them. Of a true road or even a well-worn path, there was no sign at all.

"Come on, let's have some lunch," Grant said with a chuckle.

After they had eaten a spare meal of dried beef and bread, she was the one who reminded him they had many miles yet to go, and time was wasting.

Grant remounted and waited until Glory was settled before he chirruped to Rusty and began the second leg of the day's ride.

He wouldn't have minded another hour or two under those cottonwoods. The past three weeks had been hard, physically and mentally, but they had had their compensations. There were days when he would gladly have strangled that obstinate, headstrong, determined creature who rode beside him now, only to find that her obstinacy grew on him like ivy on a stone wall, leaf by graceful leaf, so that by night, when they tumbled into bed, he could think of nothing but her. Being with her, staying with her, loving her until the end of forever.

It had to end, not because he wanted it to, but because he could see no way for it to continue. He had taught her all he could, and now it was just a matter of her applying that knowledge.

With experience added to what Grant had taught her, she'd be completely independent. He didn't like the idea at all.

She swung into her saddle and rode out of the cool shade of the cottonwoods.

"Lead the way," she ordered with an enthusiastic chuckle. "That's still one thing I can't do without you."

Grant responded with a chuckle of his own, thankful that the swish of the wind in the long grass covered up the note of bitterness.

The breeze died late in the afternoon, and the air turned crisp. Glory turned up her collar and pulled on her gloves long before Grant announced that he could see the encampment. By the time they rode into the haphazardly organized area, she could hardly wait to get a cup of hot coffee and huddle close to a roaring fire.

"Coffee can wait until after we take care of the horses," Grant reminded her.

He waited for any sound of grumbling, but she kept her gripes to herself. As usual, Glory took her job seriously and conscientiously rubbed the mare down before tying her to the picket line and seeing to it she had plenty to eat.

Grant strolled beside her as they left the horses and went in search of their own meal. The aroma of hot stew and dark bitter coffee was stirring Glory's stomach when Weed Usher approached her.

"Miz Johnson, I think you ought to come take a look at these corrals. They don't look in too good a shape to me," the foreman told her. He pointed to the temporary enclosures and Glory had no choice but to follow him to inspect them.

She didn't need Grant's opinion at all. Even in the fading daylight she could see how badly deteriorated the corrals were. They'd never hold frightened, angry cattle. Half the split rails were either missing or broken, and several posts had rotted in the damp earth until the pressure of drifted snow or a stormy wind snapped them off.

She kicked disgustedly at a fallen fence post and ordered, "Set up a three-man crew to get to work on this one first thing tomorrow, Weed." Then looking at the other two corrals, she added, "We don't have time or men enough to fix all three, so salvage what you can from the smaller of these to fix the others. After we're done, send a crew back out here to build a new one. Or maybe two. I'm not sure these will last until fall."

Grant said nothing as they walked through the twilight to the welcome brightness of the campfire. Someone had dragged a broken fencepost close to the stone-ringed blaze and Glory accepted the slightly lumpy seat as well as a plate of beans and stew that Old Ken handed her.

"Charley brought down a antelope buck," the cook explained while waiting for Glory to sample his creation. "Don't care for it myself, but most of the boys likes a change from beef or rabbit oncet in a while."

With her mouth full, Glory mumbled, "I don't think I'd care if you made it out of old saddle leather. I'm so hungry I could eat my own cooking and like it!"

They were halfway through the meal when Tom Cashion strode into the circle of firelight. The Diamond B's foreman pushed his hat back on his head and tossed a stone into the midst of the fire to raise a brilliant shower of sparks.

"When you get done here, boss, I need to talk to you."

"Something wrong?" Grant asked, knowing that there was.

"Naw, not really. Just need to go over a few instructions before I send the boys out tomorrow." Then Tom tipped his hat to Glory and turned away.

Grant took his tin plate and mug back to Old Ken, then with only the light of campfires to alleviate the pitch black night, made his way to the Diamond B encampment.

Tom and two other hands sat crosslegged on the ground around a dying fire, nursing last cups of coffee.

"Where the hell you been?" Tom asked quietly.

"I didn't want her to get nosy, so I took my time with supper and then came on over. Why? What's so damned important? And if it's that important, why didn't you just—"

"Keep your voice down," Tom warned, uncharacteristically sharp. "We got company."

"Company? Who?"

"Lonnie Hewitt."

Grant's breath of surprise whistled between his teeth.

Before he had a chance to make any comment, Tom continued.

"If I'd've known she was coming with you, I'd've told you sooner. We ran into him two weeks ago, him and a couple of friends."

"You don't sound like you approve of young Mr. Hewitt's aquaintances," Grant remarked.

"The Cooley brothers."

297

"I thought the Cooleys were in jail."

Tom shook his head.

"Nobody'd testify against 'em, and there wasn't any real evidence. So they've joined up with Lonnie, or he's joined up with them, and they're starting their own operation, hopin' to pick up some mavericks here and there."

Grant mulled over Tom's information before he said, "He's up to something. Lonnie Hewitt has never done an honest day's work in his life."

"That's what I been thinking. And you know, if he wanted to find strays, he'd have better pickings elsewhere. Hell, there's just not that many cattle this far from Cheyenne."

"I was thinking the same thing."

Jordy Finch tossed the dregs of his coffee onto the fire with a spit and sizzle, then untangled his long, skinny legs.

"I told Tom I'd keep an eye on Lonnie, if you want. He's still ridin' that paint horse and if somethin' was to happen . . ."

"You'd like to be there to lay claim to the paint," Grant finished. It's not my fight, he thought wearily. And yet I can't seem to stay out of it. "Yeah, it probably wouldn't be a bad idea to make sure Lonnie and his partners don't try to put their brand on somebody else's cattle," he conceded. "Just don't give him any excuse for a fight, hear? And that goes for you, too, Earl."

The fourth man on the far side of the campfire looked up, but there was no change in the expression on his weather-lined face. The scar that slanted across his left cheek gleamed an odd gold.

"I don't need to give him one; he owes me one already."

"He owes us all, Grant," Tom said.

Jordy and Earl left to bed down for the night, but Tom and Grant lingered. The last night had gone from the western sky, leaving a sheet of star-sprinkled blackness spread overhead. To the east, a pale yellow gold hovered

298

just below the horizon. In a few minutes, that glow would become a fat full moon, but at the moment, the only light came from the dying campfire.

Tom reached behind him for another stick of firewood and poked at the coals with it, then laid it carefully atop the glowing pile.

Grant finally broke the silence. "We've been friends too long," he said. "If you got something on your mind, spit it out. No hard feelings."

Whatever was bothering Tom was more serious than Lonnie Hewitt's return to this part of Wyoming and it required thought. Tom Cashion was like that: cautious of every word he spoke, unlike Grant. But perhaps that difference was what had kept them friends for so long, and through so much.

"We been wondering what's going on over at the LJ," he finally said. "I mean, most of the hands have been around long enough to know that if things had been different, the LJ and the Diamond B would be one operation. I guess that's what they want to know: Are you going after the LJ?"

It was a question Grant had asked himself several times over the past three weeks.

"To tell you the truth, Tom, I don't know."

"You were gonna buy it once, though, weren't you?"

The edge of the moon popped over the horizon, with a grove of trees sharply silhouetted against the growing crescent. Grant let his gaze rove over the campground as it became illuminated by the moonlight. Everything was so comfortably familiar, from the chuckwagons and the tight little bundles of cowboys wrapped in their bedrolls to the horses sleeping on their tethers and the outline of the corrals in the background. He had taken it all for granted for so many years, expecting it to go on and on, unchanged, for the rest of his life. Now everything, familiar as it was, had taken on a new aspect, moving into the unfocused future.

"When I found out Lee had left the place to his wife,

yeah, I offered to take it off her hands. I figured I'd give it to Matthew."

"And now?"

"Now? Hell, I don't know."

"Would you buy it if she was willing to sell?"

Grant looked sharply at Tom, but the foreman never took his attention from the fire. He added more wood and the flames rose higher.

"Yeah, probably."

"But that isn't really what you want to do, is it. You want her to hang onto it. Least, that's what it looks like, all the help you've been giving her."

Grant had to laugh at himself.

"I have neglected the Diamond B, haven't I? Thank God for good friends and good foremen."

At that, Tom smiled, though he still didn't look at Grant.

"Nothing came up that we couldn't handle, though it's good to have you back, boss. That is, if you're really back?"

The wood on the fire popped, and a shift of the very soft nighttime breeze brought the sparks toward the men around its perimeter. Grant brushed several off his arms, but one burned through his dungarees before he could put it out. He stood, and so did Tom, and finally the foreman let his steady eyes meet Grant's.

"I don't want to see you get burned any worse'n that, boss. And I think you're awful close to the fire."

"Do you think Matthew's wrist is as good as he says it is?" Glory asked over breakfast in the predawn darkness the next morning. She had been worrying about the boy constantly, despite all of Grant's efforts to reassure her, and now that all the hands were up and readying their horses to begin the real work of the roundup, she was looking for additional reassurances.

"I wouldn't let him go if I didn't. He's been roping for

300

almost a week now with no pain or stiffness."

"I hope you're right. You certainly were right about the chuckwagon. It's a wonder someone wasn't killed when that wheel broke."

"If anything breaks now, it won't be the wheel. We went over every inch of that contraption."

Every inch and then some, he recalled with disgust. While Old Ken stood around and grumbled that the chuckwagon had been good enough last fall for Lee, Grant and Matthew had labored all day, replacing dry rotted floor boards, greasing axles, repairing the two wheels that were salvageable, and using the other two for kindling after new ones had been installed. The canvas roofed conveyance still smelled of new lumber and axle grease, which prompted more complaints from Old Ken. He took his time reloading his supplies and utensils, until in frustration Grant pitched in to help with that chore, too.

Finally, under the light of an almost full moon, he had hitched two stout mules to the wagon and tied Matthew's mount behind, so the boy could accompany Old Ken to the campsite.

The gesture had puzzled Glory at the time, and in the hectic flurry of last minute preparations, she hadn't had a chance to ask for an explanation.

"You certainly do have the magic touch when it comes to handling Matthew," she commented. "If I had suggested he ride in the chuckwagon, he'd have balked like a mule. He hates being treated like a child."

Grant chuckled and popped the last bite of biscuit into his mouth.

"Being sent out ahead to set up camp is hardly being treated like a child. Besides," he admitted, "I told him to make sure he stayed in the wagon just until they got out of sight, and then he could ride."

"You mean you let him head out in this desolate country alone?" Glory had a sudden urge to tell the man he had sent his own son into the wilderness, but she bit

301

her tongue just in time. If he already knew, as she suspected he did, she wasn't going to give away her own knowledge. And if on the slim chance he didn't yet know, now was not the time to tell him. "Grant, he's only a boy."

"I know that. He also has Old Ken with him, who is an experienced hand with a rifle as well as a stewpot. Matthew has his own rifle, just in case, and—"

"I thought I told you before I don't want him carrying a gun. He's not old enough."

"If he's old enough to help on the roundup, he's old enough to carry a gun. This is Wyoming, my dear, not a Philadelphia drawing room."

For the thousandth time in the past few weeks, Glory had to admit Grant was right. But the idea of Matthew with a gun rankled. So did the knowledge that Grant had gone behind her back and given the boy permission to do something they both knew she would have forbidden.

Now, however, was not the time to argue. The hands from the LJ, the Diamond B, and several other outfits that had cattle on this same range were already mounting up and getting orders from their foremen. Grant got to his feet and walked up to Tom Cashion.

Glory took advantage of that break in their conversation to stand up and stretch the stiffness from her back. Sleeping on the ground was far from the exciting adventure she had imagined. Her shoulder and hip were sore enough to be bruised, and she was still so tired that she was certain she had never really slept a wink.

She took her dishes back to the chuckwagon, where Old Ken was too busy to talk to anyone, and then she headed for the picket line. Today she'd be riding a trim sorrel gelding named String, for his rather unglorious tail. He stood patiently while she saddled him and slipped the bit between his teeth, and he put up only token resistance to her mounting.

Yesterday's ride had left Glory just a bit tender, but she dismissed the discomfort and turned the horse in the direction where she had last seen Grant and Tom.

The entire camp was bathed in an eerie gloaming that made it hard for her to see very far. Lanterns lit on wagons and hung in trees shed flickering circles of light in the midst of dark. Shadows of moving horses and riders, and the pall of woodsmoke further distorted the scene until it seemed as grotesque as a nightmare.

Finally, Glory saw them, gathered in a circle under the light of a lantern mounted high in the branches of a towering cottonwood. She was about to call out to Grant, but something about the way he sat on his horse forced her to bite back the cry and pull String to a nervous halt.

Weed had joined them, as had Steve Peake and several other ranchers Glory recognized from the Christmas Eve party, though she couldn't remember all their names. Everyone seemed rather excited, which she put down to the first day of the roundup and the eagerness to get on with the most important work of the year.

She had to wait a moment while one of the numerous supply wagons lumbered between the picket line and the gathering that Grant seemed to have taken charge of. He said something, inaudible above the din of the campground, and the others nodded.

Then a man astride a fractious roan gestured into the gloomy distance, and the others followed his indication. Glory, too, strained to see what he pointed at.

Lonnie Hewitt rode jauntily into the lantern-lit circle.

Chapter Twenty-Two

"Howdy," Lonnie greeted.

Only silence answered him, until Grant said, "We got work to do, Lonnie. We'll be getting on our way."

He and the others turned their horses sharply and the circle disappeared, leaving only the man on the painted horse in the lantern's light.

Glory watched him, secure in the shadows where she knew he couldn't see her. She hardly recognized him. His clothes were battered, his once white Stetson hat stained and limp, his boots worn and scuffed. He wore a beard now, shaggy and unkempt. Even the painted horse looked down at heel. Glory felt a rush of pity for the man who had apparently hit the bottom of a long downward slide.

She considered riding out of her shadowed sanctuary to attempt a reconciliation. Surely in his present situation, Lonnie would be more amenable to a reasonable settlement. But just as Glory was about to nudge her horse forward, Grant rode up beside her. She didn't like the scowl on his features.

"I saw him," she said.

"Saw who?"

"Lonnie. And don't tell me you didn't know he was around here," she warned, then asked accusingly, "How long have you known?"

As they left the encampment and headed out onto the

trackless range in search of cattle, he told her everything he knew, including the tale of the Cooley brothers being arrested for rustling and then released. Every word he uttered rang with suspicions.

There was so much he had kept from her. Why? Hadn't he thought her capable of handling the truth? She had stood up to Lonnie more than once, and indeed it was she who had devised the scheme to thwart his move to gain possession of the ranch.

When Grant had finished, it was as though Glory needed time to digest everything he had told her. She rode on in silence.

Later, when she might have talked to him about her thoughts and feelings, there was too much work to be done. Cows with calves had to be flushed out of hiding and driven back to the corrals, where they were sorted by the mother's brand and taken to the appropriate crew for branding.

Grant had explained it all before, but there was no explanation that could prepare her for the brutality, the blood as bull calves were castrated, the stench of burned hair and hide. She reminded herself that this was part of the business of ranching. As long as folks back east clamored for western beef, this would be part of it.

The work was hard, and when Glory demanded to participate, she met with stiff resistance. But Grant was called away to attend to some problem with the Diamond B, and she took advantage of his absence to assert her authority.

Several times during the next hours, she came very close to regretting that decision.

A particularly stubborn heifer calf fought like a maddened bull when, legs wrapped securely, she was thrown to the ground to have the LJ brand burned into the flesh of her hip. Glory threw her weight against the animal's shoulder, but it wasn't enough. The calf managed to get one foreleg free and struck out, hitting her owner on the thigh with that sharp little hoof.

306

"Damn!" Glory cried out, rolling off the calf into the dust. She knelt, both hands pressed to the area of impact, and rocked back and forth as the pain raced through her. Tears beyond her control streamed down her face.

"Get her out of here!" someone ordered. "Damn woman's got no business brandin' calves."

That was all she needed to hear. The tears didn't stop, nor did the pain, but Glory crawled back to the kicking heifer and once again leaned on the animal's shoulder. Sheer determination not to be bested by a dumb creature gave her the agility to grab the flailing foreleg and the strength to hold it still.

"Get a rope on this damn thing!" she hollered. "And give me that iron. I'll let this one know who's boss of the LJ!"

She reached out a leather-gloved hand to take the red-hot branding iron from one of the new LJ cowboys. He was young, and puzzled, and he wasn't sure if he should hand over the iron to her or not. So she grabbed it and gave him a withering scowl.

Taking no chances, she plunged the heavy wrought iron into the fire once more before bringing it to the heifer's flank. The animal let out a horrified bawl and thrashed as the scent of its own flesh burning reached its sensitive nostrils. Glory, too, shuddered, and a nasty taste rose at the back of her throat that she swallowed stiffly down.

As another of the cowboys set the heifer free, Glory limped back to the fire and set the iron once again to heat. No one clapped her on the back or even asked her how her leg felt. No one said much of anything. But no one called her a damned woman again.

By late afternoon, when Glory found time to strip off her filthy clothes and bathe in the creek, the bruise was a mottled black shadow against the smooth flesh of her thigh. Wrapped in a coarse towel and shivering from the icy water, she sat down on the bank to examine the injury. At the slightest touch, the muscle beneath the skin jerked convulsively. She had ignored the pain through the afternoon, but now she could no longer push it out of her consciousness.

"How bad is it?" Grant asked as he squatted down beside her. "Mmm, nasty. And you'd better get dressed quick, or you are gonna freeze your backside."

"I'm gonna freeze more than just my backside. Here, hand me that blanket. I can't even get dressed until I warm up a little more."

He helped to wrap her in the coarse wool blanket and then rubbed her gently to speed the circulation that would bring warmth back into her chilled limbs. He wished he dared resort to another method of raising her body temperature, but this was neither the time nor the place.

"I suggest you take it easy tomorrow," he chided. "Give that leg a rest."

"Would you let a little bruise stop you from working?"

The challenge in her eyes brought a satisfied smile to his mouth.

"Damn right, I would. Even if it was on my own leg."

He jumped out of the way of her flying hand just in time. She was on her feet almost as quickly as he, but the shooting stab of pain in her thigh stopped her dead in her tracks. She crumpled, a pitiful little heap of tangled brown hair and wool blanket on the grassy bank of a gurgling cold stream.

As a peace offering, Grant handed her her clothes.

"I beat most of the dust out of them," he said as she stuck out a bare arm and snatched the garments out of his grasp.

Under the blanket, she wriggled her still wet body into the dry but not very clean clothes.

"You know, I can't help but think you did all this on purpose," she muttered just loud enough for Grant to hear. "I don't know how you could get a calf to kick me,

308

but I'm sure that if there's a way, you'd figure it out."

"Madame, you do me a grave injustice," he mocked, clapping his hat to his heart. Enough dust rose to make him sneeze. "Besides, though I admit I'd just as soon not have you wrestling calves, I wouldn't do anything that would hurt you. Why do you think I insisted on tagging along when you *had* to have a bath?"

She didn't say anything. They had seen Lonnie too many times during the day not to suspect that he was waiting for some special opportunity.

"Because you like seeing me naked," she grumbled through chattering teeth. She had the shirt on and buttoned, but the trousers were not cooperating at all. There was no alternative but to shrug off the blanket and pull the damn things up.

"Oh, that I do, Glory, that I do. But not out here where I can't do anything about it."

He hadn't really seen her anyway. Politely, because she asked him, he had turned his back as she peeled off her dirty clothes and headed for the water. He tried to focus his vision on a bush or a clump of grass, but in the fading light everything blurred. In his mind, however, he saw her as he had seen her so many times before, and the memory was as potent as the reality.

He wondered how he'd survive out here with her and not go crazy with the wanting.

He also wondered how she managed to control her own desires so completely. There had been nights at the LJ when she had been as impatient for Matthew to fall asleep as he had been. It was silly, they both knew, to keep up pretenses when the boy couldn't possibly not know what was going on, but they still waited until he was asleep before hurrying up the stairs themselves.

Even on the nights when they had been so tired they fell asleep almost the instant their heads hit the pillows, there was that unspoken acknowledgement of desire. A squeeze of their hands was enough, or sometimes Glory just curled into a tired little ball, her back to his chest, his thighs against her bottom, and he kissed her unruly hair with his last breath of consciousness.

Tonight he might have been a ladies' maid in cap and apron for all the notice she gave him, taking first the towel and then the blanket and finally her clothes from his outstretched hand. And tonight, for some strange reason, he wanted her more than ever.

"You better hurry if you want supper. Nobody saves anything for latecomers, and it's likely to be gone by the time you get your duds on."

"I'm done, I'm done. Almost."

She sat on the grass, her left leg stretched straight out in front of her, bootless. The right leg was bent, the boot half on while she pounded her foot on the ground.

"Wouldn't it be easier if you stood up and just stomped your foot in?"

She twisted her head to give him a disgusted look.

"Yes, if I could. But I can't stand on the left leg while I pound the right one, and I can't—"

"I see." He scratched his chin. She sat still, looking up at him, waiting. "I think I've got an idea."

He leaned down and grabbed her upper arms and pulled her to her feet. The jolt brought a gasp of pain from her.

"Sorry. Here, let me have that arm, and we can go over closer to the tree. Can you make it?"

One boot half on, the other forgotten, Glory grimaced with each hobbling step as the muscle knotted in protest. Grant slipped one arm behind her to take as much of her weight as he could, but she still hesitated before each step. Though the huge old cottonwood couldn't be more than five yards away, it felt like a mile.

"What good is the tree going to do?" she asked. Though chilled from her bath, she began to feel sweat on her forehead. There was an odd ringing in her ears, too, and she hoped the burning in her eyes wasn't the start of tears. The leg did hurt, but she'd be damned if she'd let him know just how much.

310

"Just sit down, and I'll show you." When she turned to lean her back against the rough bark, he told her, "No, not that way. Put your feet to the trunk, and scoot up close. I'll get your other boot."

How, she wondered with a silent groan, would she ever get through tomorrow with such agony? A good night's sleep would have to make an improvement, and if it didn't, well, she'd have to think of a way to endure.

The boot plopped down beside her, but she didn't see Grant. Instead, she felt him. He sat down behind her, his back close against hers.

"Put the boot on, and then push against the tree. That oughta do it."

It did. And more.

He swore, loudly and explicitly.

Swearing didn't help. Especially when the woman whose back was pressed quite firmly to his began to wiggle against him.

"Such language!" she exclaimed. "Grant, could you get up? You've got me so close to this tree I can't get my feet under me."

He glanced skyward, partly in vain supplication and partly to check on the progress the sun was making in setting. If he couldn't get himself under control, he didn't dare walk back into camp with his lust so blatant.

He grunted and got stiffly to his feet, then reached down to pull Glory up, too. She didn't give him her hand readily. Only after she struggled with the knot of annoying pain in her thigh did she admit defeat and grasp his assistance. Standing a bit unsteadily, she used her free hand to slap the dirt and grass from the backs of her legs and the seat of her pants.

"I'm ready when you are," she said, testing the left leg to see if she'd be able to walk the half a dozen steps to her horse unaided.

He didn't say anything; he didn't move. He couldn't. Her hand was still in his, and the feeling was akin to what he'd expect if he suddenly grabbed onto a lightning bolt.

The setting sun bathed her in a radiance that took his breath away. With her head turned to check for any remaining debris stuck to her clothes, she was completely unaware of his scrutiny, and for that he was grateful.

A strand of damp hair clung to the line of her jaw; another curled in a corkscrew on her temple. He longed to kiss it and let his tongue trace the silken spiral until he reached the sensitive whorls of her ear. She had pinned the mass of her hair onto the top of her head to keep it from getting wet while she bathed, but the short curls at the back of her neck still dripped tiny droplets onto the collar of her shirt. Glittering in the golden rays of the sun, those droplets quickened Grant's thirst.

"We've time yet," he whispered. He lifted her other hand in his and drew her closer.

"Grant, for heaven's sake, someone could see us!"

"Everyone's chowing down now," he insisted. She smelled of sunshine and icy clear mountain water, of dust and cattle, of sweat and wet wool and woman. "No one will bother us."

"But you said you were hungry, and they won't save anything for us if we're late."

He drew her up against him and wrapped his arms around her with his hands clasped at the small of her back. She sought his arousal instinctively, with no encouragement from him. Her body molded to his almost as though she were not aware of it. But the deepening glow in her eyes told him she was indeed aware.

"Grant, please, no, not here," she begged. Her plea sounded hollow even to her own ears, and her voice had gone husky and rich with the desire she fought to quell.

He slipped his hands under the edge of her jacket, into welcome and welcoming warmth. Bewildered, he shook his head before planting a loud, irreverent kiss on her forehead.

"If ever a woman said 'no' when she really meant 'yes,' that was it," he said with a rueful chuckle. "I swear, Glory Johnson, it doesn't do a man a lick of good to try to figure you out. Hell, even now, you're all hot and moving up against me."

She jumped back out of his loosened embrace, but her leg simply wouldn't hold her. She started to fall, only to be caught once more in his arms.

She looked up into those eyes of tempered steel.

"I want you, Glory," Grant whispered to her as he lifted her to her toes and then completely off the ground. "I want you here and now, whether we're alone or every cowpuncher from Montana to Texas is watching us. I want you so bad it hurts, and I can't seem to stop wanting you." His lips brushed her forehead, whispered across her eyebrows, murmured silences against her lowered lids. "And I know you want me, so there's no use denying it."

Once again, her feet made contact with solid earth, but nothing else did. She turned her mouth up for his kiss, hard, demanding, devouring. Tongues and breaths mingled frantically, even teeth met as if in an effort of two souls to join together completely. Arms and shoulders, chests and bellies and thighs and knees pushed at each other; hands and fingers grabbed and grasped and stroked and clung.

All in vain. Breathless, Glory broke the bond that held her body tight to his and opened her eyes. A cry of surprise, of fear, of recognition rose in her throat and nearly escaped before she clamped her hand over her mouth. She ran, limping, away from the man who stood, arms still raised in an echo of an embrace, and stared after her.

She untied her horse and, with tears of pain and a much deeper hurt streaming down her cheeks, pulled herself into the saddle. The sky had turned from gold to crimson, and all the wide world was in shadow. The lights of campfires and lanterns flickered in the distance, guiding her to the relative safety she sought.

Grant watched her ride away from him. Slowly, he forced his body to forget the sweet pain. Each deep breath of air, cooler now with the dying of the day, brought another measure of control back to him. He walked to his horse and mounted, satisfied that no physical trace of the woman's effect on him remained. But he knew, in the yawning hollow of his gut, that the desire would return. Indeed, the desire had never left him.

"How did they die?" Glory asked the next morning.

Weed shrugged his bony shoulders and turned his lanky grey gelding away from the nearly meatless carcasses. The brands on the scavenger-gnawed flanks were barely distinguishable as an interlocked L and J.

"Winter kill. Happens all the time."

Glory shuddered. Grant had warned her that she'd encounter dead cattle on the range, but once again, words hadn't prepared her for the reality.

"And if the calves survived, they're free for the taking, aren't they?"

Weed apparently hadn't heard. To him, a dead cow was just a pile of bones and hide and hair. To Glory, the loss was more personal and more far-reaching. She kicked Cleo and hurried to catch up to Weed.

Her bruised leg gave her little trouble except for some stiffness. She was able to forget the injury completely for long stretches. Other memories were much more persistent, despite the work Weed and Matthew put her to.

With his wrist fully recovered, Matthew proved invaluable. His skill with a rope couldn't be equaled by any other cowboy on the LJ crew. And he seemed to have an instinct for where a protective cow would hide her offspring. He was the first to comment about the dead cattle later that day when Glory and Weed stopped to rest their horses and swallow a quick lunch.

Still sitting on his horse, the boy gulped a long swig from his canteen and then splashed some on his face.

"It don't make sense," he said. "Weed, how many cows you count dead so far?"

314

The foreman shoved his hat back on his head and spread his fingers out in front of him.

"Let's see. Two back on that ridge, one by the rocks, one in the gully, another two or three maybe, I forget just where."

"And all cows."

Weed nodded.

Glory asked, "How can you tell?"

"Size, especially of the head. And another thing. You'd expect some carcasses to be really stripped, nothing but bones left, and some to be fresher, like they was weak after late calving or something. All the ones I seen so far are in about the same condition, like they all died about the same time."

They were interrupted by Young Ken, who hollered for help with a sizeable herd of cows and calves, more than one man could handle for the trip back to camp.

"Strangest thing," the cowhand told his foreman and Glory when the cattle had at last been driven into the corrals. "You count them cows? There was twenty-one of 'em. That's a lot to be in one spot."

"What kind of a spot was it?" Matthew asked.

"Nice sheltered little draw, with a spring. But that ain't the strange part."

As though some mystical power drew them, several other cowboys drifted to the picket line where Ken, Matthew, Weed, and Glory tended their horses. It had taken them too much of the afternoon to drive the cattle back to camp to be able to head out again, and Glory was grateful for the early end to the day's work.

"Twenty-two cows, but thirty calves, that's what's strange," Ken said. A ripple of whispered speculation rose from the small crowd gathered. "And it looked like they'd been there for quite a while."

"With shelter and water, why wouldn't they stay?" Glory wanted to know.

Matthew snorted "Cows ain't that smart."

"Besides, they'd ate most of the grass," Ken added. Then, as if he suddenly decided against telling his whole story to an audience, he said, "Look, we better help out with them calves if we want to get done tonight."

Glory's questions and suspicions found no resolution that afternoon or that night. First there was work to attend to, and supper, and then, utterly exhausted, she sought the meager comfort of her bedroll. She had not seen Grant since early morning, and even then he had not spoken to her. All day she had thought of him.

Nightfall brought no relief. Men talked around the campfires, cattle bawled, horses stomped and whinnied even in their sleep, and the creatures of the wilderness contributed their voices to the symphony. Unable to sleep, Glory tried to make sense out of the odd events of the past two days.

Logic told her there was no connection. Cattle did occasionally die. Perhaps a storm had killed an unusual number of them at the same time. After all, there had been plenty of storms during the past few weeks, including a freak blizzard.

But if the cows had died, why not the calves? That they hadn't died seemed obvious, from Ken's tally of livestock in the draw. More calves than cows, and even Glory knew that cattle rarely bore twins.

She watched for Grant, but saw no sign of him. Most of the Diamond B hands had come back to camp, including Tom Cashion, who had taken charge of the ruffian who started the fight. Grant, she concluded, must have wandered far afield and could just as easily have bedded down out on the open range.

He might indeed have deliberately done so, after the incident at the creek. Remembering, Glory shifted position, but there was no way to escape the discomfort of lying on hard ground—alone.

He had gotten used to her. That was the only possible explanation for the way Grant had reacted. Two weeks of making love nightly had accustomed him to the delightful luxury, and the habit refused to be broken easily. It had been the same with Melody: the more he had her, the more he wanted her.

Riding into camp long after nearly everyone else was asleep, he greeted the men on night watch and quickly took care of his horse. It was his own fault there was nothing to eat. He could put the blame on the trail of several head of cattle he had followed further than good sense dictated, only to have them turn out to be cleanly branded Rocking 4 steers, but the truth was that he had headed as far from camp as possible. He had to avoid that stubborn, irritating, exasperating, and totally irresistible woman until he had regained his immunity.

It was safely too late to worry abut running into Glory now. She'd be long asleep. He ignored the laughter of his conscience when he decided his only reason for strolling through the camp to the LJ chuckwagon was to make sure she had indeed bedded down there.

Where else would she be? that little voice inside asked him. *Sleeping with one of the cowboys?*

He didn't like the twinge of naked jealousy that raced through him at that thought. It reminded him of the way he felt whenever he had thought of Melody and Lee.

Though the night was mild for this time of year, the ground still held winter's chill. Grant found Glory curled on her side, the blankets drawn up to her chin. Just looking at her, asleep, sent desire's unmistakable warmth to his loins and he knew he should seek his own bed. Something kept him rooted to the spot, his bedroll slung over his shoulder, and then she rolled over.

"Is that you, Grant?"

He dropped the bedroll beside her and began spreading it out.

"Who else?"

"I was worried about you. Did something happen?"

He caught the reflection of firelight in her open eyes.

"Nothing except that I trailed somebody else's cows halfway to Canada."

"Oh. Well, I'm glad you're back safely."

He called himself a thousand kinds of fool for making his bed right beside her. She was fully dressed, as was he, and they were surrounded by half a hundred cowboys, including several who were wide awake and listening for anything out of the ordinary. What would be more out of the ordinary in a roundup camp than the sounds of a man making very passionate love to a woman?

But nothing, not logic or the laughter of an outraged conscience, stopped him. He lay down and pulled his blankets over himself, then turned toward her warmth.

She was asleep. Sound asleep.

His own laughter was mixed with a groan, but underneath both lay an odd satisfaction. It was almost as if she had waited up, unable to sleep until reassured of his safety.

With tangled blankets and several layers of clothing between them, he took her into his arms and buried his face in her hair. Getting unused to her was going to be damn hard.

Instinct wakened Grant long before the first birds heralded the dawn. His eyes were accustomed enough to the dark that he had little trouble making his way to the edge of the camp area to relieve himself. After emptying his bladder, he realized his stomach was even emptier. It rumbled loudly in the morning stillness.

He was about to head for the chuckwagon to search out some grub when another rumbling sound caught his attention.

He'd heard it often enough before to recognize snoring. But none of his men or the LJ boys were bedded down out here, away from the security of campfires.

The hair at the back of Grant's neck rose. His hand slid instinctively for his gun, but it wasn't there. He had left it with his bedroll, never thinking he'd need the protection of a firearm while he went to the bushes to piss.

He listened closely, and located the source of the snores no more than ten feet to his left.

318

Three slow, stealthy strides brought him to the sleeper. It was too dark yet to identify the man, who lay sprawled on his back with one arm thrown up over his eyes. Grant was about to nudge the poor fellow, when he spotted the man's hat a few feet away. With no light to reveal the stains, the hat glowed whiter in the dark than in daylight, and one silver concho reflected the faint shine of stars.

Grant swallowed convulsively. Lonnie Hewitt had no business being in camp, and less business sleeping twenty-five feet from Glory Johnson.

Neither of them said a word the next morning. Glory remembered that she had confessed her worry to Grant, and it wasn't something she wanted to discuss. She didn't even like thinking about it, or about the way he had lain beside her and taken comfortable possession of her.

For his part, Grant kept silent about Lonnie's presence. He wasn't about to give Glory anything else to lose sleep over.

Three days later, they both knew she had something far more important to worry about.

"That's not winter kill," Grant announced as he dismounted and knelt to examine the remains of another dead cow.

"How can you tell?"

"It's too recent, for one thing. Two, three days is all this cow's been dead. Scavengers have done a pretty good job picking it clean, but it's still intact. I expect, however, the real reason isn't going to be hard to find."

Using his knife, he scraped around in the moist soil under what had been the cow's shoulder. It wasn't long before the blade encountered something that rang with a dull metallic sound. Grant probed in the grass and held up his discovery, a dark, shapeless lump no larger than the end of a man's thumb.

"She was shot."

He remounted, and they rode on in silence.

319

There was no way to tell what brand the dead cow had borne, but Glory couldn't help remember the two she had seen the first day of the roundup, and she knew this one was an LJ cow as well. Two weeks ago, that same animal had had a calf trotting alongside her, a calf that could now be claimed by any cowboy on the range.

They found several more carcasses that day, enough that Glory learned the grisly details by which to distinguish old bones from new, winter kill from slaughter. The latter seemed all too common.

Day by day, the tally mounted higher, not only of calves branded and added to the asset side of the LJ's ledger, but of dead animals. There were plenty of yearling steers to be fattened for the fall consignment to St. Louis, but far fewer calves than expected.

When Glory lingered one evening over the books she had just made her entries in, Matthew strolled up and asked her what was the problem.

"We don't have all the calves I expected," she told him. "Even allowing for winter kill based on the figures Lee entered last year, we should have a lot more. I can't even account for all the cows."

"Talk to Grant about it," Matthew suggested.

If she hadn't had six months of suspicions behind her, Grant was exactly the person she'd go to. After that first day there'd been no sign of Lonnie, but that didn't mean he wasn't out there.

"No, this is our problem, not his. Anyway, we've taken advantage of him long enough. It's time we were on our own."

She fully intended to tell Grant exactly that the next day. And if they hadn't found another slaughtered cow, she would have.

The carcass lay at the bottom of a gully. The squawks and screeches of feeding vultures drew Grant's attention, or he would never have spotted the remains.

"Wait here," he ordered Glory. "I'll climb down and

320

see if she fell or if something else happened."

Holding the reins to his horse, she whispered, "Be careful."

He shook his head and laughed out loud in the growing dark. Matthew had been right. Glory was nothing like the boy's mother.

Chapter Twenty-Three

The roundup was almost over. Most of the livestock was being moved to summer pasture, which meant a good portion of the cowpunchers had left the camp, too. Thinking Matthew had ridden out with Glory and Weed, Grant was surprised to see the boy tending the horses.

"How come you're not out bringing in cows?" he asked, leaning against a tree.

"We're gettin' ready to go home," Matthew answered.

He checked over the sorrel gelding carefully, keeping the horse between himself and Grant.

"Look, Matthew, I know it's been hard for you, harder probably than for me and Glory put together. But damn it, boy, we used to be friends. What's gotten into you that you won't talk to me?"

"Nothing's wrong with me. It's her that's crazy."

Well, that was a start. As Matthew walked up, Grant ventured to put his arm around the boy's shoulders. For once, he didn't shake the gesture off.

"She took off real early with Weed, if you're wondering where she is."

Grant nodded agreeably and said, "Yeah, I was. You know where they went?"

"If you want to follow her, no, I don't know exactly. But I know what she wanted him to show her."

They were walking away from the camp, toward the

creek where Glory had bathed that first night almost two weeks ago. Grant had to force himself not to remember.

"Tell me everything," he urged.

"Even though she told me not to?"

Matthew's shifting loyalty surprised Grant.

"Especially if she told you not to."

"Okay, but only because I think she's dead wrong."

The boy eyed Grant suspiciously but went on anyway.

"She told me yesterday about the cow you found, the one that was shot. She was really upset, kind of scared but mostly just plain mad."

"At me?"

"At herself mostly, but at you, too, I think. She told Weed this morning she was tired of being so ignorant that people could lie to her and get away with it. Then she ordered him to take her out to the canyon where they found all those extra calves."

"Extra calves? What 'extra' calves?"

"You can see for yourself, Miz Johnson. There's the brush he used for a fence."

The earth in the narrow fold between two hills had been stripped of vegetation. Some grass was growing back, but the ground had been packed so hard that even weeds had trouble germinating. And everywhere were the signs of bovine habitation. The place looked and smelled like a barnyard.

Glory scowled. "So all he had to do was kill the cows and bring the calves here. But you found cows, too. I don't understand that part of it at all."

"Well, it'd look pretty strange if he showed up with a whole bunch of calves and not a single cow."

"But you found only LJ cattle here. Why would he steal only my livestock?"

Weed didn't give her the answer she expected, but his made much more sense.

"If he planned to change the cows' brands with a

running iron, he had to have all the same." Weed broke a branch off a nearby shrub and squatted down to scratch a simple design in the dry, bare earth. "I wouldn'ta thought of it, hadn't been for Matthew askin' me about the new brand. See, the LJ brand is like this, the 'L' higher than the 'J' so's they overlap."

She recognized the intersecting letters Weed drew in the dirt as the figure that was burned into the hide of every animal she owned.

"Well, yesterday Matthew wanted to know if there was some reason for his Uncle Lonnie to be usin' a Rocking 4 brand, when there's only him and the two Cooley brothers. At first I told him it was probably 'cause they had another brother who got hanged for stealin' horses, but then I got to thinkin' about it, and I think it's for a whole 'nother reason."

By extending the top of the "J" to the height of the "L," and duplicating the lower portion of the "J" on the other side, Weed created a numeral "4" with a curve under it, like the rocker on a rocking chair.

It was a very simple matter to transform the LJ brand into the Rocking 4.

Glory and Weed returned to the camp to find it much changed. Old Ken had the LJ chuckwagon packed up, with the mules sleeping in the traces. One of the new hands had the horses ready and waiting for the return trek to the LJ.

There was no sign of anyone from the Diamond B.

"They left about two hours ago," Matthew told her.

She glanced skyward to gauge the time. It was well past noon, but the days had already grown longer. She had plenty of time.

"I'll catch up to them," she promised. "No, you don't need to come with me, Matthew. Three dozen men can't be too hard to follow."

The boy hollered after her, predicting all kinds of

accidents if she took off on her own, but Glory ignored his warnings. She dug her heels into Cleo's sides and sent the long-legged buckskin racing across the range.

The trail was indeed easy to follow, and it wasn't long before Glory could see the cloud of dust raised by the horses. It hung in the still, warm spring air.

She kicked Cleo again and breathed, "Wait for me, Grant," as the mare stretched out into a dead run.

Atop a low rise, Grant watched and waited, his heart hammering in his chest. She was a fool to push the mare like that, but it didn't matter. He was glad she felt the same impatience he did.

"Hurry, Glory, hurry," he whispered.

Slowing Cleo to a lazy lope and then a walk, Glory rode up to the man silhouetted against the sky. She said nothing, just took in the wonderful sight of him, the welcoming smile he offered her.

"I couldn't leave without talking to you," Grant said after a long silence. "Tom's madder'n hell at me, but he'll get over it."

Glory laughed, still trying to catch her breath.

"Matthew's not too happy either, and Weed was calling me names again. Oh, Grant, we've got to talk. I can't go on like this."

Her eyes glittered, catching the golden glow of the westering sun, and when she turned her face up to the rising breeze, she licked her lips as though some wonderful taste lay there in memory. The wanting was plain in her face. Grant wondered if his was equally obvious.

"There's a spot down there, by the river. We can be there in an hour."

Her answer was a barely perceptible nod of her head.

They rode without speaking, down into the shallow river valley. Here, shadows lengthened even further, and the air took on a shimmering quality as the sunlight slanted through it. The horses plodded slowly, their hoofbeats muted by the thick grass. Neither Grant nor Glory seemed inclined to hurry.

He stole a sidelong glance at her, struck not for the first time by what he saw. Without the attributes of classic beauty, Glory Johnson was still beautiful. Weeks in the sun and wind had turned her fair skin a rich gold, even bringing out a dusting of freckles across her nose and on her cheekbones.

And that hair! What was a man to make of it? It swirled about her face, over her shoulders, and down her back in curls as wild and free as an evening breeze. Grant reached out, across the space between their horses, and fingered an errant strand.

"You're right," he said almost gruffly as the golden filaments slid out of his grasp and floated beyond his reach. "We have to talk. Now."

They had reached the river's edge. Here the grass was thick but short, a perfect place to kindle a fire and spread a couple of blankets. Though the sky was still bright with sunlight, stars would soon stud a moonless backdrop.

"This is as good a place to camp as any," Grant said while he dismounted.

The idea of spending the night alone with him left her feeling an odd combination of exhilaration and fear.

"I'll water the horses and stake them," she suggested. "Is there enough wood for a fire?"

"Plenty on that dead tree."

This wasn't the kind of talking he meant. Gathering firewood and ringing stones to contain it were essential tasks that must be completed while there was enough light to see. Still, he couldn't go without some appeasement for the desire building within him.

She stood between the two horses, holding the reins competently in her small hands. Thus occupied, she was helpless to avoid the kiss he planted on her surprise-parted lips.

He did not even cup her chin in his hand to hold her still; only his mouth touched her. Yet that simple contact worked like red-hot iron to brand her as his. When he broke the connection, it left her breathless, and disappointed.

"I want you, Glory," he whispered.

His silver eyes searched hers, looking for passion as undeniable as his own.

"I want you, too."

By the time they had made camp, the last sunlight was dying on the tops of the mountains. The sky to the east already glittered with stars. Grant's fire crackled merrily, sending curls of smoke and sparks into the darkening night. Two fat trout sizzled on an improvised spit over the flames.

"The fish will be burned to a crisp," Glory said as another piece of wood popped and flames licked closer to the trout. She lay back on the blanket and linked her hands behind her head.

Grant emphatically denied her worries.

"Not a chance. After what I went through to catch those damn things, I'm not about to let them burn up."

He turned the spit and then, with a long sigh of utter contentment, lay down beside Glory.

Propped on one elbow, he stared at her, holding back words that strained to escape. It had been a long time since he had told a woman he loved her, and that declaration had only led to unbearable pain. The question crossed his mind too, was he sure this was really love? It sure as hell didn't feel like what he had felt before. But he couldn't put any other name to it.

"Are you going to say something or just look at me all night?" Glory asked.

Her voice, quiet in the vast wilderness of silence that surrounded them, had broken one spell, but in doing so, it cast another. Freed of the enchantment that held him immobile while he searched for answers to questions he dared not ask, Grant willingly gave in to the magic of desire.

"I want you," his lips murmured against hers. Moving to kiss her cheek, he whispered the words against her temple, and yet again into the delicate, sensitive curves of her ear. "I want you, you golden-eyed witch, so much that it scares me."

328

He caught the lobe of her ear between his teeth and gently sucked on it, until she loosed a quiet moan. What madness was this? How had she managed to ignore all her better judgment? Why had the insistent voice of her conscience suddenly gone silent? She should never have left Weed and Matthew, never ridden off alone in search of Grant. And finding him, she should never have let him take her off into this godforsaken desolation, where she was completely at his mercy.

That voice within her had lost its strength. She heard its whisper, "never again, never again," so faint that it might have been nothing more than the chirping of crickets, or the gentle lapping of the river against its bank.

Grant unbuttoned her shirt and peeled it back to expose her breasts to the evening air. He buried his face between them, kissing her with his lips, his tongue, his teeth. She cried out when he rasped his thumbs across her nipples, but it was a cry of joy, of exultation, of freedom.

I'm free, at long last, and I'll never give that up, not even to the man I love.

"It's all right," she reassured herself as the shock of her admission spread through her body. Curling her arms around him, she cradled his head against her breast and murmured the same reassurance to him.

But her words did not reassure him. Instead, they brought a small measure of sanity back to him. With the taste of her still on his lips and tongue, Grant flopped back on the hard blanket-covered ground.

Between deep breaths that might have been gasps, he said, "No, damn it, it's not all right. We've got to talk, Glory, and I mean it."

He was right, as he had been all along.

"About what?"

"About us. About the way I can't seem to keep my hands and other parts of my body off you. About what could happen if we don't stop this."

His breathing slowed, and his heart stopped pounding

quite so hard in his chest. But the ache of arousal still pulsed through him as strong and vital as ever. There was only one way of easing that ache.

Glory took a deep breath and swallowed hard before answering.

"I'm not going to have a baby." Her face burned even in the cool night air. "Considering how much time we, uh, spent together and how little effect it had, I can't see why this time should be any different."

With her free hand she reached for the buttons on his shirt and slowly undid them.

Grabbing her hand and forcing it away, he begged, "Stop it, Glory. I can't talk reasonably when you do this to me, and you know it. And I'm not going to let you get away with it again."

Never again. The words echoed more firmly in her mind now, and she understood their warning.

She leaned over him to brush her lips across him. He groaned, but though he did not turn his head away from her kiss, neither did he draw her closer.

She whispered, "I don't intend to be reasonable."

"Somebody's got to be."

The bitterness in his voice cut through the haze of passion and sent Glory flopping onto her back, too.

"That wasn't exactly the reaction I expected," she told him. "You weren't so concerned a few weeks ago."

"Things were different then."

"Now who's being unreasonable!"

They lay in silence for several minutes. The last light had gone from the sky, save for the millions of stars that shimmered in the blackness. The fire had died to a rich, warm bed of coals. Grant sat up and turned the fish on their spit again, then rested his forearms on his knees and stared into the pulsating glow.

"I'm thirty-eight years old, Glory. I've lived alone more than twenty of those years. Staying with you those couple of weeks reminded me of how much I've missed."

She had made a confession of her own, but only to

330

herself. Grant was making his confession to her, and she wondered how long he had lived with it held silent within.

She wondered, too, what life would be like when she returned to the routine at the LJ—without Grant. Had she become so accustomed to him that she wouldn't be able to live without him? No, she vowed, that would never happen. The whole reason for having his help had been to make her no longer need him.

But if she didn't need him anymore, why did she want him so much?

Rising slowly, Glory knelt behind Grant and wrapped her arms around him.

"I love you," she whispered.

He let out a funny little chuckle that had not the slightest trace of humor in it.

"I love you, too, Glory."

"Well, you don't have to sound so glum about it."

"I think the fish are burnt," he said, poking at one of them with a stick.

"I told you so."

"And is that what I'm supposed to say when you turn up fat as a Christmas goose with my baby in your belly?"

He spun to face her, still on his knees, but it wasn't his attitude of supplication that drew a rasping cry of shock from her. She could almost have sworn the gleam in his silver-fire eyes came from tears. And there were tears in his voice, too.

"For Christ's sake, woman, don't you think I'd have some feelings about it? Or am I just supposed to treat it like your precious ranch: help put it securely in your little hands and then walk away without a second thought?"

Guilt stabbed her. Was the anguish that tortured his features born of knowledge or only suspicion? Did he know that Matthew was his, or had Melody's secret gone with her to her grave?

"Oh, God, Grant, did you think I'd . . ."

"I don't know what to think any more. I *can't* think, not when I'm around you."

He drew a long breath and held it before slowly exhaling with a sigh of regret.

"I can't live with you, and I can't live without you," he grumbled. "Every time I'm near you, I want you. And when I'm not near you, I want you even more."

"Do you think it's any different for me? How do you think I felt all that time I tried to believe you were responsible for sabotaging the LJ?"

"You did *what?*" he shouted. "You thought I cut your fences and stampeded your steers?"

His anger echoed in the night's stillness. He struggled to his feet and stomped off into the dark. For a moment there was only silence, and a furious silhouette against the stars.

She had hurt him, and hurt herself in the process. But the truth had to be told, all of it. She had believed too many lies, of her own making.

"I said I tried to believe it," she dared to whisper. "I didn't say I succeeded."

"But you wanted to. Good God, Glory, you believed me capable of all that? Setting the fire, too?"

Admitting it even to herself hurt, and she knew telling him would be like a knife in his heart. "Everything. I tried to make myself blame you because I thought I wouldn't fall in love with a man who could do that. I failed there, too." She waited for a response, but he just threw his head back and let out a long, slow sigh of a man trying to come to grips with something completely beyond his comprehension.

"Please, Grant, come here. I don't like trying to reason with a man I can't see."

"Reason with *me!* Hell, I've been trying to reason with you for months, and look where it's got me."

"Out in the middle of nowhere with a woman who loves you?"

Her voice was small, and guilty, but it didn't change

the way he felt. What he wanted from her was more than she could give; what he was willing to give was more than she wanted.

"We both thought so many things wrong."

He turned to face her then, but she didn't like what she saw. His eyes were cold, hard, even in the uneven firelight. The mouth that had kissed her was drawn into a tight line. And at his sides, the hands that had given her such pleasure were clenched into fists.

"Then let me set this straight for you, Glory Johnson. I'll admit that when a man takes a woman for pleasure, he doesn't much care about the consequences."

"A baby, you mean? That's really what we're talking about, isn't it?"

"Yes, a baby. Only when a man gets serious about the woman, it's not just 'a' baby. It's his child, his family, his future, his immortality."

She longed to cry out to him, Oh Grant, you have your immortality. You have a son who worships the ground you walk on.

But she couldn't tell him, not tonight. This was their time, theirs alone, to find the truth and learn to live with its consequences.

He was wallowing in self-pity, and he knew it. But if there was a chance that she, the proud and selfish and beautiful Glory Johnson, would take pity on him, he'd grovel. He'd do anything.

"I wouldn't want to think that I had a child somewhere that I'd never know, never be able to acknowledge, never be able to put on a horse for the first time or paddle his butt when he put soap bubbles in my favorite pipe."

She felt her throat constrict with tears she dared not shed.

"You don't smoke a pipe," she reminded him, hoping to bring him out of his funk. "Besides, you've got Matthew."

She held her breath, waiting for his reaction to reveal how much or how little he knew.

But there was no telling. If Grant Brookington displayed any reaction to her statement, she could not see it.

He walked back across the blanket and leaned down to pick up another chunk of wood for the fire. It was something to do, something to occupy his hands for a moment, since he couldn't do with those hands what he really wanted to do. If he touched her now, he'd be completely in thrall to her, to the love that threatened to consume him as the fire consumed the wood.

"Yeah, I've got Matthew," he admitted, still with no emotion either in his voice or his features. "Poor kid. I used to resent him, especially when he'd show up and ask me things his daddy shoulda taught him. It was a long time before I saw Matthew as a little boy looking for help. He was always just Lee's kid, the son Lee stole from me the way he stole Melody. And then he stole you, too."

"No, Grant, there you're wrong. He never stole me." She stood, ignoring the way the cool night air raised gooseflesh on her arms, back, and belly. "I've been yours always. And I will be yours—always."

The fire flared, the fresh wood blazing to bathe the woman before him in firelight. The wild honey hair was aflame and flowed like molten gold about her in the breeze. He reached out to grasp a loose strand, but she tossed her head and the lock flew beyond his fingers.

"I am no child, Grant Brookington. I have neither father nor brother nor guardian uncle to come after you with a shotgun should I be found 'ruined.'"

The tawny eyes flashed and raked his body with undisguised longing.

"I have the means to raise a child by myself, but that does not mean I would exclude the father. I'd never steal your son, Grant. Never. And I love you more than I thought possible, but . . ."

"But what?"

He grabbed her upper arms and pulled her roughly to him. Her nipples were hard against his chest, her breasts

334

soft, as his mouth slanted across hers. She was stubborn, and proud, and as hungry for this passion as he. And he'd know the reason why she was denying it all, if it was the last thing he did.

"Oh, Grant, I can't give it up," Tears she never expected welled up in her eyes and spilled over before she had a chance to blink them back. "All my life, I've had to put my trust in a man, not because I wanted to but because I had no choice. And every time, I lost more and more of myself."

She tried to break away from him and hide her tears, but he wouldn't let her go.

"Tell me, Glory," he demanded. "Tell me all of it."

She was sobbing, but the words came clearly as she remembered, "I wanted so badly to make my father proud of me. I learned everything he taught me, until there wasn't a man who worked for him who was better. But when the War went against us, and Papa knew he was dying, he made one last deal. But it didn't work out."

"He sold you?"

Glory laughed, even through her tears.

"Quite the opposite. He bought me a husband. He turned the company, the warehouses, everything over to Phllip Beaumont in exchange for Phillip's promise that I'd be allowed to run things after the War."

"Except Phillip was killed, wasn't he?"

She nodded, and he released her arms so she could wipe the tears from her cheeks.

"It didn't matter by then. Everything was gone. Phillip's brother, Terrence, came down from Philadelphia and took me to live there, with his parents, his wife, and children."

His listened, only half hearing her words, as she poured out the tale of her complete subjugation by the Beaumont family, her decisions always ignored simply because she was female. And even Lee, whom she had seen as her savior, refused to allow her to be anything more than an ornament.

"I wanted to be his wife, not because I loved him, but because I simply wanted to be what I wanted to be. Oh, hell." She buried her face in her hands. "I'm not making any sense at all, and I've ruined this night that I wanted so desperately to be perfect."

"It is, Glory. It is perfect."

This time his hands were gentle, resting lightly on her shoulders until she tumbled into his arms.

Her golden eyes looked up into his.

"I love you, Grant, but I can't give up myself, not again. Please, can you understand that?"

His vision blurred for a moment. He had to hold her face with his trembling hands to be sure he saw her.

With a groan, he possessed her. He pushed her shirt off her shoulders and somehow managed to strip off his own until her flesh was warm and yielding against his.

"All I understand is that I love you, Glorianna," he murmured. Her arms went around his waist and held him as tightly as if he were a lifeline and she were drowning. "Jesus God, woman, but I love you."

His hands, warm and strong, curved to embrace her breasts. He kissed one perfect nipple and then sucked it between his teeth. Glory cried out, her voice clear and high with passion, and clasped him to her.

She realized then that that was what she wanted most, to hold him to her forever. And she knew also that she had lost him—forever. She could not give him what he wanted. Belonging to him meant surrendering herself, and that she could not do, not even for his love. But tonight, for one last time . . .

He could not let her go, not even to remove the rest of his clothing, so it was Glory whose hands freed the buttons and pushed his pants down over his hips. Pulling off boots and pants tangled around their ankles wasn't easy, and it even brought muffled laughter, but somehow they managed it without breaking the bond of that ferocious kiss.

Only when they lay warm and naked together did they

separate, to draw great gulps of air into starving lungs.

"Love me," Glory breathed, tugging at his shoulders. This would be the last time, it had to be.

His hands seemed to be everywhere at once, teasing her, arousing her, taunting her every nerve ending with pleasure.

His palms circled her breasts until the peaks were hard as pebbles.

He slid one hand down her belly to cup the warm nest of curls between her thighs. She groaned, and her fingers tightened on his shoulders until he could feel the nails digging into his flesh.

"You want me, and I know it," he whispered. She was pushing against his hand, until he felt the moist heat on his palm. "You want me now, when spring is driving everyone crazy, but when it's winter again and the nights are cold and dark, you'll think of tonight and want me even more. Marry me, Glory."

"Oh, God, Grant, don't, please," she begged. "Just love me now, tonight. Don't think . . ."

"About tomorrow? How can I not?" He found the tenderest, most sensitive place and touched it, stroked it, until she writhed and cried out in the agony of pleasure. "And I'm going to make sure you think about it, too. Not just tomorrow, but every night of your life."

He wondered if she had drawn blood, but the pain in his shoulders was nothing compared to the pain of holding back his own need while he drove hers to fever pitch.

"Scream, Glory, scream how much you need me," he taunted. "There's no one to hear but me."

But she didn't scream. She cried out, mindless with exquisite torment, and asked him, "Why, Grant, why? Love me, please now. Not like this. Love me, love me . . ."

Then he, too, could bear it no longer. Her hands were cool on his heat, soft on his hardness, drawing him to her inexorably. Instinctively, he found her and plunged

337

within the welcoming warmth with a cry of his own.

That first savage lovemaking left them sated yet empty, and no words could fill the void. There had been anger and distrust, pain and hurt. In the darkness, some of it faded, and as one hand sought another, the longing pushed everything else away.

The night grew cold, so that they sought each other's warmth. Warmth led to desire, so they made love again, and again, knowing each time that it would never be enough.

Dawn crept up on them, like the sliver of new moon that preceded the sun. Exhausted, Glory stared at the narrow crescent and knew that the time had come.

She rose, hating the frosty air on her skin but needing it to keep her resolve. Grant watched her every move as she bent to find her scattered clothing and pull the wrinkled, cold garments on.

"You're leaving?" he asked.

"I have to." Dear God, don't let me break now, don't let me cry. "The others will be back at the LJ and I don't want them to worry."

Her teeth were chattering with the cold, and her fingers couldn't do up the buttons quickly enough.

He lay on his side, the coarse wool blanket pulled only to his waist. He couldn't be impervious to the cold; his slow, steady breathing left puffs in the morning air. Yet he seemed comfortable, almost casual, except for his eyes.

Flint? Granite? Steel? No, those grey eyes were harder and colder than any substance known to man.

"Matthew was wrong," Grant said slowly, his voice carefully controlled.

"Wrong? About what?"

"About you, and Melody. He said you were different, but you're not. You're just like her."

Glory knew she looked absurd, standing in the dull light of an overcast morning, with her mouth open and no words for it to speak.

"You take and take and take, and never give. Security,

that's the name of your game. Don't take risks; play it safe."

His statement was even more absurd than her appearance, and Glory tried to fight back a bitter laugh but couldn't.

"If all I wanted was security, I'd have married you the minute you asked me. Or I'd have taken your money when you first tried to buy the LJ. You don't think there were risks involved in my trying to run the ranch?"

He remained unperturbed. His very calm disturbed her, until she lashed out unexpectedly at him.

"Damn your smugness, Grant Brookington. If I'm just like Melody, then maybe you're just like Lee. You don't want me to be a person, you just want an ornament, a bed partner, and maybe a broodmare. Well, damn it, I don't have to be that!"

Her tears were hot on cold cheeks, but she made no attempt to stop them.

"I'm not stupid, Grant. And I'm not afraid of hard work. Look at my hands. Take a good look. I'm damn proud of the calluses, the blisters, the burns. They're the rewards of hard work, work no one ever thought I could do."

She took a deep breath and tried to speak more rationally, but all the emotion she felt infused each word.

"Don't blame me for Melody's mistakes, or for those you made with her. Did you ever consider that maybe what went wrong between you was your fault, too?"

She turned away then, and strode, still sobbing, to saddle Cleo. She expected Grant to get up from his cold bed and confront her. He didn't. From the corner of her eye Glory saw him lie back down on the blanket and lock his hands behind his head. At first she thought he was just ignoring her. Well, fine, then I'll just ignore him, she told herself as she threw Cleo's saddle on the mare's back.

But Grant wasn't ignoring her. He was struggling with her accusation, and with the pain it had inflicted on his already open wounds.

Don't walk away, he wanted to beg her. I said we

339

needed to talk, and we do. Last night wasn't enough. It could never be enough.

But he said nothing, and the next thing he knew, she was astride the big buckskin, a sad, hurt silhouette against the grey sky.

"I love you, Grant Brookington," she confessed, sobs breaking her voice into rough-edged whispers. "Maybe not enough, or maybe too much. But I can't give up what I've worked so hard for. Do you—can you—understand that?"

He turned his head away from the tormenting image. She could ride away now, and he had no chance of catching her. Maybe it was better to let her go without another word.

She was proud and stubborn and prized her independence above everything else. Not like Melody at all, and Grant knew it. He had known it even before he made that stupid and utterly inaccurate comparison. There was nothing he could say to erase the damage. More words would only hurt more.

Except for a warning. And a plea.

"Watch out for Lonnie," he said, still not looking at her. "He's not through with you yet."

"I know. And I will."

"One more thing."

Hurry, Grant, she pleaded silently. If I don't go now I never will.

"What's that?"

"If there's a baby this time, don't bother naming him after me."

340

Chapter Twenty-Four

The morning's overcast remained, a perfect gloom to match Glory's mood on the long, lonely ride back to the LJ. She arrived late in the afternoon. Her head pounded, her eyes and throat ached from all the crying, and she wanted nothing more than a hot bath and an uninterrupted night's sleep.

Weed was waiting for her in the stableyard, fists on his skinny hips.

"'Bout time," he greeted. "You got company."

Glory swung down and relinquished the reins to her foreman when he offered. Clearly the visitor was someone who oughtn't to be kept waiting.

"Lonnie?" she asked in a small voice.

"Nope. Some friend of yours."

Not inclined to say more, Weed led the mare toward the stable and left Glory standing, alone and feeling vulnerable, in the yard.

She gathered her courage during the walk to the back porch, but her hand was trembling when she placed it on the door handle. What friend of hers could possibly have Weed in such a state of disgust? She had made no friends since coming to Wyoming, unless one counted Grant and Nancy Reynolds. Recalling that last conversation with Nancy, Glory concluded there'd be no friendship from that quarter, and she had completely alienated Grant.

One step into the kitchen, however, she had no doubt about the identity of her guest.

The room was a disaster. Every pot and pan, every bowl and skillet, every dish and glass and piece of silverware cluttered the place. The trestle table was covered. A cast iron skillet containing a mixing bowl with several spoons sat on one of the benches.

The stove was cold, the only blessing. Something had been spilled down the front of it and burned to a black crust, and the whole top of the range was a patchwork of grease spatters. Had there been a fire going, the kitchen would have filled with smoke, and that was if the whole house didn't go up in flames.

Lingering in the air, like smoke after a holocaust, was an instantly familiar fragrance: sandalwood-scented hair oil.

"Is that you, Anna?" an equally familiar voice called from the parlor. "I've been waiting for you."

Terrence Beaumont rose gracefully to his feet at her entrance and even extended her the courtesy of a mocking bow. All the while, his eyes surveyed her, from the weather-beaten hat to the tangled hair and swollen eyes, from the worn jacket to the denim trousers and dusty boots.

"What the *hell* are you doing here?" Glory exploded.

Terrence was oblivious to her animosity, just as he had been oblivious to everything else important about her.

"I wrote, but apparently you haven't picked up your mail for several weeks," he began to explain, once again taking a comfortable pose on the sofa. "Goodness, Anna, how does one survive without the basics of civilization like mail?"

He might just as well never have left Philadelphia, or Richmond, for that matter. From the carefully combed dark hair and soft white hands to the polished shoes, he was every inch a "gentleman."

"Mankind survived a long time without post offices. Now, back to my question."

"Oh, do sit down, Anna. You needn't—"

"I am filthy dirty, in case you hadn't noticed. I am not so far removed from civilization that I intend to deposit my dirty carcass on my own furniture."

Terrence Beaumont, of all people! Glory could think of no one who represented the exact opposite of Grant Brookington better than Terrence. Yet even they had one thing in common, and she wasn't about to dwell on that.

"I'm waiting for an answer. And you'd better make it quick, because I intend to take a hot bath and then go to bed."

"All right then. In my letter I explained it all. Sadie passed away in February and—"

"Oh, Terrence, I'm so sorry! Forgive me, I didn't know."

Now she felt like a complete fool. Good God, the man had lost his wife, the mother of his children, and she was chewing him out.

"Sadie was never strong, and we had a very hard winter. She took cold, and one night she just didn't wake up."

He was so matter-of-fact about the tragedy that Glory felt even more awkward. She searched the little parlor for a place to sit down, but there was no place, except the stone hearth in front of the fireplace. Wearily, she sank down onto it and wondered if she'd find the strength to rise again.

"What about the children? And your parents?"

"Sadie's sister Beatrice, from Baltimore, has taken them." He sounded quite relieved of the responsibility. "It was my suggestion that, there being empty rooms in the house now, Father offer some of them to rent, to suitable boarders, of course. Mama was appalled at first, naturally, but I located some exiled Virginians who could benefit from her generosity."

Your suggestion my foot, Glory longed to remind him. She had proposed that the Beaumonts consider converting the extra rooms for boarders, but Terrence and

343

his horrified parents would have none of it. Glory wondered what had happened to change their minds. Probably the prospect of pennilessness.

"And what about you? Why in hell, I repeat, are you here?"

Terrence shrugged his narrow shoulders.

"The adventure seemed to have agreed with you, so I thought perhaps I might give it a try."

She laughed, and once started, she couldn't seem to stop. The very idea of Terrence Beaumont living the life of a rancher, much less an ordinary cowpuncher, was truly hysterical.

"What's wrong?" he demanded petulantly. "Certainly if you can do it, why not I?"

"Oh, Terrence, you can't even dirty your hands enough to wash dishes. I saw you turn your nose up at the way I smell; you'd die before you'd let yourself smell the same way. There are no bathtubs on the range, or mirrors so you can make sure your moustache is perfectly symmetrical."

A look of concern flashed across his face, and he couldn't resist raising a hand to smooth the carefully waxed decoration below his nose.

Glory pushed herself to her feet and headed back to the kitchen. She almost had to close her eyes to walk through the mess, but she forced herself to ignore it and promised to tackle it only *after* she had bathed and slept at least twelve hours. Even the prospect of washing in cold water wasn't enough to prod her into starting a fire in that stove until it had been scoured.

Glory slept as one dead, and when she wakened, she thanked God for the exhaustion that had kept her from dreaming. Other nights might not be so restful, but she had desperately needed this one.

After dressing quickly in dungarees, flannel shirt, and boots, she checked Matthew's room to confirm a niggling

344

suspicion. As expected, the room was as much a shambles as the kitchen: Terrence had taken over. Shirts and trousers and even his underclothes lay hither and thither, on the floor, under the bed, hanging from a bureau drawer, draped on the back of a chair.

"Damn you," she growled as she headed for the stairs.

The kitchen was cold, since no one had started a fire. The blaze in the parlor seemed to be within Terrence's limits of what a gentleman could lower himself to tend, but the stove was clearly woman's work.

"Where'd you get that coffee?" Glory asked.

Terrence offered her a dazzling smile and drawled, "Good morning, Anna. Cooking isn't one of my talents, so I've been relying on the boys in the bunkhouse to provide a cup or two in the morning."

They probably gave it to him to keep him from hanging around them, too, she thought.

"And where's Matthew? I see you kicked him out of his room."

Terrence stroked his moustache and took another sip of coffee. Glory hoped it was Old Ken's blackest and strongest. By the little grimace her guest made, she suspected he found it a bit blacker and stronger than he was accustomed to.

"Your stepson was gracious enough to allow me the use of his quarters. I'm sure he's quite comfortable with the others."

She muttered something that she hoped he took for an obscenity and then stormed to the door. Her only explanation as she grabbed her coat from its peg and thrust her arms into it was, "Matthew isn't a horse, to be moved from one stall to another for your convenience. I suggest you gather up your belongings while I find him."

It took her considerably less time than expected. When she opened the back door, Matthew was just coming up the porch steps. Glory took one look at the bitter scowl on the boy's face and pulled the door shut behind her.

345

"Out to the barn," she ordered in a voice that indicated she wasn't going to listen to any arguments. "We've got to talk."

They took three or four steps away from the house before Matthew asked, "Where's Grant?"

"I presume he's at the Diamond B. At any rate, he's no concern of ours right now. Terrence Beaumont is. And we've got to decide what to do with him."

"'We'?" Matthew echoed. "I'm afraid this Mr. Beaumont is your problem. I didn't bring him here, and it ain't my ranch, remember?"

He walked away from her, toward the barn, forcing her to run to catch up with him.

"I didn't bring Terrence here either. All I'm trying to do now is—"

"You sent him the money, didn't you?"

"Well, yes, but I never intended him to—"

"And you told him how well off we are out here, didn't you?"

Vanity had made her hand pen those words, puffing up her meager accomplishments so that the people who had never let her use her skills would be forced to acknowledge her competence.

Her voice was more contrite now, and she avoided trying to justify her errors.

"Yes, I did brag a little."

"Then I guess it's your own fault he took your bragging for an invitation. And by the way, he hired a buggy from the livery when he came here two weeks ago, and he ain't taken it back yet."

Glory had no idea how much it cost to rent a buggy for two weeks, but she was certain the sum would be considerable. Terrence was already beginning to drain her. Her contrition turned to anger.

"All right, I'll admit part of it was my fault. But, Matthew, right now I'm only trying to help you get back what's rightfully yours. You shouldn't have to give up your bedroom and sleep out in the bunkhouse."

He turned to face her squarely. He was several inches taller than she, and the growing resemblance to his father made her flinch. Matthew's eyes were bluer than Grant's, but just as hard. And though his features lacked the weathering and maturity, his cheekbones were just as high and square, his jaw just as firm and stubborn.

"Try some of your own medicine, lady," he retorted. "If you don't have to take help you don't want, why should I?"

The next two weeks brought relief to some of Glory's problems, but others only got worse.

Matthew helped her rearrange the contents of the two upstairs storage rooms so that one could be converted into a comfortable chamber for Terrence. But that was the extent of the boy's assistance. He refused to return the rented buggy. Glory had to take time out of her schedule to hitch Lucy to the back of the vehicle and then, after completing several errands, ride the horse back to the LJ.

The kitchen required most of a day to put back in order, and even then Terrence grumbled about it. He continued the same grumbling every night, over dinner served in the dining room. He considered eating in the kitchen undignified.

"You really should not be doing this kind of work, Anna," he'd scolded her while she served pan-fried steak and mashed potatoes. "Do you have anymore of those pickles?"

"In the pantry," she sighed, knowing that telling him where they were would not get him off his butt to fetch them for himself.

After finding another jar of Melody's pickles and opening them for Terrence, Glory sank down onto a chair across from him. She had spent most of the day in the garden plot, where the first seeds had sprouted, and every bone and joint and muscle in her body ached. Scrubbing her hands hadn't been enough to get rid of all the dirt, and the raking had added new blisters.

"Terrence," she said wearily, "we must come to an understanding." Even food didn't appeal to her, but she ate dutifully, a bite of beef, a mouthful of potatoes, a slice of crisp pickle. "We are not back in Virginia. The LJ is a ranch, not a plantation."

Terrence looked hurt and brushed his fingers across his moustache.

"Anna, the Beaumonts were never planters."

"No, you owned city property in Richmond and collected outrageous rents on it."

He puffed himself up in what he considered righteous indignation. His Virginia drawl, prominent under normal circumstances, thickened even further.

"We were fair landlords. We charged no more than any other landlord in the city."

Arguing with Terrence was worse than arguing with Grant. Grant could be frustrating and mule-headed, but Terrence was just plain stupid.

"It doesn't matter what you charged, Terrence. The point is that you never had to work."

"I worked in the bank in Philadelphia."

"And nearly wept if you got ink stains on your lily white hand."

"Anna! Your talk is most unbecoming a lady!"

A rash of unbidden tears blurred her vision.

"Oh, damn it, Terrence, I'm not a lady anymore, not by your standards. This isn't Richmond, it's Wyoming. Out here we work, and sometimes we work very hard. Those who aren't willing to work, well, they either die or they go back East."

Sniffling and hiccuping, she finished her supper without another word to him, then left the dining room, dishes still on the table, and ran to her room to cry herself to sleep.

Grant shaded his eyes against the sun and scanned the entire expanse of blue. Not a single cloud broke the azure perfection.

"No rain today," he told Tom as they urged their horses forward. "Better get the market steers moved again. That creek'll be dry by the end of the week."

"I've never seen it this dry so early. Cripe, we cut hay two weeks ago and it ain't grown back yet. Gonna be hard gettin' through next winter without it."

"I know."

Two weeks without rain could hardly be called a drought, but Grant was still worried.

"It'll rain eventually," he said. "Always does."

Glory stood and pressed her hands to the small of her back. The garden was doing as well as could be expected. With no rain for over a month, she had been carrying water to the plants nearly every day. The beans were up nicely, and the peas had started blossoming, though the carrots were little more than a green fringe in their rows.

Grasping the two wooden buckets, she headed back to the yard and the pump. One more trip, and that should do it for today. And maybe it would rain tonight. Yesterday there had been clouds on the horizon at sundown.

Between the garden plot and the house was the row of fruit trees, two each of cherry, apple, peach, and pear. A few weeks ago, they had been covered with blossoms, clouds of pink and white so fragrant that the bees had caused an almost constant hum. Now the few petals that clung to the branches were brown and withered, and small fruit had begun to form. But as Glory set down the buckets to check the fruit on the lower branches, she wondered if any would be harvested. Without rain, nothing could grow.

Except for one thing. If she had been sure no one was around to see her, she'd have pressed a hand to her still flat belly, but when there could be any one of a dozen ranch hands watching, to say nothing of Terrence or Matthew, she resisted the urge and picked up the buckets once more.

She'd keep the baby a secret as long as she could,

especially from Terrence. He was already hinting at marriage, using his presence in her house as a reason for the gossip that followed her everywhere. If he found out she was pregnant, he'd be capable of anything. And she'd be ten times more vulnerable.

The weather that had been cool for weeks had turned suddenly hot. Tired of carrying water buckets, and battling again the tears that seemed always just below the surface, Glory sank down in the shade on the back porch.

Matthew came out the back door a moment later.

"Oh, there you are."

Four words in a row. That was a lot for Matthew these days.

"What is it now?" Glory asked, anticipating yet another disaster.

"Nothin'. His highness was askin' about dinner. Told him to fix it hisself."

"Good for you," she said, with a weak smile, but by then Matthew had already walked past her, down the steps and into the yard.

Grant backed the skittish horse away from the watering hole. He had seen enough, and the stench from the rotting carcass was more than he could take.

"Shot too?" Tom asked. This was the third they'd found.

"Probably. I wasn't going to get close enough to tell for sure."

"Lonnie?"

"Well, this one's in Diamond B water, but all three steers were LJ animals. And it's just what he'd think of doing. Make it hard for her, but not jeopardize the ranch itself."

The two men rode on in silence for a while, frequently casting glances to the clouds massing above the mountains. This wouldn't be the first time the promise had gone unfulfilled, but there was always hope.

"I'll see Matthew in the morning and let him know

we've found another one," Grant said finally, when they were well away from the fouled watering hole. "Might just as well let this one dry up and leave the carcass for the wolves."

"Do you think he's telling her the truth?"

The grey eyes narrowed and stared unseeing at the mountains again.

"Maybe, maybe not. The problem is whether she believes him."

The room was like an oven, even at dawn. There had been no rain last night, either, though the air had seemed heavy with it when Glory staggered into bed. She had hardly slept, not only because of the oppressive heat, but because Matthew had brought her more worries.

And he did not deny where the information about the fouled watering places came from.

She lay in the wide bed and fought back the tears yet again. The morning sickness Sadie had suffered would have been preferable to the almost constant weeping. Poor Sadie. So trusting, so willing to do what anyone told her. So afraid to say anything in her own defense. Looking back on it now, Glory could see how miserable Terrence's wife had been in Philadelphia, with neither friends nor family, with all of her old way of life gone forever.

"Well, so is mine," Glory whispered to herself as she slowly swung her legs out of bed. "And there's no going back."

It would be another day just like so many before it, and delaying the start would only force her to squeeze the same amount of work out of fewer hours.

She came into the parlor to find Terrence, as usual, lounging on the sofa, a cup of coffee balanced rather precariously on the arm. He was quite absorbed in the newspaper and didn't look up until she asked him, "Where did you get that?"

"Oh, this? Your neighbor dropped it off, along with

351

some mail. Said he picked it up in town yesterday and—"

"Grant was here? When? This morning?"

She rushed to the window and pulled aside the curtain to see if he were still there. There wasn't even dust hanging in the air.

"About an hour ago, I'd say. I didn't catch his name, though. Grant, did you say? Tall fellow, rather crude looking, desperately in need of a haircut?"

Glory stepped back from the window and before her knees gave out completely, she sank down onto Lee's wing chair by the fireplace. At least now she could knot her hands against her stomach and not draw undue attention.

"I asked him to stay for coffee, but he said he was in a hurry."

"Oh, God," Glory breathed, blinking back tears. He'll never believe me, she thought. Panic tightened in her throat. I've got to tell him now, before it's too late. "I'm going out, Terrence. I'll be gone most of the day."

"But, Anna, my dear, you've not eaten breakfast."

She wiped nervous hands on her skirt and sent stubborn resolve to her knees.

Then she calmly stood directly in front of Terrence until he laid his newspaper aside and granted her his full attention.

"What you're really concerned about, Mr. Beaumont, is your own breakfast, which I haven't prepared yet, and your lunch, and your supper. To that I can only say, Fix it yourself, or do without. I've waited on you hand and foot long enough."

She was saddling Lucy when Weed came up behind her.

"You goin' somewheres?"

The lanky foreman leaned against the rough-hewn post and chewed a long stalk of grass.

"Yes, I have some business with Mr. Brookington that can't wait. Why? Is something wrong?"

"Not yet, but I think there might be." He stopped

chewing long enough to sniff, like a hound on a scent. "We got a storm comin', finally, and it's gonna be a duck-choker. You'd best wait."

Leaving Lucy in her stall, Glory followed Weed outside once again. Sure enough, clouds were billowing over the mountains. Instead of the fleecy wisps and puffs of so many dry days and nights in the past, these were huge and dark and as heavy with moisture as the night air had been.

"You got at least three creeks to cross to the Diamond B, and any one of 'em could wash you clean away in a flash flood," Weed warned.

Again Glory had to fight down the urge to clasp protective hands over the growing life within her. One more day won't make any difference, she told herself. The damage has already been done.

The day grew more oppressive as the clouds continued to pile upon themselves. Any hint of breeze died. The chickens refused to leave their roosts, and the horses huddled in tiny bunches as though they, too, knew there was a vicious storm on the way.

Glory went about her usual routine of watering the garden, fixing lunch, washing laundry, and whatever other chores could be found to occupy her time. Terrence moved, with his newspaper, to the front porch.

When he asked her to clean off the wicker rocking chair, she threw a wet rag at him, then burst into tears and fled to her room. The whole house shook with the slamming of her door.

With the front of his vest disfigured by a huge wet spot, Terrence returned to the parlor. The rag in his hand dripped steadily onto the floor.

"Where'd you get that?" Matthew asked.

"She—she threw it at me. At me! And demanded I clean the chair myself."

Matthew cocked his head to one side and gave the intruder an almost comical look.

"Consider yourself lucky. Most people she wouldn't even ask for help."

In her room directly over the parlor, Glory heard the exchange. It brought on a fresh torrent of uncontrollable weeping that ended only when she fell asleep.

Matthew spurred his mount mercilessly, though the gelding was giving every ounce of speed within him. In the distance, lightning flashed out of the roiling clouds. Overhead, where the noon sun still shone bright, the sky was a stagnant blue. But the air smelled of rain, rich and fresh and tantalizing.

The boy spotted the familiar horses and riders and yelled at the top of his lungs. The red horse pulled up sharply, then turned toward Matthew. Soon the other followed. Satisfied that he'd been seen, Matthew let his own mount slow and come to a complete halt halfway down the low hill.

"You shouldn't be out here alone," Grant scolded.

"Well, if you send me back now, I'll still be alone, so you either let me stay, or you come with me."

Grant didn't know whether to laugh at the boy's perverse logic, or admire it. Over the past few weeks Matthew had grown increasingly difficult to manage, and more difficult to understand. But he was Grant's only link to the strange goings on at the LJ, his only link to the woman who had haunted his days and nights for two long and lonely months.

"Look, Matthew, I stopped by this morning to bring some mail I picked up in town yesterday. That Mr. Beaumont seemed—"

"Things might not be exactly what they seem," Tom Cashion interrupted. "Go on, Matthew. Just give Grant a break today; it's been a rough one."

"Not another water hole?"

Cashion nodded, and gave his employer a look that clearly indicated he wanted no more interruptions until the boy had had his say.

"Look, Grant, this time you gotta come. Me 'n Weed've been moving the cattle, and so far we haven't had any problems, except for those two steers. But we lost another hand yesterday, so we're gettin' short again."

"Have you told her?"

Matthew shook his head emphatically.

"Are you kiddin'? That's why I said you gotta come. I didn't tell her about the two dead steers or the hands that quit or the fouled water, and if you'd take one look at her, you'd know why."

Grant pulled Rusty up short.

"What's wrong with her?"

There was something of a child's wail in Matthew's voice when he answered, "I don't know! That's why I been beggin' you to come and see her! She's always tellin' Terrence that he could give her a little help with things, but he don't lift a damn finger, 'cept to make coffee. And when he don't help, she gets all mad and starts to cry. Hell, yesterday I saw her carryin' water to that garden of hers and all of a sudden she just set them buckets down and plopped herself in the grass and started bawlin' like a branded calf."

A queer thought blew through Grant's mind, and he dared to ask, "Has she been sick?"

He tried not to hope, but when Matthew's answer came, Grant couldn't hide his disappointment.

"No, not that I know of. She's killin' herself with work, though, waitin' on Terrence all the time. He's got her so worn down she's been takin' a nap in the afternoon the past few days. It's like she just can't keep up with him anymore."

That's not Glory, Grant thought with some alarm.

He remembered the days on the range, riding after calves from dawn to dusk, wrestling the stubborn creatures to the ground and burning the mark of ownership into the hides. Glory had been tired at the end of those days, as had every other cowboy, but each morning she had been ready for more.

What the hell was this Beaumont fop doing to her? Grant's blood simmered at the image of that pomaded priss in Glory's parlor. She'd wait on him hand and foot, and then beg for his help until he drove her to tears, but would she ever come to the one man who would willingly give her all the help she needed?

He was about to let her stew in her own pot, until Matthew reminded him of one salient point.

"If Lonnie tried anything now, she'd be no match for him," the boy said, and with that parting remark turned his little gelding back toward the LJ without so much as a good-bye.

Grant let him go, his own thughts too confused to allow for rational action. When he turned to his best friend, he found Tom sitting quite comfortably on his big grey Morgan mare, hat slid back, and a very silly grin on his face.

"For Christ's sake, Cashion, what's got into you now?"

"I was just thinking how that boy is damn near as stubborn as his father."

"And am I supposed to—"

The sharp explosion rippled through the heavy, still air, and drew both men's gaze to the dark western horizon, where the mountains had all but disappeared behind the storm clouds.

Against the charcoal sky, another even darker cloud rose, oily and fast-moving.

"It's too far away for us to do anything about it," Grant observed angrily. "Hell, if it ain't flood or blizzards, it's damn drought and brush fires."

He looked ahead and saw that Matthew, too, had heard the rumble of lightning striking the ground. The gelding was skittish and would much rather have headed for his

356

home stable, but the boy manhandled him around and headed back to Grant.

"Go on back to the Diamond B, Tom," Grant ordered. "If you run into anyone on the way, send 'em up here."

His instructions were interrupted by another ground-shaking rumble. A second spire of dense smoke rose above the dry rangeland.

There had been no flash of lightning, nor any answering clap of thunder.

"That goddamn bastard set the grass on fire," Grant cursed.

Chapter Twenty-Five

She felt the difference even before she opened her eyes. The room was darker, the air more stifling than when she had drifted off. But there was something else, something almost tangible.

She stretched and rubbed her eyes. It was the storm, building in intensity until the moment it would break and bring blessed relief. Glory listened for the boom of thunder, the rush of wind, or the patter of raindrops, but there was only a deep, stagnant silence.

Then a door downstairs opened and slammed shut. Glory sat bolt upright, every nerve atingle with apprehension.

She heard a voice, too, angry and impatient. Then footsteps bounded through from the kitchen to the parlor and up the stairs.

Breathless, his face smudged with dirt, Matthew burst into her room without knocking.

"What in heaven's name—"

"It's a fire," he interrupted. "A bad one. North of here, and a little west."

"Where we moved the cattle last week?"

The boy nodded.

"I already sent as many hands as we can spare out there. There's no wind to speak of, so it's not going to spread fast, but with the storm coming, the wind could kick up in a hurry. We got to take advantage of it before the storm hits."

A slow-spreading brush fire, though a serious occurrence, shouldn't be enough to have Matthew this agitated. With one hand on the doorknob, he was already leaning toward the stairs, poised to rush back to the field of battle.

"What else?" Glory asked while she pulled on her boots. There wasn't time to change from the comfort of a loose-fitting calico housedress to dungarees.

Matthew walked nervously to the small window, as though he had to keep moving to give the energy an outlet. Glory followed his gaze and could see the enormous columns of smoke. The way the billowy black masses moved suggested the storm wind was rising, pushing the fire ahead of it.

"C'mon," the boy urged. "Grant's saddling a horse for you. He can explain everything on the way."

The instant Glory had her boots on, Matthew raced down the stairs again, and Glory wasn't far behind him. Terrence, waiting at the bottom with the fingers of his left hand nattily tucked into a vest pocket, demanded an explanation.

"Get out of my way, Terrence," Glory spat at him. "We have a fire to put out."

He tried to follow her, asking, "Don't you have firemen for that sort of work?" but she had no time even to laugh at the absurdity of his question.

"If you have any brains at all, you'll be gone before we get back," she told him firmly.

Though the clouds were darker and thicker and moving more swiftly from their mountain birthplace, the smoke nearly obscured them. Where a few hours earlier the scent of rain had been a tantalizing promise on the still air, now the acrid odor of burnt grass and charred soil stung the nose and eyes.

"How bad is it?" Glory yelled at Grant as their horses sped over the uneven ground.

"Bad. Usually a fire like this starts in one spot, from a lightning strike. With no wind, we should have been able to contain it quickly."

"What put this one out of control?"

"It was set, deliberately. A trail of black powder to a mason jar of coal oil, and bang! We never had a chance. And it's in the one area of open range where any of us— the LJ, the Diamond B, the Witch's Hat, half a dozen others— had plenty of good water to wait out the drought."

He didn't need to say anymore on that subject. A short distance ahead, Glory could see the cattle, in small, patchy groups being frantically driven away from the fire.

Grant broke off the conversation to shout orders to several of the LJ hands who had accompanied them from the ranch. Young Ken, Charley, and two others veered off to join the crew working the panicked cattle. That left just Weed and Matthew.

Weed would have gone with the others, but Matthew staunchly refused.

"No, I'm stayin' with you," he insisted to Grant, and dug his heels into his horse.

They reached the river not long after. The horses plunged into the shallow stream and galloped across with little difficulty. Even at its center, the river was no more than three or four feet deep, with little current. But as they emerged on the other side, Glory hazarded a glance backward, knowing that they could now be trapped. If rain on the higher ground swelled the water to a torrent before the fire was put out, she and Grant and Matthew and all the others would have no escape route.

As it was, they rode into a nightmare.

"Jake, take the horses!" Grant shouted as he jumped off Rusty and threw the reins to a black-faced hand. "Where's Tom? How's the ditch coming? Matthew, get

Glory out of here. Take her back by the oxbow. Weed, they can use those shovels up on the high ground."

The wind was coming up. He could taste the smoke now. In just a few minutes the air would be thick with sparks and bits of burned vegetation. He grabbed a proffered bucket and dumped the contents over his head. Soaking wet, his clothing was less apt to catch fire from a stray spark.

Sputtering, he turned to hand the bucket back and saw Glory hurrying to catch up with him.

Her hair was a mess, all tangled and dusty. Dust streaked her face, too, where tears, from either the wind or the smoke or something else, had run down her cheeks. Gone were the dungarees that had hugged her hips and thighs like a caress. In their place she wore the ugliest, most shapeless cotton rag he'd ever seen.

And she was still the most beautiful sight in all this madness.

"I told you to go back," he mumbled against her hair when he held her tight in his arms.

"I couldn't leave you. Not again. Never again."

He was just about to kiss her when pounding hooves and shouts from Tom Cashion burst through the pandemonium.

"Stop 'em, Grant! Stop the sons of bitches before they get away!"

The paint horse charged so close to Glory that if Grant hadn't jerked her out of its path, she might have been trampled. But there was no stopping Lonnie, nor his cohort. The men fighting the fire were all afoot; those who had set the blaze knew they had the devil on their tails.

Grant pushed Glory away from him and searched wildly for a horse, any horse.

"No!" she screamed, clutching at his arm. "Let them go! For God's sake, Grant, worry about the fire first."

Smoke, borne on rain-laden wind, swirled all about

362

them, blurring his vision of the golden eyes turned beseechingly to his.

It was like a battlefield, the shouts, the cries, the boom of thunder that echoed like cannonfire. All those years ago he had fought not to claim something but to escape it. This time, he vowed, he'd hold on.

He had to scream above the noise. "All right! We'll fight it together! If Lonnie headed for the oxbow, he's trapped anyway!"

Glory hardly heard him. Someone thrust a shovel into her hands. She immediately joined the line of men and boys clawing at the hard dry earth with picks, shovels, any implement they could get their hands on to cut a ditch across the fire's path. When complete, they would break through to the river and flood the ditch, putting the most formidable barrier of all to work for them.

And all around, the roar increased with every second. Men shouted orders, sometimes countermanding each other. Horses screamed, terrified by the smoke and the panic. Through the dense smoke lightning flashed in eerie streaks of purple and blue, followed by violent claps of thunder. Yet still there was no rain.

Glory pushed her foot against the spade and loosened a pitifully small clump of earth. Frustration welled up in her and those damnable tears threatened again. She tossed the dirt aside and stabbed again. Where was the rain? She could smell it, almost taste it, and yet it held back.

Another bolt of lightning split the air. Its sizzle still ran along taut nerve endings when the thunder exploded just above everyone's head.

"It hit!" someone shouted. "We got another fire here!"

No, not fire, Glory begged. The smoke, the dust, the storm, all that she could stand, but not the flames. Why didn't it rain?

But not a drop fell. She wiped the salty rivulets from

her eyes and drove the spade into the earth one more time. An odd vibration travelled up her arms, like the shock wave from the lightning only stronger, and more sustained.

The whole earth was shaking, with the pounding of not hundreds but thousands of hooves.

"Outta the way! They're runnin' the cattle through!"

Someone grabbed her arm and half dragged her across the ditch. She stumbled, but something kept her feet under her, moving until she collapsed alongside her rescuer.

Now the frantic bawling of the cattle added to the din, and the whoops and hollers of the men driving them.

Terrified, Glory rolled face down on the ground and covered her head with her hands. She could smell the stink of the cattle, their fear, the heat of their bodies, the wind of their passing.

But it wasn't the passing of the cattle that stirred the air so. It was the storm wind, rising to a keen howl.

"Get up, Glory!" Matthew was screaming at her, choking, as he tried to pull her once more to her feet. "They got the cattle across the river, now we gotta move."

She uncovered her head and looked around her.

She could see nothing. The rampaging cattle had churned the dry earth to a suffocating cloud of dust that the wind now drove relentlessly. It stung the skin and burned the eyes and shredded fragile clothing.

"C'mon, we gotta get back across the ditch. The water's comin', and when it floods this, we'll be caught between it and the fire if we don't hurry."

The boy was a phantom of soot and dirt in a world of dust and smoke. She could barely see him, and it suddenly occurred to her that the day itself was fading. And Grant was nowhere in sight.

"Oh, God, Matthew, where's Grant?"

"He's up by the oxbow to get Lonnie. C'mon, the rain's on its way, and river's rising, so we gotta . . ."

Whatever he was going to say was drowned by the roar, not of the storm or the fire, but of the water. It built so quickly from nothing to deafening, that neither Glory nor the boy pulling on her arm was prepared for it. For a split instant they both froze, paralyzed in the growing dark.

Then the wind was on them, pushing them before it like a hurricane. It seemed to lift them over the rough ground. They barely noticed the ditch as they crossed it and then ran on until they could run no further.

"Look!" Matthew gasped, pointing to the ditch, now some ten yards behind them. "It worked! Even if the rain doesn't come this far, the water did, and the fire can't cross it."

Glory blinked and rubbed the stinging dust and smoke from her eyes. That first gust of wind had been the herald. Behind it came a stiff, steady breeze that would fulfill the promise of rain. It blew her hair away from her face and blew away, too, some of the smoke. She could see the ditch rapidly filling with churning river water. As the glittering ribbon stretched further across the threatened grassland, it spilled over its manmade banks, further protection against the ravages of the flames.

Though the fire had not abated and smoke still filled the sky, the wind had driven off the dust raised by the cattle. Now Glory could see exactly where she was and exactly what had been done.

From a quarter mile to her left came the now muted roar of the swollen river. The quiet trickle had become a torrent, and still rising. The cattle would have floundered in it and died; they had indeed crossed just in time.

But where the river looped around a tree-crowned hillock, another confrontation had just begun.

The jubilant cheers of the firefighters slowly died, as their attention swung to the men at the base of the hill and those who had taken shelter in the dense copse of trees on its summit.

"It's over, Lonnie," Steve Peake bellowed. "Hank

Cooley's dead, and we got you cornered."

Glory inched closer, along with the rest of the crowd. "What's he talking about?" she asked Matthew.

Matthew shrugged, but a sooty-faced cowboy next to him explained, "Dan French and Stu Mackey caught 'em, all three of 'em, turnin' an LJ brand into their Rockin' 4. Hank Cooley drew a gun, and Dan didn't have no choice but to shoot back."

Glory's stomach turned over twice, and she felt the blood drain from her face, but she didn't know how close she had come to fainting until she felt Matthew's arms around her waist.

"I think that's enough, Pete," the boy hinted.

Pete shrugged and said, "Anyways, Hank's dead, but Harv Cooley and Lonnie got away."

If Pete intended to say more, he forgot it as Steve Peake shouted to the fugitives again.

"Don't be a fool, Harv," the deep voice rang out over the muted rumble of the river. "You're fifteen years old. We know you just been takin' orders from Hank and Lonnie. Give yourself up."

The fire, still flaring on the other side of the ditch, was virtually forgotten as the new drama claimed everyone's attention. The storm, too, seemed to have abated. The lightning was as bright as ever, but the time between flashes stretched longer and longer each time. The reverberating thunder followed so closely that no one doubted the rain was far behind.

The day was dying, leaving only the weakening glow from the fire and the intermittent brilliance of the lightning to illuminate the scene. Glory searched for Grant as she wove between the exhausted onlookers, but she saw no sign of him. Even when she was close enough to the front to make out Steve Peake's unmistakable silhouette, she could not find Grant.

It was a scrap of conversation to her left during the lull following a thunderclap that seemed too close for comfort that helped her locate him.

"The water's gonna break through any minute, Grant. It'll be an island, a death trap."

She turned in the direction of the unknown voice just as the next bolt sizzled from the clouds.

In that moment of atmospheric incandescence, she would never have recognized the man beside the prancing red horse, but she knew Rusty immediately. Grant was as smoke-blackened as the others who had battled the blaze, except that he had at some point shed his shirt. Even his arms and chest and back were filthy, striped where splashes of water had run down through the grime.

"I'm gonna get that bastard, once and for all," he growled as he placed one foot in the stirrup. "For God's sake, Glory, get out of here. Where's Matthew? I told him to keep an eye on you."

"Please, Grant, don't go. Lonnie isn't worth it." Her eyes followed his to the gun he wore at his hip. Then she glanced at the grim-faced people who surrounded them. The men on the oxbow were thieves, not only of cattle, but of the way of life those cattle represented. "I know this isn't the place or the time, but I've got—"

"Not now."

He swung aboard the nervous gelding and took a moment to calm the horse. Then he blanked everything out of his mind but the task ahead. If he dared to let the woman into his thoughts for so much as a second, he'd back away. Oh, Jesus, but he wanted her, not just tonight but forever. Whatever she wanted, or didn't want from him, it was hers, on her terms, on any terms.

The horse tensed beneath him, a subtle warning, but nothing could have prepared Grant for the explosion of light and sound as the jagged bolt arched from the storm clouds to the crown of the oxbow.

The old tree shattered, its trunk riven clean down the middle, and then erupted in flame. The Cooley boy, further from the strike than Lonnie, nearly lost his seat as his horse reared in terror, but he held on as the animal

367

bolted down the hill and charged into the crowd.

Accustomed to yearling calves, the cowpunchers had little trouble gaining control of the rustler's horse and wrestling the young man to the ground. Glory saw none of the action. Her attention was rivetted on the fire-lit scene at the top of the oxbow.

The pinto horse had reared in terror and then galloped for safety, unseating Lonnie and leaving him to fend for himself. By the light of the blazing tree, Glory saw he was wounded, but she took no comfort from his incapacity. He was as dangerous as ever.

Rusty sidestepped and tossed his head, refusing to go nearer the flames. Though Grant needed both hands to control the big horse effectively, he held the reins in one hand and extended the other to his enemy.

"Don't bother reaching for the gun, Lonnie," he warned. "Your right arm's broken and you can't hardly pull a trigger with the left; you'd never outdraw me."

But Lonnie didn't give up.

"I ain't gonna hang, Brookington. Them cattle were mine."

"If you don't let me get you off this oxbow, you're gonna be just as dead as hangin'. We cut that ditch as close as we could, and there's too much water. It's gonna run a new channel any second."

Lonnie laughed and took a step backward, closer to the burning tree.

"Then it looks to me like you'd be trapped here with me, and we could fight it out once and for all, just the two of us."

Grant felt the first drop of rain on his shoulder. It was a cold, sweet blessing, and yet he hoped it would delay just another minute or two. It had waited so long already, what were a few more seconds?

"I'm not going to fight with you, Lonnie, and you know it." Grant slowly removed his gun from its holster and tossed it to the ground. "Now, let me give you a hand up before it's too late."

Another enormous splat of rain hit him, this time on the head. It sent a shiver down his spine, but he didn't waver.

And then the lightning struck another tree. Like the first, it exploded, sending a deadly shower of sparks into the air. As the fragments landed, the still dry grass on the hill began to flare.

Rusty reared and snorted. Flaming bits of twigs and leaves landed on his hide, and fire erupted all around him.

"Now, for God's sake!" Grant screamed. Lonnie didn't move, frozen by the horror all around him. Grant inched Rusty closer, but his quarry remained out of reach. "You want to be roasted alive?"

Finally, knowing he had no other choice, Lonnie grasped the proffered hand of his enemy just as the clouds opened up.

The cowboys who had fought the fire sent up a cheer as the huge drops pelted them. The rain would finish the fire, and replenish the grassland that was their life's blood. They danced, and clapped each other on dirty wet backs, and for a moment forgot the two men on the hill, where the rain had not yet put out the angry glow of two burning trees.

Glory alone did not turn from the scene.

Startled by the downpour, the big red gelding shied again. Lonnie, struggling now in blind panic, let go of Grant's rain-slick hand and grabbed for his arm. His purchase there was no more secure.

Neither was Grant's. In only a few seconds the rain had made the saddle and the reins slippery. If he didn't get Lonnie up behind him soon, he'd have to leave him. At least the rain had eliminated the danger of the fire.

But Lonnie hadn't realized that yet, or if he had, he became even more desperate to leave the high ground nestled in the river's loop. He clawed his way up, finally placing one foot in Grant's stirrup.

The thunder and lightning was constant as the core of

369

the storm moved directly overhead. The rain was almost blinding. It dripped off noses and the brims of sodden hats, and the wind drove it into unprotected flesh like needles. Hatless, coatless, Glory hugged her arms about herself and waited.

This was all her doing. Her pride, her stubbornness had set everything in motion. She could have let Grant buy her out months ago, and she'd be comfortably settled in Philadelphia, where range fires and flash floods were foreign words. All along, Grant knew Lonnie was at the bottom of her troubles, but she hadn't listened to him, and that gave Lonnie one opportunity after another.

And now he had another more deadly than any before.

"I said I won't hang!" he screamed into Grant's ear while he pounded his good arm into the rancher's ribs. "Gimme the horse, damn you!'"

Grant took the blow to his side with a grunt, and tugged on Rusty's reins to head the gelding back to the crowd. But now the ground was slippery too, and the big horse had trouble keeping his footing. He jerked and bucked and slid on his haunches, and both Grant and his passenger were almost unseated.

"Somebody help him!" Glory shrieked, but no one paid her any attention. Even Matthew had disappeared, and she felt as though she stood alone. Tears filled her eyes, warm where the rain was cold.

Then she spotted the horses, Cleo among them, picketed just a few yards away. Matthew, Weed, and another man were struggling to bring the frightened animals under control, with little success.

She tried to run but couldn't, not on such treacherous footing. It seemed forever before she was at Matthew's side, jerking the reins to Cleo's bridle from his hands.

"I'm going to help your father!" she shouted above the screams of the horses and the din of the storm. More lightning flashed, and the air reverberated with thunder.

"Don't be a fool!" Weed hollered back. He, like Matthew, tried to stop her, but she had led the mare away from the picket line before they could calm the other horses enough to leave them.

Her dress was saturated and seemed to drag her down as she struggled to mount. Even her hair, hanging in a sodden mass down her back, added extra weight. But Cloo, away from the contagious panic of the other horses, settled enough that Glory finally got one foot in the stirrup and swung up.

She wished she had a gun, but once she saw the struggle on the hill, she knew no one could have controlled a shot. The two men and the red horse were one twisting, plunging creature. A single bullet could have killed all three.

It was a fight no one was willing to surrender. Lonnie's broken arm was useless, but Grant had half a ton of angry horse beneath him. That left the two men almost equally disadvantaged. And if Lonnie had been afraid of the fire, he was more afraid of the crowd waiting at the foot of the hill.

"Hewitt, you damn fool!" Grant swore when Lonnie's fist connected with his ribs again. "You're in no shape to control Rusty, even if I was fool enough to let you have him!"

"I ain't gonna hang! I was just takin' what was mine!"

"Fine! Then hold still, damn it, and you can tell it to a judge! You keep this up and neither of us is gonna get off this oxbow alive!"

There was a split second of silence, then another of those blinding bolts of light arced down from the sky. In that moment of brilliance, Grant saw a shadowy form moving toward him through the rain.

"Oh, Jesus God, get back, Glory!" he cried, but the words sounded faint to his storm-deafened ears.

A ground-shaking clap of thunder should have followed the lightning almost instantly, but instead a soft, low murmur filled the electric void.

The water was coming, bridging the hastily thrown up levee that had shifted it into the fire-stopping ditch. In

371

minutes, seconds perhaps, the oxbow would be an island surrounded by deadly flood waters.

He felt the force of Lonnie's fist against his temple, but Grant shook it off and turned all his efforts to getting Rusty under control. In the light of the almost constant lightning he saw now that Glory and the mare had entered just the edge of the water.

He screamed at her again, "Get out of here!" but knew the storm had torn the words away from her.

The water at the horse's feet was rising rapidly. There was no time left. Hoping that the presence of the relatively calm Cleo would have a beneficial effect on the bay gelding, Glory headed the mare in Grant's direction.

And she raised her weapon—the shovel she had dug the ditch with.

Lonnie was weakening. So was Grant. The pain in his ribs and the throbbing in his head were taking a terrible toll. It didn't help any that he had Glory to worry about, too. Damn the woman! He was all set to scream at her again when Lonnie hit him with the gun.

The water was up to Cleo's knees, fast and swirling and with slick grassy mud underneath. Glory saw Lonnie raise his arm and then bring the butt of his revolver down on the top of Grant's head, but there was nothing she could do. Except to kick and beg and plead with the horse beneath her to plunge into the strengthening current.

"Please, dear God," she prayed hysterically. "Not again, please, not again. I can't lose him, I just can't."

Lonnie saw her and let fly a stream of curses.

"You goddamn bitch! You stole everything, everything that should have been mine!" He lifted the gun again and aimed it at her in his weakened, shaking left hand. "You won't get it! I swear to God you'll never have it!"

Grant struggled through the haze of pain and exhaustion. He heard the threats shouted almost into his ear, but his body seemed reluctant to react. Then, suddenly, Rusty heaved beneath him, fighting the

372

encroaching water. It was all Grant could do to keep his seat, clasping the rain-slick saddle horn like the rankest tenderfoot. He felt Lonnie's hold on him loosen as the horse struggled to free himself of the water's clutches.

Glory screamed, as she reached over to grab Rusty's bridle and hauled the red horse across the raging torrent.

With nothing to hang on to, Lonnie slid off Rusty's streaming back. He screamed a short, sharp cry that was quickly drowned by the stormflood as he disappeared beneath it.

Chapter Twenty-Six

They didn't reach the Diamond B until almost dawn. Even the smallest creeks were swollen, forcing long detours. There was no hope of getting dry, but no one seemed to care. Least of all the man and woman on the tired bay gelding.

"That was the damnedest fool thing you've ever done," Grant scolded her a thousand times during the long trek.

"It saved your life didn't it?"

For a few minutes he'd be quiet, content just to hold her against him, feeling her warm and close and wonderful in his arms again.

The arrival of nearly a hundred cowboys at the Diamond B caused hardly a flutter from Maxim, but when Grant carried a dripping wet Glory into the house, the Frenchman shook his head and wagged a scolding finger.

"You do this to her, Brookeengton, you better be keepeeng her."

"I intend to, Maxim," Grant replied with a laugh, though it made his head hurt like hell.

He carried her up the stairs to his own room. Maxim rushed in behind them, to light lamps, lay out dry clothes for Grant and, with a wink, an extra shirt for Glory. Matthew, standing in the doorway, waited silently, but when the Frenchman was finished, he shooed everyone out of his way and shut the door.

"Wait a minute, Maxim," the boy complained when he discovered the Frenchman blocking the door. "Grant's my—"

"You theenk I don't know who he is?" One black eyebrow arched. "You theenk I can't see when a boy grows to a man and looks just like his papa?" Maxim snorted and puffed out his chest. "I am not blind, like some people."

Grant waited until the voices had faded and the footsteps followed, then he turned to the woman lying on his bed.

He stared for just a moment before stretching out beside her and drawing her cold and wet into his arms once more.

"Oh, Grant, I thought I'd never hold you again," Glory whispered, fighting tears, as always these days.

"I know. I'm so glad to have you here again I can't hardly let you go. And if I don't get you out of these clothes, you're going to catch pneumonia."

He wouldn't even let her get out of the bed, which made stripping off the soggy cotton dress a bit awkward. He got it unbuttoned and pushed it off her shoulders, but getting it past her hips required some rather ungraceful manipulations that left Glory hiccuping with laughter, though tears rolled down her cheeks.

"What are you crying for?" Grant asked. He helped her to sit up so he could pull her equally sodden shift over her head.

"I can't help it. These past few weeks, it seems like all I do is cry."

"Never again," Grant promised, wrapping a huge fluffy towel around her shoulders to dry her skin and warm her after the storm. Through the soft fabric his hands found her breasts and he took their full, voluptuous weight in his palms. "Like I said," he teased, "nice breasts."

In the soft lamplight she blushed furiously, but when he parted the towel and rubbed his thumbs across the nipples, she sighed with pleasure, remembered and anticipated.

He tucked his arms around her and lay her back into the softness of the bed. His fingers slid into the damp tangles of her hair to cup the back of her head. Waiting for his kiss, her eyes grew darker, smokier with passion.

"I love you," her lips whispered against his.

"I know you love me," he responded between half a dozen tiny kisses that left her panting, aching for the pressure of his mouth on hers. "You've told me that before." Now his lips trailed to her cheeks, her nose, her eyelids still wet with tears. "But enough to marry me? Damn it, Glory, I don't think I can—"

"Yes," she breathed, and silenced any further conversation with the kiss she had been waiting for.

He slid one hand down her side and fumbled with the tie on her underdrawers. The cotton cord was wet, and the knot wouldn't release no matter how he tugged at it.

And then someone knocked on the closed door.

"Damn!"

Maxim's voice was only vaguely apologetic.

"I brought you some hot coffee. And Mr. Matthew is waiteeng to see you both."

"In a minute, in a minute," Grant answered, rolling reluctantly away from Glory. While he got even more reluctantly to his feet, he muttered, "Good God, what does that matchmaking little brat want now?"

"Grant! That's no way to talk about your—"

She caught herself, but too late. Drawing the towel more closely about her shoulders, she cowered away from the man who stood beside the bed. His silver steel eyes pierced through all her defenses.

"Out with it, woman. Now, before I make an even bigger fool of myself."

"I think you'd better sit down first."

He was furious, but beneath that, Glory detected the faintest hint of fear, as though he suspected the truth but just couldn't quite face it yet.

He sat down on the edge of the bed, near enough that her hands could reach out and touch him. Her gentle fingers traced the twisted line of the scar on his arm, then moved to his shoulders to knead and soothe the tension away.

"He's my son, isn't he?"

She gave up trying to control the tears. Though she tilted her head back and blinked, they still came, until one dripped off the end of her chin and splashed on Grant's shoulder. He snaked one arm behind him to draw her close.

"Does he know?"

She mumbled a pathetic "yes" before succumbing to the tears again. Grant let her cry; he almost wished he could do the same himself. Instead, he went to the door and took the tray with the pot of coffee and two cups from Maxim, and told the servant it would be a while before Matthew could visit. Maxim made a face to indicate the young man would not be pleased, but he didn't argue.

Grant set the tray on the floor beside the bed and then sat down again. There was a different weariness about him now. The broad, strong shoulders seemed slumped.

Glory sniffled and settled back against the pillows. It was an uncomfortable situation in which to tell him about the letter she had found, but she could not delay any longer. Grant listened, with no visible reaction, while she told him everything, including her suspicions that Grant knew all along.

He shook his head. "No, I didn't. I never guessed."

"I'm sorry. I felt so horrible that night after the roundup, when you accused me of stealing so much that had been yours."

"Well, I felt guilty, too. And pretty damn stupid." He

378

paused for a few seconds before adding, in an even more subdued voice, "And pigheaded, too."

"Almost as pigheaded as I?"

He chuckled, a warm, wonderful sound in the lamplit room.

"No one is as pigheaded as you!"

She sat up, ready to retaliate physically if necessary, when the door crashed inward. Matthew, shivering in his wet clothes, glowered at Grant just long enough for Glory to grab the edge of the quilt and wrap it around her.

"Children shouldn't barge into their parents' bedroom," Grant scolded, rising to his bare feet.

"She ain't my ma!"

"No, but I'm your pa, and you better learn better manners, which includes knocking before you come into this room!"

Stunned, Matthew froze. His eyes never wavered from his father's face as they both let the truth and the acceptance of it sink in.

They looked so much alike, especially now that they were angry and indulging in their favorite pastime of being stubborn as mules. Matthew's hair was lighter, and it didn't curl quite as much as Grant's when it got longer, but he had that same belligerent stance, the same strong chin, even the same wrinkle between his eyes when he frowned.

Their embrace was cautious at first, but then both succumbed to the longing of so many years. Grant clasped his son in his arms and hoped Glory's tears blinded her to his own.

Then he held Matthew at arm's length and gave the boy a real once-over.

"You get yourself cleaned up, tell Maxim to fix you a big breakfast, and then I want you in bed. And if this door is closed, don't you *ever* come in without knocking."

Matthew completely ignored the sternness in Grant's voice and grinned broadly.

379

"This mean you two're getting married?"

Grant tried to turn the boy toward the door.

"I don't think that's any of your business."

"Hell, yes, it is. Cripe, Grant, I been tryin' for months to get you two to open your eyes. She's perfect for you. Not like Ma."

Matthew walked past Grant and stood beside the bed where Glory cowered in her quilt and towel.

"I'm sorry," he apologized meekly. "I was pretty rotten to you. But after Ma told me about Grant, all I wanted was to be with him, and I hated her because I couldn't. Then when you came along and married Lee, well, I figured you were just like her."

"She's not," Grant interrupted. "Now, scoot, son, and let Glory and me get some details straightened out."

"Then you *are* getting married?"

"If Grant stills wants to, yes," Glory piped up. "I guess that means you'll get the LJ after all."

"*What?*" both man and boy cried in the same breath.

Confused, she glanced from one to the other.

"Well, isn't that what you wanted? That Matthew would inherit the LJ?"

Grant opened his mouth to answer, but suddenly realized he didn't know what to say. Matthew, however, did.

"I got a funny feeling you two did something really stupid." He leaned his weight on one leg and rested his hands on his hip, just as Grant did whenever he felt superior to the rest of the world. "Everybody always thinks they know what's best for kids, that we can't make our own decisions. Well, I'm here to say that I'm almost fifteen years old, same as Harv Cooley."

"Oh, God, Matthew, don't tell me you've decided to become a cattle rustler!" Grant teased.

The boy shook his head.

"Nope. I don't even want to be a rancher. Too damn much work." He started to grin at the looks of shock on both their faces. "I'd kinda like to be a lawyer. Get to

380

wear fancy suits, ride in a snappy buggy all over the county. I thought about being a doctor, but that means messin' around with dead people, and that doesn't sound like fun."

"Well, you certainly talk enough for a lawyer," Grant complimented. "We can talk about it later. Now, get out of here."

And finally they were alone again, getting sleepy as the energy that had sustained them through the long night began to ebb. Grant slipped out of his pants and managed to open the bed without forcing Glory to leave it. She yawned several times while he struggled to untie the knot that held her drawers on. Then he turned down the lamps and crawled in beside her between the crisp, cool sheets.

"You really want to marry me?" he asked softly as she snuggled naked against him. She was warm and her rain-washed skin was smooth under his drifting fingers.

"Yes. I'll give up the LJ, if you want me to. Anything, so long as I never again have to say good-bye to you the way I did two months ago."

He tightened his embrace on her. Her head lay on his shoulder, her hair still cool and damp and untamed as ever spilling over his arm. It, too, smelled as fresh as the summer rain now falling gently outside the window. Morning was coming; the window was a grey rectangle in the dark.

"No, the LJ is yours, to do with as you want. Lee may have given it to you to spite me, but you earned it."

He was so tired he knew he ought to be sleeping, but having Glory in his arms once more was too much temptation for any man, much less one who had done without the woman he loved for two months. Involuntarily, he was stroking the soft flesh of her hip, and the his hand moved to her belly.

She curled tighter against him, the warmth of desire slowly spreading through her. One leg slithered over Grant's, opening her to his searching fingers.

"Matthew was right; you're nothing like Melody."

Glory lifted her head sharply and looked into the eyes that were growing silver in the increasing light.

"Now's a hell of a time to talk about her."

"Maybe. But it's true. She used me for her own ends, just as she used Lee and Lonnie and every other person in her life."

"I used you, too."

"That was different. You asked first. She just took. Exactly like I'm going to take now."

He covered her mouth with his, dipping his tongue into the sweetness her surprise offered him. He was hers, all hers, and never again, never ever again, would she be parted from him. Her arms pulled him closer even as more tears welled up in her tightly shut eyes.

"Love me, Grant," she murmured, the words slurred as she ran the tip of her tongue out to touch his. She did not have to ask him twice.

He filled her swiftly, sweetly, knowing that the night's exertion and their own pent up desire would bring them too quickly to a far from satisfactory climax. But when they had reached that delicious pinnacle and savored its fleeting pleasure in expectation of yet further delights, Grant lay still within her.

"Jesus God, but I love you," he whispered as he leaned down to kiss her cheek. It was wet and salty, despite the smile that turned up her open lips. "Why are you crying? Did I do something?"

She laughed, and felt him push himself more securely inside her, as though afraid of losing her.

"I cry a lot these days," she chuckled. "Maybe it's only temporary, like morning sickness."

If she hadn't tightened her legs around his hips, he'd have withdrawn completely.

"Fine time to tell me. What if I . . . ?"

"No, it's perfectly safe. At least for now. Later, well, I'll have to ask a doctor about that, but we have plenty of time."

Plenty of time. She moved against him, pushing

thoughts of caution from his mind until, in the soft early light of a rainy day, they lay completely spent in each other's arms.

"Do you want a boy or a girl?" Glory asked, her voice slurred with sleep. She tried to open her eyes but simply couldn't.

"You haven't given me much time to think about it. I mean, I just found out I've got a half-grown son, and now you expect me to decide what I want this one to be?"

"Well, at least you had a hand in raising Matthew, even if you didn't know he was yours. And I must say, that's one of the reasons I decided to marry you: I do believe you'll make a good father."

He wanted to slap her, but exhaustion had conquered him completely. It was enough just to hold her against him and let sleep creep up.

"Since I'm so good with boys, maybe we ought to have another. But a girl would be nice, too. Maybe she'd turn out just like you."

They both groaned and laughed.

"Stubborn as a mule?" Glory asked.

He looked into her sleepy eyes, the lashes still wet with tears, and he smiled with the deepest, most contented peace he had ever known.

"Stubborn, and independent, too." He squeezed her gently, tucking her head securely under his chin. "I hope I don't have to be hit over the head every time, but I learned one hell of lesson out there last night. I knew exactly what it felt like to be at someone else's mercy. I knew how you must have felt, not just for a few minutes, but for years and years and years."

He thought for a minute she had fallen asleep, but the soft caress of her hand on his belly told him she was listening, and listening carefully.

"I learned something, too," she said quietly. "I realized all my independence wasn't worth a plug nickel if it made me such a slave I wasn't even free to love. Nothing, not the ranch, not the cattle, *nothing* is more important to me than spending the rest of my life with you."

He kissed the top of her head, and yawned again, and then he simply couldn't make another conscious move. And as sleep crept up and claimed them both, Glory smiled at the fading whisper. Never again. Never ever again would she be alone.